MW00992379

The Arachnid

New Eden – book 2

KISHORE TIPIRNENI

Copyright © 2020 Kishore Tipirneni
All rights reserved.
ISBN: 978-0-578-72452-2

DEDICATION

For my father, Dr. Eswara Tipirneni,
who instilled in me my love of science.

ACKNOWLEDGMENTS

Thanks to William Hammett whose help was once again invaluable.

Thanks to Lee Goettl for his inspired narration of the audiobook.

The cover illustrations for the book were created by Guillermo Herrera.

Two possibilities exist: either we are alone in the universe or we are not. Both are equally terrifying.

- Arthur C. Clarke

THE STORY SO FAR

New Eden is a story I'd culminated over many years. Even though I'd never written a novel before, the plot, scientific concepts, and resulting philosophical dilemmas were so compelling to me that I felt I had to write and release it for a general readership. I've been both thrilled and humbled by the response that *New Eden* has received. Many readers have asked for a sequel, and I'm pleased to be able to present *The Arachnid*.

In writing *The Arachnid*, I wanted the content to encompass new material and not repeat details from *New Eden* wherever possible. Because of this goal, *The Arachnid* is written from the perspective of someone familiar with the original story. I have purposefully not used any part of the narrative to explain concepts that were revealed in *New Eden* except when absolutely necessary, and even then, only in the form of brief summary or allusions. For those who have read *New Eden* and want to refresh their memories of the major plot points, I've included the following synopsis of the first novel, although it is not meant to be a replacement for reading it. If you've not read *New Eden*, I strongly encourage you to do so to have the proper context for *The Arachnid*. For those who are entirely familiar with the plot and don't require a synopsis, please feel free to skip to the first chapter.

Here is the story so far . . ..

*　　　　　*　　　　　*

Dr. Henry Bowman, a professor of particle physics at Berkeley, delivers a lecture on a new type of quantumly entangled particle that he has created called the spookyon. Entangled spookyon pairs allow for instantaneous communication at any distance, proving that Einstein was wrong about nothing being able to travel faster than the speed of light. Bowman demonstrates the ability to control a rover on Mars with no time delay using spookyon technology. Bowman is assisted by his PhD student, **Joshua Andrews**, during the demonstration. At the end of his lecture, Bowman dies suddenly from a ruptured aneurysm. Trying to comfort the dying Bowman, Joshua hears Bowman's last words: Everything is information.

Five years later, Joshua is in charge of the new Bowman Particle Research Center, created by the university to further Bowman's research. Joshua is visited by scientific journalist **Rachael Miller**. Subsequently, Joshua captures a new pair of spookyons that are contained in glass receptacles called Bowman spheres. While testing this latest pair of spookyons along with Joshua's PhD student, **Rodrigo Torres**, Joshua and Rachael discover an intelligent signal emanating from one of the particles, a signal transmitted by an alien source. They later realize that spookyons were created at the time of the Big Bang, and with the expansion of the universe, they created a built-in instantaneous communication system.

They enlist the help of Rachael's friend **Vinod Bhakti**, an information theorist, who created an algorithm based on math and science to allow for communication with aliens. Due to their advanced intelligence, the aliens are able to learn English in a matter of minutes using the algorithm. **Seth**, a member of a highly advanced alien race called the petrins, begins conversing with the trio (Joshua, Rachael, and Vinod), and they find out that petrins, DNA-based lifeforms, use DNA to engineer their species and environment. Petrins are able to grow any living organism they choose simply by coding the DNA required for it. Due to the non-directional nature of entangled particle transmission, they are able to speak with Seth, but neither party knows where the other is physically located in the universe. To celebrate their discovery, the trio goes to a night club, where Joshua and Rachael become romantically involved.

When Joshua tells NASA about their discovery, the U.S. government takes over the project. The White House chief of staff, **Dina Williams**, the director of NASA, **Dr. Robert Langdon**, and the chairman of the joint chiefs, **General Mitchell Porter,** meet with the trio. They explain that the government has purchased the research center from the university and proceed to shroud the discovery of the petrins in secrecy. However, they retain the trio to work on a secret project to discover more about the aliens. The trio learns about Petri, the alien home world, and the petrins' philosophy regarding matters of life and death. Seth explains that petrins believe that life is simply data—purposeful information—and that death is the loss of the last copy of data from this universe that defined a specific living entity.

A few months later, Seth requests that an android body be constructed for him so that he can remotely view Earth via a spookyon connection and learn more about its culture. The humans initially deny this request, but when the secret of the alien communication is leaked on the Internet, with other countries demanding equal time with the aliens, the government decides to create the android. They believe he will be easier to control and monitor as an android rather than in digital form.

Rachael and Joshua further their relationship and become engaged while scientists at NASA construct a very human-looking android. When it's activated for the first time and Seth is given control of it, project leaders are shocked at how completely human-like his movements are. Physically, android Seth is indistinguishable from an African man. Seth, who is always accompanied by a security team and who can only be active while in close proximity to specially designed tether watches that his handlers wear, visits world leaders and spends time with his close friends, the trio. On one trip, Seth visits Las Vegas and is able to cause dice at a craps table to come up the numbers he chooses due to his extreme intelligence and knowledge of physics.

While driving in the mountains, the trio and Seth are involved in an accident in which their car goes over a bridge into a river. Seth is able to save Joshua and Vinod, but Rachael dies. Joshua is devastated, and Rachael's body is frozen in a cryo facility according to her wishes.

A few months later, humans ask for Seth's help in eradicating a newly discovered virus that is projected to kill almost the entire human population. Seth is initially hesitant but finally agrees on the condition that a private lab be built for him so that he can keep his methods secret.

When Joshua visits Seth in the lab, he is shocked to see that Seth is growing petrins. Seth then interfaces with Joshua's brain by pouring interface cells he has created called biograins over Joshua's head. These penetrate his skin and interface with his cranial nerves and spinal cord. Seth proceeds to tell Joshua that the petrins are the creators of humans. Billions of years ago, they engineered DNA and the cell and have used them to seed life throughout the universe after discovering they were the only intelligent species in the cosmos. They never left their planet but nevertheless seeded life on thousands of planets, expanding their civilization by using spookyon transmission. Seth explains that petrins plan on using the Earth as a new distribution point to disseminate more cells but have terraformed another planet, New Eden, where humans can be relocated. Using spookyon transmission and the interface to Joshua's brain, Seth instantly transports Joshua to New Eden, a planet genetically engineered from the ground up. Once at New Eden, Joshua is overjoyed when he sees that Seth has recreated Rachael by scanning the information in her frozen brain on Earth. Seth wants Joshua to explore New Eden with Rachael for three days to show him how much of a paradise it is. The plan is for Joshua to return to Earth and convince humanity that it is desirable and safe to be relocated to New Eden.

Rachael and Joshua explore New Eden, a mind-boggling paradise that shows the power of genetic engineering. Everything in New Eden has been genetically engineered, including the house they live in, as well as creatures called arachnids that act as flying transports. Joshua and Rachael use the arachnids to explore the new world. Despite New Eden being a true paradise for humans, Rachael wants Joshua to destroy the spookyon inside of Seth when he returns to Earth to end their communication with the petrins. She feels that humanity would not be truly free in New Eden since it would be under the governance of the petrins and face no challenges to evolve as a species and determine its own fate. Joshua is torn since severing the communication with Seth would also mean the death of Rachael on New Eden and billions of others on Earth due to the virus.

When Joshua is returned to Earth by Seth, he destroys the Bowman sphere inside of Seth with much anguish, ending their connection with the petrins. After the connection is cut, the petrins growing in the lab are destroyed. Seth, showing his empathy for humanity, reveals via a pre-recorded message that he has left a cure for the virus and that he has recreated Rachael on Earth. Like children going against their parents' wishes, humanity has shunned its creators and decided to risk forging its own future.

Chapter One
The Chase

Rodrigo Torres ran through the forest as if his life depended on it—because it did. He was being hunted by a creature that was definitely not from this world, a creature that he knew he had no chance of evading, but he wasn't going to give in without a fight.

Severely out of breath, Rodrigo stopped, hands on the knees of his obese body as he gazed behind him, looking for any motion in the thicket of trees. There was a slight breeze, but he heard and saw nothing, not even the chirping of birds or the buzzing of any insects. He grabbed a dried leaf from the forest floor and tossed it in the air in an attempt to see which way the breeze was blowing. He then continued his sprint in the direction of the faint breath of wind since he knew that the creature chasing him had a keen sense of smell, one more acute than even a dog's, and he definitely wanted to be upwind of it. He pumped his fat legs hard as his body hurtled forward.

Rodrigo had no idea how much of a head start he had on the creature, but he knew that regardless of the distance, it wouldn't be enough. As he lumbered across the forest floor littered with fallen branches and pine needles, his mind raced, thinking of how he had gotten into such a hopeless predicament. The money he had received for his lab work from the foreign government had seemed like a fortune at the time, but no amount of money was worth being killed for. He knew that he alone was the reason that the creature chasing him now roamed the forest. Out of greed, he had taken an enormous financial gamble, but what had he unleashed on humanity?

The sun had set below the canopy of the forest, but Rodrigo could still see fairly well in the fading light of dusk. He stopped once again to catch his breath—years of greasy tacos and pizzas had caught up with him—before looking behind him, listening for the slightest snap of a twig. Still nothing. Had the creature stopped chasing him? Had it given up? Given its relentless pursuit, he wasn't going to take any chances. He would keep running as fast and as far as he could. His instinct for self-preservation had taken over, and he decided to keep hauling ass.

After agonizing minutes of running, Rodrigo halted and leaned against a pine tree; his obese body demanded it since he was definitely no marathon runner. In fact, he couldn't remember the last time he had done any exercise at all, not that it would have mattered in the situation he was in. He doubted that any human, no matter his physical condition, could outrun what was chasing him.

Cocking his head, Rodrigo heard the loud buzz of an insect close to his right ear. He instinctively slapped the side of his face, stunning the creature, which landed at his feet. Rodrigo peered closely at the stunned insect, which was still moving, and his heart sank. He knew that the creature chasing him would now know his location.

About to continue his dash through the forest, he heard a faint sound, like the hoofbeats of galloping horses, but this was no horse. He still saw nothing behind him, but terror filled his heart as he realized the creature was getting closer. He broke into a run, his strides now more urgent.

Rodrigo realized yet again that he had no chance of outrunning the beast. His only hope was to hide in the tangle of shadows afforded by the forest. But how could one hide from something with sensory acuity unlike any creature, or even any machine, on Earth? His mind searched for an escape plan as he ran. His considerable intelligence was the only resource at his disposal.

The hoofbeats grew louder as he spotted a large pond in the clearing ahead. With fat stubby fingers, he felt in his pants pocket for a ballpoint pen he had used earlier that day and ran to the edge of the pond, producing the pen. Breathing heavily, Rodrigo removed the ink and ballpoint cartridge and quickly discarded it. He then removed the end cap, leaving the hollow plastic exterior. Rodrigo glanced behind him and heard the ominous sound of tree branches breaking, a slight cloud of dust visible through the foliage. The creature made no secret of its location as it barreled through the forest, snapping branches with loud cracks as its elephant-sized body hurled forward. It had no need for stealth and was afraid of nothing.

Grabbing large rocks from the edge of the pond, Rodrigo urgently filled his pants pockets with the heavy stones and slowly waded into the frigid water. As he moved farther into the pond, the water up to his neck, he looked back one final time in the direction of the noise. After taking several deep breaths—he was wheezing from exertion—he placed one end of the pen shell into his mouth, moved deeper into the pond, and slipped beneath the water, using the pen as a straw through which he could breathe. The ripples in the pond created by his entrance dissipated as he stood motionless on the muddy bottom in the murky water, the only evidence of his presence being the tip of the pen sticking slightly above the waterline.

*   *   *

The creature erupted from the tree line and moved to the edge of the pond, where it stopped. Eight articulated legs connected to a central carapace remained motionless. On top of the carapace, eight tentacles scanned the surrounding area with methodical precision. The sky had grown darker, but the eyes at the end of its tentacles could see perfectly since they had the ability to scan far into both infrared and ultraviolet wavelengths.

Despite its sensory and physical prowess, the creature had but a rudimentary brain, one that operated more on instinct than intelligence. It knew but one simple purpose endowed by its creator: survive, replicate, and conquer at any cost.

Its infrared eyes caught sight of a single point of heat rising from the surface of the pond, one that was easy to discern given the fact that the water was cool. It saw the breath of its prey rising from the tip of the long hollow object and focused all of its sensory tentacles in that direction. Taking notice of a slight increase in the water temperature beneath the surface, it made out the figure of a human standing on the bottom of the pond. It had found its target.

The creature's biologic brain, which contained no higher-level thought processes, was well-adapted for making almost instantaneous mathematical calculations and targeting its prey. It calculated the density of the disparate fluids of the atmosphere and the water through which its projectile would need to travel. It took little time to accomplish this, and it launched a small projectile at high speed from one of its tentacles. There was a loud crack as the tiny missile ripped the air with supersonic speed and entered the pond. The projectile made an arc in the water as it turned and sliced through the throat of its prey, severing both carotid arteries in one swift motion. A second projectile emerged from another of the creature's tentacles and mercifully severed the spinal cord just below the cranium and ended the life of its prey.

The creature watched as the surface of the pond turned red with blood as the heat signature of its prey's breath disappeared. It paused for a few minutes to make sure the lifeform was dead before retreating into the North Korean forest.

Chapter Two
Unannounced Invader

Dr. Robert Langdon, director of NASA, walked down the stairway of a private jet at Washington's Reagan National Airport, shielding his head from a steady rain with his briefcase. Standing next to a black SUV was an envoy, umbrella in hand, waiting for him on the tarmac.

"Dr. Langdon, I'm Sheila Peters," the envoy said, extending a hand while covering Langdon's head with the umbrella. "I'm going to escort you to the Eisenhower Executive Building next to the White House. Ms. Williams will meet you there."

Langdon, a tall man in his fifties, greeted the envoy and climbed into the back of the SUV. "Do you know what's going on?" Langdon asked as the SUV drove away. "Dina insisted that I come to Washington right away."

"No, sir," Peters replied. "I was told to deliver you to the Eisenhower, nothing more."

As he watched the streets of the rainy capital drift by, Langdon wondered why Dina Williams, White House chief of staff, wanted to meet with him so urgently. Williams hadn't told him anything on the cryptic phone call he had received a few hours earlier, but she had insisted that he get on the private jet and fly directly to Washington.

When they arrived at the executive building, the envoy escorted Langdon to a conference room on the third floor. There was a window in the room which afforded a commanding view of the White House. Dina Williams and Mitchel Porter, chairman of the joint chiefs of the military, were already seated at a conference table. Williams was a slender African American in her forties; Porter was an imposing figure in his sixties, his face weathered from a lifetime of service and dangerous missions. A third person sat at the table, someone who Langdon didn't recognize. He was an African American male in his forties with short-cut hair in a Navy dress uniform.

"Thanks, Sheila," Williams said before the envoy exited the room, closing the door behind her.

"Well, it's been a while since I've seen the two of you in person," Langdon stated as he took a seat.

"Yes, it's been a while," Williams responded. "Thank you for coming on such short notice." Williams motioned to the man in the Navy uniform. "Dr. Langdon, I want to introduce Commander Theodore Johnson. He's the commander of Navy Seal Team Four stationed out of Virginia. Commander, this is Dr. Robert Langdon, director of NASA."

"Pleased to meet you, sir," Johnson replied with a southern accent as he stood and shook Langdon's hand.

"You as well," Langdon stated. "Well, Dina, what was so urgent that you had me flown here on a private jet?"

"This," Williams replied as she took photographs from her briefcase and laid them on the table.

Langdon picked up one of the pictures and examined it. The photo showed an aerial view of an arachnid in the clearing of a forest. It was an eight-legged creature about the size of an elephant. Its eight articulated legs were attached to a central carapace, which was the body of the arachnid. On top of the carapace were eight, thick, snake-like tentacles.

"It's an arachnid," Langdon said, "but I don't recognize this particular one. I extensively reviewed all of the images of arachnids that Seth sent us from Petri, but this one isn't familiar to me."

"That's because this image isn't from Petri," Porter stated. "It was taken by one of our spy satellites over North Korea a few hours ago."

Langdon's eyes widened. "North Korea?" he asked, shocked. "What the hell is an arachnid doing in North Korea?"

"We don't know," Williams answered calmly. "We were as surprised as you when we first saw these images. That's why I wanted you here. I realize that you and your scientific team reviewed extensively all of the images of arachnids from Petri, so I needed your expertise on what we should do with this new information."

"Have you asked the North Koreans about this?" Langdon inquired, still examining the photographs.

"We've tried," Porter answered. "They're not saying anything. We've had absolutely no communication from them."

Langdon picked up another photograph from the table and studied it. "This is definitely an arachnid of petrin origin," he stated, "but this one looks more substantial, more rugged than the others. Also, this arachnid has eight tentacles on its carapace, while all the others I've seen from Petri have only four." Langdon placed the photo on the table. "How the hell did it get here? Dr. Andrews severed our connection with the petrins years ago."

"That's what we need to find out," Williams replied. "We need to learn how and why an arachnid is in North Korea. General Porter is worried that it may be some kind of weapon, which would obviously make it a threat to the United States and possibly the Earth." Williams sat back in her chair, her hands joined in front of her, fingertip to fingertip. "Robert, what do you think our initial course of action should be?"

Langdon was still in shock at the thought of an arachnid being discovered in North Korea. It took him a few moments to let the situation sink in. "In light of the fact that the North Koreans aren't saying anything," Langdon replied, "if we need to find out more about this creature and how and why it's here, then the answer is obvious: we need to send some kind of team to North Korea. We'll have to observe it in person to get any reliable information about it. Given their communications blackout, I'm highly suspicious of the North Koreans. I'm sure they had something to do with this."

"We all concur on those points, Dr. Langdon," Williams responded. "We're in agreement that we definitely need to send a team to North Korea, but what do you suggest we do once we're there? How should we deal with this arachnid?"

Langdon stroked his graying hair as he thought about the question. "We'll have to communicate with it somehow—try to find out its intentions."

"Its intentions?" Porter asked.

"Yes. We don't know at this point if the arachnid is hostile or not. I would think that trying to communicate with it would be our first priority."

"It's an unannounced invader, doctor," Porter said tersely. "To me, that suggests its intensions *are* hostile. We should deal with it accordingly."

"Accordingly?" Langdon asked. "What do you mean?"

Porter stared at Langdon without saying anything.

"You want to just destroy it, general?" Langdon asked.

"Absolutely," Porter replied. "We should kill the thing first, and then you scientists can figure out how and why it's here."

"I disagree," Langdon said. "Until we know for sure it's a threat, we shouldn't destroy it. We may lose any chance of gaining valuable information about it if we simply blow it up. Besides, whoever or whatever sent it here may view that as a hostile act, which may have further detrimental consequences."

"Shouldn't we view *this* as a hostile act?" Porter asked. "Having an alien creature suddenly appear on Earth?"

"It very well could be hostile," Langdon acquiesced, "but we don't know that for sure. I think it would be hasty on our part to simply destroy it."

The two men turned to Dina Williams, who had the president's ear and would be the final decision maker.

"I agree with you, Robert," Williams stated. "We need to proceed cautiously and not make any rash decisions, but if the creature isn't friendly, then it must be destroyed. It's not a natural part of the ecosystem of this planet. It simply doesn't belong here."

"I understand," Langdon said. "So how do you want to proceed?"

Williams crossed her arms. "I think we definitely need to send a team to North Korea to deal with the arachnid as you suggested. This team needs to represent a collaboration between military and scientific personnel. The military component should be run by one of our special forces. That's why I've invited Commander Johnson to this meeting. I want his seal team to handle the military operations. General Porter will, of course, be in charge of the military team. Dr. Langdon, I want you to be in charge of the scientific team. Any ideas on who you might choose for this mission?"

Langdon leaned his head back, mentally going over candidates for the assignment. "Dr. Joshua Andrews and Rachael Miller should definitely be part of the scientific team. They have the most experience with the petrins and petrin technology. They're the only humans who have actually interacted with an arachnid, so their input would be invaluable. Also, since communicating with an alien entity may be involved, Vinod Bhakti would be helpful. He wrote the algorithm that allowed us to communicate with the petrins in the first place. Additionally, I'd also like to have someone with expertise in alien biology, preferably an exobiologist. In fact, I have someone in mind—Dr. Elizabeth Yang. She's an MD and a PhD out of the University of Washington."

"All logical choices," Williams responded. "I want you to get your team and all of the necessary equipment assembled as quickly as possible, but I do have a question for you. You mentioned trying to communicate with the arachnid. From the reports I've read from Dr. Andrews and Miss Miller, they didn't have any direct communication with the arachnids they encountered on New Eden. They were just animals, more or less. What if communication with this creature isn't possible? What would be your course of action in that event?"

Langdon pondered the question for a moment before answering. "Then I'd suggest trying to capture the creature so that we can study it in a more controlled environment."

"You want to try to capture the goddamn thing?" Porter said. "It's the size of an elephant, for Christ's sake. How the hell are we supposed to capture it?"

"I'd like to capture it *if possible*," Langdon replied. "I really don't have an idea at present on *how* to do it. We need more information from scientific observation before we can formulate such a plan, but I think we'd need some type of container constructed for the arachnid if capture is indeed possible."

"Container?" Williams said. "Like a cage of some sort?"

"Yes," Langdon said. "I'm sure we can extrapolate the approximate size and strength of the arachnid from these photographs. Maybe the Army Corps of Engineers can construct an appropriate cage given this information."

Williams and Langdon looked to Porter for an answer.

"I'm sure they can," Porter said. "I can get on that right away."

Williams turned to Commander Johnson. "Commander, what type of personnel from your seal team do you think we'll need?"

"It's difficult to say," Johnson replied. "From what I've gathered today, the mission objective is to communicate with, capture, or destroy this arachnid. We'll also have to provide security for the civilians—the scientific team—but there are still a lot of unknowns here. We'll have to be ready for all possible scenarios." The commander paused as he thought of the manpower needed. "We have eight platoons as part of our team. I'd want at least six members from each platoon, each with different skill sets, to be part of this operation."

"Close to fifty men," Williams said, clearly satisfied with what she'd heard. "I'm okay with that. I want you to return to your base and get your men ready. I also want you to assemble all of the equipment you feel they'll need and then wait for further instructions."

"Yes, ma'am," Johnson replied.

Given the immediate nature of the problem, Williams had no doubt that she could sell the mission to the president. Like most White House chiefs of staff, she had far more power than the vice president or cabinet members.

"General Porter and I have already discussed the logistics of this mission," Williams continued. "We need a base of operations, and the USS Gerald R. Ford carrier is already positioned in the Sea of Japan near the

North Korean coast. I want all personnel and equipment transported to the carrier as soon as possible. Dr. Langdon, I think it's best if the general and I fly back with you to Berkeley to brief the scientific team. From there we can arrange to transport the team to Korea. I've also ordered for increased aerial surveillance of the area where the arachnid was spotted in order to glean more information. This, in essence, is our initial plan. Any questions?"

There were none.

"Okay," Williams said as she stood. "It seems we have an appointment with an arachnid."

Chapter Three
Return from Eden

Dr. Elizabeth Yang sat alone in front of a long, polished mahogany table in a conference room at the Bowman Particle Research Center. She was a full twenty minutes early for her scheduled meeting, so it was no surprise that the room was empty. Dr. Yang, or Liz as she liked to be called, fidgeted nervously with her visitor's badge that the British receptionist had given her when she'd walked into the center.

In her mid-thirties, Liz was a slim woman of Asian descent. As she stared out the lone window of the second-floor room which looked over the courtyard, she thought of the cryptic phone call she'd received the day before from Dr. Robert Langdon. He had insisted that she get on the next flight from Seattle to Oakland to attend the meeting. Langdon hadn't given her any details about why she'd been summoned, only that he was in dire need of her expertise as an exobiologist. He did mention, however, the others who would be present at the meeting: Dr. Joshua Andrews, Rachael Miller, and Vinod Bhakti. Liz was excited and somewhat nervous to meet the three people on Earth who had made first contact with an alien intelligence. She wondered if her expertise as an exobiologist would live up to the expectations of people who had actually seen an alien world firsthand.

Liz got up from her chair and retrieved a bottle of water from a cart next to the conference table. She sat down, fiddled with her badge again, and waited for the others.

*   *   *

Vinod Bhakti, a man of Indian descent in his late twenties, entered the atrium of the NASA Bowman Particle Research Center. It had been a long while since he had been inside the building, but he was happy to see the familiar surroundings. Not much had changed, including the receptionist.

"Mr. Bhakti, so nice to see you again," Charlotte Lloyd said in her usual British accent. "Welcome back. It's been a while since you've been here."

"Over three years, Charlotte," Vinod remarked as he took a visitor's badge from the receptionist and attached it to his shirt. He was dressed in jeans and the obligatory rock tee shirt, which today was a cover from Pink Floyd's *The Wall*. His hair was cut short as usual.

"Your meeting is in conference room two," Charlotte stated.

"I'm going to meet up with Rach before the meeting," Vinod said. "Is she in the same office as before?"

"Yes. I'm sure you know the way there."

Vinod walked through the bustling corridors of the center, interrupted occasionally by researchers who gave him a high five or a fist bump to celebrate his return. Eventually, he made his way to Rachael's office and glanced at the placard on the door: RACHAEL MILLER, DIRECTOR of PR. He saw Rachael, her back turned, looking at a large whiteboard with various terms scribbled on it. Vinod made a cursory knock on the door, which caused Rachael to turn and exclaim, "Vinod!" She rushed to give her old friend a hug. Slender and attractive, Rachael was five foot six and had brunette hair and high cheekbones.

"I see you won the fight on the last name thing," Vinod said, looking at the placard on the door again.

"Yeah, but it wasn't really a fight. I told Josh that I wanted to keep my last name, and he agreed."

"Right," Vinod said sarcastically. "More like he wimped out."

"Besides," Rachael said with a smirk, "I didn't know how permanent this arrangement would be. I didn't want to change my name back if things didn't work out."

"Right," Vinod said with a chuckle. He knew Rachael was kidding and that she and Joshua were soul mates. Their marriage a year earlier was one that he knew would survive any obstacle. "'Til death do us part" really didn't seem to apply to them. After all, Rachael had indeed died, but they were still a couple, nonetheless. If Rachael and Joshua weren't the perfect couple—two people meant to be together—he didn't know who that might be.

"You're moving up in the world," Rachael remarked as they sat on a vegan leather couch in her office. "I hear you're the CTO for a new AI startup. Well deserved, in my opinion."

"Mo money, mo problems," Vinod said. "But obviously the pay is good, and the stock options aren't bad either. So what's with the powwow? I haven't been in this place in over three years. What does the ever-secretive Dina Williams want to talk to us about?"

"Beats me. They haven't told us anything yet, but it's good to have the gang back together again. I hear that Langdon and Porter are going to be present."

"Langdon and Porter?" Vinod said, eyebrows raised. "Just like old times. Maybe I can ruffle that old dude Porter's feathers just for kicks."

"Behave yourself."

Dr. Joshua Andrews entered the room, dressed in a button-down shirt, jeans, and a white lab coat. "Vinod!" he exclaimed, giving Vinod a handshake and a bear hug. "Long time no see." Tall and handsome, Joshua was in his early thirties.

"Yeah, dude. It's been a while. Looks like you're doing well."

"Well, this one keeps me on my toes," Joshua said as he gave Rachael a hug.

"Rachael and I were discussing why we were summoned," Vinod said. "Do you think they changed their minds about releasing the security code left by Seth?"

Joshua knew immediately what Vinod was speaking about. It had been over three years since he and Rachael had returned from New Eden, the immediate aftermath of which had been fraught with much controversy. Joshua, true to his convictions, had insisted that nothing be hidden from the public about why Seth had sent him and Rachael to New Eden, what had transpired there, and his decision to break the Bowman sphere containing the spookyon connected to the petrins. Joshua's stance had received much pushback from the governmental team consisting of Mitchell Porter, Robert Langdon, and Dina Williams. He reflected on their initial meeting after he and Rachael had returned to Earth from New Eden.

*   *   *

Three years earlier, the day after Joshua and Rachael had returned from New Eden, Joshua called an emergency meeting of the executive group at the Bowman Particle Research Center consisting of himself, Vinod, Williams, Langdon, and Porter. Rachael, of course, had been a member of the group, but since the others still believed she was dead, he didn't want her present at the start of the meeting, believing that her appearance would overwhelm the others. No, it was best to keep her hidden until they had a chance to hear the events of the past few days.

Joshua had insisted that the meeting be held as soon as possible, with all members physically present due to the highly sensitive nature of the briefing. With all members assembled in a conference room, Joshua was ready to tell his tale. Not one to mince words, Joshua started with, "I've shattered the Bowman sphere in Seth."

The group stared at him in disbelief, unable to speak as the gravity of the statement sank in. The others had hoped that Joshua was going to deliver news that Seth had created a cure for the current viral pandemic that was projected to kill almost all humans on Earth. Breaking the sphere, and therefore permanently severing their contact with Seth and the petrins, would end any possibility for a cure.

"What!" Williams said. "Why?"

Joshua requested that no questions be asked until he had finished his story. He then methodically related what had happened the night he visited Seth at the lab. He told them about the biograins, and how they'd interfaced with his cranial nerves and spinal cord in an ultimate demonstration of virtual reality. He also related what Seth had told him about the petrins being the creators of the cell and humans before describing his adventures with Rachael on New Eden. He further related what had brought them to their decision to have Joshua rupture the sphere to end contact with the petrins. He did not, however, relate the content of the final recorded message from Seth or the fact that Rachael was back on Earth. He had strategically left this information out in order to get an unbiased opinion of what the group thought of his decision.

The others in the group sat in stone silence, finding it difficult to believe what they had heard. Porter was the first to speak. "If you broke that sphere, then we're all screwed. This viral pandemic is going to do us in. There's no stopping it now." Porter was referring to the deadly viral outbreak that threatened Earth at the time Joshua and Rachael had made contact with Seth.

"Are you saying I made the wrong decision by breaking the sphere?" Joshua asked. "Would any of you have allowed Seth to transport humanity to New Eden? Would you have wanted the petrins to have control over human destiny?"

There were a few moments of silence, finally broken by Dina Williams.

"Joshua, I'm not sure what to think. Maybe you made the right decision, but maybe you didn't. However, I don't think it was a decision you should've made by yourself. I think you should've consulted with the rest of us prior to breaking the sphere."

"I understand your sentiment," Joshua stated, "but for me there *was* a sense of urgency. The petrins in the tank had grown much larger during the three days I was on New Eden, and I wasn't sure what else Seth had done in my absence. I wanted to end the petrins' influence on Earth as quickly as possible." He glanced at Porter. "It's a decision I think the general would have made in a heartbeat."

Porter, appearing pensive, nodded. "I can't argue with that."

There was silence again, this time broken by Robert Langdon.

"Josh, I think that, given the decision you had to make, you made the right one. Who knows what would have happened if you had let the petrins grow larger? After all, even if we hadn't made contact with Seth, we'd still be in the same predicament we're in now with this virus. Seth was giving humanity a way out, but apparently one with strings attached."

"I suppose so," Williams said, "but you made a tough, long-term decision, one you thought was best for humanity. I also realize the sacrifice you made. You knew that breaking the sphere would mean the death of Rachael, but you did it anyway, which showed conviction. I'm not sure that many people would have made such a sacrifice, but I know you felt you were doing it for the good of humanity."

"Thanks, Dina." Joshua glanced at Vinod. If anyone would be opposed to breaking contact with Seth, it would be Vinod. He was, after all, one of the 103 club—fans of Seth and the petrins—who looked to Seth as a guru, someone with incredible wisdom and a person who he cherished deeply. "What do you think, Vinod?"

"Josh, you know how I feel about Seth, but I also know how deeply you felt about Rachael. If you sacrificed being with her by breaking the sphere, I know you made an enormous sacrifice. Who am I to second-guess this decision? What's done is done. You know I support you and Rachael in this. After all, wasn't it *her* decision to break the sphere? Didn't she convince you to do so?" Vinod's voice became emotional as he thought of Rachael. "We must all recognize that *she* made the ultimate sacrifice in the end. She sacrificed herself for what she thought was best for humanity."

Joshua had gotten the information that he had been looking for. From the team's reaction, he knew that no one would have done anything differently given the same choice. In their minds, he had made the correct decision.

"I'm glad you all understand. It's very important to me that you know why I did what I did."

"Something still bothers me, Josh," Vinod said. "I can't believe Seth would allow this to happen."

"What do you mean?" Joshua asked.

"Seth must have known there was a possibility that you would break the sphere. He should have anticipated that. I mean, for a guy who was worried about stepping on some ants, I can't believe he would let humanity succumb to this virus. He's leaving the fate of billions of people to chance."

Joshua smiled at Vinod. He definitely had a deep understanding of Seth, maybe even deeper than his or Rachael's. "Oh, he didn't leave it to chance."

"How so?" Langdon inquired.

"Because Seth left a cure for the virus in the lab."

The group stared wide-eyed at Joshua. "What?" they said in unison.

Joshua relayed the content of the recorded message Seth had left regarding the cure for the virus and how petrins considered humans their offspring—how they wanted the best for their children even if they hadn't picked the path the petrins had recommended for humanity.

"My boy Seth came through for us after all!" Vinod exclaimed. "Shit! An android saving humanity! Who would've thought?"

Vinod's elation was not shared by Porter, who by nature was suspicious. "I find all of this very difficult to swallow," he retorted. "Dr. Andrews, you've told us an incredible tale. Some would say unbelievable. How do we know if what Seth left for us in the lab is a cure for the virus? How do you know it's not some type of biologic agent meant to kill everything here so that the petrins can take over Earth?"

"Mitchell," Robert Langdon said, "of course we'll test the cure in a controlled and quarantined environment before we release it. But I for one believe in Seth's good intentions. If he'd had nefarious motives, he had more than enough opportunity to carry them out. The fact that he didn't leads me to trust him."

"Trust is not something I give as easily as you do," Porter said. "To believe this story requires a leap of faith I'm not sure I can take. How do we know that what Dr. Andrews told us is the truth? There's no physical evidence. For all we know, there may not even be a place called New Eden. Seth could have injected the entire experience into his mind. There is also the possibility that Dr. Andrews made this whole story up as an excuse for breaking the sphere."

Vinod glared at Porter and immediately came to Joshua's defense. "Screw you, Porter!" he exclaimed. "Are you accusing Josh of lying?"

"I have to consider all possibilities," Porter replied, leaning back in his chair, a smug look on his face. "That's what I'm paid to do."

Joshua cut off Vinod before he could speak again.

"It's okay, Vinod. I know that what I've told the group is hard to believe. It's still difficult for *me* to believe even though I was the one who experienced it, but it's important that you all *do* believe it." Joshua turned to Porter. "General, you want proof? You want physical evidence of New Eden? Well, I have proof, and it's just outside." Joshua turned towards the door of the conference room. "Come on in," he said loudly.

The door opened and Rachael walked in. There were audible gasps from around the table, but no one said a word. Rachael grinned as she spoke. "'Sup guys?"

"Rach!" Vinod exclaimed as he raced to embrace his friend. "Is it really you?" he asked with tears in his eyes.

"It's really me."

The others also got up from their seats and greeted Rachael. Had they just seen a ghost, a miracle of genetic engineering?

"My God!" Langdon exclaimed. "How is this possible?"

They were still in shock as they made their way back to the table and sat, this time with Rachael.

"She's a gift," Joshua replied. "A parting gift left for me from my friend. Seth cloned her body in the lab from her DNA and injected into her brain the information from her frozen body at the cryo facility."

"Simply amazing!" Langdon stated, still in shock at seeing Rachael. "The petrins can bring back someone who has died. Their technology is so much more advanced than we ever imagined."

"But she wasn't really dead," Vinod corrected. "At least not according to the petrin definition of death. Remember, her last copy was never erased."

"Are you really Rachael?" Williams asked. Was the clone of a person injected with information from the original individual still the same person?

"I believe so," Rachael replied. "My physical body is the same, and all of my thoughts and memories are intact. I don't feel different than any other time I've been alive. It's just me."

"The petrins are true masters of genetic engineering and information transfer," Langdon said. "The idea of them inventing the cell seems more plausible to me now."

Over the next hour, the group asked Joshua and Rachael to explain more about their time on New Eden and about what had transpired in the lab after their return to Earth. The couple answered their questions in detail.

"At this point, Mitchell," Langdon said after the question and answer session, "I have no reason to doubt that everything Joshua and Rachael have told us is true."

"I concur," Williams agreed.

All eyes turned to Porter for a response. He scanned the faces staring at him and stopped at Rachael's. "Given the current evidence, there's no reason to doubt Dr. Andrew's account of events."

"I'm glad we're all in agreement," Williams said, looking relieved. "I want to formulate a plan on how to proceed. I think our first priority should be to go about testing the cure for the virus and to formulate a method for distributing it."

"Seth left instructions on a flash drive for the most effective way of distributing the cure," Joshua said. "There's also one more thing on the flash drive."

"What else?" Langdon asked.

"There's a digital security key. It's something that Seth said should be used to ensure that we're speaking to the petrins if we ever decide to reestablish contact with them. He seemed quite adamant on that point."

"Security key?" Porter said, perking up. "Dina, that's definitely a strategic advantage for us. It means that only *we* would have access to the petrins. We need to keep that key for ourselves."

"I don't think that's how the key works." Joshua replied. "It's meant to make sure that whoever we're talking to are the petrins and not some other sentient race."

"Still a strategic advantage," Porter insisted.

"I think the key should be made public," Joshua said. "Seth meant it to be for all humanity. It's not right to keep it from other nations."

"Hold on a minute," Williams said. "I'm not sure that we should make *any* of this information public, let alone the key."

"I agree," Porter said. "The less we disclose, the more advantage for us."

"Are you kidding?" Rachael asked incredulously. "You're not going to make any of this public? Nothing about New Eden, the origin of life on Earth, or the fact that the petrins and Seth saved humanity from the virus?"

Rachael eyed Josh and sat straight, a resolute look on her face. In her estimation, such secrecy would be immoral.

"It's what I'm considering," Williams replied.

Joshua was apoplectic. "We must reveal *everything* to the public!" he exclaimed. "I insist. I for one will not be a part of hiding vital information from public consumption. I don't care what you do to me. This information is going to be made public, and if *you* don't release it—*all* of it—*I* will. We have no right to hide the origin of life on Earth from the very life that is the result."

"I tend to side with Joshua and Rachael on this," Langdon said. "Dina, this is too important to hide from the public. Besides, it's not right to release a foreign substance on the public without their knowledge, even if it *is* a cure for the virus. I believe there's a principle in medicine called informed consent."

"We don't have to disclose shit!" Porter shot back. "*We* own this information. It came about as the result of Seth using *our* lab and *our* resources. Those other nations have no right to it."

All eyes turned to Williams. They knew in the end that this would be her decision since she had the president's ear. Whatever she recommended would be rubberstamped by the administration.

"What makes this decision difficult is that it has to be all or nothing," Williams said, choosing her words carefully. "If we don't release all of it, there would be gaps in the information that would make the public suspicious. We can't really hide the fact that Miss Miller has been revived since the public was informed of her death. If we release this to the public, we would have to disclose *all* of it: New Eden, the origin of life, the viral cure, and even the resurrection of Rachael. Frankly, Mitchell, as I see it, it would be nearly impossible to keep this a secret. There'd be too many holes in any story we made up. After all, scientists in other nations know about our current viral infection. They'd wonder how it was miraculously cured. I'm leaning towards releasing everything."

Porter glowered at Williams, his teeth clenched. "Fine," he replied after regaining his composure. "But there's no need to share the security key with anyone. We *must* keep that a secret. Only *we* should have the ability to contact the petrins if the need arises. It's a strategic advantage that we can't give up."

Williams thought about the decision and finally rendered what she believed to be a fair compromise. "Okay. Dr. Andrews, we will hide nothing from the public according to your wishes. You will tell your entire story, including the origin of life on Earth, your experience on New Eden with Rachael, your ending contact with the petrins, and the cure they left us."

Joshua was elated. The petrins and Seth would be judged in light of the facts. They had, after all, saved humanity, and it was important for Joshua that mankind know about it.

"I'm so happy you agree," he said.

"However, I see no reason to make the security key public," Williams added. "Doing so might encourage others to contact the petrins, which at this point is something we don't want. We'll keep the key for ourselves."

Porter leaned back smugly in his chair, satisfied with the decision.

Chapter Four
Satellite Images

Joshua, Rachael, and Vinod walked through the halls of the research center towards conference room two, where another emergency meeting called by Dina Williams would take place.

"How's this whole marriage thing working out for you two?" Vinod asked. "Is it still happily ever after?"

"We're finding that a good marriage is possible, but it does take effort," Rachael replied. "There has to be some give and take on both sides. There's always some tension, but as long as we have mutual respect, we can get over any disagreements. Right, Josh?"

"Right," Joshua said as he reached out and grasped Rachael's hand.

Vinod made a vomiting sound, his index finger aimed at his open mouth. "Come on, guys. You know how I feel about PDA."

The couple paid Vinod no heed as they continued down the hallway hand-in-hand.

"Alright," Vinod said. "I see you two are still in love. So how come there are no miniature Andrews-Millers or Miller-Andrews or whatever running around? I'd love to be greeted by someone as Uncle Vinod."

Joshua and Rachael looked at each other with pained expressions on their faces, expressions that Vinod did not pick up on as he walked behind them. This was definitely a difficult topic for the couple. They had tried for the first year of their marriage to conceive a child, but without success. Initially, Joshua thought it would happen eventually, but as the negative pregnancy tests piled up, they both decided to see a fertility specialist, who revealed crushing news to the couple: Joshua was sterile. Due to a viral infection, probably during childhood, he was unable to produce any sperm, and even in vitro fertilization was out of the question without viable sperm.

The news had been devastating for Joshua and Rachael. In fact, they had not told anyone else, even their families, about this revelation. In the time since they had learned the news, they had come to grips with the fact that they could not have biological children, but they were starting to entertain the idea of adoption.

"We're just not ready for that yet," Rachael said in order to end Vinod's line of questioning.

Thankfully, Vinod made no more inquires on the subject.

The trio reached conference room two and entered to find Langdon, Porter, and Williams seated at the table. There was also another person seated at the table, a slim Asian woman in her mid-thirties, her straight black hair cut shoulder-length. The three newcomers joined them.

Williams started the meeting.

"I want to thank all of you for coming on such short notice. I'd like to introduce Dr. Elizabeth Yang. She is an MD and PhD and is one of our country's most preeminent exobiologists. Dr. Yang, this is Dr. Joshua Andrews, Rachael Miller, and Vinod Bhakti."

"I'm honored to meet you all," Elizabeth said with no accent. "I've read and heard much about all three of you. Please call me Liz, by the way."

"Damn," Vinod remarked. "An MD and a PhD and exobiology? Did you do anything else besides study up to this point?"

Rachael shot Vinod an admonishing glance. "You'll have to excuse Vinod, Liz. He tends to be fairly informal."

"No problem," Liz said as she looked at Vinod's *The Wall* tee shirt. "Yes, Mr. Bhakti, I did have a tendency to hit the books, but there were times that I liked to get comfortably numb."

Vinod's face perked up at the obvious Pink Floyd reference as Liz gave him a wink. The allusion to the song "Comfortably Numb" escaped Williams, Porter, and Langdon.

"What was so urgent that we had to meet?" Joshua asked.

"This," Williams answered as she took an eight-by-ten black and white photograph out of her briefcase and slid it across the table.

Joshua, Rachael, and Vinod studied the photo. It was the same image that Williams had shown to Langdon in D.C. earlier.

"Is this one of the images received from Seth?" Joshua asked.

"I wish it was," Williams responded. "This photograph was taken twenty hours ago by one of our spy satellites pointed at a remote region of North Korea."

"What?" Vinod exclaimed. "There's an arachnid in North Korea?"

"It certainly looks that way," Williams replied.

Joshua and Rachael exchanged shocked glances. They had encountered arachnids on New Eden and had even ridden them as they'd toured a portion of the planet to evaluate it as a potential new home for mankind. To see such a creature on Earth was unsettling given that it was assumed that all contact with Petri had ended three years earlier.

"Are you sure this isn't a statue?" Joshua asked. "Maybe it's some kind of attraction. Is it even alive?"

"Oh, it's definitely alive," Williams remarked as she took more photographs from her briefcase and placed them on the table. Each showed an image of the creature from a different angle, its legs and tentacles in various positions.

"But how is that possible?" Rachael asked after looking at the additional pictures.

"Don't know," Porter said, looking accusatorily at Rachael and Joshua. "We thought you two could explain it to us."

Langdon glared at Porter. This was not something they had discussed in D.C. Was he testing the couple for their reaction? To Langdon, Joshua and Rachael were above reproach.

"Are you joking?" Joshua asked. "You think Rachael and I had something to do with this?"

"Come on, Mitchell," Langdon protested. "You're jumping to unwarranted conclusions."

Porter continued staring at Joshua, not blinking. "You two are the only ones that have seen an arachnid up close. Why shouldn't we believe you had something to do with this?"

Joshua and Rachael looked at each other in disbelief. Were they really being accused of somehow bringing an arachnid to Earth? The very idea seemed ludicrous. The Bowman sphere had been broken, and Porter knew it.

Langdon came to their defense. "Mitchell, don't jump to conclusions. We don't know how or why this creature ended up in North Korea. That's what we're trying to figure out."

"What *he* said!" Vinod exclaimed in order to protect his friends. "Porter, you've got a lot of nerve thinking they had something to do with this."

As usual, Williams was the calm and collected moderator of the discussion. "Look, we don't know how or why an arachnid is in North Korea and hence this meeting. I want to get ideas and opinions from everyone around the table. This is also the reason Dr. Langdon invited Dr. Yang to the meeting today. He thought her expertise as an exobiologist would be beneficial. So, Joshua and Rachael, is this creature similar to what you saw on New Eden?"

Rachael composed herself and examined the photographs. "There are similarities, but this creature is much different. It's general size and layout is the same with eight legs and a carapace with sensory tentacles, but the arachnids we rode on New Eden had only two tentacles, and their legs were much thinner."

"That's right," Joshua added. "Also, there are no handles on this creature like the ones on New Eden. We used the handles to control them. This is definitely an arachnid, but not like the ones we saw."

"I came to the same conclusions when I first saw the images," Langdon remarked. "But do you have any reason to believe they were not built from the same technology as those you used to travel on New Eden?"

Joshua sorted through the photographs. "No. This creature is too similar to the arachnids we encountered on New Eden. It must be petrin technology."

Joshua's statement caused the room to grow silent. There was now petrin technology on Earth, the origin and the purpose of which no one knew. The simple concept of unknown technology roaming the Earth was sobering for all in the conference room.

"How can petrin technology exist here?" Vinod asked. "Joshua broke the sphere, which was our only connection to the collective. The information transfer from them stopped at that point."

"There are only two logical possibilities," Langdon answered. "Either the information for this technology was transmitted here by the sphere before it was broken, or someone has re-established contact with the collective."

Always the observer, Williams patiently listened to the debate, weighing each remark from people she deeply respected.

"Are you saying that Seth somehow caused this to happen before the sphere was broken?" Rachael asked.

"Why not?" Porter asked defiantly. "If he created those reconnaissance insects that scanned your frozen body to bring you back from the dead, who knows what else he could have unleashed."

Rachael's voice betrayed her defensiveness. "No way. I can't believe Seth is behind this," she said shaking her head. "Remember, he left us with a cure for the virus that ultimately saved humanity and everyone in this room. The message he left in the lab was one of true empathy for humans. I can't believe he could be behind this."

"Miss Miller," Porter began, "I find it hard to accept your impartiality on this subject given the fact that the only reason you are here with us is because of Seth."

Joshua jumped to Rachael's defense. "Look, Porter, she didn't have anything to do with this, and neither did I. Your insinuation is a personal affront to me and my wife."

"What about the second possibility?" Langdon asked, trying to keep tempers from flaring. "Could someone else have captured a spookyon that's connected to the collective?"

"How could that happen?" Vinod asked. "Joshua is the only one who knows the formulation of the lids that capture primordial spookyons."

"That's not entirely true." Williams responded. "Didn't your PhD student, Rodrigo Torres, also know this formulation?"

"Yes," Joshua replied hesitantly. "Do you think he has something to do with this? I haven't had contact with him in over a year. He said he was going to work in the private sector to make more money."

"That, Dr. Andrews, is our current working hypothesis. The CIA has been monitoring Mr. Torres since we took possession of the original Bowman sphere from your lab."

"You've been monitoring Rodrigo?" Vinod asked. "Why does that not surprise me? You're probably also monitoring everyone else here. Typical Big Brother shit."

Williams continued, ignoring Vinod's remark. "We intercepted communications by Mr. Torres from multiple foreign IP addresses which the NSA believe originated in North Korea, but we were unable to decrypt the messages. For the last nine months, there has been complete radio silence—no activity at all that we can attribute to Mr. Torres."

"So you really think Rodrigo has something to do with this arachnid?" Joshua asked.

"We don't know," Williams answered. "There's much we don't know. Why is this creature on Earth? What is its purpose? How did it get here? The government is arranging a top-secret mission to North Korea to find some answers. It will be a joint scientific and military operation. The military portion will be handled by General Porter, and I want you, Joshua, Rachael, Vinod, and Liz to be part of the scientific team, which will be led by Dr. Langdon."

"Military?" Vinod said. "That's definitely outside my comfort zone. I want nothing to do with this. Why do you want us to go anyway? We don't have any military experience."

"No, you don't," Williams said sternly. "But you three are the most familiar with the petrins and their technology. Joshua and Rachael are the only humans who have experienced it directly, and as far as you're concerned, Mr. Bhakti, like it or not, you and your algorithm are best-equipped to make communication possible with whatever we find in North Korea." Williams softened her tone. "But I understand your concern. This is not a risk-free endeavor. All of the physical aspects of this mission will be handled by General Porter's military team. The four of you will have an advisory and scientific role only. You won't be put in harm's way."

"Famous last words," Vinod said, folding his arms.

"You're going to try to communicate with or capture the arachnid?" Joshua asked.

"If possible," Porter answered. He strategically didn't mention anything about the possibility of destroying the creature. He felt that doing so might lessen the cooperation of the scientific team. "Do you have a better plan?"

Joshua took some time to let the current situation sink in as he re-examined the photographs. "No, I don't," he replied with resignation. "Have you contacted the North Koreans about this? What do they have to say?"

"We've tried all channels." Williams replied. "Complete silence. They're not saying anything, and the most recent satellite photos we've obtained of the surrounding region show the roads are packed with traffic moving away from the area where the arachnid was spotted."

"We think they're evacuating the population," Langdon added. "But as to why . . . we have no idea. What's interesting is that they're not waving us off—not telling us to stay away even though they are aware of our knowledge of the arachnid."

"You want to send us into an area that they're evacuating?" Vinod asked, his voice strained, eyes wide. "Sounds pretty sketch to me."

"Definitely risky," Williams replied. "But as we've said, this is primarily going to be a military mission. We're not going to send in the scientific team until we've established a safety zone using the military. We don't have any other viable options since we can't let this creature roam free. That's riskier in my opinion." Williams returned the photographs to her briefcase. "Look, we're not going to *force* anyone to do anything, but we *are* asking for your help in assessing what we perceive as a threat to the security of not just our nation, but the whole world."

Rachael took a few moments to let Williams' words sink in before turning to Joshua, Vinod, and Liz, who gave her affirmative nods. "Okay, we're in," she announced.

Skeptical at first, Joshua and Rachael knew that decisive action needed to be taken. Both suspected alien influence of some kind, and with the world's welfare at stake, they felt committed to the mission. In truth, they were the best qualified for the job, plus someone needed to be present to keep the military in check to the extent that they could.

"Great," Williams said, looking relieved. "We have a transport to take us to the USS Gerald R Ford aircraft carrier, which is now positioned in the Sea of Japan. The transport will be leaving in four hours, so get ready."

Chapter Five
The Overachiever

Rachael peered out the window of a transport helicopter at the turbulent ocean below. Whitecaps extended in broken rows as far as the eye could see, and the copter was jolted by strong, gusty winds. *Certainly not the best weather for a helicopter flight or a landing on the deck of a rolling carrier,* she thought. The last few hours had been a whirlwind. They had boarded a military transport in San Francisco, which had taken them to a military base in Seoul. From there, their entourage had boarded a military copter that was now en route to the deck of the USS Gerald R. Ford.

"Almost there," the pilot announced over the headphones that each passenger wore. Rachael looked towards the horizon and saw the silhouette of the Navy's latest nuclear-powered carrier against the orange sky of the nearing dusk. The ship was a long, gray, floating city with state-of-the-art weapons systems and the navy's latest magnetic induction catapult launchers. The conning tower and bridge were located well to the stern of the flight deck.

"Going to be a bumpy landing because of the weather," the pilot cautioned. "Everyone grab hold of something."

The copter made multiple attempts to land on the heaving deck of the carrier, finally succeeding on its third attempt. Rachael grasped Joshua's hand as the passengers, which included the rest of the team, disembarked, keeping their heads low to evade the still moving rotors as they moved a safe distance away. After the last passenger had disembarked, they turned and watched the copter take off into the dusk and bank over the dark sea.

Once on the flight deck, they were escorted below, where they descended by elevators and ladders into the bowels of the ship. They walked through a maze of hatchways and narrow corridors, passing dozens of Navy personnel in khakis or blue work suits. They were led by the ships XO—the executive officer—who was obviously proud of his vessel. He explained that it had a water displacement of over 100,000 tons and had replaced the Enterprise and Nimitz-class carriers.

The sleeping arrangements on the carrier were less than ideal. Most of the bunks were arranged in large groups for which privacy was not a priority. Rachael was told she would bunk with Liz in a private cabin, a rare luxury aboard such a ship. Even though it was small, with two bunk beds and no windows, she and Liz were grateful that they had better accommodations than their male companions, who would bunk with male crewmembers, although she figured that Porter would have his own suite.

Rachael unpacked her gear and stowed it in a tan metal cabinet as Liz did the same in another. Rachael glanced at her watch, which read almost 11:00 p.m. local time, but she wasn't the least bit sleepy due to the time change.

"Liz, what time did Porter say the briefing was?"

"0800. We should get some rest. We need to be fully on point tomorrow."

Rachael donned her pajamas and jumped into the lower bunk, hoping that Liz would be okay with the choice. The vessel was still rocking due to the heavy seas, and Rachael felt nauseated. This was not, after all, a Caribbean cruise ship, and she figured that the lower bunk would afford less motion. "You okay if I take the lower bunk?" she asked.

"No problem," Liz replied as she turned out the light and climbed into the top bunk. The cabin was dimly lit by a small night light plugged into a receptacle by the door.

Unable to sleep, Rachael lay on her back, staring at the bunk above. Her thoughts wandered to their mission. No one had been given further details about what the mission would entail, but she assumed they would be covered in the morning briefing. An arachnid on Earth? She and Joshua had had an amazing experience with their arachnids on New Eden, which had been genetically engineered to serve humans. But how had this one come to Earth and what was its purpose?

Still unable to sleep, Rachael's thoughts turned to her roommate, who was not much older than she. She was familiar with the rest of the scientific team, but Dr. Elizabeth Yang was a stranger who she wanted to become more acquainted with. Rachael was a reporter at heart, and gathering information was in her nature.

"Liz, you still awake?" she asked in a hushed voice.

"Yup."

"I can't seem to go to sleep."

"Me neither. I think it may be the time change—or the fact that our floating hotel has enough firepower to start a world war."

The informality put Rachael at ease. "So an MD and a PhD, huh? Did you ever practice medicine?"

"Not really," Liz replied as she stared at the ceiling from the top bunk. "I finished my residency in pulmonary and critical care, but I found that I wasn't interested in clinical medicine. The PhD part of me took over. I acquired an academic position in the medical department at the University of Washington, so my day job now is as a professor of medicine and biology. I love research. It's where my heart is."

"How did you get interested in exobiology?"

"I was always interested in space and the planets. In fact, I minored in astrophysics during my undergrad at UCLA. After I got my position at UW, I hooked up with the astrophysics department and have been consulting for them in exobiology."

"Astrophysics, huh? You and Josh may have some interesting discussions. I can see why they wanted you on the team. You have amazing qualifications."

"Also probably didn't hurt that I speak fluent Korean."

Liz's gentle sarcasm caused Rachael to laugh out loud.

"Are you Korean?" Rachael asked. "You certainly don't have an accent."

Liz had heard the question many times before. Most Asians would be able to discern the subtle physical differences between a Korean person and a Chinese person, but westerners were not so savvy.

"No, I'm Chinese by origin. My parents emigrated to the U.S. from China when I was four years old. I'm an only child, which is not surprising given China's single child policy at the time. When we moved to the U.S., my parents ran a convenience store and worked long hours. I spent much of my childhood by myself—a latchkey kid, so to speak. I hit the books during my youth. You know . . . tiger mom and all."

Rachael chuckled at the mention of the stereotype. "How is it then that you know Korean?"

"My college roommate—my best friend really—was Korean. We made a pact that I would teach her Mandarin and she would teach me Korean by the end of our undergraduate studies."

Liz slowly rolled on her side, peered over the railing of her bed, and looked down at her roommate. Rachael had quickly become a celebrity after returning from New Eden, and Liz was somewhat intimidated by her. It was refreshing that Rachael was so cordial, and she wanted to take advantage of the opportunity of being alone with her. Rachael was the only person to be brought back from the dead, although she hadn't actually been dead if one subscribed to the petrin definition of life. "So what was it like?" Liz asked, her tone more casual.

"What was *what* like?"

"You know, being dead, being brought back to life, visiting a foreign planet?"

"Wow, that's a lot in one question," Rachael laughed, "but I'll try my best. Being dead was like nothing—literally nothing. One moment I was in an accident on a bridge, and the next moment I woke up on New Eden. I had no recollection of the passage of time even though many months had gone by. Even the transition back to Earth from New Eden was instantaneous. One moment I was lying next to Josh on our bed there, and the next I was getting up from a stretcher in the lab. Being dead for me was like . . . nothing. As far as what New Eden was like, I've written a detailed report of our adventures there for the government. I'm sure you have the security clearance to read it, but suffice to say it was a true paradise, albeit one with strings attached. I felt that Seth and the petrins were trying to do what they believed was in the best interest of humanity, but I wasn't sure humanity was ready for it. I felt that mankind needed challenges."

Liz's hair, bunched into a short ponytail, fell to her shoulder as she propped herself on her elbow.

Rachael was glad that she was getting better acquainted with the highly intelligent but somewhat intimidating Elizabeth Yang. "My turn for a question. Are you married? Any kids?"

This was a question—a common one unfortunately—that brought much anguish to Liz. She turned away and stared at the ceiling again. She didn't want Rachael to see the tears welling up in her eyes as memories of Bojing came rushing back.

*   *   *

In her late twenties, Liz had been engaged to Bojing, a man her age who her parents had set her up with. It wasn't an arranged marriage per se, but it *was* an arranged meeting. At first Liz had been dismissive of the cultural convention. "I want to find my own partner," she informed her parents when they told her about Bojing. "I don't want to be set up with someone you pick. This is America, not China. I want to make my own decisions about who I marry."

"But why?" her parents asked her. "He is very suitable for you. He comes from a good family, and he's also going to be a doctor like you. You have a lot in common."

"You don't know what's best for me," she'd responded succinctly.

"Why don't you give him a chance?" her mother asked. "You may like him. He was born in China but has grown up in America, just like you. Besides," her mom said with a sly smile, "he's very handsome. What's the harm in meeting him?"

Liz's parents could be demanding and overbearing at times, but they were nothing but logical—and loving. She knew they were doing what they felt was in her best interest, but Liz was independent, the result of growing up in an American culture that was very different from the highly-scripted life in China.

"Fine," Liz had finally responded. "I'll meet with him, but if I'm not interested, you can't pressure me or be disappointed. I'm doing this only because you're asking me and for no other reason. Don't have unrealistic expectations."

"That's fine," her father said. "No expectations. Just meet him but have an open mind. If you don't like him, we'll be okay with your decision. In the end, we just want you to be happy. That's the most any parent can wish for their children."

Liz met Bojing, and at first it was awkward. They'd met at her home, with both their parents having what she considered "formal conversations." She noted, however, that Bojing was indeed handsome. He was tall and slim, with a genuine and disarming smile. Soon the couple were left to themselves, their parents, not so inconspicuously, having gone to the kitchen to allegedly check on dinner. Liz remembered the first thing Bojing told her when they were alone. "This is terribly awkward. What do they expect? For us to form some kind of connection in this scripted setting?"

Liz looked at him, surprised and relieved. He felt uncomfortable too? "Yeah, it's definitely awkward. To tell you the truth, I was against this setup."

"So was I," he'd said with a warm smile.

Liz thought at the time that she should give the guy a chance. He was not so different from her, and he was definitely handsome, just as her mother had said.

Their relationship blossomed over the months following their initial meeting. Bojing was a gentle, intelligent soul, one that Liz fell in love with. He was very respectful of Liz, someone who he considered his equal, his partner. He didn't have the chauvinistic tendencies of many men of Chinese upbringing. When they finally announced that they wanted to get married, Liz's parents were overjoyed. "See, sometimes your parents know what you like," her father said to her.

"Don't get cocky," she replied.

Unfortunately, their joy was short-lived. Six months before their wedding, Bojing became sick. He started having abdominal pain that the couple initially attributed to indigestion, but the symptoms persisted. He finally got a CT scan that showed multiple masses throughout his abdomen that were later diagnosed as metastatic colon cancer. It was little consolation to the couple that it was very rare for someone of Bojing's age to get the disease. Despite treatment, Bojing passed away a month before they were to be married, leaving Liz devastated. It was over a year after Bojing's death before she went on another date. Her pain had faded over the years, but there were still moments when those old feelings resurfaced.

*   *   *

"No, not married," Liz said wistfully. "But I was engaged once."

"What happened?" Rachael asked.

Liz contemplated about how much she wanted to say about Bojing. She had just met Rachael and didn't feel like explaining one of the most painful periods of her life. "It just didn't work out," Liz finally said, desiring to change the topic to happier thoughts. "So what's it like being married? Josh seems like a great person. You two seem perfect together."

Rachael smiled as she thought of her marriage to Joshua. "I'm not sure any relationship is perfect, but I feel fortunate to have found him. He's intelligent and caring. He has his own opinions, which I respect, but he also respects mine even if they differ from his. We're different people in many ways, but in the end we've found much common ground. We have a great respect and adoration for each other, which is the most I could have asked for."

Rachael didn't speak for the next few moments, the hum of machinery and the life of the carrier audible but distant. She reflected on how lucky she and Joshua had been to have met each other. Given her religious beliefs, she was convinced that providence of some kind had brought them together, although she had never revealed this to Joshua.

"Did you find anyone else after your engagement didn't work out?" Rachael asked, her thoughts brought back to the conversation at hand by the latest noise coming from behind some distant bulkhead.

"No, not really," Liz answered. "I haven't given romance much effort since then. I guess you could say that I'm married to my work. I've had a few boyfriends, but things didn't go much beyond the early stages. It seems to me that many men feel intimidated by a well-educated and successful woman. Has that been your experience as well?"

Rachael pondered the question for a while. "We're both strong intelligent women. I guess some men find that intimidating, but I can't say that all men do. So what kind of men are you attracted to?"

Liz thought the question was somewhat personal coming from someone she had just met, but there was something disarming about Rachael. She seemed genuine, with no ulterior motives. Talking to her about deeply personal matters gave Liz comfort. "They would have to be intelligent, of course," she replied.

"Like a scientist?"

"Maybe."

"How about physical looks? Are they important to you?"

"I guess so. If I had to pick physical attributes, I'd say I'm attracted to the tall, dark, and handsome type. Speaking of which, tell me more about Vinod."

"Vinod?" Rachael said, taken aback. "You're attracted to Vinod?"

"I'd say intrigued would be a better word. He's a bit quirky. He seems like someone who doesn't have much respect for authority and is his own person. It takes confidence to ignore what everyone else thinks and go your own way. Also, what's with those rock tee shirts he's always wearing?"

Rachael knew that Liz and Vinod had no chance of being a couple given Vinod's sexual orientation, but Rachael had a mischievous streak in her that popped up from time to time. This was one of those times. She was going to let this play out and watch for the fallout.

"Vinod's a great guy. We've been the best of friends since college. He's a brilliant information theorist, and he invented the algorithm that allowed us to establish contact with the petrins. He's also a huge classic rock fan. As far as he's concerned, music stopped being great after the nineties. And you're right—he's very much an individual. A great person all around." The women lay in silence, Rachael with a slight grin on her face as she thought of the ramifications of her words.

"You're fortunate to have found someone like Joshua," Liz said, breaking the silence. "Many people have a tough time in a relationship with someone who's equally successful. It's refreshing to see that you two have figured it out. Have any children yet?"

Rachael's grin disappeared. This was a subject that had been brought up by two people in the past twenty-four hours. She guessed it was only natural for others to inquire about children for a couple that had been married over a year. "No, not yet, but eventually we would love to have some." It was Rachael's turn to change the subject. "So what do you like to do for fun? What are your hobbies?"

"I like music, mostly the classical variety. I'm pretty good on the piano. I also like to read."

"Read?" Rachael asked. "What are your favorite genres?"

"I like everything really, from fiction to nonfiction, but I'm a huge fan of science fiction. It goes well with my love of astrophysics."

Rachael's eyes lit up. "Sci-fi? I'm a huge fan too!" Maybe she and Liz had more in common than she thought. "Who are your favorite authors?"

"I like the classics. Jules Verne, Isaac Asimov, and, of course, Arthur C. Clarke."

"Some of my favorites as well," Rachael said. "I've read most of their works. They had amazing imaginations. Just think about what they would come up with today given recent advancements in science." Rachael continued her questioning. "Any other hobbies?"

"There is one other thing I like to do."

"What?"

"I like to go paramotoring."

"Paramotoring?"

"You know, it's where you have a backpack with an engine on it, and you're connected to a paraglider wing."

"I've seen some videos of it. You just run, take off, and fly like a bird."

"Yes, it's an amazing feeling. Simply flying over the landscape with your feet dangling from the seat. The ultimate freedom."

Rachael thought of her experience of riding an arachnid on New Eden and the complete freedom it afforded her. "I think I know the feeling." Rachael placed her hand behind her head as she reflected on soaring over the immaculate landscape of New Eden.

The ship still made odd noises—clicks, thumps, and an occasional whine followed by a muffled roar—that told the women that night patrols over the Sea of Japan were being launched many decks above them.

Liz noticed the tattoo on Rachael's wrist that was revealed when she'd placed her hand behind her head. "What's the tattoo on your wrist?"

"It's a Christian cross."

Of course, this wasn't the original one she'd had since college. That one was frozen in a cryo facility in Phoenix. She'd received this one shortly after her return from New Eden. "You have any tattoos?"

Without saying a word, Liz rolled, leaned her right arm over the railing, and lifted the sleeve of her right forearm, exposing a tattoo. Even in the dim light, Rachael clearly saw the number 103 tattooed in blue ink.

Rachael was more than a little surprised by the tattoo. One hundred and three was a reference to a session number during which Seth had been interviewed via spookyon transmission. This was the session that Seth had revealed the petrin definitions for life and death. The petrins viewed life as simply just purposeful information and death as the loss of the last copy of the purposeful information that defined an entity. Devotees of the alien and his beliefs regarding life and death had become known as the 103 Club, and the cult had grown worldwide. That the very academic and scientific Elizabeth Yang would have had the number tattooed on her body was revealing.

Rachael looked at the tattoo again. Vinod also had a similar 103 tattoo on his arm. Maybe she and Vinod really *were* kindred spirits regardless of sexual orientation.

Chapter Six
Mission Plan

The next morning, Rachael walked onto the hanger deck, where the briefing was to take place. The deck had been cleared of aircraft, and there were rows of gray metal folding chairs occupied by numerous military personnel in their fatigues. In front of the chairs was a podium with a large LCD display behind it. The aircraft that normally occupied the hanger had been moved to the flight deck except for two F-35 fighters in the corner, and the room had the distinct odor of jet fuel.

The USS Gerald R Ford had what was termed an open hangar deck design, with large openings in the hull on the starboard and port sides of the ship that allowed multiple jets to throttle their engines and warm up before being lifted by elevator to the flight deck. These gaps also afforded a spectacular view of the ocean, although the briefing area was far from the nearest opening.

What dominated the space, however, was an enormous metal cage, twenty feet tall, to the right of the display. It had solid top and bottom square panels made of one-inch steel. The sides of the cage were comprised of thick steel rods spaced a few inches apart. It was reminiscent of cages from old-fashioned zoos before the era of the modern animal habitats. This cage, however, was clean, polished, and exhibited modern technology in its construction.

Rachael approached the cage and ran her fingers along the smooth rods and looked at the steel top of the structure twenty feet above her. She marveled at the size of the cage and its purpose. It gave her some perspective on the creature they were endeavoring to study or capture on this mission. She turned away from the cage and took a seat in an empty row towards the front.

Joshua and Vinod walked in and sat on either side of Rachael. Joshua gave Rachael a kiss on the cheek and asked, "How was your night? Did you get some sleep?"

"Yeah," Vinod chimed in before Rachael could answer. "Rach, how was the girls' slumber party? Josh and I barely got a wink with the time change and the close quarters. It's tough to sleep when there are dozens of men snoring right next to you."

"To be honest," Rachael replied, "I didn't get a lot of sleep either. I think I'm still jet-lagged from the trip."

"What was it like bunking with Dr. Liz?" Vinod asked. "Were you two cozy in your private suite?"

"I wouldn't exactly call it a suite," Rachael answered, "but I'm sure we were more comfortable than you."

"Did you gals have some girl talk?" Vinod asked with a smirk.

"I guess."

Vinod rolled his eyes and patted Joshua on the shoulder. "Typical. They must have talked about men because she's pretty tight-lipped about their conversation."

Porter, Landon, and Williams walked into the hanger, Porter took a place in front of the podium as Langdon and Williams took seats in the front row.

"Where is Liz anyway?" Joshua asked, scanning the seats to see if the exobiologist was nearby.

"She'll be here soon," Rachael replied. "Just stopped to get some coffee."

On cue, Liz walked into the hangar, coffee in hand, and Rachael motioned for her to take the empty seat next to Vinod.

"So what did you gals talk about?" Vinod inquired, unwilling to drop the topic.

"Girls stuff," Rachael replied with a slight grin.

As Liz was almost to her seat, Rachael whispered into Vinod's ear, "I think she's got the hots for you."

"What? But you did tell her that . . .." Vinod couldn't finish his sentence. He was interrupted by Liz who sat down next to Vinod.

"Morning guys. Hello Mr. Bhakti."

"Rach...," Vinod whispered back to Rachael, but was interrupted once again by the voice of Mitchell Porter starting the meeting.

"Good morning, everyone," Porter began. "I'd like to start with some introductions. First, I'd like to introduce the captain of this carrier— Captain Nathaniel Pierce."

A tall, lanky man in his late fifties and wearing a khaki Navy uniform stood up and gave a peremptory wave from the front row.

"Most of the military personnel in this room are part of Navy Seal Team Four stationed out of Virginia," Porter continued. "All eight platoons are represented here, consisting of forty-eight soldiers. Their commander is also with us—Commander Theodore Johnson." Porter pointed to the front row. "Commander, can you please stand?"

Commander Johnson, dressed in fatigues, stood, turned, and waved to the gathering.

Porter then introduced the scientific team and Dina Williams.

The LCD screen switched to a display of satellite images of the arachnid. Some showed close-ups—these lacked clear resolution—while others showed it from higher perspectives in order to convey scale and location.

"I want to speak about the mission," Porter stated. "First, I'd like everyone to get more information on what we're dealing with. Dr. Andrews, you and Miss Miller are the only ones who have had actual contact with an arachnid. Can you share with the group your analysis of the images?"

Joshua stood and walked to the podium. He and Rachael had closely examined the satellite images on the plane trip to Seoul and had reached a few preliminary conclusions.

"After analyzing these images," he said, "we believe that this is indeed an arachnid of petrin technology. There are too many similarities to the images of arachnids provided to us by Seth and those we encountered on New Eden to conclude otherwise. But there are also significant differences." Joshua used a laser pointer to indicate certain features on the screen. "First, this creature seems to have eight tentacles on its carapace, while those from Petri have four. The ones on New Eden had only two. Also, the legs on this creature are much thicker, the purpose of which is unknown. Another difference is that this arachnid seems to have two rows of slots, almost like gills, on top of its carapace. Again, the significance of this is unknown. The final difference we noticed after careful observation is that both the arachnids on Petri and New Eden had a small orifice towards the front of their carapace, which was a kind of mouth. It's where they connected to nectar trees to gain nourishment. However, even after close inspection, this creature doesn't seem to have an orifice at all. There's a small round opening on top of its carapace near the front, but we don't feel it's a mouth. It's not located in any position that would make it easy for the creature to feed itself."

Heads in the audience craned left and right to better view the image of the large spider-like creature. Despite its resemblance to earthly arachnids, it had an otherworldly appearance, one that, to most, was quite menacing.

"Then how the hell does this thing eat?" Porter asked brusquely.

Joshua wasn't surprised that the general's abrupt manner had not changed since their initial encounter with him shortly after first contact with the petrins had been made. He was perennially gruff, suspicious, and prone to outbursts.

"Unknown," Joshua replied.

"Dr. Andrews, the arachnids from New Eden were capable of flight," Langdon said from the audience. "Do you think this creature can fly as well?"

"It's a good question," Joshua answered, "and one that Rachael and I had much discussion about. We can't know for sure, but we don't believe this creature is capable of flight. The thickness of its legs and overall density make flight highly unlikely."

"Anything else?" Porter said.

"No, that's about it," Joshua answered. "This is the best analysis we can give at the present time given the extreme distance at which these photographs were taken." Joshua returned to his seat.

"Obviously there's much we don't know about this creature," Porter said, now back at the podium. "This is the purpose of our mission—to get as much information about it as we can. The *main* goal of the mission, however, will be to communicate with or capture this creature, and if that isn't possible, to *destroy* it."

"Destroy it?" Rachael asked taken aback by Porter's last statement. No one had mentioned the destruction of the arachnid in the meeting they'd had in Berkeley. "If we do that, we'll lose any chance to study it or know why it's here."

"The more things change," Joshua sighed, "the more they remain the same."

"Typical military shit," Vinod added under his breath. "Same ole same ole."

"Like I said, Miss Miller," Porter continued, "we'll try to communicate or capture *if possible*, but this creature is not native to Earth. It's an invader and must not be allowed to roam free. This is not only my opinion, but the mission directive which comes directly from the president."

"We don't have any reason to think it's an invader," Vinod said, his hand waving dismissively. "Otherwise, why are we bothering to gather information in the first place?"

Vinod had made a valid point, and all heads turned to Porter.

"It's going to be treated as such as a precautionary measure," Porter said. "Don't parse words with me, Bhakti."

"Whatever," Vinod said, folding his arms defensively.

Porter waited for further comments, but there was none.

Porter then pointed to his right. "We've had this cage constructed of high-strength steel in order to capture the arachnid. Our engineers made calculations as to the physical strength of the creature given its size and presumed biological origin. This cage was designed to withstand five times the theoretical maximum strength of the creature and should afford safe containment for it."

"How the hell are we supposed to get it in there?" Vinod asked with skepticism. "You gonna tie a leash on it and ask it to go for a walk?"

The comment drew laughter from the audience, and Liz turned to Vinod with a wink. As usual, Vinod had the ability to irritate Porter in a comedic way.

"Some of the details, Mr. Bhakti," Porter stated with irritation, "have not been worked out yet. Our plan is to do close-up reconnaissance of the arachnid before trying to capture it. Frankly, that's going to be the job of the scientific team—to try to figure out if there's some kind of bait we can use to lure the creature into the cage."

"Right," Vinod whispered into Rachael's ear. "Bait for a creature with no mouth. Somehow I feel like *we're* going to end up being the bait."

Porter brought up a new image obviously taken from a satellite. The image was of a group of three buildings, all in close proximity to each other.

"This image is of a complex that's near the last known location of the arachnid. The complex has been scrutinized by our satellites for years, but our intelligence services noticed a large increase in activity around the area beginning one year ago. There has been no recent activity, however, and we now feel that the facility, whatever its original purpose, has been abandoned. We'll use it as a base from which to conduct our mission if it checks out as safe."

All eyes were on Porter as he went into the details of the mission. His arms were braced against the podium, and his voice echoed through the cavernous hangar deck.

"The mission will consist of four phases. Phase one will involve the seal team. They will be shuttled to the area of the buildings by helicopter—fully-armed of course—and search and secure the complex. Once the complex is secure, they will create a one-kilometer perimeter around the structure, at which time phase two will begin. During phase two, the scientific team, as well as the equipment needed for the mission, will be transported to the complex. Also during this phase, the scientific team will examine the complex to determine its purpose while the seal team sets up its equipment and gets ready for phase three. Phase three will be to search for the creature and establish a plan for either communication, capture, or destruction. The final phase will be to execute one of the three options. What I've given you is a general overview of the mission. We all realize that its objectives are broad and dynamic, but there are too many unknowns for us to formulate a more specific mission plan. Further details for these phases will be provided to the individual teams. Are there any questions?"

The room was silent as the group considered the ambitious nature of the mission. Although Porter had concisely explained the entire operation, there was an uneasy feeling that its execution might prove far more difficult than it sounded. The mission had multiple possible outcomes, and more than one military officer present worried that their deployment might end in mission creep, which was every commander's worst nightmare.

"Phase one will begin at 1200 today. I want the seal team to get its equipment ready while the scientific team assembles in the operations center of the carrier. Each seal team member will be equipped with a camera and headset that will transmit to the operations center what they see in real time. I want continual analysis from the scientific team via the transmitted video during phase one."

Porter had finished his presentation, and team members stood, talking in low tones about the daunting tasks ahead of them. A warning siren blared, indicating that one of the large deck elevators used to transport planes and equipment to the flight deck was about to be activated.

"How about we grab some breakfast?" Vinod asked Joshua and Rachael as the group dispersed. "There's not much we need to do before 1200. Most of the preparation is for the Seals."

"Sure," Rachael replied. "Liz, please join us."

*   *   *

The four gathered at a table in a mess hall of the carrier, enjoying their breakfast. Rachael and Joshua sat on one side of a long table, Liz and Vinod on the other. Vinod's tee shirt du jour was a cover of Tesla's *Mechanical Resonance* album. His outfit of jeans and rock tee shirt drew more than a few stares from uniformed sailors.

"I'm surprised that Porter didn't have you adhere to the military dress code," Rachael told Vinod.

"Like I've told you before Rach, that dude's all bark and no bite."

"Don't get overconfident," Joshua remarked. "Porter's got *plenty* of bite. I think he's giving us a lot of leeway since we're not military, and he needs our help."

"Tesla?" Liz asked glancing at Vinod's t-shirt. "As in Nikola Tesla?"

"No, it's the name of a rock band," Vinod said, "but I'm sure the band got its name from Nikola Tesla just like the car company did. You've never heard of Tesla the rock band?"

"Not really," Liz said. "I'm more of a classical music person, but I'm open to new experiences."

Vinod was pleasantly surprised and leaned closer to the exobiologist. "You're not familiar with classic rock? Then how come the 'Comfortably Numb' reference yesterday?"

"I'm not familiar with classic rock," Liz said, "but I did go to college. 'Comfortably Numb' is a campus staple."

Rachael rolled her eyes. "Wrong answer, Liz. You just opened Pandora's box, which is the Vinod Bhakti School of Classic Rock."

"Whoa, Rach," Vinod shot back defensively. "I didn't hear you complaining when *you* attended that school."

"Oh, I enjoyed your teaching, master," Rachael responded wryly, "but let new pupils beware. Attending Vinod's school is like going down the rabbit hole."

Vinod smiled and cocked his head as he and Rachael spoke simultaneously. "'White Rabbit' by Jefferson Airplane."

"Don't you think Liz has more important things to do than learn about classic rock?" Joshua asked with a sigh.

"Oh, I don't mind," Liz said. "I'm very good at multitasking. I can listen in my spare time." Liz turned to Vinod, "I'm assuming that your love of classic rock was the result of some influence by someone one generation removed from us? I mean, it's definitely before our time."

"You're correct," Vinod said. "My uncle provided my introduction to classic rock. I grew up in Cleveland, and he was the manager of a Radio Shack and made sure the music in the store was always tuned to a classic rock station. I used to hang out in the store after school while my parents were working."

"That explains a lot," Rachael remarked. "Electronics, computers, and classic rock all in one location during your formative years. The recipe for Vinod."

"Absolutely," Vinod responded. "Definitely an influential period in my life."

"I was never exposed to classic rock," Liz confessed. "My parents immigrated from China, and I think they would refer to such music as noise."

Vinod was crestfallen. "Noise?" He put down his fork. "Okay, the Vinod Bhakti School of Classic Rock is officially open. Hand me your phone. I'm going to create a playlist for you. Just a few songs. It's important, though, that when you listen to them, you read the lyrics. As much as the music, the lyrics have so much emotion and nuance tied to them. Some are downright poetic."

"And so it begins," Rachael joked.

"Okay," Liz said as she handed Vinod her phone.

Vinod spent a few minutes adding songs to a new playlist named "Vinod Lesson One" and handed the phone to Liz.

Commander Theodore Johnson, breakfast tray in hand, approached the group and asked, "Mind of I join y'all?"

"Be our guest," Joshua replied.

The commander took a seat next to Vinod.

Rachael eyed Johnson as he sat. He looked to be in his late forties, with the obligatory military crew cut. His short hair had gray stubble near his temples that, to Rachael, made him look mature and dignified. He was definitely career military, but his demeanor was far more palatable than Porter's.

*   *   *

Ted Johnson had grown up in Grand Isle, Louisiana. His mother and father had run a seafood restaurant in the small coastal town near the mouth of the Mississippi River, and his father had done most of the shrimping and fishing to obtain fare for his menu. Ted had excelled in sports, especially football, and like most residents he learned how to fish, hunt, and trap at an early age. Having weathered many Gulf hurricanes over the years, he wasn't easily intimidated by adversity. His uncle had served in Vietnam and Iraq, and Ted gravitated to the military after school. He had an adventurous spirit that yearned to travel beyond the confines of Grand Isle, and he wanted to serve his country and make his family proud. He'd risen through the ranks quickly and had become a specialist in counterterrorism. Still, at the end of the day, Ted liked to kick back and relax like anybody else. He was laidback and affable, but in the field he was a fierce warrior who was known for his resolve and lack of hesitation in giving an order. He was highly decorated but never tried to claim the spotlight. For him, every mission was about his duty and his men. His years spent in the swamps, bayous, and backwoods of Louisiana made him not only an excellent commander of the Seals, but also the perfect man for the mission at hand.

*   *   *

"Commander," Rachael said, "is your team ready for phase one?"

"They're getting there," Johnson said with a southern drawl. "I think we'll be ready to go by 1200. Y'all can call me Ted, by the way. Those military people call me commander, but I'm more comfortable with you civvies calling me by my Christian name. Where I come from, they call me a bayou rat. I'm not one to stand on formality." He paused and raised his eyebrows. "Unless the situation calls for it, of course."

"Okay, Ted," Rachael said. "Are you from the south? I detect a southern accent."

"Sure am, ma'am," Ted responded. "Louisiana, born and bred."

"Ma'am?" Rachael said. "I know you're just trying to be polite, southern upbringing and all, but please call me Rachael, and this is Josh, Vinod, and Liz."

"'Morning all," Ted replied as he took a bite of eggs. "So what did you guys think of the briefing?"

"I thought it sucked," Vinod replied succinctly.

Rachael's face flushed with embarrassment. Vinod definitely was a unique person, but sometimes *too* unique. They were speaking with a person raised in the south, someone who was surely used to respect and decorum. She felt that she had to atone for Vinod's frankness.

"You'll have to excuse Vinod," she said, shooting her friend an admonishing look. "He's a great guy but sometimes doesn't have much of a filter."

"No offense taken," Ted said. "So what sucked about the briefing, Vinod?"

"There were no details," Vinod answered. "How the hell are we supposed to freaking capture some elephant-sized arachnid in a cage? It looks to me like we're going to have to make this stuff up as we go along. No offense, Ted, but this lacks Porter's usual military precision."

"General Porter is a good man," Ted said, "and it's a difficult operation. As far as making up stuff in the field, that's part of our training. It's called working the problem."

"I'm not sure they had much of a choice," Joshua conceded, taking the contrarian viewpoint as he was frequently apt to do. "I mean we *are* dealing with a lot of unknowns here. Their plan seems logical and the best course of action given what little information we have. Why? Do *you* have a better plan, Vinod?"

"I don't know. Maybe."

"Like what?" Joshua asked, somewhat bemused.

"How about if we just fire up our buddy Seth the android. I'm sure he could tell us what's going on."

Joshua's eyes shifted to Rachael. They'd had a discussion on the plane about the possibility of trying to contact Seth, but attempting to do so would violate the quarantine that the United Nations had implemented on using primordial spookyons to contact life beyond Earth. The quarantine had been deemed necessary because humanity had learned there was life on other planets. The consensus among nations was that humanity was just fine knowing it was not alone in the universe but didn't want to risk outside interference in its evolution and development. It was therefore determined that capturing primordial spookyons—those created by the Big Bang—and attempting to communicate with the petrins or any other civilization would be strictly forbidden. However, research on non-primordial spookyon technology used for instantaneous communication was still permitted since it had many theoretical applications. This, in fact, was what Joshua and his team continued to work on at the Bowman Particle Research Center.

Knowing what her husband was thinking, Rachael gave Joshua an imperceptible nod. The less mention of Seth, the better.

"Look, Vinod," Joshua said, "we all know that contacting Seth would involve breaking the moratorium on capturing primordial spookyons. Besides, even if we did have permission, it would probably take weeks, if not months, to capture one, and we wouldn't even know if that one was connected to the petrins. I think that, given the urgency of the situation, we're taking the best course of action."

"Yeah, I suppose," Vinod responded, acquiescing, "but it sure would be great to have our buddy Seth back with us. I miss that guy."

"We all do," Rachael said, suddenly emotional. She knew that the only reason she was on Earth, or even alive for that matter, was because of Seth's kindness.

Liz scrolled through her new playlist and donned ear buds as she evaluated the conversation. Both Joshua and Vinod had made valid points. It was going to be an interesting mission, but she was worried that everyone wasn't on the same page. More than anything, she didn't know what to make of Vinod, the man who'd made contact with the petrins possible.

Chapter Seven
Phase One

With the Sea of Japan shining a bluish-green because of algae stirred up by the carrier's wake, waves glazed by the sun, the scientific team stood on the deck of the USS Gerald R Ford at 1130 and watched three MV-24B osprey helicopters take off carrying Seal Team Four and its equipment. The osprey was a hybrid between a helicopter and a plane in that it had two rotating engines on its wings, which meant that the rotors could be placed vertically for vertical take-offs and landings but could also rotate to the horizontal for faster flight. Initially, the rotors of the copters were set in the vertical position, and the group watched the machines lift off and rotate their engines after they had gained sufficient altitude.

The osprey, despite its technological prowess, was not stealthy. It could easily be picked up on North Korean radar, but this was not a concern for the military commanders who had planned the mission. There had been complete radio silence from the North Koreans since the U.S. had tried to contact them regarding the satellite images of the arachnid. This, along with the fact that the North Koreans seemed to be evacuating the area around the arachnid, led the U.S. to believe that the Koreans were hoping for help from other nations, albeit without officially asking for it. As a precaution, the U.S. had made known their intentions of embarking on a military mission to deal with the arachnid, but they'd received no response. Since the U.S. was sure the message had gotten through, they were not expecting any resistance from North Korea.

"I'm not big on the military," Vinod remarked while standing on deck, watching the ospreys in the distance as they headed towards the North Korean coast. "But damn! They do have some amazing technology."

"You can say that again," Joshua said as he marveled at the physics and engineering needed to create such machines.

"You two are forgetting those brave, well-trained men up there," Rachael remarked. "They're more valuable than the machinery."

"Quite right," Joshua said.

Promptly at 1200, the scientific team, as requested, was seated in the command center of the carrier. The center was a fully-enclosed space in the bowels of the ship and was outfitted with controls and computerized displays that governed the operations of the carrier as well as its weapon systems and all sensory equipment. Numerous technicians sat in front of digital controls and displays, monitoring their consoles and screens with a minimum of talk. Screens showed aircraft, drones, feeds from various ground targets in Asia and the Pacific, tactical displays, maps, weather patterns, and a dozen news feeds from television stations around the world. The center, bathed in low-level recessed lighting in the ceiling, was a command post no different from situation rooms at NORAD or the Pentagon. During times of high alert, the lights dimmed completely, replaced by red lights that cast an eerie glow throughout the high-tech space.

Towards one side of the center, two enormous LCD displays were mounted on stands, each showing video feeds from the helmet cameras of the Seals—twenty-four on each screen in a six-by-four matrix. The videos currently showed various angles of the inside of the ospreys since the Seals were still en route to the Korean complex.

Porter sat closest to the displays and wore a headset with microphone, a wireless keyboard with trackpad in his lap.

"These are the live video feeds from the helmets of each seal team member," he explained. "The numbers in the lower left corners represent which platoon each member is a part of and who that person is." Porter pointed to a feed on the LCD on the left. "For example, this feed has 4-6 at the lower left. That means that the feed is from member six of the fourth platoon. I felt this was easier than using the actual names of the soldiers."

"Impersonal bastard," Vinod whispered to Liz, who was seated next to him.

"Your job," Porter continued, "is to scan the feeds for anything you feel is important. If you see something, shout it out and I can bring that feed front and center."

Porter tapped a few keys on his keyboard, which brought feed 4-6 full-screen on the left display. The other feeds transitioned to smaller windows surrounding the main feed. He then tapped more keys, causing the feeds to revert to their original orientation.

"All of the feeds are being recorded, of course, so that we can do more detailed analysis in the future, but I want you all to be studying the feeds so we can get immediate feedback."

Liz looked at the feeds on the two screens. "Why is there one feed that simply has a C on it?" she asked.

"That's the feed from Commander Johnson's helmet," Porter explained. "Each team member also has a microphone that's connected directly to the speakers in this room, but these are currently set to 'push to talk' mode so that we don't have a jumble of audio coming through all at once. If any member wants to talk or ask a question, he pushes a button on his headset to enable it, like a walkie talkie. Additionally, I can talk to the entire group at once using my headset. Any questions?" Porter surveyed the center, his jaw set and resolute. It was clear he was accustomed to being in command.

"What are we looking for?" Joshua asked.

"I have no idea," Porter said, turning to Joshua. "You're the scientific experts. Analyze. Look for the unexpected or unfamiliar."

Porter explained what would happen once the copters set down. The complex consisted of one large building and two smaller ones in close proximity. Platoons one through four were in charge of patrolling the exterior and then the interior of the main building. Platoons five and six would do likewise for the other two buildings. Their mission was to engage and capture any people they found, as well as conduct a thorough inspection of all rooms and hallways to look for any threats.

"They're descending," Porter announced as seal 2-4 peered out the open door of the osprey, revealing an aerial view of the complex.

The ospreys landed in a grass field adjacent to the main building, and their occupants quickly piled out, weapons drawn. The first two ospreys to land held platoons one through four, which swiftly assembled in front of the main building. The third osprey held platoons five and six, which moved to the other two buildings. The Seals were dressed in dark grey and black camo and were well-armed with automatic weapons, ammunition, body armor, and grenades.

The surrounding landscape was a cool-temperate coniferous forest consisting of spruce, Siberian fir, pine, and Korean pine trees. Tall jagged mountains rose in the distance, their slopes heavily wooded. Beyond the complex, foliage was dense, with dark green scrub occupying much of the forest floor. It was hot and humid, with the sun already climbing to its zenith, when the area would heat up further.

The three ospreys took off after the last occupant had disembarked and headed back to the carrier, leaving the Seals in the eerie silence of the forest.

The scientific team on the carrier inspected the video feeds of the exteriors of the three buildings. Their architecture was strictly utilitarian. The buildings were rectangular-shaped and had exteriors made of cement blocks. There were few windows, all of which had metal bars covering them, shutters sealed. From above, the structures resembled three stone rectangles devoid of ornamentation or landscaping. The overall impression conveyed to the scientific team was that the buildings were barren and sterile, at least from a cursory view of their exteriors.

"They look like prisons," Vinod remarked. "Drab and secure."

The main building was three stories tall and was approximately 300 feet by 200 feet. The other two buildings were two stories tall and were smaller, only 150 feet by 100 feet. The buildings occupied a clearing in the otherwise thick forest. Unkempt grass dotted with weeds surrounded the buildings and extended for a distance to the forest edge. A single dirt road snaked from the woods and ended in a dirt parking lot in front of the main building. There were no vehicles present, however.

Ted was heard over the speakers in the command center. "Commence the perimeter sweep."

The platoons walked slowly around the buildings in opposite directions, weapons at the ready. The smaller buildings had one main entrance, with smaller doors to the side.

The larger building had a main entrance set in an alcove with two large wooden doors. It, too, had smaller doors, but the side of the building adjacent to the dirt parking lot had a large, metal, industrial garage door two stories high that rolled up.

The platoons completed their perimeter sweeps of the buildings with no incident. There were no external threats or signs of life around the buildings.

"Perimeter secured," Ted announced in clipped syllables used during a military operation.

"Any signs of life?" Porter asked.

"Negative," Ted replied. "No sounds at all. Dead quiet. Platoon two, take position in front of the main entrance and get ready to go in."

Ted took up a position behind the Seals. "Check the door," he ordered.

A member of platoon two pulled on the handle of the door, which swung open a crack. "It's unlocked," he announced.

"They didn't even bother to secure the facility," Joshua commented. "Very strange."

"But who are *they*?" Rachael asked.

Joshua shook his head, eyes fixed on the feed.

"Proceed inside," Ted commanded.

Platoon two stormed into the main entrance, ready to engage anything hostile, but no threats were found.

"It's dark in here," 2-3 announced.

"Switch on your helmet lamps," Ted said.

The video feeds from the platoon were now bright spotlights shining on what appeared to be a lobby with metal chairs randomly dispersed around the concrete floor.

"I think I see a lighting panel," 2-2 announced as his video feed illuminated a wall-mounted white rectangle. He flipped numerous switches but got no response. "Looks like the power's out."

"Platoons five and six," Ted said, "commence your interior sweeps."

Like the main building, the other two were unlocked, and the platoons entered without incident.

Platoons one through four, along with their commander, entered the lobby of the main building. There were two hallways on either end of the space that led into the interior of the building, which was unnaturally silent. The floor was dusty, and it was obvious that none of the buildings had seen any cleaning or maintenance for a long time. The walls were constructed of featureless tan cinderblocks. Signs in Korean obviously indicated directions or the functions of various areas in the building.

"Platoons one and two, take the hallway to the left," Ted said. "I'm going with platoons three and four into the right hallway. Look for any stairwells. I want platoon two to sweep the second floor while platoon three sweeps the third floor. If we find a basement, that will be for platoon four. Platoon one will sweep the main floor." Ted's voice was steady and bore little resemblance to his conversational tone when off-duty.

The platoons split up into two groups and explored the hallways.

The scientific teams examined the video feeds from the three buildings, which were rapidly-moving spotlights playing over the interior of the buildings. The feeds from one of the two smaller buildings, which was being swept by platoon five, showed multiple dormitory-style rooms with bunk beds and bathrooms, all without ornament. There was also a large central area that looked to be a dining room. Bowls with chopsticks were still on some of the long brown tables, and the bowls contained food covered in mold.

"Living quarters," Langdon surmised.

"Yeah," Vinod said, "and it looks like the occupants left in a hurry. Didn't even bother to clean up."

"Pretty Spartan," Liz commented. "I wonder what they were up to."

"That's what we're here to find out," Porter said.

The video feeds from the second small building revealed something much different. It looked to be a biological laboratory with numerous machines and shelves filled with chemicals, all with Korean labels.

"Can you read those, Dr. Yang?" Porter asked.

"Bring up feed 6-4," Liz said.

Porter obliged and feed 6-4 showed prominently on the right LCD screen of the command center as Liz read the labels on the canisters.

"Potassium hydroxide, acetic acid, sulfur, hydrochloric acid. They seem to be chemical reagents."

The feed from 6-4 shone on additional containers on the shelves, all with various chemical agents that Liz translated. The feed next showed large barrels of chemicals on the floor, also with labels in Korean.

"Definitely a lab of some sort," Rachael remarked.

Feed 6-2 was in a different room on the second floor of the same building, which housed a large modern laboratory with machines.

"Bring up feed 6-2, please," Liz requested.

"This is laboratory equipment. Centrifuges, biological freezers, and . . .," Liz paused as she examined the feed.

"And what?" Porter asked impatiently.

"DNA sequencers," Liz answered.

"Genetic engineering?" Langdon said, glancing at Joshua. "Damn."

"I think so," Liz said. "I also see genetic analyzers, spliceosome units, and microfluidic dispensers. Pretty sophisticated stuff, and it's all used for genetic research."

The scientific team grew more apprehensive by the moment. What were they dealing with? A lab conducting genetic engineering? Rachael put her hand on Joshua's arm, their thoughts on the technology of the petrins, although neither understood why such equipment would be found in a North Korean forest.

Members of platoon one swept the ground floor of the main building. Their feeds revealed numerous administrative rooms furnished with simple wooden desks and chairs. Otherwise, the rooms were bare, with no documents or books of any kind.

"No way to know what the hell they were doing," Vinod remarked.

"At least not yet, Bhakti," Porter said. "Let the men do their jobs."

Platoon two found a stairwell in the main building and was sweeping the second floor. There were more administrative rooms, but there was a large railing that surrounded an opening in the floor that looked down upon a concrete surface on the first level of the structure. At one end of the space was the rolling garage door they had seen from the outside. The space within the railing extended to the third floor, which also had a railing. The result was a three-story area that was accessed by the two-story tall garage door. The space itself was empty, with no vehicles present.

Platoon six continued exploring the second floor of their building, which was the laboratory building. Something glimmering on the floor on one of the feeds caught Rachael's eye.

"What was that on feed 6-5?" she asked.

Porter enlarged the feed.

"Looks like shattered glass," 6-5 responded. He knelt and picked up a piece to examine it more closely. "Whatever it is, it looks like it was spherical in shape."

The thought sent a chill up Joshua's spine. "Wait, what is that on feed 6-6?" he asked.

When Porter brought the feed up, a large rectangular glass tank appeared. One of its walls had an irregular-shaped hole. The bottom of the tank was covered with a semi-translucent gelatinous material, some of which had oozed through the hole and spilled onto the floor.

"Oh, my God!" Joshua gasped.

"What are we looking at, Dr. Andrews?" Porter asked with urgency.

"I'm not sure," Joshua replied, "but it looks very similar to the material I saw the embryonic petrins suspended in when I was in the lab at the research center."

"Don't touch that material," Porter ordered the Seals.

"Something strange about the hole in the tank though," Joshua remarked.

"What?" Porter asked.

"That tank is made of glass, but there's a hole in it, and the rest of the glass is intact."

"So?" Porter said.

"A hole made by a projectile or by some type of hit to the glass would cause shattering. This looks like something intentionally cut a hole directly into the glass. Very unusual."

The platoons continued their sweeps of the buildings. Platoon three was on the third floor of the main building. It seemed to be a storage area for equipment that was covered with dust and white tarps. Seal 3-3 lifted one of the tarps to show the equipment underneath as Porter brought the feed front and center. It showed a myriad of outdated equipment.

"Looks like really old electronics," Langdon remarked.

"Old?" Vinod said. "More like ancient. I'm talking vacuum tube ancient. I think these are old radio devices from way back when. Why would they be here?"

"Hell," Portered answered, "this complex has been under surveillance for decades. The equipment may have been there for quite some time. Maybe they just moved it to the third floor to make room for more modern equipment."

"You may be right," Vinod said. "Do you see that layer of dust on those tarps? Could have been there for decades."

"The main building has a basement," Ted announced. "I'm heading down with platoon four."

Porter switched to the feed from Ted's helmet camera as he descended a stairwell to the basement two flights down. Ted opened the door at the bottom and walked into a cavernous opening two stories tall. His spotlight focused on a large metal curving wall in the center of the space, with numerous metal pipes and wires on its surface.

"What are we looking at?" Porter asked.

"You tell me, man," Ted answered as he examined the pipes. "You have the scientists."

Joshua felt a gnawing in the pit of his stomach. "I recognize that," he said nervously. "It's a tokamak."

Chapter Eight
Larry, Moe, and Curly

Joshua, Rachael, Vinod, and Liz climbed aboard an osprey sitting on the deck of the carrier. They, along with various other military personnel, were ready to depart for the complex where the seal team was keeping vigil. Langdon and Williams would remain on board the carrier, but Porter had insisted on being with his men, so he was on the osprey as well.

It had been a full day since the Seals had secured the complex, and over the past few hours, as per the mission plan, they had established a secure one-kilometer perimeter around the complex without incident.

The osprey's engines roared as it took off and flew over the Sea of Japan. There had been a constant stream of helicopters leaving the deck for the past several hours, each delivering tons of equipment and supplies to the complex, including the cage that hopefully would be able to hold the arachnid if captured.

It was late afternoon when the occupants of the osprey got their first glimpse of the complex as the aircraft descended slowly. It was similar to the satellite images except for the fact that equipment and supplies—some crated and some exposed—now surrounded the buildings.

Upon landing, the scientific team learned that the Seals had given nicknames to each of the buildings to make them easier to identify: Larry, Moe, and Curly. Larry was the laboratory, Curly was the residence with bunks and dining hall, and Moe was the main building that housed the tokamak.

The team set up residence in Curly and unpacked their belongings. Liz and Rachael shared a dorm room, while Joshua and Vinod took another.

"Couldn't they come up with better names for these buildings?" Vinod asked Joshua as they settled into their room.

"Like what?"

"How about Emerson, Lake, and Palmer?"

Joshua laughed at yet another classic rock reference, not that he was surprised by the answer.

Porter announced that the scientific team would meet at 0800 the next morning in the lobby of Moe to go over the details for the next stage of the mission. This would give military personnel and technicians time to unpack and set up equipment still being airlifted to the site.

Joshua and Vinod went to bed early in order to be refreshed for the meeting, but their sleep was interrupted around 2:00 a.m. as the light in their room came on.

"Looks like they got us power," Joshua mumbled as he got out of bed to turn off the light switch.

In the morning, after a breakfast of canned military rations in the dining area, Joshua and Vinod left Curly to make the short walk to Moe for the meeting. They heard the rumble of copter blades in the sky as they saw two CH-53E super stallion helicopters carrying military tanks suspended on cables.

"Tanks?" Vinod asked incredulously.

"Porter isn't messing around," Joshua said as the copters placed their loads on the ground, kicking up clouds of dust as they hovered.

Vinod noted that the tanks were skeletonized, their armor having been removed.

"The tanks aren't complete," he said as the copters departed.

"The tanks were probably too heavy to lift intact. I suspect they'll transport the armor separately and reassemble the tanks onsite."

The tanks joined numerous other vehicles occupying the dirt parking lot next to Moe. There were Humvees equipped with large-caliber machine guns, as well as smaller vehicles like military-style four-wheel ATVs. Next to the vehicles stood the cage, two stories tall.

"Shit," Vinod exclaimed. "Porter's brought a small army here." The duo walked over to the cage to examine it more closely. "You think this can hold that creature?"

"Looks pretty strong," Joshua replied. "I think it'll do the job. It reminds me of something from *Jurassic Park*. It looks like it could contain a velociraptor."

As they walked farther, Vinod noticed that a large array of solar panels had been assembled on the grass adjacent to the dirt lot. "Looks like that's where we're getting our power," he said. "They must have the solar array connected to a battery storage unit since we had power last night. These panels can only produce electricity during the day."

Next to the solar array was a large satellite dish that a technician was still in the process of hooking up.

"What's this for?" Vinod asked the technician.

"It's the main communications array," the technician answered as he connected various wires. "This'll be your primary method of communicating with the ship. It'll handle all data transmission, including audio and video."

"Porter's thought of everything," Joshua commented as the two entered the main lobby of Moe. "Looks like phase two of the mission is well underway."

Liz and Rachael were seated on metal chairs in the lobby as Joshua and Vinod walked in.

"Morning, gals," Joshua said as he and Vinod took their seats. "How was your night?"

"Uneventful," Rachael responded. "It's nice that we now have power."

"I'm sure it is, Rach," Vinod replied sarcastically. "Now you two can use your curling irons."

"Hilarious," Rachael shot back with equal sarcasm. "You know, Vinod, there are a lot of times when you're a really funny guy . . . and then there's now."

Liz looked at Vinod's tee shirt, which was the cover from Billy Thorpe's *Children of the Sun* album. "Billy Thorpe? Was that on my playlist?"

"No," Vinod replied. "What I gave you were the basics. Thorpe is, shall we say, a subject for advanced students. Have you had a chance to listen to any of it?"

"A couple of songs last night. One called 'For What It's Worth' by someone named Buffalo Springfield."

"Oh, that's a classic from the Vietnam era," Vinod said excitedly. "It's about . . . .."

Joshua and Rachael were relieved as Vinod was interrupted by Porter's entrance. He took a seat facing the other four.

"Damn, general," Vinod said. "You certainly brought some serious firepower here."

"In my opinion," Porter answered, "there's no such thing as too much firepower. The technicians are almost finished setting up the equipment and weapons systems. Once they're done, they'll head back to the ship. Then it will just be us and the Seals to deal with the arachnid. We have enough food, water, and supplies for a week and can requisition more from the carrier if needed."

"Like summer camp," Vinod said.

Porter ignored the humor. He'd never grown accustomed to Vinod's glib attitude, but Williams valued his skill set, and that was enough to keep him on the team.

"Any more sightings of the arachnid from the satellites?" Joshua asked.

"No," Porter answered. "We feel it may be hiding in the foliage."

"So we don't know its location?" Rachael asked.

"We know its general vicinity, but it will be the job of the Seals to run reconnaissance and obtain its precise location."

"What do you want us to do?" Liz asked.

"The Seals will be starting their scouting mission tomorrow to search for the arachnid," Porter replied. "I want them to have as much information as possible about this complex and what it contains before they start. I want you to explore the buildings and gather any relevant details. What I'm looking for is information on what the North Koreans were doing here, as well as what caused them to abandon it."

"We already know that the North Koreans cleaned out the place," Vinod pointed out. "Files and documents and what have you."

"Then give me your best guess," Porter countered. "Brainstorm. You're the scientific team, so earn your pay."

Vinod nodded.

"There's not much valuable information to be gleaned from Curly," Porter said. "It seems to be a simple dormitory complex, so I want you to concentrate on Moe and Larry. Miss Miller, I want you and Dr. Yang to explore Larry. Dr. Andrews, you and Mr. Bhakti explore Moe. I'd like all of you to report back to me and Commander Johnson at this time tomorrow with your findings."

*   *   *

Joshua and Vinod stood in the basement of Moe next to the tokamak. Joshua could now explore the workings of the complex machine in greater detail. He was very familiar with tokamaks since it was the same type of instrument that he used for creating spookyons back in the lab in Berkeley.

The tokamak was an extremely large machine that contained a torus, a compartment shaped like a hollow donut. Powerful electromagnets surrounded the torus, with the magnet used to create superheated plasma. The entire machine was wrapped in field coils cooled by liquid helium. Its purpose was to force hydrogen nuclei to fuse in order to form helium. The collision of the nuclei was partially responsible for the creation of spookyons. The inside of the torus was lined with smooth metal plates conforming to its donut shape.

"Pretty shoddy construction, if you ask me," Joshua stated after examining the pipes and wires. Some of the connections are coming apart, and the whole thing looks jury-rigged."

"I don't think the North Koreans are known for their technological prowess," Vinod said. "They're infamous for knocking off other people's tech."

"Don't be so sure. Remember, they exploded a nuclear device recently even though the yield was low. Still, this tokamak doesn't pass muster for me."

"You think you can fire this thing up?"

"No. The solar panels may provide enough energy to turn the lights on, but there's nowhere near enough power to operate a tokamak. But why would I want to?"

"I don't know. Just asking. Do you think they were trying to capture primordial spookyons? You know, going against the UN moratorium on such activity?"

"The fact that there's an arachnid close by leads me to no other conclusion. They're not known for playing by the rules."

Joshua and Vinod circled the machine. When they had almost made a complete circuit, they found the control room from which the tokamak was operated. There were desks and panels with numerous gauges and switches, but Vinod was attracted to a rack full of servers near the back. Pulling a rolling chair close, Vinod sat at a workstation near the server rack.

"You know enough Korean to be able to access that?" Joshua asked.

"Korean?" Vinod said. "That's high-level shit. I operate at the low level directly with the OS and the CPU. There hasn't been a computer system invented—on Earth anyway—that I can't hack. Let's see if this thing will boot."

Fortunately, the power afforded to the complex was enough to activate the workstation. Vinod typed feverishly on the keyboard as Joshua stood behind him and watched.

*   *   *

In the lab, Liz and Rachael stared at racks of chemical reagents on the first floor of Larry.

"Looks like they have a whole chemistry lab here," Rachael remarked.

"Certainly complete," Liz said as she read Korean labels on jars and canisters. "I think it would be prudent if I catalogue what items are present." Liz took out her phone and started typing the names of the compounds into her notes app.

"Cataloging all these chemicals could take a while given the number of containers," Rachael said.

"Definitely going to take some time, but we need to have *something* to give Porter." Liz laughed halfheartedly. "For our best guess, as he calls it."

"While you're doing that, I'm going to explore upstairs."

Rachael climbed the stairs to the second floor, where it appeared that most of the lab's activity had taken place since it contained laboratory equipment and workbenches. She paused at the spot where the seal team had discovered the broken glass and examined a large piece with its spherical contour. She was familiar with it since it had the same contour she'd seen at a lecture given many years earlier at Wheeler auditorium when she was an undergraduate at Berkeley. Rachael was sure that what she held in her hand was a broken piece of a Bowman sphere. She'd seen Joshua for the first time that day, and she had to force her thoughts away from the eventful lecture in order to focus on the shard in her hand.

She was convinced that the North Koreans were using the complex to attempt spookyon transmission, but for what purpose, she had no idea. Her suspicions were confirmed during her continued exploration when she spotted a black instrument sitting on one of the lab tables. Turned on its side, it was a cylinder with attachment points for a sphere. It was a spookyon detector, the kind she and Joshua had used in the underground chamber below the particle center, one nicknamed the Bat Cave. She was lost in thought again. She'd been an up-and-coming journalist who had wanted to interview the handsome young scientist. Instead of conducting an interview, the two had accidentally contacted the petrins.

*　　　　*　　　　*

"You get anything yet?" Joshua asked. It had been a full twenty minutes since Vinod had sat at the terminal.

"Almost there," Vinod replied. "I think I've got access to the file system. I'm bringing up a file list . . . now." He didn't say a word, his eyes growing large as he read the list of files.

"What is it?" Joshua asked.

"What the hell?" Vinod exclaimed.

"Do you recognize the files?"

"Of course I recognize the files," Vinod replied, exasperated. "*I* wrote them. They're my algorithm for communicating with aliens."

Chapter Nine
Prime Suspect

"Goddamn it!" Vinod shouted as Porter entered their scheduled meeting the next morning. The scientific team and Ted had been present for a while, Vinod nervously swaying his foot in anticipation of Porter's arrival.

"Mr. Bhakti," Porter said as he took a seat, "what're you so upset about?"

"You damn government guys!" Vinod exclaimed.

"What about us?" Porter asked, his tone bellicose.

"You confiscate my algorithm for communicating with aliens and tell me—" Vinod paused, cleared his throat, and mimicked Porter's voice. 'Don't worry, Mr. Bhakti, your code will be safe with us.' What a load of bullshit!"

"*Your* code?" Porter asked, brows furrowed. "Your algorithm for communicating with aliens? It's stored on a hard drive at the research center in Berkeley. The drive is locked in a safe, so I think it's very secure."

"Secure, my ass," Vinod said with indignation. "Then explain why I found my algorithm on a server at this facility?"

"What?" Porter asked, his face pale. "Your code is *here*?" The general was clearly troubled by the revelation.

"Yes," Vinod replied. "Josh and I found it on servers next to the tokamak. Your security protocols suck! First you had the data breach that allowed our communication with Seth to become public, and now this. I would've been better off leaving the protocol on the servers in my apartment. At least Layla could've kept an eye on it." Layla was Vinod's personal version of Alexa, his custom-designed virtual assistant named after the legendary song by Derek and the Dominos.

"How the hell could someone have gotten access to *that* code?" Porter asked. "It's not even connected to the Internet. There's no way it could have been hacked." In a rare moment of consternation, the general inhaled and rubbed his right hand over the top of his head. "That code was one of the most carefully guarded secrets on the planet."

"Then it must have been an inside job," Rachael concluded. "Who had access to the safe?"

"Very few people," Porter answered as he pondered the list of people who had clearance to view the protocol. "I do have one prime suspect though. Dr. Andrews, have you had any recent contact with Rodrigo Torres?"

"No," Joshua replied. "Like I told you at the lab, I haven't spoken to him in over a year. He kinda fell off the face of the Earth—complete radio silence. Last thing he told me was that he was going to work for more money in the private sector. Do you think *he* stole Vinod's code?"

"Quite possibly," Porter answered. "Look, only you and he know the formulation for the lids used in the tokamak to capture primordial spookyons. As I mentioned, the FBI has been investigating his whereabouts. They recently found that he traveled to Beijing about fourteen months ago, and his location subsequent to that trip is unknown. No email address, credit card statements, cell phone pings—nothing."

"With *his* tech skills, Rodrigo is more than capable of staying off the grid," Joshua conceded.

"China is one of the countries from which you can get into North Korea fairly easily," Liz commented. "I think there's still train service between the two countries."

"Precisely," Porter answered. "His presence in Beijing—that's the smoking gun."

"You really think Rodrigo is behind all this?" Joshua asked. "I always trusted him implicitly given the classified nature of our work. He was thoroughly vetted by the FBI after we made contact with Seth. Hell, the particle center was practically in lockdown."

"He's the only one that makes sense," Porter answered, "and his disappearance roughly coincides with the time you lost contact with him."

Rachael was clearly upset. She and Rodrigo had built a rapport since she had first met him. The two had often spoken Spanish in Joshua's presence just to get under his skin. "Why would Rodrigo do such a thing? He and Josh were tight." She thought of how the two men had worked long hours in the bat cave in an attempt to create entangled spookyons.

"Money," Porter answered. "It's *always* about money. The FBI is looking into financial transactions between North Korea and anonymous bank accounts in the Caymans, but they haven't found anything conclusively linking the accounts to Mr. Torres, but I'll bet the stars on my uniform that they will."

Porter turned to the information theorist. "Look, Vinod, I . . .."

Vinod was surprised that Porter had called him by his first name. He'd never heard that from the ever-official Mitchell Porter before.

"I'm genuinely sorry your algorithm was stolen," Porter continued. "Believe me, we'll investigate this completely. I know the importance of that algorithm, and frankly I'm embarrassed that it was stolen on my watch." Porter lowered his eyes, unwilling to look directly at Vinod.

Vinod stared at Porter, his anger quenched by the general's rare display of sincerity. He fought the urge to say something nice to Porter, a man he'd disdained ever since their first meeting three years earlier. "Whatever. What's done is done. I guess we just have to move forward."

Porter raised his head and nodded in agreement. He turned to Joshua. "Dr. Andrews, what has the scientific team found while exploring Moe and Larry. Do you have any insights into what the North Koreans were doing?"

"The scientific team met last night," Joshua answered, "and we came up with a hypothesis. There's no doubt that the Koreans were trying to capture primordial spookyons. They built a tokamak to capture the spookyons, and we discovered a spookyon detector in the lab. And to be honest, the subject of Rodrigo was discussed by the scientific team since he was the only one besides me who knew the formulation of the lids needed to capture primordial spookyons."

Joshua was referring to the lids inside a tokamak that were used to attract spookyons. The lids were funnel-shaped metallic objects that were the covers for cylinders that housed Bowman spheres. The lids attracted spookyons and directed them into the glass spheres. There was a specific combination of heavy metal elements that were needed to attract primordial spookyons, and only he and Rodrigo knew the formulation.

"We can now reluctantly conclude that the Koreans, with Rodrigo's help, were successful in capturing a primordial spookyon and establishing communication with . . . someone. We're fairly confident that the DNA sequence for the arachnid was transmitted to Earth via a primordial spookyon, and that the Koreans used that DNA sequence to start growing something in the lab. The rest of what I'm about to say is more speculative. We believe that what they were growing somehow turned on them. The tank we found in the lab—the one with a hole in the glass and with no evidence of shattering—leads me to believe that whatever they were growing escaped and eventually grew into the arachnid."

"A solid hypothesis," Porter said. "But why did the Koreans embark on this endeavor in the first place? What was their intent? They had to know that we'd be breathing down their necks given the UN moratorium if we ever found out. They took a hell of a gamble."

"We simply don't know," Joshua replied. "Rodrigo might be the only person who can answer that."

"Could they have been developing a weapons system?" Ted asked. "That's definitely their MO. Things are usually what they seem. When you see a gator's eyes poking out of the water, you know what lies beneath—a lot of teeth with a hell of a bite."

"My thoughts exactly," Porter affirmed. "Maybe they were using the petrins to gain an advantage on the rest of the world. Definitely wouldn't put that beyond the bastards."

"I . . . don't think so," Rachael said, drawing out her words thoughtfully. "Why would Seth or the petrins want to give the Koreans an unfair advantage? Seth's purpose for wanting to transport humanity to New Eden was to preserve mankind and prevent its self-destruction. Why would they suddenly agree to give the Koreans a weapons system, one that would destroy large parts of our society? It doesn't make sense, nor does it tally with the petrin prime directive of noninterference in other cultures."

"Maybe Seth changed his mind," Porter suggested. "Maybe after Dr. Andrews broke the sphere in the lab and cut the connection with the petrins, he had a change of heart."

Vinod drummed his fingers on the table, obviously agitated at Porter's conclusion.

"No way," he said. "If Seth wanted to get us, he could easily have done so in the lab. He had ample opportunity. Also, aren't we forgetting the fact that Seth was the one who gave us the cure for the virus? He anticipated the possibility of the connection being cut, and hence the recorded message he left us. *He* was the one that saved billions of lives. No way he would unleash a biological weapon on Earth. I just don't believe it."

"Precisely," Rachael said. "It doesn't conform to anything we learned about petrin culture, and we talked with Seth at length about that."

"Maybe the Koreans got the technology from the petrins and simply botched the job," Porter countered. "Perhaps the petrins didn't know the reason behind the request."

"You're missing the point," Joshua said. "Seth would have found it suspicious that the North Koreans would want an arachnid, and he wouldn't have helped them regardless of what rational they gave him. It would violate their ethics."

"Maybe there's another reason the Koreans contacted the petrins," Liz suggested, her hand and index finger raised to emphasize her point.

"Like what?" Ted asked.

"Maybe they weren't trying to create a weapons system at all," Liz said. "Hear me out. Aren't there rumors that the North Korean leader has been sick? I've heard that he's been battling prostate cancer."

"I can confirm those rumors," Porter added. "Our intel sources in the CIA have briefed us that the Korean leader has been ill for quite some time." He nodded, clearly impressed with Liz's idea. He was glad that Langdon had assigned her to the team. She was thoughtful and showed respect and deference to the way the mission was being conducted.

Liz continued her train of thought. "The North Korean leader is a dictator. In fact, the people in this country think of him as some kind of deity. They would do anything for him. Maybe they were looking to see if the petrins could find a cure for his condition the same way that Seth found a cure for our previous viral outbreak. I'm sure that given petrin technology in the biological sciences, it would be a piece of cake for them."

"Liz," Rachael said, "you're saying that the Koreans were looking for a medical cure for their leader and somehow ended up creating this arachnid?"

"Yes. I'm just trying to think of other plausible reasons the Koreans would have had for trying to connect with the petrins other than trying to obtain a weapon of some type."

"It is plausible," Porter agreed. "We have to consider all possibilities."

"You make a reasonable argument, Liz," Joshua said, "but something still doesn't sit right with me. The petrins wouldn't trick the Koreans and unleash the arachnid. Why not just give them the cure they were looking for?"

"Maybe they thought they were helping us in some way," Vinod said. "At this point, we don't know for sure if this arachnid is hostile or not. For all we know, it could be something that's meant to serve humanity like the ones Josh and Rachael encountered on New Eden."

"No, that would also violate their noninterference directive," Joshua said, "plus there's a gap in the logic. Rachael's right. The North Koreans ask for a medical cure and receive an arachnid instead. Somehow I don't feel that we're dealing with the petrins at all. I think the Koreans . . . well, they may have contacted some other alien intelligence without knowing it."

Everyone at the table sat up straighter.

"Why, Dr. Andrews?" Porter asked, a worried look creasing his forehead. "Need I remind you that you yourself told us that, given the physical similarity of this creature to the ones on Petri and New Eden, you felt that this has to be petrin technology?"

"That's true," Joshua said, his hand stroking his chin. "But we've discovered new information since then. Vinod's algorithm for establishing communication with aliens is here in North Korea. What use would the Koreans have for the algorithm if they had made contact with the petrins? After all, petrins already know English and multiple other human languages. What I'm getting at is that Seth said there are thousands of species that communicate by using primordial spookyons. It's possible, even likely, that not all extraterrestrials operate according to petrin morality, and I suspect that's why Seth wanted to make sure we contacted the petrins and not another species assuming we ever changed our minds about the moratorium. That may be his reason for leaving us the security key."

"It's definitely a possibility," Rachael said after pondering Joshua's statement. "As usual, Josh, your logic is impeccable."

"It's all just conjecture at this point, but you may be right," Porter said. "Anything else you have to report?"

"That's about it," Joshua replied as he turned to Ted. "Commander, I'm not sure how much of what I've said is going to help you and your Seals, but it's the best we have at this point. I know you have a difficult mission ahead. I speak for the entire team in wishing you good luck."

"Thanks," Ted said. "We'll need it. The Seals and I are going to embark on phase three in a few hours—to find that overgrown spider. We're goin' arachnid hunting, and the gear and tackle are in the box." He grinned broadly. "So to speak."

Chapter Ten
Recon

The day was bright and sunny, and the sky was bright blue interspersed with the occasional slow-moving white cloud.

The Seals were positioned to begin phase three. They spread out around the perimeter established during phase one but were now prepared to venture farther in order to locate the arachnid and observe its actions at a safe distance. Each platoon was tasked with exploring a "slice" of a pie-shape area that radiated from the complex. Their camo allowed them to blend seamlessly into the forest surrounding the three buildings.

The Seals were fully armed and attached to their belts were devices that measured radiation levels. The teams didn't anticipate discovering anything radioactive, but the devices were issued nonetheless out of an abundance of caution. Additionally, General Porter had made sure to go over the rules of engagement for this phase with all Seals, including Commander Johnson. They would not be allowed to take any hostile action against the arachnid unless they found themselves in imminent danger. The possibility of contact and communication had to be exhausted before more dire actions against the creature were contemplated.

The scientific team and Porter gathered in the lobby of Moe, where two LCD screens were positioned so that the team could get live video feeds from each seal team member. As before, each feed was labeled, and any single feed could be enlarged. There was also a speaker in the lobby to allow conversation to and from the teams to be heard, and once again Porter, outfitted with headset and mic, controlled the display of the feeds using a wireless keyboard. The video feeds and the conversations would be relayed to the carrier, where Langdon and Williams would observe operations on the ground. If any change in the mission plan was necessary, Williams would issue the final authorization.

"Looks like everyone's in position," Ted announced. "Permission to proceed?"

"Permission granted," Porter responded.

Crouching, the Seals slowly advanced into the forest, weapons drawn.

Even though the scientific team examined the feeds intently, nothing was discovered for the first forty minutes except dense forest interspersed by the occasional clearing. At the forty-one-minute mark, seal 4-3's feed revealed freshly-broken branches on the lower trunks of adjacent trees.

"Looks like something big squeezed through here," he remarked as Porter enlarged his feed. "*Really* big."

"We're on the right track," Porter commented. "Proceed carefully."

Although the Seals were looking for footprints, they didn't expect to find any. The forest floor was covered with a thick layer of pine needles which made finding footprints near impossible. Also, it hadn't rained in this portion of the country for over a month, which meant the ground was dry and hard.

At the forty-seven-minute mark, seal 3-1 bent down to look at a rust-colored object slightly smaller than a baseball.

"What is that?" Rachael asked as Porter enlarged the feed.

"3-1," Porter said into his headset, "what is it you're looking at?"

"I don't know," 3-1 responded. "There are a couple more of these lying around." He panned his camera to show two similar objects resting on a bed of pine needles. "I think it's metallic. Looks like there's rust on it. Should I pick it up?"

"What's his radiation detector registering?" Joshua asked.

Porter relayed the question to the seal, who glanced at the meter on his belt. "Nothing. No radiation."

"Then I guess it's okay to pick it up," Joshua remarked. "But make sure he wears his gloves."

The seal took out a pair of blue latex gloves from one of his pockets and put them on. He then picked up the object, which was not a perfect sphere. "It's heavy for something so small," he reported. As he turned the object over in his hand, he noticed the rust color was not uniform. The portion of the sphere that had touched the ground had less rust and was darker. "It's definitely metallic, and this sure looks like rust," he said, rubbing his fingers together.

"Is it a grenade?" Ted asked.

"Negative, commander. There's no pin."

"Could be a piece of discarded Korean military equipment," Joshua suggested. "Maybe from a soldier or a jeep."

"Possible," Porter replied.

"Jesus," Vinod remarked looking at the discoloration on the fingertips of the gloves of the seal. "I hope that's only rust. He's got that shit all over his gloves."

"I want you to discard those gloves when you take them off," Porter told the soldier.

"All Seals will be going through a rigorous decontamination procedure when they return," Liz stated. "We're dealing with alien technology, and there could be biohazards."

Porter had explained the decontamination procedure prior to the Seals' departure. One of the showers in Curly had been cordoned off with plastic sheeting and contained numerous spray bottles filled with a powerful disinfectant. The Seals were to thoroughly spray any exposed areas with the disinfectant and then shower before being allowed back into the common areas of the complex. They didn't wear the airtight space suits seen in numerous pandemic movies, but it was the best the military could muster given the rapid deployment of forces.

On the carrier, Liz had floated the idea of outfitting the Seals with full respirators and gas masks given that what they were dealing with was biological in nature, but this was vetoed by Porter, who said it would take too much time to procure the equipment. They didn't have months to prepare for the mission; it was urgent that they get *some* firsthand information about what they were dealing with as soon as possible. The Seals and the scientific team knew that the mission was dangerous given its many unknowns, and the best they could do was mitigate as much risk as possible. Delaying the mission had not been an option.

"Could it be some type of ammunition?" Porter asked, his attention focused on the object. "Like a cannon ball?"

"I don't think so," Joshua said. "Look at its irregular shape. It would have horrible aerodynamic properties. Even cannon balls in the Dark Ages were spherical so that they could be aimed properly. Not sure *what* that thing is."

"We should examine it more closely in the lab," Joshua said. "Let's bring it in."

"3-1, we want you to collect that object for further analysis," Porter said.

3-1 took a Ziploc bag from his pocket and deposited the object in it before tossing it into the side pouch of his fatigues. He then carefully took off the rust-covered gloves, turning them inside out in the process, and tossed them on the ground before continuing with his patrol.

A few minutes later, seal 5-3 heard the loud buzzing of an insect near his right ear. He instinctively slapped the creature, which was smashed against the side of his neck before falling to the ground. He knelt to look at the insect while rubbing away the pain from the slap on his skin. "Guys, take a look at this," he said over his radio.

The seal bent close to the creature, which was still slowly flapping its wings, but was mortally wounded as evidenced by white gelatinous material spilling from a rupture in its exoskeleton.

Porter enlarged the feed from the seal.

"Never seen a bug like that," Vinod said. "Looks like something from a video game."

As the scientific team examined the video feed on the screen, they noticed that the insect was the size of a large dragonfly. It had four long wings that were a semi-transparent blue, two on each side of a central abdomen, which was black and spherical. Positioned at numerous spots on the abdomen were small clear spheres of various sizes, each partially embedded in the larger one. What the scientific team found curious was not what the creature contained, but what it lacked. It had no legs or head, just a central sphere connected to four wings.

Its wings moved slower still, disturbing the sandy grit upon which it lay. The uneven movement of its wings caused it to rotate one hundred and eighty degrees.

"No way that thing's from this planet," Vinod remarked.

"I've never seen anything like it," Liz said. "It's definitely biologic, but it doesn't follow any basic body pattern of any insect on Earth."

"It's beautiful," Rachael remarked, mesmerized by the image of the insect. "Are those small clear blue spheres eyes?"

"Possibly," Liz answered. "They're spherical, which would match the overall shape of something created for capturing and focusing light." Liz felt an adrenaline rush like never before as she stared at the image on the screen. This was her first chance as an exobiologist to actually examine what very well could be biology not indigenous to Earth. "Rachael, did you or Joshua encounter anything similar to this on New Eden?"

"No," Rachael replied. "In fact, we noted that there were no insects at all on New Eden."

"I definitely want to examine that under a microscope," Liz said.

"I think it's dead," 5-3 relayed as the creature now exhibited no motion at all.

"General," Liz said, "tell him to collect the object, but not to touch it with his hands. Just scoop it up with the Ziploc bag and seal it."

Porter relayed the instructions to seal 5-3 who scooped up the insect into a bag and placed it in one of his pockets.

"It's a nice precaution, Liz," Vinod commented. "You know—not having him pick it up with his fingers—but you do realize that he just smacked that creature with his hand, and if there's any kind of contaminant on it, and you bring it into the lab, we're all screwed."

"Don't worry, Vinod," Liz answered with a smile. "I know how to follow isolation protocols—or the best semblance of them given what I've got to work with."

"I hope so. I'm getting freaked out by this alien shit. Rusted metal balls and a spheroid insect. Too much for me. Rach, I don't know how you and Josh handled being on an alien planet by yourselves with no other humans within light years. My anxiety would have gotten the best of me."

"We felt very safe on New Eden," Rachael said. "Seth told us there was nothing there that could harm us, and we trusted him."

"You feeling safe *now?*" Vinod asked.

Rachael and Joshua exchanged glances before she responded. "Not exactly. None of this conforms to what we saw on New Eden."

Porter took personal offense at the statement and glared at Rachael. "Miss Miller, you have forty-eight of the finest, best-equipped soldiers on the planet protecting you. Please remember that."

"Not what I meant, general. I'm extremely grateful for the Seals and their courage but being in an unknown situation is bound to cause *some* anxiety."

Porter turned back to the LCD screens without comment.

Rachael's anxiety was soon heightened by the next discovery made by the Seals. As seal 2-2 neared a small pond, he spied a large object on the opposite side of the water. "I think I see something," the seal declared, which caused his feed to be enlarged as he circled the pond to get a closer look at the object. "Holy crap. I think it's a body. Stinks to high hell," he said as he put his hand over his nose as he moved closer.

The corpse floated near tall reeds at the edge of the muddy brown water as the seal waded ankle-deep to get closer still. The bloated body was face down, arms and legs splayed. It was clothed in wet tattered jeans and a dirty yellow pullover shirt.

"Fuck!" Vinod exclaimed. "A dead guy. This can't be good."

The anxiety level of the observers at the complex was now considerably elevated. Rachael reached out to hold Joshua's hand as she was prone to do in moments of stress.

Seal 2-2 grabbed the right arm of the cadaver and, with much effort, rolled it over, causing a splash and sending ripples across the surface of the pond. His feed showed the swollen face of the victim, one that, in spite of its distortion, Rachael recognized immediately.

"Oh, my God!" she exclaimed as tears filled her eyes. "It's Rodrigo!"

Chapter Eleven
The Alabaster Tree

The macabre image on the screen shocked Joshua, Rachael, and Vinod. They'd respected Rodrigo. He had always been personable, and in the end, he had been the one who discovered how to create non-primordial spookyons, which in their minds proved his talent. He had discovered Dr. Henry Bowman's elusive secret that he'd committed to notebooks that had never been found. They hadn't been best friends, but the image on the screen was nevertheless hard for the trio to bear.

"Oh, Rodrigo," Rachael whispered, her hands covering her mouth.

"I can't believe it," Vinod said. "I mean . . .." His voice trailed away as all eyes remained focused on the screen.

"Rodrigo, what happened?" Joshua said rhetorically. Joshua was, after all, the person who had hired Rodrigo to be his PhD student just as Henry Bowman had done for him. How was it that he was looking at the dead body of his former assistant at the edge of a pond in North Korea?

"Well, I think that one theory has been confirmed," Porter said. "Rodrigo Torres *was* working with the North Koreans."

Vinod bristled at Porter's callousness. "Don't gloat, Porter. We're in no position to determine what led up to this. Have some respect. Rodrigo was a friend of ours."

"Just making an observation," Porter said, emotionless.

The mood in the room had previously been one of excitement mixed with anxiety, but now there was palpable grief among team members.

"Continue your patrol," Porter told 2-2 over his headset.

"I've got another body here," seal 1-3 said a few minutes later.

The seal's video feed revealed a North Korean soldier, fully uniformed and lying on his back, a rifle near his head. There was a pool of dried blood on the forest floor that had obviously flowed from a wound on his neck.

"Can you tell how he died?" Porter asked.

The seal inspected the body. "It looks to me like he was stabbed in the neck."

"Stabbed or shot?" Porter asked.

"Stabbed," the seal replied. "The entrance wound is just a small slit, much different than a gunshot entrance wound."

"He's right," Liz agreed upon viewing a close-up of the neck. "The wound is very clean, without jagged edges. It looks like it was made by a sharp, penetrating object."

"The wound seems relatively small," Joshua observed. "Doesn't seem likely that a wound that small would kill him. Maybe it's the entrance point for something else, like a toxin."

"You mean like a snakebite?" Vinod said.

"Yes, something like that."

"I disagree," Liz remarked. "Look at the location of the wound. It's right over the carotid artery. Judging by the amount of external blood, it's highly probable that his artery was severed, which would definitely cause death, and rapidly."

"You could be right," Joshua said, acquiescing. His expertise was in physics; Liz was the medical expert.

As the afternoon progressed, the Seals found several more dead North Korean soldiers, each killed with what appeared to be small stab wounds to various parts of their bodies. These findings caused the anxiety in both the Seals and the scientific team to increase further. Everyone had a clearer understanding of the extreme danger the Seals were in since the mission had uncovered new alien technology—technology that was quite probably lethal.

"Guess we know why this area was evacuated," Vinod remarked. "Kind of wish I could be evacuated too."

"We have a job to do," Porter responded tersely, "and we are going to do it, Mr. Bhakti. You included. I also think we can dismiss your idea of the arachnid being benign petrin technology. The dead bodies prove otherwise."

A few minutes later, seal 4-3, the one who had noted the broken branches, caught sight of a tall structure in the distance. "I may have found something," he announced. "It looks like the trunk and branches of a tree, but it's pure white." He headed in the direction of the tree, crouching to be as inconspicuous as possible.

Porter and the scientific team watched with anticipation as his enlarged video feed showed what looked to be a tall, slender white tree, partially obscured by intervening branches and shrubs.

"What the hell *is* that?" Joshua asked. "Is it even a tree?"

"Don't know, man," Vinod said. "What kind of tree is perfectly white?"

As 4-3 cautiously advanced, he entered a small clearing rimmed by tall Korean pines. His video panned down and revealed more rust balls on the dirt floor of the clearing. As he pushed away pine branches to get a clearer view of the white tree, his attention was drawn to an elephant-sized dark grey object—almost black—a few feet from the odd white growth.

"Target located," he announced with a hushed voice. "I think I've found the arachnid."

*   *   *

The scientific group stared at the creature, that up until this point, had only been visible on satellite images. The arachnid lay motionless, its dark grey form resembling an enormous crab from Jules Verne's *Mysterious Island*. Its legs were folded in segments next to its body, and the tentacles on its carapace were curled in neat spirals.

The group stared at the arachnid for a few moments, looking for some sign of life—some movement that would indicate its intentions—but nothing happened. The creature continued sitting motionless in the tall weeds and grass.

"Is it dead?" Vinod asked.

"Maybe it's sleeping," Joshua theorized.

"Target located," Porter relayed to the other Seals. "What is your position, 4-3?"

4-3 responded with GPS coordinates as he continued to focus on the creature.

"Everyone establish a perimeter around those coordinates," Ted announced. "But don't get too close. No one get within half a klick of it."

It took thirty minutes for the Seals to surround the area. They moved quickly, but with stealth. Some stood, others knelt, and some lay on the forest floor, their weapons and helmet cameras focused on the arachnid. The highly-trained soldiers were as motionless and silent as the creature— the only sound being the wind rustling through the trees.

The scientific team had multiple video feeds of the arachnid, showing it from all angles. It appeared large and forbidding even from half a klick away.

"Looks like it's covered in some kind of armor," Joshua observed.

The creature's lower legs had oblong-shaped panels that resembled shields, and its tentacles were circumscribed with metallic-looking concentric plates.

"Does it look like the arachnids on New Eden?" Liz asked.

"The overall form is similar," Rachael answered, "but this one is much different. First, our arachnids were brownish in color. This creature is almost black. Second, it's much bigger. Much more . . . forbidding."

"I concur," Joshua added, studying the construction of the arachnid. "There's no way that that this creature was designed for flight. It's built more like a tank."

"A tank is a military weapon, Dr. Andrews," Porter pointed out. "You think this could be some kind of weapon?"

"I don't know, but it definitely looks armored."

They sat anxiously, waiting for movement—some sign of life—but there was none.

"Do you really think it's dead, Vinod?" Rachael asked.

"Well, it certainly isn't moving, but that may not mean anything."

Porter magnified the feed of the seal who had the most direct view of the creature.

"I don't see any sign of breathing if, in fact, it has such a capability," Joshua remarked.

"No mouth to eat, no breathing," Vinod said. "What is its source of power?"

"Nuclear?" Rachael speculated.

"I doubt it," Liz said. "A nuclear power source would have to be heavily shielded in order not to give off radiation. That creature is definitely biologic, and biologic structures like cells and DNA are easily damaged by radiation. I doubt that there's some kind of nuclear reactor in there."

"Commander, any radiation being detected out there?" Porter asked.

"Nope, nothing at all," Ted replied while looking at the detector on his belt.

"It must have *some* source of power," Joshua commented. "Otherwise, it would go against the laws of physics, and I don't think even the petrins are capable of that."

"How about solar?" Vinod questioned. "Maybe it has some form of photosynthesis going on in that dark skin."

"Possible, but improbable," Joshua replied. "I'm assuming that the creature is mobile since it has legs, and if it's mobile, it would require a lot of energy to move that massive frame. The amount of energy coming from the sun over the relatively small area that its shadow encompasses isn't enough to allow it to move for any significant period of time."

"He's correct," Liz agreed. "Just think of other creatures on Earth. Animals don't create their own energy. They feed on energy stored by other organisms, like plants, since it would be highly inefficient for them to get energy directly from sunlight. I don't think this creature is solar-powered. What *does* power that thing, however, is a complete mystery to me."

Porter switched his view to a feed aimed at the white tree behind the creature, enabling the team to see it in more detail. It was thirty feet tall and had a slender trunk, which gave way to multiple, cascading branches, but there were no leaves. Instead, at the ends of terminal branches were circular-shaped paddles the size of the head of a tennis racquet. The entire structure—trunk, branches, and paddles—was motionless, not affected by the slight breeze that gently swayed the limbs of surrounding trees. Despite its unusual configuration, what struck the scientific team most was its pristine white color—trunk, branches, and paddles.

"What the hell *is* that thing?" Vinod asked.

"No idea," Joshua answered. "It must be made of a pretty stiff material though. It's not moving at all despite the breeze."

Porter switched back to a close-up of the creature. He further magnified the image, which revealed slight motion—almost a shifting mist—at one end of the arachnid.

"What's that?" Porter asked. "We don't have enough resolution to see what's going on."

Ted had carefully taken a position closest to the creature. His eyesight was much better than the resolution of the video feed observed by the scientific team in Moe.

"There are insects going to and from the creature," he reported. "They're strange looking, with blue wings."

"Flying back and forth?" Porter asked.

"Yes. Some are going towards the creature, while others are leaving."

"Like a beehive," Liz remarked.

"What do you think they're doing?" Rachael asked.

"Not sure," Liz answered, "but they're going in and out of the arachnid just as Ted described. They look like identical to the dragonfly insect we saw earlier."

"Could it be some kind of feeding mechanism?" Joshua asked. "Maybe the insects gather nutrition for the arachnid and, like bees with nectar, return to feed the creature. That may explain where it gets its energy."

"Possible," Liz responded. "There's ample precedent for such activity in biology on Earth, but this . . . who knows?"

"I don't think so," Vinod said. "The insect that the seal found a few minutes ago had no mouth, so how can it gather nectar? No, I don't think it's *feeding* activity. I think it's some kind of *surveillance* mechanism. Remember, Rach thought that the insect's body was covered with eyes."

"What do you mean a surveillance mechanism?" Joshua asked.

"It's like an aircraft carrier," Vinod explained. "A carrier uses its planes to launch surveillance missions to search for targets. The planes then return to the carrier for refueling. I think those insects are being used for surveillance. They're the remote eyes, and possibly other senses, for the arachnid. They fly around and check out the surroundings and then communicate with the creature." Vinod, absorbed by what he was looking at, folded his arms and nodded his head. "Yep, I'm sure of it."

"Communicate?" Liz said. "How?"

"They could be using spookyons," Joshua replied, his voice filled with excitement. "Not the primordial type, mind you. Just paired spookyons like the ones we create in our lab. There could be one spookyon of an entangled pair in the insect and another in the arachnid. That way, the insect could communicate directly with the arachnid. It would certainly be consistent with petrin technology."

"So you're saying that the arachnid is creating spookyon pairs and these insects, and then sending them out for surveillance?" Liz asked.

"It's a real possibility. When Rachael and I were on New Eden, our entire existence and experience were transmitted as information via spookyons. Seth referred to a structure he called a neural nest that was located in our craniums that interfaced with spookyons. Remember that petrin technology is biologic and DNA-based. It wouldn't surprise me if this creature communicated with these insects via spookyon pairs."

"If they communicate via spookyons, why do they have to return to the arachnid?" Liz asked.

"It's like the carrier and why the planes return to it," Vinod reiterated. "Refueling."

"It's an interesting concept," Liz said. "Unlike bees that return nourishment back to the hive, these creatures get *replenished* by the hive."

"Don't think of them as bees," Vinod said. "Think of them as biological drones."

"Mr. Bhakti," Porter said, "I'm not one to agree with you on many occasions, but in this instance I do." Porter pointed to the image of the arachnid. "This creature is definitely a military instrument of some kind. I just know it. And information and surveillance are key for any military endeavor. I think you're spot on. Those insects are remote sensors for the arachnid. Biological drones, as you say. They're the arachnid's AWACS system."

Porter was interrupted by the voice of Commander Johnson. "General, what do you want us to do? This thing hasn't moved in over an hour."

"Nothing," Porter responded. "Let's just observe it a while longer."

For another hour, the Seals maintained their positions around the arachnid and white tree while Porter switched between video feeds, giving different angles of both, but nothing changed. There was no motion from the tree or the creature as the insects continued their constant back and forth flight.

"General," Ted said, "the batteries on our transmitters are getting low. We'll have to return soon. What are your orders?"

Porter didn't respond immediately. A bead of sweat trickled down from his short hair. "Alright, I want one of you to get a closer look. Try approaching the arachnid."

"General," Joshua said, "are you sure that's safe?"

"I don't know," Porter said, "but we have to do *something*. Our mission is to find out what this creature's purpose is. We can't do that by just staring at it, especially since it's not doing anything."

"I'm going closer," Ted announced. He was used to waiting in duck blinds and deer stands back home, but he also knew how to move through densely-wooded areas and approach his prey without a sound.

He slowly left the cover of the forest and crept into the clearing, his firearm pointed straight ahead. He got within ten feet of the creature and began to circle it. He stood near the front of the arachnid, and as he looked up, the scientific team could see the constant stream of insects coming and leaving. He made it three quarters of the way around and was getting close to the white tree, which he trained his helmet camera on. Suddenly, the tip of one of the tentacles sprang to life with a sharp crack and pointed directly at Ted, like a cobra about to strike.

"Look out!" Vinod shouted.

Porter remained collected and calmly said, "Commander, back away slowly."

Ted stared at the end of the menacing tentacle, a single eye with what appeared to be a horizontal mouth staring back at him. *That's one hell of a combination*, he thought. His heartbeat pounding in his neck, he backed away slowly, glancing over his shoulder occasionally so as not to trip. As he moved, the tentacle floated in the air and followed him. As he entered the forest, Ted knelt, and the tentacle curled back to its original position. He let out a long, silent sigh of relief.

"At least we know it's not dead," Joshua said.

"Porter," Vinod said, "get your men out of there. I've seen enough for one day."

"I agree," Porter said. "Retreat slowly."

The Seals carefully moved away from the creature until it was out of camera range. Their movements were slow and methodical so as not to arouse the suspicion of their enigmatic foe.

"Commander," Porter said after the Seals were a safe distance away, "have your men return to base, but I want you to retrieve a few bodies. Get Torres as well as a couple of the dead North Korean soldiers. I need to know exactly how they were killed."

Chapter Twelve
Postmortem

The Seals had returned safely and had been decontaminated. They had retrieved specimens for the scientific team to examine, which included the rusted metal ball, the dead insect, and three dead bodies, one of which was Rodrigo. Porter told the scientific team that they had until noon the following day to provide an analysis of the items, which meant they would be working late into the night.

Since the exact location of the arachnid was now known, Porter had one of the Seals climb to the roof of the tallest building—Moe—with a long-distance telescope to see if they could maintain a visual on the creature to detect any movement. The arachnid was shrouded by trees, which meant that satellites couldn't view it. Luckily, the seal assigned with the task was able to sight the creature with the telescope. A soldier would be posted throughout the night and would use a night vision attachment after dusk to monitor the arachnid.

Later that evening, the scientific team sat in the dining area of Curly for dinner, which consisted of more military rations.

"So who wants to help me with the autopsies?" Liz asked with a bite of food in her mouth.

"Autopsies?" Vinod asked. "Come on, Liz. We're eating here. Carving up dead bodies in the middle of the night in some spooky Korean lab isn't my cup of tea. It's like a B horror movie."

Liz turned to Joshua.

"Don't look at me," Joshua said, shaking his head. "I'm a physicist, not a physician. Definitely not in my comfort zone."

"I'll do it," Rachael offered.

"Yeah," Vinod said, almost gleeful. "Let Rach do it."

Rachael glared at Vinod. "Very chivalrous of you, Vinod." She turned to Liz. "I'm not a physician either, but I'm willing to help you."

"Thanks, Rach. I just need an extra pair of hands. I'll walk you through it." Liz put another bite of food in her mouth. "I see how it works on this team. The weak men leave the dirty work to us strong women."

"Perfectly fine with that," Vinod replied.

"Me too," Joshua added. "Besides, Vinod and I are going to do some testing on that metallic ball the Seals retrieved."

"May be the only balls you have tonight," Liz chided.

"Wicked, Liz," Rachael said with a smile.

"How about the insect?" Joshua inquired. "Who's going to examine *that*?"

"That's going to be me as well," Liz said. "It's in my wheelhouse. I'll get to that first thing in the morning."

"Jesus, Liz," Vinod said. "You gonna be able to get any sleep tonight?"

"Probably not."

"I don't know how you function like that," Vinod said. "I need at least eight hours, or I'm a zombie the next day."

"How's that different than any other day?" Rachael asked.

"Brutal!" Liz said as she and Rachael gave each other a high five.

"Man, we're getting roasted tonight, Josh," Vinod muttered.

"Vinod, you forget that I went through a critical care residency," Liz said. "Going nights without sleep is something I'm accustomed to."

The group noticed Commander Johnson walking towards them while carrying two large cans.

"What you got there, Ted?" Vinod asked.

"A couple of cans of molasses."

"For what?" Rachael asked.

"I'm working on a special project." Ted had a mischievous gleam in his eye.

"For Porter?" Rachael asked.

"Naw, for myself."

"What's the project?" Joshua asked.

"Oh, it's kind of a secret," Ted said with a wink, "but I'll let y'all in on it a little later. Not related to the arachnid or the mission though. Just something I'm doing to kill time."

"Okay," Joshua said.

"Ted," Rachael said, "I want to thank you and your team for the job you did today. It was simply excellent and very courageous."

"Thanks ma'am—I mean Rach, Just doing my duty."

"You want to join us for dinner?" Liz asked.

"Naw, I already ate. Oh, I almost forgot. I have something for Vinod." Ted reached into his shirt pocket and produced an SD card. "The Seals that retrieved Mr. Torres' body found this in one of his pockets. General Porter wanted me to give it to Vinod for examination."

"It looks intact from the outside," Vinod said, taking the card, "but if it was in Rodrigo's pocket, it may have been submerged for quite some time. I don't know if any data can be read from it."

"I know," Ted said, "but General Porter said that if anyone can retrieve data from it, it would be you."

"I'll try my best." Vinod stated. "Maybe I'm winning Porter over."

"I'll catch y'all later," Ted said, holding up the cans. "My project awaits."

*   *   *

Donned in surgical attire, Rachael and Liz stood over body of one of the Korean soldiers in a lab room on the second floor of Larry. The room was as drab as the others. An overhead lamp with a green metal dome was suspended from the ceiling, although the women had procured auxiliary lighting. Against the cinderblock walls were tables with metal instruments. The room was warm even though the thermostat was on its coolest setting, and a portable oscillating fan sat on the floor.

Rachael insisted that they start with one of the soldiers since the thought of dissecting a dead body was bad enough, but dissecting the body of a friend would be too much for her in the beginning. She knew that the examination of Rodrigo would be coming up soon, and she was trying to mentally prepare for it.

The stench of the partially-decomposed body was overwhelming, even for Liz, and both women wore surgical masks to mitigate it. Liz had sprayed perfume on the interior of the masks, which only helped a little.

They began by removing the soldier's clothes in order to do an exterior inspection of the body. There was a puncture wound on the neck, but the rest of the skin was intact.

"Guess we'll start at the neck wound," Liz said, using a scalpel to extend the original wound.

"Why did I eat before we started this?" Rachael asked.

"You okay?" Liz said, continuing her work without looking up.

"Guess so," Rachael responded as she held retractors in the wound while Liz explored the neck more deeply using Metzenbaum scissors.

"The carotid has definitely been transected," Liz said. "Sliced in half, like with a scalpel."

"Yeah, but sliced by what?" Rachael asked.

"Unknown."

Liz's gloved hands worked with dexterity and precision, and Rachael was impressed with how routine the exobiologist made the autopsy look.

As Liz dissected deeper, she got close to the anterior bodies of the cervical vertebrae and ran her finger through the tissue planes utilizing a blunt dissection technique. As she palpated the vertebrae, she felt something sharp. "There's something lodged in this vertebral body. Rach, can you swing that light in here so I can get a better look?"

Rachael adjusted a portable spotlight to shine directly onto the wound. Liz used gauze sponges to wipe away dried blood to better examine the object.

"It's something metallic," Liz observed. "Can you hand me a pair of those needle holders?"

"Needle holders?"

"It's that instrument with the two loops on the handle," Liz said as she pointed to a tray containing multiple instruments that had been delivered from the carrier as part of their medical supplies. "It's used to hold metal suture needles during surgery. I think I can extract whatever this object is with those."

Liz introduced the instrument into the wound.

"I think I got it," Liz said, and with a stiff tug on the holders, she extracted the foreign body, which she held up for examination. She used a gauze sponge to clean blood from the object, revealing a silver metallic finish.

It was a thin sliver of metal about two centimeters wide, two centimeters tall, and two millimeters thick. The metal was shaped like the delta wing of a combat aircraft, with a triangular leading edge and accompanying trailing edges, the trailing edges having less acute angles.

To Rachael, the object looked like a wide metallic arrowhead. "What is it?" she asked.

"Looks like some kind of projectile. Definitely has an aerodynamic shape." Liz examined the leading edge of the projectile more closely and noticed it had been honed to a sharp edge. "The front looks like a scalpel."

Still grasping the object with the needle holders, Liz ran the leading edge over skin on the chest of the cadaver. The edge sliced through the skin easily, like a knife through soft butter.

"Razor sharp," Rachael commented.

Liz shifted her eyes from the projectile to Rachael. "Small but deadly, and it's definitely what killed this man."

"A lucky shot," Rachael commented. "Hitting the carotid, that is."

Liz returned to work. "Maybe not. The location of the wound is too coincidental."

Liz and Rachael dissected the second dead Korean soldier, who had multiple similar-sized wounds on his body, five in all. Judging by their location, Liz figured that four of them were paired, meaning they were both the entrance and exit wounds made by a single projectile. The women therefore concentrated on the fifth wound, which was located on the soldier's right arm. After a few minutes, they discovered a second projectile, identical to the first, lodged in the distal radius bone.

"Feeling better?" Liz asked as Rachael turned away to get a breath of fresh air after removing her surgical mask.

"A little. Pretty gruesome stuff."

"All medical students lose their lunch when they dissect their cadavers for the first time, but you get used to it. You're doing great."

Rodrigo was the final dissection. Rachael asked Liz to put a towel over his face to make the procedure easier for her. Rodrigo had three wounds, all in his neck. As before, Liz calculated that two wounds represented entrance and exit wounds, so she concentrated her dissection on the third. Not surprisingly, they found a third projectile lodged in the odontoid process of the C2 vertebrae.

"This one severed his spinal cord," Liz said dispassionately as she laid the third projectile in a cup with the others. "I think the autopsies are finished. We know these men were killed by penetration of the projectiles."

"What should we do with the projectiles?" Rachael asked.

"Let's clean them up and take them to Josh and Vinod. They may have better insight into how or why they were used."

"I have to take a shower first," Rachael said. "I've got to get this smell out of my hair." Rachael shuddered as she removed her surgical gown and made a guttural sound in her throat. "Ugh! This was gross."

Liz smiled at Rachael. Liz had been accustomed to going home smelling of her occupation. In the first year of medical school, she smelled formaldehyde wherever she went. It was the chemical that preserved cadavers used in the study of human anatomy.

"Fine, I'll take these to the guys while you shower. But meet me back here afterwards. We have a date with an insect."

*   *   *

Liz walked into another lab in Larry where Vinod sat on a stool in front of a computer workstation. "Where's Josh?" she asked.

The room was as warm and plain as the others.

"He took the metal ball to the Seals to see if they had tools to cut it in half. I'm trying to recover data from the SD card that Ted gave me."

"Any luck?"

"Some," Vinod replied. "I recovered most of the files, but some have corrupt sectors, which I'm trying to interpolate."

"What kind of files are they?"

"They seem to be video files, but I haven't opened them yet."

"What about the metal ball?" Liz asked. "What've you guys found out about it?"

"Not much," Vinod said, swiveling to face Liz, his head raised. "The surface of the object is covered in ferrous oxide."

"Rust, just like we thought."

"Yup, and we measured its dimensions, which are irregular and don't fit any pattern I'm familiar with. We also calculated its density, which exactly matches the density of iron. We've also learned that it's ferro-magnetic."

"So essentially you're saying that it's just a piece of iron."

"Looks that way. Not very interesting—unless there's something inside it, of course."

"Well, I have much more interesting pieces of metal for you two to examine." Liz handed Vinod the cup containing the projectiles. "Beautiful but deadly."

"What are they?" Vinod's eyes narrowed as he looked into the cup.

"They're the cause of death of the people we dissected—projectiles that sliced through their skin and did mortal damage. With surgical precision I might add."

Vinod started to reach into the cup to retrieve one of the projectiles.

"Don't touch them!" Liz cautioned. "The front edge is razor-sharp. It could cut you easily."

"Whoa, lethal!" Vinod said, backing away.

"I have some needle holders so you can handle them." She handed Vinod the instrument, and Vinod turned away from her and placed the cup on the table in front of him. Liz moved behind him, peering over his shoulder.

Vinod carefully retrieved one of the projectiles from the cup. Liz's closeness made him uncomfortable. She was a likeable person, but why was she breathing down his neck? Did she really have a thing for him?

"We figured that you and Josh can do a better job of analyzing these than we can. Besides, we still have to examine the insect, and it's almost dawn. Time's running short." Liz put her hand on Vinod's shoulder, which increased his discomfort.

Vinod spun around on his stool to face Liz. "Look, Liz, there's something I've got to tell you."

"What?"

"I'm gay."

"Gay?" Liz responded with a puzzled look. "I *know* you're gay. Why'd you feel the need to tell me that?"

"You know I'm gay?" Vinod said, surprised. "But . . . well, I told you because Rach said you had the hots for me."

"She said *what*?" Liz asked. "What gave her that idea?"

"She said something about you being interested in me."

Hands on her hips, Liz shook her head as a smile crossed her face." I'm interested in you *as a person* Vinod. You're a very unique individual, full of many quirks, and you're very independent. I feel that you have little respect for authority, which I admire, but I'm not attracted to you in a sexual way."

"That's good . . . I guess."

Liz was still puzzled. "Why would Rachael not tell me herself that you were gay if she thought I was interested you?"

Vinod smiled sheepishly. "Rach is kind of a prankster sometimes. I think she did it to play a trick on me, and apparently on you too. I love Rachael more than anything, but she does have a mischievous streak."

"A prank, huh?" Liz said with a wry smile. "You know, one good prank deserves another."

"You want to get her back?" Vinod asked excitedly. "I'm in. What do you propose?"

"I have an idea."

*   *   *

It was just past daybreak, and the eastern horizon was orange and crimson. The night watch had confirmed that the arachnid was in the same location and had exhibited no movement at all. The entire forest, in fact, was preternaturally quiet.

Liz began her inspection of the insect. She had taken some tissue from the insect and had prepared a glass slide from a razor thin section. She and Rachael sat next to a microscope, which was equipped with a camera that allowed its image to be displayed on a monitor situated next to the microscope.

Liz loaded the slide on the microscope adjusted the magnification and stage and zoomed in on a single cell. "Looks like a fairly typical cell. There's a nucleus, cytoplasm, and organelles, although some of the organelles are unfamiliar to me."

"What part of the insect did this cell come from?" Rachael asked.

"The circulatory system."

"Is it like a blood cell in humans?"

"Maybe. Red blood cells in humans don't contain a nucleus, but other species on Earth have nucleated blood cells."

"What do you think its purpose is?"

"Don't know for sure," Liz replied. "It could be used like a blood cell that transports oxygen in humans and animals, but there are many different types of cells in blood, all with various functions."

Rachael hadn't looked through a microscope since biology class in college. She gazed in wonder at the image on the screen. "It amazes me that the petrins were able to engineer something so small, yet so intricate. It's beautiful in its own way."

"Maybe you should have become a biologist instead of a reporter," Liz said. "You have a keen eye, and your comments at the briefings are always insightful."

"Oh, I've always been interested in cells. In fact, Josh and I had an argument the first night we met about how I thought the cell was too complex to have evolved randomly, but he thought it could." Rachael continued staring at the screen. "It's just a single part of a whole," she said wistfully.

"What do you mean?" Liz asked.

"This cell is just part of a larger creature, the insect. It has a specific function, whatever that function is, that benefits the whole creature, but there are other entities—unicellular organisms, for example—in which a single cell *is* the entire organism. I've often wondered what the difference is between a cell that's part of a larger organism and one that's an organism unto itself. If the first kind were sentient, would it know that there's a higher purpose for its existence? That it performs its function for a higher purpose, or does it perform its task without knowing why it's doing it?"

Liz was surprised by the philosophical nature of the question. It was welcome, however, since Liz occasionally liked to explore the larger ramifications of scientific discoveries. "You're asking if this cell knows that it's part of an organism or what the purpose of that organism is?"

"Exactly," Rachael said. "For that matter, what exactly is an organism?

One could consider this cell by itself an organism of sorts, or one could consider the insect that it's part of as an organism as well. It depends on your perspective. But even the insect that this cell came from is just part of the arachnid. The arachnid creates the insects that work in tandem for a single purpose, so maybe the arachnid and the insects are one single organism. The insect is acting just like this cell. Perhaps it performs *its* function without knowing what the eventual purpose of the arachnid is. But the arachnid itself may be part of another organism that it's unaware of. If that's true, the arachnid wouldn't necessarily know what *that* organism's purpose is. It's life in layer upon layer that builds to higher and higher complexity."

Liz was impressed by Rachael's ability to grasp the larger implications of what they were studying in the lab. "Rachael, do you consider humans to be organisms?"

"Of course. Humans are organisms, but we perform specialized tasks that help humanity as a whole. You're a physician and a biologist. I'm a reporter and a PR person. But are we just like the cell? Is humanity an organism? Are we performing specific functions for a larger entity? And like this cell, do we know what our higher purpose is?"

Liz was enjoying the conversation, which had taken an unexpected metaphysical turn. Rachael was definitely a unique person, someone who was a scientist at heart but still had prevailing religious and philosophical views.

"You've mentioned that you're a religious person," Liz said. "Are you intimating that only a creator can know what the ultimate purpose is for an organism? Are we all just tiny cells that do the jobs for which we are created, but will never really know the ultimate purpose of our actions?"

"That *is* what I believe," Rachael answered, happy that her partner had grasped her meaning. "Only the creator knows the ultimate purpose of why we're here."

Rachael held up her wrist, the one with the tattoo of a Christian cross. "It's still my core belief even though Joshua doesn't agree."

"What about the petrins?" Liz asked. "Do you think they have insight into the mind of your creator? They're millions of years ahead of us. Maybe billions."

"I've given that a lot of thought," Rachael replied. "Is each petrin an individual, or is the entire collective a single organism made up of individual petrins like this insect is made of individual cells? After meeting Seth and learning something about his species, I believe that petrins primarily look at the collective as a single entity. They're just like cells that

93

serve a larger purpose. The petrins are interconnected by information flow via spookyons, so the collective certainly functions like a single entity. As far as your question about whether or not the petrins know the ultimate purpose of the universe—why any of us are here at all—they may have some insights, but I don't believe even *they* know for sure. Hopefully we'll find out some day."

Chapter Thirteen
Rodrigo's Story

The scientific team was bleary-eyed from lack of sleep as they shuffled into the lobby of Moe at noon and sat around a long table, ready to brief General Porter and Commander Johnson.

"Well, who wants to start?" Porter asked. "Bhakti, were you able to retrieve any data from the SD card?"

"Yes," Vinod answered. "There was data degradation on some of the files, but I was able to interpolate the missing data from what remained."

"What kind of data was it?" Porter asked.

"They were personal video logs that Rodrigo recorded using the camera on his laptop. They tell quite a story."

"A video log?" Porter replied. "That could be valuable. What kind of story?"

"Instead of explaining it to you, it would be better if you saw the files yourself. There aren't too many, and it won't take long to view. Besides, the inflection in his voice reveals as much as the content."

"Okay. Let's see them."

Vinod connected his laptop to one of the LCD monitors in the room. He then inserted the SD card into the computer, opened the folder, and played the first video file. An image of Rodrigo, sitting in one of Larry's laboratories, appeared on the screen. The trio felt as if they were looking at a ghost. Indeed, Rachael grew emotional at the image of Rodrigo. Just a few hours earlier she had helped with his autopsy. Seeing and hearing him now—his face, his voice, his mannerisms—was definitely jarring.

"Day one. My first day here. The Koreans have shown me around the complex, and it's not a bad facility. They've done a decent job with the construction of the tokamak. It's nowhere near as nice as the one at

Berkeley, but it'll do the job. I just hope that I'm able to capture a primordial spookyon so I can connect with the petrins. I have some trepidation about breaking the moratorium on capturing primordial spookyons, but I feel it's for a good cause. The Koreans have assured me that once they get a cure for what's ailing their leader, the connection will be severed, and no one will know the better."

"That's the end of the first video log," Vinod stated. "I'm going to play the others in order."

"You were right, Liz," Rachael commented as Vinod got the next video file ready. "The Koreans *were* trying to find a cure for their leader."

Vinod played the second file. The setting for this video was the same as the first.

"Day twenty-eight. I was finally able to capture a primordial spookyon today, which was a small victory. Unfortunately, the spookyon didn't have any signal—no mathematical carrier. It must not have been connected to anyone. I feel like I did back in Berkeley when Dr. Andrews and I were trying to create spookyons for the first time. We had many failures, but we did finally succeed. I know with enough effort I can succeed. I'll keep trying.

"Day forty-five. Not much progress to report, I'm afraid. I've captured four primordial spookyons, but none of them have been connected to anyone either. The Koreans are becoming impatient with me. They've asked me to increase the number of hours that I work, and I'm tired. I'm only getting about four hours of sleep per night. I hope that I can connect with the petrins soon."

Rodrigo's fatigue was obvious. His voice was weary, and there were dark circles under his eyes.

"Day fifty-one. Success! I captured a spookyon with a connection that has a mathematical carrier signal, although this signal was slightly different than the one Dr. Andrews found in Berkeley. Josh and Rachael discovered that the ratio between the segments of the first signal was pi. The ratio I found is the square root of two, but it's definitely a mathematical signal. Unfortunately, I haven't been able to communicate using the spookyon yet. I don't get any response to simple text-based queries, and I'm not sure why. I'm going to try Vinod Bhakti's algorithm on the spookyon tomorrow and see what happens.

"Day fifty-two. More success. Vinod's algorithm worked! I was able to speak via text to a petrin! I asked to speak with Seth, but they told me that he was busy on another project. The petrin that I'm connected to doesn't have a name. He said his name was digital, which is something Seth also told us. But I'm fairly certain that I've reestablished connection to the petrins and the collective since he relayed the exact same story of how they had seeded life throughout the universe using cells. I've confirmed that they are highly advanced with DNA technology. Tomorrow I'm going to ask about finding a cure for the North Korean leader. I hope he'll help us."

"I told you so," Porter announced. "The petrins are behind all of this. Mr. Torres was convinced of it."

"Still doesn't make sense to me," Joshua replied. "If it was the petrins why did Rodrigo need to use Vinod's algorithm to communicate with them? Let's wait to see all of the videos before jumping to conclusions."

"Day fifty-three. Another great day! I was able to convince the petrin I'm connected with to help cure the Korean leader. I've transmitted to him all of the Korean leader's medical information including the DNA sequences of his normal cells and the genetic information of his cancer cells. He thinks he's found a cure! He's going to transmit to us the DNA sequence for an organism which would be able to eradicate the cancer growing inside of him. They said that the creature, when fully grown, would be able to scan his body and selectively eradicate the cancer cells. He gave me specific instructions on how to grow the creature, which the biologists here at the lab will be in charge of. He told me that it would take a few weeks for the creature to grow and become mature. Everything is going as planned. After the cure is verified, I plan on breaking the sphere and ending the connection.

"Day sixty-five. The plan is progressing nicely. The biologists in the lab were successful in sequencing the DNA given by the petrin, and the cure is now growing in the lab. Hopefully it will mature soon, and I can leave this country. I'm getting tired of being here. It's becoming like a prison for me. I told the Koreans that there's nothing more for me to do, but they insist that they want to make sure the cure works before letting me leave. I miss being home. I would kill for a plate of hot tamales at this point. Korean food is getting old.

"Day sixty-seven. Something's wrong. The tank which contained the cure has a hole in it, and the organism growing inside can't be located. This is definitely not good. I've spoken to the petrin, and he said that we screwed up the cultivation process somehow. He suggested that we start the entire process again. I have much trepidation at this point, and I'm not sure we're doing the right thing. We've lost control of alien DNA. Not sure what the long-term implications of that will be. The Koreans are monitoring for any biological pathogens but haven't found any which I suppose is a good sign. Part of me just wants to break the sphere and end the connection, but the

Koreans won't allow it. I'm going to try to convince the Koreans not to start over with the DNA replication process. I don't feel comfortable moving forward until we account for the missing creature."

"Stupid bastards," Porter stated. "They let the goddamn thing escape. What kind of shitty security protocols did they have?"

"Probably similar to the same shitty protocols that allowed my algorithm to be stolen," Vinod retorted.

"Day eighty. Things have gone from bad to worse. The petrin I've been communicating with has stopped responding to me. No message I send via the spookyon gets a response, and the Koreans are at the limits of their patience. They still haven't found any evidence of biological pathogens like foreign bacteria or viruses which give me some solace. There's also been no sign of any radiation which I'm also grateful for. I wish I was back in the U.S. Why did I agree to this in the first place? I can't even ask for help. The Koreans have cut all of my communication channels, so I'm stuck in limbo."

"At least even the Koreans didn't find any evidence of biological pathogens," Liz remarked trying to be hopeful. "We haven't encountered any either."

"No biological pathogens?" Porter asked. "Then what do you consider that arachnid sitting out there in the forest?"

"Point taken," Liz responded.

The next video showed Rodrigo in a different environment. He was in one of the dorm rooms of Curly and spoke with a hushed voice.

"Day ninety-five. Situation terrible. A village close to this complex was attacked by an arachnid! The images were horrible. So many dead people. I know what I need to do. I need to break the sphere. I need to end the connection with the petrins. What have I done?"

"This is the final video," Vinod stated as he played the last file. The video was set in a laboratory, and Rodrigo was out of breath as he spoke.

"Day ninety-six. I've ruptured the sphere. The connection is cut. The Koreans have dispatched an army unit to deal with the arachnid. I just hope . . .."

Rodrigo never finished his sentence. Two Korean soldiers appeared on the video and grabbed him by the arms, uttering something in Korean as they dragged him away. The final image was one of Korean soldiers approaching the laptop and shutting it.

*   *   *

"This explains a hell of a lot," Joshua said, "and partially exonerates Rodrigo."

"We wouldn't be here if Torres hadn't tried helping a North Korean dictator," Porter countered. "Who the hell cares whether the son of a bitch lived or died? My men are in harm's way because of his actions."

No one spoke as they assimilated Torres' video log. Although Rodrigo had been instrumental in enabling the creation of the arachnid, the trio felt that he had clearly expressed remorse for his actions.

"That son of a bitch, as you put it, was our friend," Vinod stated. "He thought he was saving someone's life. Maybe he even thought that the cure could be used for others with cancer."

Porter was unmoved. "You heard the video yourself," he said. "He knew he'd gotten in over his head. He regretted his decision."

"Screw you, Porter!"

"Listen Bhakti, I don't want to hear anymore—"

"It's a moot point," Joshua interrupted to end the argument. "He's dead, so let's move on. We now know how and why the arachnid is here in North Korea."

There was brief silence as Porter cleared his throat while Vinod looked away.

"Dr. Yang, what did the Korean soldiers say in the last video," Porter asked as Vinod disconnected his laptop from the LCD screen.

"We're taking you into custody."

"He obviously escaped," Rachael said.

"Yeah," Vinod said, "but not for very long."

Chapter Fourteen
Airfoils

The discussion had moved past Rodrigo's fate, his ghostly image no longer on the LCD screen. Whether he was a conspirator or an unwilling dupe was irrelevant to the group, which needed to focus on the mission. The deadly creature in the forest was sitting uncomfortably near, and it had been established beyond any doubt that its intentions were hostile. But at least one goal of the mission had been accomplished: the military and scientific teams knew how and why an arachnid of petrin technology was on North Korean soil.

"It's pretty much like we surmised," Vinod stated. "The Koreans were trying to find a cure for their leader and were tricked into downloading DNA blueprints for the arachnid."

"We now have confirmation of *how* things happened," Porter said, "but we're still left with the original problem—what to do with the arachnid. We either have to capture it or destroy it. There are no other options since I have no intention of trying to communicate with a highly armored killing machine. We have to continue with our mission. What have you discovered after examining the objects retrieved from yesterday's operation?"

"I'll start with the metal ball," Joshua replied. "Vinod and I cut it open using a hacksaw provided by the Seals. As far as we can tell, it's made of pure iron and nothing else. The orange coloration on the surface was indeed ferrous oxide—the result of the spheroid's exposure to the elements. The object's dimensions are not uniform and therefore we don't think it was a projectile. As I indicated earlier, it's not aerodynamically stable."

"Then what is its purpose?" Porter asked.

"Completely unknown," Joshua answered. "We have no idea."

"So just a lump of iron then?" Ted said, jotting notes on a yellow legal pad as the meeting progressed. Using a number two pencil, he sketched the ball from memory. He was listening, but as a trained artist, he found that getting things down on paper helped him to concentrate better.

"As far as we can tell," Joshua said.

"Where did it come from?" Porter asked. "Surely it's somehow connected to the arachnid."

"Again, unknown," Joshua answered. "This region has no significant deposits of iron ore, but your point is well taken—namely, that it was probably created by the arachnid."

"Not much help, Dr. Andrews," Porter said, disappointed. "Who's next? Dr. Yang, do you have an idea what killed those people?"

"Yes," Liz replied. "These did." She dumped the contents of the cup in front of her onto the table. "Don't touch the projectiles. They're very sharp."

"Projectiles?" Porter said, eyeing the arrowhead-shaped pieces of metal.

"We think they're some type of weapon," Liz said. "A projectile shot through the air for the express purpose of killing its target."

"A razor-sharp bullet?" Ted asked. "Pretty deadly."

"We found these in the three dead men," Liz continued. "They do lethal damage when they enter the body. They're definitely the cause of death in each case: internal hemorrhage caused by the penetration of these objects. It's strange, they seem to be like smart weapons. They know exactly where to inflict the most damage to their victims."

"What do you think fired them?" Porter asked. "I mean, do you think this arachnid has the ability to fire projectiles?"

"That's our current theory," Vinod replied.

Ted stared closely at one of the projectiles, trying to ascertain its width. He was sketching an enlarged representation of them on his pad. "I think you're right, Vinod. These came from the creature."

"Why do you think so, commander?" Porter inquired.

"Yesterday, when the arachnid pointed one of its tentacles at me, the end of it had two structures. One was definitely an eye."

"That's similar to both the arachnids on Petri and those on New Eden," Rachael added. "It's how they see."

"Right," Ted said, "but there was something else. There was an opening just below the eye, a horizontal slit slightly wider than these projectiles."

"Commander," Porter began, "are you saying that you believe the arachnid shoots these from its tentacles?"

"Yes, it makes sense. The tentacles are the only parts of the arachnid that are truly mobile—the only parts that could aim a projectile at its target. If it does shoot these things, they have to come from that slit at the end of the tentacles. Plus the North Korean army has no ordnance that fits the description of these projectiles. They must have come from the arachnid."

"Shit!" Vinod remarked. "That thing's got eight tentacles. That's a lot of firepower."

"It gets worse," Joshua added.

"Worse?" Vinod said. "How?"

Joshua had not briefed the rest of the scientific team about his research on the projectiles, which he'd conducted while Vinod worked on extracting data from the SD card.

"I did extensive analysis of the projectiles. They're made of an alloy of iron, similar to steel. All three appear similar on the outside, but I examined them under a stereoscope and made precise measurements with a micrometer. There are differences among the three, and they're not random differences either. There are slight variations in the thickness and curvature of their sides. But here's the kicker. I believe they were *purposefully* manufactured with slight differences in their shapes. Liz is correct. They appear to be custom-designed weapons."

"Purposely manufactured?" Ted asked. "For what purpose?"

"Look at the shape of the projectiles," Joshua said. "Do they look somewhat familiar to any of you?"

The group stared closely at the objects, but no one offered a response.

"Not sure what you're getting at, Dr. Andrews," Porter said. "They appear to be nothing more than small arrowheads."

"To me, they look like wings. I'm sure you're familiar with the shape of the B2 stealth bomber. Doesn't this shape remind you of it?"

"I see the similarity, but what does it mean?" Porter asked.

"They have a similar shape to the bomber because they have a similar purpose," Joshua explained. "They're airfoils. They're meant to fly through a fluid medium like air, and that makes them a lot more sophisticated than a metal arrowhead."

"Are you telling me these things fly?" Porter asked.

"Not fly exactly," Joshua answered. "The shape of these wings was not meant to create lift, like the wings of an aircraft. The variations in the shape of each wing allow the airfoil to turn while in flight."

The group was stunned by the implications of Joshua's theory.

"Josh," Vinod said, "are you saying that these things are like guided missiles—that they can fly in curves in order to hit their target?"

"Yes, but not exactly like guided missiles. Guided missiles can reorient their direction in flight if their target moves. The shape of these objects is fixed once they leave the arachnid's tentacle. The shape of the airfoil, along with its speed and the fluid that it travels through, determines its ultimate destination. Depending on its shape, it can fly in a straight line or any variety of curved paths to reach its target."

"But what's the usefulness of having a projectile that takes a curved path?" Ted asked. "It seems to me that if you want a projectile to hit a target, the projectile would get there the fastest if it took a straight path."

"You're correct, commander. A straight line is always the fastest route, but these airfoils have a big advantage over an ordinary projectile. When you target something using your rifle, you use line of sight. You point your weapon directly at your target because the projectile you're firing—the bullet—is shaped to travel in a straight line. That works fine as long as your target is directly in front of you, but if your target is behind another object, like a tree for example, you wouldn't be able to hit it using line of sight. Since these projectiles can be programmed to take a curved path, they can fly around trees or other objects to hit their targets. It's small but ingenious."

The group let the implications of Joshua's statement sink in. The technology was sophisticated in the extreme. Would capture or extermination of the arachnid be possible given the creature's unique targeting system?

"Fuck!" Vinod exclaimed. "A razor-sharp, guided missile-shooting, eight-armed arachnid? That's what we're dealing with here?"

"I believe so," Joshua said soberly, leaning back in his chair, arms folded.

"Something still puzzles me," Rachael said. "Josh, if each airfoil is shaped to follow a certain path, there are millions of different trajectories that the creature could program. Its target could be at various distances and behind numerous types of objects. That would mean the arachnid has to carry an enormous arsenal of airfoils, all with slight variations in shape. Each time it fires, it would have to pick one with the specific configuration needed for a particular target. I know the arachnid is large, but it doesn't seem big enough to hold all of the airfoils necessary for its purposes."

Joshua grinned. "Smart girl. I knew there was a reason I married you." He leaned forward, elbows on the table. "I thought of that too, but unfortunately there *is* a solution to that problem. The creature may contain numerous *generic* airfoils not shaped to fly in any specific direction. As it targets something, it quickly shapes one of the generic ones as needed before shooting it."

"Reshaping a piece of metal on the fly?" Ted said. "That would take some time, don't you think?"

"Possibly," Joshua answered.

"At least *that* seems like an advantage for us," Ted said. "Our automatic weapons can fire multiple rounds per second."

"But remember that we don't know *how* this creature is reshaping the airfoils, if that is indeed what it's doing," Joshua cautioned. "It might have the ability to do it very quickly."

"But Josh," Vinod chimed in, "the number of calculations per second needed to shape these airfoils is vast. The creature would have to account for multiple variables at once—the density of the air, the wind direction, the distance to the target, and the velocity at which the airfoil needed be fired. How could it make so many calculations in a nanosecond? Seems implausible to me."

Porter followed the debate closely, gazing at each speaker as he or she tendered an opinion. This was why the scientific team was so crucial to the mission. He didn't always appreciate their personalities, but they knew how to do their jobs efficiently. More importantly, they got results.

"It's just physics," Joshua said. "Isn't that what Seth told us when we asked him how he was able to make the dice at the craps table in Vegas come up any number he chose? If you have enough calculating power, it can be accomplished. Just think of a professional tennis player. How many calculations per second does their brain make in order to hit a ball with a racquet so that it takes a curved path and lands close to a line of his or her choosing? Difficult, but not impossible."

"Josh?" Ted said, "do you think our Kevlar body armor will protect us from these airfoils?"

"It depends on the velocity of the airfoils, which determines the amount of kinetic energy they contain. It's not a linear relationship. If you double the velocity of an object, you increase its kinetic energy by a factor of four."

"Okay," Ted said. "I get it. How about if the airfoils are traveling at the same velocity as a bullet shot from an average gun, which our armor currently protects us against. Would our Kevlar still be effective against these airfoils?"

"I don't think so," Joshua replied after some thought. "Kevlar is designed with high tensile strength. A regular bullet penetrates a substance by trying to plough its way through it. Relatively speaking, a bullet has a large area of contact. This causes the Kevlar fibers to retain cohesion rather than stretch. That's how your armor works. It uses the tensile strength of Kevlar strands to stop a bullet. These airfoils, on the other hand, with their triangular shape and sharp front edges, would simply slice through your armor. Think of a strand of Kevlar. You can't pull it apart, but if you take a sharp pair of scissors, you could cut it easily."

"Josh, you're definitely a buzz kill today," Vinod remarked. "You got any more good news for us?"

"Nope, that's all I have."

"But we're making progress, people." Porter noted.

"I've got another question," Rachael stated. "Theoretically, the arachnid has to have a finite number of airfoils—a limited amount of ammunition, so to speak. They're metal, but can a biological creature manufacture metal objects as the need arises?"

"It's possible," Liz answered. "Even humans contain iron in their bodies. It's associated with hemoglobin and helps in the transport of oxygen. It's conceivable that the creature's tissue aggregates iron to form these airfoils, but there's still the question of where it's getting the iron. It can't just make it out of thin air." She clasped her hands on the table, her mind racing. "It must ingest it somehow."

"Maybe it eats the iron balls," Vinod suggested.

"Seems logical, but where do the iron balls come from?" Joshua asked.

"Maybe some creature we haven't seen yet is producing them for the arachnid," Vinod said. "Who knows what else Rodrigo may have accidentally created? We've only staged one day of reconnaissance."

"I guess it's possible," Joshua said, "but then we're even farther down the rabbit hole. Where is this hypothetical other creature getting *its* iron from? We've already established that there's no iron-rich geology here."

"It's an ironclad mystery," Vinod joked, which brought smiles to the faces around the table.

"Let's move on," Porter stated, not amused. "Liz, what can you tell us about the insect?"

"I had a chance to examine it under the microscope this morning. Definitely not from this world. Anatomically speaking, it's a fairly simple creature. It's biological and made of cells. The cells themselves are fairly typical, with nuclei and organelles. As far as the creature as a whole, I believe the tiny clear spheres surrounding the central abdomen are visual devices, like eyes. They're filled with a clear gelatinous material like the vitreous humor in our eyes. There's a tiny lens in each one to focus light on a light-sensitive material that makes up the rear of each sphere, which is covered with what I presume is a membrane similar to a retina. Each of these eyes has a neural bundle that emanates from its rear and connects to a central neural structure."

"Like a brain?" Vinod said.

"I wouldn't consider it a brain per se. It's too small. More like a nexus of neurons that surrounds a tiny black speck about the size of a grain of sand, but the speck isn't cellular. It's made of a really hard material that I couldn't slice through."

"A nexus of neurons," Joshua repeated. "It's a neural nest!"

"A what?" Liz asked.

"A neural nest. It's the term Seth used to describe the interface I had in my brain on New Eden that allowed the spookyon inside to interface with my nervous system."

"It makes sense," Liz said. "The visual information from the various eyes could be transmitting information to this neural nest, as you call it, and maybe the black grain of sand is the structure that contains a spookyon. What's also interesting is that I found no other systems involved. No digestive or respiratory systems—nothing. This leads me to believe that it's not an independent creature. It's a parasite that is completely dependent on its host and may have a symbiotic relationship with it. The host is obviously the arachnid."

"What kind of symbiosis?" Rachael asked.

"I believe the insects are dependent on the arachnid for their energy source," Liz explained. "In turn, the arachnid receives visual and sensory information from the insects."

"So you believe Vinod's theory that these insects are some kind of surveillance system for the arachnid," Porter said.

"Yes," Liz said. "Having seen the anatomy of the creatures, it's the only purpose that makes sense." She brushed hair away from her forehead and looked at Porter and Joshua. "The airfoils, the insects—they're all extremely sophisticated."

"What's the range of these insects?" Porter asked. "How far does the arachnid's sensing ability go?"

"That's difficult to determine, but the fact that the insects have no legs leads me to believe that they have to be in continual flight, which is a large energy drain. Given the size of the insects and the limited amount of energy they can store, I can't imagine that they could fly more than a kilometer from the arachnid before having to refuel."

"Good analysis, Dr. Yang." Porter said. "That's valuable and actionable information."

Liz smiled at the rare accolade from General Porter. Although she, like the rest, was troubled by the team's findings, she was enjoying the mission and the opportunity to use her expertise in unexpected ways. Everything the team had presented was on the cutting edge of exobiology.

"The final item on the agenda," Porter continued, "is to discuss the white tree-like structure. Does anyone have an idea what it is?"

The room was silent as each member considered the question, but there was no answer.

"Beats me what that thing is," Vinod said, "but we all know that petrins can create some weird shit."

"It's definitely a biologic entity of some kind," Liz offered. "It looks like something that was grown rather than manufactured, but as to what its purpose is, I have no idea. It seems unrelated to anything we've discussed thus far."

"I saw the thing up close yesterday," Ted said. "We have white cypress trees back home, but nothing like this. I got the impression that the arachnid was protecting it."

"What makes you say that?" Porter asked.

"Because of the creature's actions. The arachnid didn't move at all as I walked around it. Fairly close, I might add. But as soon as I got near the tree, the arachnid pointed one of its tentacles at me, like a momma bear protecting its cub. I think the reason the arachnid isn't moving is because it's guarding the structure."

"I could definitely interpret the creature's actions as being protective," Rachael said, "but does anyone have a clue as to what the purpose of the tree could be?"

Team members shook their heads. They could offer nothing as to its function or its relationship to the arachnid.

"Okay," Porter said after some silence, "now that we have the scientific analysis, we need to come up with a game plan on how to deal with the arachnid. I still don't see any way of communicating with it, so that part of the plan is out of the question. We know from the dead bodies that it's definitely hostile, and we'll therefore stick to the original goal of trying to capture it, but I won't hesitate to destroy it if necessary. Any comments?"

Porter looked around the table for any dissension, but there was none. After seeing numerous dead bodies the day before and learning more about the arachnid's capabilities, the scientific team was not opposed to the creature's destruction if that became necessary.

"I want ideas, people, on how to proceed given the information we have. I want you to formulate a plan of action. I'm giving you until tomorrow noon to come up with suggestions. I'll discuss the situation further with Dr. Langdon and Miss Williams for their insights. Dismissed."

Chapter Fifteen
The Special Project

The scientific team spent most of the afternoon resting and catching up on much-needed sleep. They agreed to meet for dinner and invited Ted to join them.

"Man, I'm getting tired of these military rations," Vinod complained as the group ate dinner in the dining area of Curly. "I don't know how you do it, Ted. Eating this stuff all the time would kill me."

"These are rations, not what we normally eat," Ted said. "The regular food in the military is actually very good. They want to keep us happy. You know the old saying—an army moves on its stomach. That having been said, I could go for some gumbo about now. Maybe red beans and rice or jambalaya washed down with Abita beer."

"Are those your favorites?" Rachael asked.

"Y'all know I'm from Louisiana, right? Cajun food is my favorite, no question, but there are an infinite number of ways to make gumbo or jambalaya. Every family has its own recipe, which is what makes Louisiana cuisine so unique. And the hotter, the better."

"Well, this food is a long way from Cajun," Vinod remarked as he took a spoonful of corned beef hash from a can.

Joshua was also having difficulty with the food. He was a vegetarian, and the military was not well equipped to handle his diet. "I know what you mean, Vinod. These mashed potatoes don't have much flavor."

"Hold on a sec," Ted said as he rummaged through one of the pockets of his fatigues. "Got something for ya." He produced a bottle of Tabasco sauce. "This will spice it up. If you can handle it, that is. It's made on Avery Island by the descendants of the Mcilhenney family."

Joshua gladly accepted the red sauce and dripped some on his potatoes.

"You're full of surprises, Ted," Liz commented. "Have any more condiments in your fatigues?"

"No, but speaking of surprises, I have one more for y'all." Ted reached into his backpack on the floor and produced two large bottles filled with a clear liquid.

"What's that?" Rachael asked.

"It's the special project I've been working on for the past couple of days."

"What's in the bottles?" Liz asked.

"Rum." Ted folded his arms and smiled.

"Rum!" Vinod exclaimed.

"Yes, rum. But not just any ole rum."

"How did you get booze?" Rachael asked. "Did it come with the supplies? I thought the military frowned on alcohol, especially on a mission."

"Naw, didn't come with the supplies. I made it right here. I noticed that the North Koreans left some yeast in the kitchen pantry. There was also molasses in our supplies from the ship, so I fermented the molasses with the yeast for a couple of days to get alcohol production going. Then I used some of the distillation equipment in the lab this afternoon to extract the alcohol."

"Awesome!" Vinod said, giving Ted a high five. "The man can cook!"

"Where'd you learn how to make rum?" Rachael asked.

"In the bayou. My daddy had a still deep in the swamp. As a kid, I'd help him make real Louisiana moonshine. Would y'all like to try some?"

"Louisiana moonshine? Sure," Vinod answered enthusiastically as he left and retrieved five cups and placed them on the table.

Making his way around the table, Ted filled each cup with a shot of alcohol. "Lessaiz les bons temps rouler. That means let the good times roll."

"We need a toast," Rachael announced, picking up her cup.

"How about to the Seals?" Joshua suggested. "They're the ones doing the toughest job. They're keeping us safe."

"To the Seals," the group said in unison as they downed their shots.

Vinod's face contorted after he swallowed his portion. "Damn, Ted, that's some strong shit. Probably combustible."

"I'm guessing about a hundred proof," Ted said. "So not combustible."

"My eyes are watering," Joshua stammered. "This stuff is going to eat my stomach lining and shut down my liver."

"It's definitely got a kick, son," Ted conceded.

"Hey, I've got an idea," Vinod stated.

"Oh, no," Rachael muttered, holding her arms out and shaking her head. "I think I know where this is going. Buyer beware."

"How about a little dorm party tonight?" Vinod asked. "Ted, you bring your rum and I'll provide the music. I brought my Bluetooth speaker for the tunes. We can have it in my room."

"Vinod," Joshua remarked, "you know it's my room too, right? Besides, we have a meeting scheduled with Porter tomorrow."

"There goes the old worry wart Joshua again," Vinod said. "The meeting's not until noon, doc. Besides, the alcohol may give us some creative ideas on how to deal with the creature."

"I seriously doubt that," Rachael proclaimed, "but we've all been under a lot of stress lately. Maybe a little stress relief is in order."

"I'm game," Ted replied. "Moonshine is mother's milk to me."

"Liz?" Vinod asked, eyes raised.

"Sure, why not?" Liz said, shrugging her shoulders. "Haven't been to a dorm room party since med school."

"Oh, it's on, Josh," Vinod said enthusiastically. "You need to get with the program, dude."

"Okay, fine," Joshua acquiesced, "but we can't stay up too late, and you need to take it easy. I don't want another episode like the time we went to the Rock Candy. You know, like how I had to carry you out from the stall in the men's room."

"Yes, mother," Vinod replied in a mocking voice. "Hey, you guys ever played quarters?"

"Heard of it," Ted answered. "Never played."

"Nope," Liz replied.

"Liz," Vinod said, "you're going to get an education tonight. Classic rock and quarters."

"Quarters?" Rachael said. "A drinking game? I thought you just agreed to take it easy? Quarters with hundred proof alcohol doesn't seem like taking it easy."

"Mother 2.0," Vinod said, pointing at Rachael, reverting to his mocking voice. "Look, we'll dilute the rum with juice. What's up with you two? Is this what marriage does to a couple? Turns them into buzz kills?"

"My buzz is definitely not killed," Rachael responded, now starting to feel the effect of the first shot. "Let the games begin."

*   *   *

An hour later, the group sat in Joshua and Vinod's dorm room around a circular table dragged in from the dining area. Vinod had made sure to pick a table whose surface was hard enough to allow a quarter to bounce on it easily. Vinod's Bluetooth speaker blared from a shelf in the corner of the room, blasting out a steady stream of classic rock. As per his habit at the start of any new song, Vinod announced the artist, the name of the song, and the album from which it came.

The group took turns bouncing a quarter on the table and trying to get it to land into a cup at the center of the table filled part way with rum mixed with orange juice. Vinod was acquainted with more advanced versions of quarters like chandeliers, or power quarters, but since most in the group weren't familiar with the game, he decided to keep the rules simple. If someone made the quarter in the cup, then that person could pick the person who would have to drink the liquid in the cup in order to get the quarter back out. Then the turn would move to the next person.

An hour into the game, two bottles of rum were almost empty, and everyone in the group was heavily buzzed. It was Vinod's turn, and as he had done many times during the evening, he rolled the quarter off the bridge of his nose, the coin bouncing off the table and clinking into the cup.

"Josh," Vinod said, pointing at Joshua, meaning that he had picked him to drink the contents of the cup.

"This is a ridiculous game," Joshua said before downing the drink and extracting the quarter from his mouth. "Why did I ever agree to this? Vinod, if I had a nose like yours, I'd get it in every time."

Liz laughed at Joshua's remark, her usual reserved manner replaced by one more uninhibited. "I love this game. It should be called how to get a doctor wasted. Good call, Vinod."

"Y'all are funny," Ted said. "You like to roast on each other, don't you?"

"All part of the friendship, Tabasco man," Vinod replied. "Hold the game for a sec. Gotta take a leak."

"Make sure you come back this time," Joshua shouted at him as he left the room referring to the night at the Rock Candy.

"Tabasco man, huh?" Joshua said.

"I'm down with it," Ted replied. "And I suppose it's accurate."

"That gives me an idea," Joshua stated. "You got more Tabasco?"

"Sure," Ted replied, retrieving the bottle from his pants.

"Josh, what're you thinking of doing?" Liz asked. "I see trouble coming."

"Vinod just had his turn," Joshua said, uncapping the bottle of

Tabasco, "So the four of us have to go before he gets a turn again." Joshua dripped a copious amount of Tabasco into the cup.

"What the hell are you doing?" Rachael asked.

"I'm getting back at Vinod for giving me all those shots. I'm sure you all noticed that he gave me more than the rest of you. Just a little payback for our IT specialist." Joshua added orange juice and the last of the rum to the glass and gave it a stir. Due to the opacity of the juice, the Tabasco was inconspicuous. "The four of us need to make a pact. If any of us gets the quarter in, we have to give the shot to Vinod."

"What happens if we all miss?" Liz asked. "One of us will get tortured if Vinod makes it in."

"It's four versus one," Joshua stated. "The odds are on our side."

"Kind of mean," Rachael remarked, trying to protect her friend. "Don't you think?"

"Come on, Rachael," Joshua said. "I know Vinod's your buddy but play along with me on this."

"Fine," she said. "I've come this far. Proceed, Dr. Andrews."

A minute later, Vinod walked in and took his seat. "Ted, you're up."

Ted shot the quarter and missed, as did Liz. It was now Joshua's turn. He took extra time to aim his quarter before shooting. The quarter bounced in the air, hit the rim of the cup, and bounced out.

"Rim shot," Vinod commented. "Rach, your turn."

The four were a little anxious. If Rachael didn't make the shot, one of them would surely have to down the Tabasco-laden drink given Vinod's expertise in bouncing quarters. Rachael steadied herself and calmly bounced the quarter off the table. It flew through the air and into the center of the cup with a splash.

All eyes turned to Rachael for her decision.

"Rach," Vinod said, "you get to pick the last person. No more rum left."

Rachael dramatically scanned the faces around the table, her gaze stopping on Vinod before she spoke. "Josh."

Liz and Ted exploded in howls of laughter at the look of shock that occupied Joshua's face.

"Oh, snap!" Ted exclaimed through fits of laughter. "Brutal."

"Oh, God!" Liz said. "Well played, Rach!"

"What's so funny?" Vinod asked.

"Take your drink, Josh," Rachael said with a Cheshire cat grin.

Joshua stared at Rachael, knowing he'd been had. "Full of surprises tonight, aren't we?"

"I'm an unpredictable girl," Rachael said with a wink.

Joshua picked up the drink and downed it, trying his best not to alter the expression on his face after he had finished swallowing. "Can someone please hand me some water?" he asked. "I'm dyin' here."

"What's so funny?" Vinod asked. "Did I miss something?"

"Inside joke," Rachael replied, handing Joshua a tall glass of tap water.

The song on Vinod's speaker transitioned to "Sweet Home Alabama" by Lynyrd Skynyrd.

"I love this song," Rachael said dreamily. "It's even better with a hundred proof rum."

"Everyone get up!" Vinod ordered. "I'm moving the table out to get the dance floor open."

"Dance floor?" Liz said.

"No one throws a party like Vinod," he said, referring to himself in the third person. He took the table back to the dining room and moved the chairs into the corner. "Gotta set the mood," he said as he turned the room lights off and flipped a switch on his Bluetooth speaker which caused LED lights to emanate from a clear ball on the top. The lights swept all areas of the room, flashing and strobing in time to the music.

"Man, you've thought of everything, Vinod," Ted remarked. "You'd fit right in on Bourbon Street."

"Always prepared for a party," Vinod said. "Your rum was amazing, by the way. Thanks. It's high-powered ammo."

"No probs," Ted replied. "Y'all know how to have fun. Just glad to be here."

"Josh, let's dance," Rachael requested.

"I think I've embarrassed myself enough tonight."

"Talk about a buzz kill." Rachael turned to Ted. "Ted, dance with me."

"Ain't Louisiana, but this song's still southern," Ted said as he danced with Rachael. The other three observed that Ted was an excellent dancer, moving in perfect time to the music.

"Damn, Tabasco!" Vinod exclaimed. "You got some moves!"

"It's the jitterbug mixed with a Cajun two-step. Don't know what it's called, but it dances real good!"

Liz grabbed Vinod's hand. "Let's go," she said.

She and Vinod joined Ted and Rachael on the makeshift dance floor. The quartet danced to multiple songs as Joshua watched, sitting on his chair, arms folded.

The song transitioned to "We Are Family" by Sister Sledge.

"Come on Josh," Rachael requested, motioning with her hand. "Join us."

Joshua reluctantly got up from his seat and joined the revelry. A few verses into the song, he started dancing to the lyrics with gusto, his previous embarrassing episode forgotten. The other four formed a small circle to give him a mini-stage. Joshua moved with emotion as the others played background dancers to his lead role. It was a welcome, joyous break from the serious mission they were on. The impromptu party allowed them, for the moment, to forget the danger and uncertainty lurking outside the complex in the dark North Korean forest.

It was midnight when the song finished and transitioned to "You Sexy Thing" from Hot Chocolate. Joshua, Rachael, and Ted took a break from dancing and sat down, watching Liz and Vinod, who continued their moves on the dance floor. They got more sultry as the song progressed, with Vinod moving his hands sensually across the curves of Liz's waist, back, and shoulders.

Rachael elbowed Joshua as the sexy dance continued. "What's up with *that?*"

"Who knows?" Joshua answered with a shrug. "It's not like anyone here is sober."

The song changed to "Waiting for a Girl Like You" by Foreigner. Vinod and Liz slow-danced face-to-face.

Rachael watched the couple dancing with their arms around each other. "Josh, are you seeing this?"

"Yes. Curiouser and curiouser."

"Damn," Ted said to Rachael. "They gettin' it on. Those two a couple?"

"Um . . . no," Rachael said.

"They may be before the night's done," Ted said with a wink.

After the song finished, Vinod and Liz walked over to the others, beads of sweat covering their foreheads as Vinod turned off the speaker and switched the room lights on. "I think the party's over, guys. We have to function tomorrow."

"Y'all sure know how to party," Ted said as he exited the room. "I'll see y'all at noon."

"Josh?" Vinod asked sheepishly. "You okay staying in Rachael's room tonight?"

Joshua and Rachael stared wide-eyed at Vinod and Liz, who were holding hands. Were they going to spend the night together?

"Uh, sure," Joshua replied hesitantly as he grabbed Rachael's hand, her mouth still agape, and led her out of the room.

Vinod closed the door and waited long enough for the couple to reach their room before laughing hysterically, bent over. "Mission accomplished," he said as he and Liz gave each other a high five.

"Did you see the looks on their faces?" Liz asked, laughing out loud.

"The look on Rachael's was classic," Vinod said. "She was as white as a ghost despite the rum."

"We make a good team, Vinod."

"We're *all* a good team," he said, giving her a hug.

*   *   *

"What the hell just happened?" Rachael said.

"Not sure."

"Do you think Vinod's . . . *bi*?" Rachael asked.

"Anything's possible," Joshua answered, lying on the bottom bunk in Rachael and Liz's room.

"I don't believe it," Rachael said.

"Why not?"

"I've known Vinod longer than I've known you. He's never mentioned any kind of attraction to a woman."

Joshua contemplated the statement for a while and looked at Rachael from his bed. "You sound jealous."

"Jealous?" Rachael asked defensively. "Jealous how?"

"Jealous like 'why is Vinod making moves on Liz when I've known him longer, and he's never been attracted to me'?"

"You're out of your mind."

"Perhaps, but the room is spinning, and I need to shut my eyes. I've done enough analysis for one day."

Am I jealous? Rachael wondered before turning out the light and climbing into the lower bunk next to Joshua.

*   *   *

Seal 4-3 volunteered for the night watch to keep an eye on the arachnid. He attached a night vision lens to the telescope on the roof of Moe, dropped a backpack with a few provisions at his feet, and peered through the eyepiece. The arachnid hadn't changed position, nor were its tentacles exhibiting any kind of movement. He noted the creature's current status in an electronic log and looked into the eyepiece, taking an occasional break to eat his rations or survey the dark countryside through night vision

115

binoculars. The arachnid was full of surprises, and acting on orders from
General Porter, he made a sweep of the area surrounding the complex to
make sure that no other threat presented itself. It was not out of the realm
of possibility that the alien life form could manufacture other objects or
creatures similar to airfoils and insects. If it did, he was to relay the
information immediately to the commander on night watch. Soldiers were
also stationed on the roofs of Curly and Larry to make sure all areas near the
compound received equal coverage.

The seal backed away from the telescope and rubbed his eyes before
taking a bite of rations, which tasted like spam even though it was labeled as
ground beef. He then looked up at the night sky and was dazzled by the
array of stars shining brightly since the complex was not running external
lights, both to conserve power and maintain stealth in order to avoid notice
from the arachnid. He couldn't pick out the constellations or even name
any of the brighter stars. Like most of Earth's population, however, he had
turned his head to the night sky numerous evenings after the official
announcement had been made three years earlier that intelligent life had
been discovered outside the solar system and that, even more remarkably,
contact had been made with a planet called Petri. The dialogue with the
distant planet had been made possible by something called quantum
entanglement, meaning that two paired particles separated by any distance,
near or far, could communicate with each other instantaneously. He had no
grasp of the science whatsoever, but that left him in no less awe that an
advanced civilization was out there . . . somewhere. It was his understanding
that Petri could be circling a nearby star in the Milky Way or, more likely, a
star in a galaxy billions of light years away. That was really all he'd
understood about the discovery that had changed human history forever.
He'd never bothered to join the 103 Club, a worldwide group devoted to
following the teachings of Android Seth. It was ironic, therefore, that it was
his job to keep an eye on a piece of technology that had been manufactured
using genetic instructions from the petrins.

He returned to the telescope and checked on the arachnid. For a
moment he thought he saw movement—had a tentacle uncurled and
floated through the night air? Or had the creature unfolded its legs, ready to
stand and possibly advance through the forest? He swung the mouthpiece of
his helmet in front of his lips, ready to radio the news, but he exhaled a sigh
of relief when he saw that what had disturbed the branches of a distant pine
was only a deer foraging in the tall grass.

The rest of his watch was uneventful, and that suited him fine. He'd
been in the field and knew that the arachnid had the capacity for great

destruction. He'd seen the dead Korean soldiers, and while he was startled by the sophistication of the alien technology, he was committed to the mission, which was to contain or destroy the arachnid. Personally, he hoped that the teams or their carrier support would be given a single unambiguous order: destroy the lousy son of a bitch.

*   *   *

Langdon and Williams stood on the observation deck of the carrier, observing night launches of F-18 Super Hornet fighter jets that patrolled airspace within 200 nautical miles of the carrier. The launches were mesmerizing to both individuals as the planes were catapulted from the flight deck by the Electromagnetic Aircraft Launch System, or EMALS, which took up far less room below decks than traditional steam catapults on Nimitz-class carriers. The jets raced from the carrier deck, dipping slightly towards the sea for a few seconds until their engines were fully engaged, circles of yellow light glowing brightly from the tails of planes as they gained altitude and banked over the Sea of Japan. Some of the fighters were instructed to patrol the Korean coastline, but they were to avoid any flyovers of the complex where the Seals had been deployed so as not to awaken the arachnid, which appeared to be in a state of hibernation.

"It's a hell of an operation," Langdon commented. "The fighters and flight deck crew are in perfect sync with the operations tower."

"Impressive," Williams said. "The Navy knows what it's doing. We have the greatest fleet in the world."

"Amen," Langdon said. "I think—"

The conversation was interrupted by the ship's XO.

"Excuse me," he told the pair, "but Captain Pierce would like to see you in his ready room."

"Anything serious?" Williams inquired.

"I don't know, ma'am. I was just told to escort you there."

The three figures disappeared into the maze of corridors within the carrier, climbing ladders and making their way through hatchways just as the science team had done after landing on the carrier. Ten minutes later, they emerged into a wider passage in a section of the ship where executive offices and briefing rooms were located. On one door was a placard that read CAPTAIN NATHANIEL PIERCE. The XO knocked twice, after which a voice within said, "Come." The three figures entered, and the XO left, shutting the door behind him.

"Good evening, captain," Langdon said. "To what do we owe the pleasure? I hope you're going to offer us some pricey bourbon instead of telling us there's a crisis on the mainland."

Pierce smiled thinly and motioned for the two visitors to take seats opposite his desk. "Make yourselves comfortable," he said. "No crisis to report, although I do have an update I thought you should hear."

"We're all ears, captain," Williams said. "What do you have for us?"

Pierce leaned back in his leather chair and placed his hands on the armrests.

"I received word from General Porter," he said. "You two will get a full briefing tomorrow before the noon meeting, and I don't want to step on the science team's toes by relaying information that I still don't fully comprehend myself, but I'll give you the gist. It's a heads-up from Mitch so I can keep operations at sea at the proper stage of alert." He paused, smiled, and glanced at the chief of staff. "I wanted to relay the information to you instead of telling the president directly. I wouldn't want to alarm him."

"Believe me," Williams said, "he always appreciates that sentiment."

"I'm sure he does. What Porter relayed, and what you'll hear more about tomorrow, was that they've determined the cause of death of the bodies they retrieved yesterday. The arachnid apparently killed them all and has some impressive offensive capabilities. Its tentacles can shoot some kind of metal dart that one doesn't want to be on the receiving end of. It also deploys high-tech insects for the purposes of reconnaissance. It's still in its non-threatening posture though, with its legs folded and tentacles neatly curled against its carapace."

"So things are well, in hand," Langdon said, appearing relieved.

"For the time being," Pierce said, "but I'm concerned that, after tomorrow's briefing, we may be moving onto the next phase of the mission, namely capture or extermination. We've planned for these contingencies as much as is humanly possible given the limited amount of intel we had going in, but . . .."

"Yes," Williams said.

"I'm disturbed by the fact that the creature has demonstrated lethal force using advanced technology that we may not fully understand yet. The briefing tomorrow will tell us what kind of analysis the scientific team has been able to make, if any."

"Your point, captain," Williams said, her tone of voice more concerned.

"I think we have to be proactive since it takes time to move ships and forces around. What I'd like you to recommend to the joint chiefs and the president, Ms. Williams, is that we bring a nuclear submarine into the vicinity. It's equipped with both cruise and ballistic missiles. I'm also putting some long-range bombers on alert. We have patrols, but I'd like to have some heavy firepower ready so as to cover all the bases."

"Ballistic missiles carry nuclear warheads," Langdon said. "What's your thinking, captain?"

"It doesn't appear as if the arachnid—or petrin technology, for that matter—has demonstrated the best intentions to the North Koreans. I don't want to jump to any conclusions, but the preliminary reports from Porter give me pause. I don't think it would be prudent to wait until after the scientific team delivers its briefing to start redeploying vessels from their current patrol routes. The Navy's tactical posture in such situations is to keep ahead of the curve. Ships can be recalled. Human lives can't."

"In other words," Langdon said, "don't get caught with your pants down."

Pierce smiled broadly. "Believe it or not, that's a philosophy taught at the Naval War College."

"I'll put a call into the president tonight," Williams stated. "I'll make sure he knows how you'd like to proceed out of an abundance of caution."

"Excellent," Pierce said as he opened the bottom left drawer of his desk. "Now then, it just so happens that I do indeed have some pretty fine sippin' whiskey. Bourbon, as requested. A quick nightcap before we head for bed. Tomorrow may be a long day."

The captain produced three glasses and poured the drinks.

Langdon couldn't suppress a laugh. "It's another way to be prepared. Do they teach this at the war college too?"

"As a matter of fact they do," Pierce replied, taking a sip of bourbon.

Chapter Sixteen
Game Plan

The group reassembled at noon the next day in the lobby of Moe. Porter had a laptop open to a video conference with the carrier, allowing Langdon and Williams to join in. The scientific team and Ted looked alert despite their late-night party.

"The purpose of this meeting is to establish a plan of action for phase four of the mission," Porter stated. "I've briefed Dr. Langdon and Miss Williams on what we've learned about the arachnid over the past couple of days. They're in agreement that we'll try to capture the creature if possible, but given its lethality, it will be destroyed if it can't be done. We also agree that it will be destroyed if the Seals are in danger. But let's turn our attention to capturing this beast. Who's got ideas?"

Liz spoke first. "What if we subdue it using a powerful tranquilizer like they do with elephants? I noted that the Koreans have Ketamine in the lab. It's a powerful sedative."

"A nice, easy solution if it works," Langdon said through the laptop. "Commander, do you have a gun that can shoot a tranquilizer?"

"I'm sure we can rustle one up," Ted said.

"A good idea," Joshua commented, "but there are some potential problems. First, we don't know how strong the creature's armor is, which seems to cover its entire body. I don't know if we could get a steel needle to penetrate it. That would be necessary to deliver the drug."

"True," Ted said. "But Josh, if you had your choice of the weakest spot on the creature, where would you aim?"

"At a transition area. Mechanically, transition zones are always the weakest. If I were to pick a point, I'd pick the junction between the carapace and one of its tentacles."

"That's a pretty small area," Vinod commented. "Ted, can your guys hit that?"

"Pretty sure we can. One of my men is a sharpshooter. He would need practice shooting a dart to get used to the trajectory, but it's definitely possible."

"There's another problem with this tranquilizer idea," Joshua stated. "We don't know what makes the creature tick. Hell, we don't even know its power source. Its chemistry may be vastly different than anything we've encountered. We don't know if Ketamine will affect it."

"Definitely could be an issue," Liz said, "but one thing we do know is that this is a biological entity. It was grown from DNA transmitted to Earth. I think Ketamine is worth a try, and it presents minimal risk to us. If it works, it works."

"I agree," Williams said. "It's a good first step, but we also have to plan for what to do if it *doesn't* work. Does anyone have ideas on getting that thing into the cage."

"If it wasn't tranquilized, we'd have to lure it somehow," Rachael said.

"Rach, I don't think that thing is just going to walk into a cage for no reason," Vinod stated.

"I don't think so either," Rachael said. "We need to hide the cage. Maybe we can dig a hole, bury the cage, and then camouflage the opening. Then we lure the creature over the opening."

"Like a pit trap," Ted responded. "We do it all the time in Louisiana."

"Yeah, but how're you going to lure it over the trap?" Vinod asked. "What's the bait? We don't even know what this thing lives on."

Ted looked at the others before speaking. "Unfortunately, I think the bait is going to have to be us."

"What do you mean *us*?" Porter asked.

"General," Ted began, "we know that if that thing gets pissed off, it's going to come after us, the Seals. We saw what it did to those North Korean soldiers. So we let it chase us, but we lead it to the trap."

"No offense, commander," Joshua stated, "but that sounds crazy and dangerous. I don't think you can outrun that thing. You or your men would get killed by the airfoils just like the Koreans did."

"How fast do you think it can run?" Ted asked.

Joshua thought of the speed at which the arachnids were able to run on New Eden. "I'd estimate the max speed to be about thirty to forty miles per hour. No way you could outrun it."

"Then we use one of our vehicles," Ted suggested. "The hummers could do it."

The group contemplated the idea, playing out the scenario in their minds.

"How much do the hummers weigh?" Rachael asked.

"I'd say about four tons, including armor."

"Then I don't think it's going to work," Rachael said. "If we bury that cage in the ground and cover its opening to camouflage it, that covering must be weak enough to break if the arachnid is standing on it. The only way I see the arachnid going over the hole is if whatever it's chasing also goes over the same path. If the hummer goes over the hole first, it would fall in due to its weight, not the creature."

"How much do you think that thing weighs?" Ted asked.

"It's biological," Liz answered, "and about the size of an elephant. I'd say about the same as the hummer, about four tons."

"Okay," Ted continued. "We make the cover of the buried cage strong enough so that it holds about a ton before collapsing. We can lure the arachnid using one of the quads. A rider on a quad is less than a ton, and I think the quads can do about fifty."

"Quad?" Joshua said. "Like the ones people go off-roading with?"

"Yeah," Ted answered. "You know, those small four-wheeled, single-rider vehicles. We got a couple here."

"You'd be a sitting duck on a quad," Vinod said. "There's no armor, no protection. Those airfoils would slice right through you."

"Maybe we can fit it with some metal shielding," Ted suggested. He turned to Joshua. "How thick do you think metal needs to be to stop those airfoils, doc?"

"It depends on their velocity. At typical bullet speeds, I think a half-inch-thick piece of metal would do the trick."

"Fine," Ted said. "We'll weld some metal plates to the quads as shields for the rider. We'll make the shield three-sided—left, right, and back. Got to leave the front open so the driver can see."

"Don't forget the top," Vinod said. "Remember the curving airfoils. Also, you'll have to protect the tires."

"Good point," Ted said. "We'll cover the top with metal too. We'll also place metal panels along the wheel wells to prevent the tires from getting hit. It'll be like a mini-tank. Even with the added weight of the armor, it still won't be heavy enough to collapse the camouflaged covering over the cage."

"Speaking of metal," Porter added, "I want your men better protected. I want to replace your Kevlar vests with some type of metal armor. It's going to be heavier, but I don't want your men out there without *some* type of enhanced protection against the airfoils. I'm sure the military has heavier shielding that your men can wear. I'll look into it."

"Sounds good," Ted said. "We'll need all the protection we can get."

As before, Ted made notes, this time on the quad enhancements and the armor plating. He'd sketched the quads and the dimensions for the metal panels that would be added. On a separate sheet of paper, he drew a picture of the arachnid in exacting detail since he anticipated encountering the creature very soon and wanted to have a mental image of the arachnid before engaging it. As he was fond of saying, "I play hard, I work hard." His mind was totally focused on the mission.

"There's something I've been thinking about," Vinod said pensively. "I've made some calculations on how much processing power the creature needs to shoot airfoils and shape them to reach the desired target. It has to make a tremendous number of calculations, but the creature can't have *unlimited* processing power. It has to somehow reduce the number of variables to make the calculations simpler."

"What are you getting at?" Rachael asked.

"If the creature's chasing you, it's moving," Vinod explained. "We have to assume that its target is moving too, not to mention the wind, let's say at thirty miles per hour. Bullets are one thing, but the airfoils have to fly a designated path. According to my calculations, it would be extremely difficult for the creature to shoot airfoils at a moving target. In order to reduce the number of calculations, it would have to be standing still."

"You're saying that the creature can't shoot while moving?" Ted asked.

"Well, to shoot with any precision, it needs to be stationary," Vinod replied. "That's what I think given the amount of information processing needed."

"Solid reasoning," Joshua said. "Even at the craps table, Seth had to recruit additional petrins to help him get the dice to land how he wanted."

"But what if this creature has a primordial spookyon in it?" Rachael asked. "It could be connected to other individuals to help with calculations that are instantaneous."

"If it does," Vinod said, "then all bets are off. It'd have unlimited computing power like Seth had at the craps table."

"I think it highly unlikely this arachnid is connected to a network using a primordial spookyon," Joshua commented.

"Why not?" Liz asked.

Joshua explained his reasoning. "Remember, this thing was created in a lab and then grew into an arachnid. Unlike regular spookyons, like those we create at Berkeley, there are only a finite number of primordial spookyons that were created at the moment of the Big Bang, and they're randomly dispersed throughout the universe. Even if this creature could capture one, it would be highly unlikely that one would be connected to whatever network the creature needed. For that reason, I don't think this creature is being remote-controlled like Android Seth was. I believe it's a completely independent entity."

"What about the spookyon that Rodrigo captured?" Vinod asked. "Could it have gotten access to that one?"

"I don't think so," Joshua replied. "Rodrigo broke the Bowman sphere in the lab, the one that contained the spookyon he captured. Once that sphere was broken, the spookyon mixed with molecules of air. There's no way it could have been recaptured, not even by an advanced creature like the arachnid."

"All of this could work to our favor," Porter said.

"It's just speculation, general," Joshua said. "There could be other variables we're not accounting for."

"I have faith in your scientific team," Porter answered with an almost imperceptible grin. "Otherwise, I wouldn't have brought you here."

The general stood and started pacing. "Alright, I want to summarize our plan thus far. First, we're going to get better armor for the Seals and weld some metal panels to the quads. We're also going to need to clear a path through the forest to reach the creature. The tanks can help with that, but I don't want the arachnid to know about them. We would lose our strategic advantage. Our estimate is that the drone insects have a range of about a kilometer. The tanks can create a path up to that point, but the Seals will have to do the rest with saws. We can curve the path to utilize the clearings so there's less tree cutting to be done. Most importantly, we need to dig a hole along the path and bury the cage. I think the hole will have to be outside the one-kilometer sensing limit since we don't want the creature to know about the trap." Porter ceased pacing and faced the team. "Then we move in some firepower. I want the hummers with their fifty-caliber guns to take positions in the forest and surround the creature. I also want some Seals with RPGs surrounding the creature."

"RPGs?" Liz asked.

"Rocket propelled grenades," Porter explained. "They're essentially shoulder fired missiles that pack a serious punch. The tanks will be positioned just outside the one-kilometer limit and will be brought in as a last resort."

"What about aerial support?" Vinod asked. "Like drones or helicopters."

"I thought about that," Porter answered. "It may do more harm than good. The drones would have to fly very high in order not to be heard, and the accuracy of their weapons would be diminished at that height. With helicopters, we'd lose any semblance of stealth. They're easily heard and seen. Besides, if the creature goes into the forest, it would be hidden from both drones and helicopters, and I wouldn't want them firing randomly into the forest since our men will be in there. We can use drones to monitor the situation, but we won't use their firepower. This is going to have to be a ground-based operation. If something goes drastically wrong, we'll have fighters ready to roll from the carrier. With their supersonic speed, they can be here in a few minutes."

All team members were now making notes on what would be a complex but well-orchestrated operation.

Porter continued elaborating on the plan. "Once all the equipment is in place, we'll move our men into position. First, we try to knock that thing out with the tranquilizer. If that doesn't work, we lure it to the trap with a rider on an armored quad. If anything goes wrong, we roll in the tanks and blast the thing to smithereens."

"I'm good with it," Langdon said over the laptop.

"A solid plan, general," Williams commented. "I'll get approval from the president."

"It's going to take a few days to get everything in place," Porter said. "We're going to need more supplies and equipment from the carrier."

"I'll arrange for that," Williams said. "Any movement from the creature, or is it still guarding the white tree?"

"Our scout on the roof says there's no movement," Porter replied.

"Let's hope it stays dormant," Vinod said. "We can't possibly be ready if it moves or advances on the complex."

No one spoke. Vinod was right. The entire plan hinged on the arachnid's current placement remaining unchanged.

Chapter Seventeen
Preparations

The Seals were busy getting ready for phase four of the operation. More food and supplies were delivered from the carrier by the ospreys and deposited in the clearing around the complex. Using satellite maps, a route was created, leading from the complex to the creature's location. It had many curves, allowing the team to take advantage of the natural landscape and minimize the need for cutting down trees.

Tanks ploughed through the forest, cutting a path up to the one-kilometer sensing limit, which is when the Seals took over with chainsaws. As they neared the creature, armed scouts watched for any movement, but it remained motionless despite the noise from the loud buzzing of the saws.

"Why do you think it's not moving?" Vinod asked Joshua from the roof of Moe as he peered through the telescope.

"No idea. It may be in some kind of regenerative state."

"But it must know what we're doing. I spoke to some of the Seals cutting down trees. They occasionally see the sensing insects buzzing around."

"It may have something to do with the white tree," Joshua speculated, "which is why the Seals are staying clear of it. The arachnid apparently doesn't want to leave it unguarded. Or maybe the creature doesn't view the Seals as a threat. I wonder what the Koreans did to piss it off."

"Hopefully not what we're planning on doing."

The next day, Joshua and Vinod prepared to drive with one of the Seals in a hummer to the site where the cage was being buried. Porter had ordered that the hummers, four in all, and the two tanks be driven to an area beyond where the hole was being dug since the hummers and tanks were too heavy to go over the trap. They were about to deliver the final hummer.

"Damn, that's a big gun," Vinod remarked as he looked at the automatic weapon mounted on the rear of the vehicle.

"Fifty caliber," Joshua said. "Plenty of firepower. Porter's not messing around."

The hole for the cage had been dug using numerous Seals with shovels and pickaxes, and the cage was being lowered in place by helicopter as their hummer arrived at the site. After the cage was deposited in the hole, the tethering lines were disconnected, and the hummer drove over the closed lid of the buried cage with no problem.

"At least we know the cage can support four tons," Vinod noted after they had crossed and had gotten out of the hummer.

"I'm sure it can support much more than that," Joshua said. "Did you see how thick its steel is? Probably could support more than twenty tons."

The work for the helicopter was not finished. The top of the cage, a solid steel slab, was connected at one side with hinges that allowed the top to swing open. The three non-hinged sides of the top contained latching mechanisms that caused it to automatically lock when closed. Three groups of Seals worked to unlatch the locking mechanisms before attaching cables from the still-hovering copter to the top of the cage on the side opposite the hinges. The copter rose higher, which caused the unlocked lid to swing open. The copter then lifted the lid and moved laterally and down, positioning it on the ground adjacent to the hole.

Joshua and Vinod walked towards a group of Seals digging out dirt beneath the area where the lid now rested.

"Man, that lid looks heavy," Vinod commented.

"It is," one of the Seals said. "About a thousand pounds."

"How the hell are you going to close it when the arachnid falls in?" Vinod asked.

"That's what we're working on. We're digging a channel under this edge of the lid. The channel's going to be filled with C-4 high explosive. The detonator for the explosive will be linked to a pressure sensor at the bottom of the cage. When the creature falls in and activates the sensor, it'll blow the lid closed. It automatically latches when shut. Presto! Trapped arachnid."

"Ingenious," Joshua remarked.

"All you guys have to do is put the false lid on top of the opening, camouflage the whole thing, and the trap is set," Vinod said.

"Correct."

The false lid would break if anything greater than a thousand pounds passed over it. It would support a rider on a quad, but the arachnid would definitely fall through. It was being constructed at the complex using wood timbers to exact specifications provided by mechanical engineers on board the carrier. After it was placed over the opening, the wooden structure and the lid would be covered with a small layer of dirt and pine needles to camouflage the trap.

Their transport having been delivered to the opposite side of the trap, Vinod and Joshua, accompanied by heavily armed Seals, walked back to the complex. They knew they were not in any real danger since the arachnid was over a kilometer away, closely watched by a group of Seals who would radio at any sign of movement.

"Looks like everything's all set for tomorrow," Joshua remarked.

"As set as it can be," Vinod said. "Somehow I feel that everything's not going to go as planned. We're still dealing with a lot of unknowns here."

"True. However, I think we've done the best we can in planning for phase four, which is scheduled to start at 1200 tomorrow. We'll just have to see what happens."

"Nothing has ever really gone according to plan when petrin technology was involved," Vinod pointed out.

Joshua said nothing. Vinod was absolutely right.

Chapter Eighteen
Hell on Earth

Williams, Langdon, and Pierce stood on the bridge of the carrier. They had an expansive view of the Sea of Japan as well as the flight deck, where fighter jets had been positioned for immediate departure. The bright glimmers of sunlight that gilded the wave crests betrayed the seriousness of the tactical situation for the troops on the mainland.

"If we launch, what are the chances your fighters will kill this creature?" Williams asked.

"I'd say our chances are excellent at destroying the arachnid," Pierce answered. "The hornets carry AMRAAMS, or Advanced Medium Range Air-to-Air Missiles as well as infrared imaging Maverick air-to-ground missiles. They pack a considerable punch. The creature's armor can't possibly withstand these weapons. I think we can vaporize the thing."

"What about the range of the fighters' weapons?" Langdon inquired. "Can they fire before the airfoils have the opportunity to damage the aircraft?"

"From what we know, the airfoils have limited range compared to the missiles we carry. They're simple metallic projectiles that have no internal propulsion. We can fire long before we're anywhere close to the arachnid's weapons range."

"The arachnid has fooled us before," Langdon warned, arms folded as he gazed at the sea.

Williams' eye shifted to the captain for a response.

"I can't argue the point," Pierce said, "but the F-18 is an amazing aircraft. I'll place my bets on its superior firepower. In fact—"

The captain was interrupted by a bridge officer.

"Captain, you and Ms. Williams and Dr. Langdon are needed in the command center below. The mission is about to proceed."

*   *   *

The scientific team and General Porter gathered in Moe and sat in front of two LCD screens that displayed video feeds from the Seals' cameras. The feeds, as before, were also relayed to the carrier. The team sat quietly, with no banter or conversation. They knew that the success of the mission, though planned with meticulous detail, hinged on several steps being executed in quick succession and without a hitch.

Everyone on the ground was in position. There were numerous Seals, some kneeling, some standing behind trees shouldering RPG launchers and automatic weapons aimed at the arachnid. The four Humvees and their fifty-caliber guns were stationed around the edge of the clearing where the arachnid maintained its eerily motionless posture. Two tanks were positioned in front of the trap and were ready to roll if given the command.

The tanks themselves weren't manned by Seals. Tanks were Army artillery, so Army personnel were part of the expanded mission in the North Korean forest. There had been discussion as to what kind of ammunition the tanks would fire since different types of shells could be loaded into their main cannons depending on the target. General Porter had ordered two types of rounds for the tanks: explosive rounds that would detonate when a target was hit, and armor-piercing rounds that would hopefully penetrate the exoskeleton of the creature.

The tank commanders communicated via radio, engines running, waiting for the command to advance if necessary. The radio chatter, rendered in military jargon, was brief and relayed location, tactical assessments, and status.

"We're in position," Ted said over his radio. He knelt next to seal 5-3, the sharpshooter, who held the rifle that would shoot the Ketamine-loaded dart. The sharpshooter lay on the ground, his rifle propped on a fallen pine trunk. He loaded the first of five Ketamine rounds, prepared by Liz, into the chamber and waited for the order to fire. The sharpshooter had practiced with the rifle for the past three days and had honed his accuracy. The sight on his rifle was aimed at the junction between the arachnid's carapace and the rear tentacle on its left side. Although the tentacle was still coiled like a length of thick rope, its attachment point to the carapace was clearly visible. The rifle he held was a variation of the military's fifty-caliber JM dart rifle, which fired ballistic tranquilizer darts that delivered anesthetic agents such as Ketamine via compressed gas. The sharpshooter's rifle was a larger and sturdier version of the JM and could fire multiple steel needles loaded with the tranquilizer.

"Make the first round count," Ted whispered. "Once it's riled up, you may not get a clear shot at one of those junctions near the carapace again."

"Yes, commander."

Next to Ted was one of the two quads that had been fitted with metal plates. The rider's seat had been surrounded with armor on all sides except the front, and its tires were shielded with half-inch plating. The path through the forest had been made as smooth as possible since the protective armor extended to within two inches of the ground. The quad wouldn't be able to handle large bumps easily without losing maneuverability.

Porter scanned the video feeds carefully for anything out of place, anything that needed to be corrected, but he saw nothing. The soldiers were ready for the operation to commence, their weapons aimed at the massive dark-gray creature.

"Are the fighters ready for launch?" Porter asked into his headset.

"Ready to go," Captain Pierce replied over the radio.

The tension in Moe was palpable. Every team member sat straight; breath suspended in their chests. The shot would be the first of many steps to capture a creature that literally had otherworldly capabilities.

Steel in his voice, Porter gave the command into his headset. "You may fire, commander."

*   *   *

The sharpshooter slowly squeezed the trigger, and the dart flew through the air, hitting its target at the intended site, but it couldn't penetrate the arachnid's exoskeleton. The dart ricocheted off the armor at high speed and smacked a lower limb of the white tree. The branch shattered as if made of glass and dropped to the forest floor.

The arachnid immediately rose, all eight tentacles unfurled and scanned its surroundings. It was as if it was on high alert, searching for whatever had harmed the tree. Its tentacles moved high and low, left and right as they sought the attacker. Its legs unfolded further as it stood, the carapace rising higher into the air.

"Shit!" Vinod exclaimed. "I think we pissed it off."

"That was our intention," Porter said.

"We may have been lulled into complacency by its lack of movement," Rachael said.

131

What followed was nothing the teams could have foreseen in their planning. The creature unleashed a barrage of airfoils from its tentacles at various targets in all directions. They left the tentacles at supersonic speed, which caused each to create a high-pitched *crack*, a mini-sonic boom as it sped through the air. The resulting effect was the sound of a thousand whips being cracked.

"We're taking fire!" Ted screamed into his microphone. He knelt in the tall grass, his shaded helmet visor down.

"Fire back!" Porter yelled. "Light that damn thing up!"

The Seals opened up with automatic weapons, their ammunition bouncing off the creature's armor in sparks. The arachnid stood tall in the clearing, continuing to discharge its barrage of airfoils as its tentacles sought out Seals in every direction. Its legs extended and compressed rhythmically to raise and lower its carapace in order to give its tentacles further scanning range.

The Seals with the RPG launchers fired their rockets at the creature. The rockets flew through the air leaving long grey streaks of exhaust fumes in their wake. The projectiles exploded in midair in large fireballs before reaching the arachnid.

Ted watched as the RPGs exploded in quick succession in midflight. "The goddamn thing is picking off the RPGs midflight with its airfoils!" he shouted into his headset. "They're completely ineffective!"

Seeing that the bullets and RPGs had no effect on the arachnid, Porter spoke into his microphone. "Roll the tanks! Open up with the fifties!"

The Seals on the hummers opened fire with their fifty calibers, filling the forest with deafening sound as rapid-fire rounds tore through the air. They had no effect on the arachnid, the bullets no match for the creature's seemingly impenetrable armor. Hundreds of empty shell casings littered the forest floor.

"Goddamn!" Ted yelled over the din of the weapons. "What the hell is that thing made of?"

"Reminds me of the alien machines in *War of the Worlds*," Joshua said. "They hovered over streets as they fired in every direction, a large eye on the end of a mechanical neck scanning for targets."

"That's pretty much what's happening," Vinod said. "A war with an alien species."

The arachnid targeted the Humvees, showering them with airfoils that left its tentacles at a rate of four per second. The projectiles hit their marks with deadly accuracy, mangling the Seals operating the guns as their bodies grew limp, the weapons silenced.

The scientific team watched in horror, their hands over their mouths as, one by one, the video feeds from the Seals stopped moving as the seal wearing them got hit. Many feeds now showed only static images pointed in random directions—some at the ground, others at the sky, and others at odd angles at the arachnid which continued its unabated attack.

"They're getting slaughtered, Porter!" Joshua cried. "Get them out of there!"

"Commander, fall back!" Porter shouted. "*Everyone* fall back!"

"Where the hell are the tanks?" Vinod asked.

The surviving Seals retreated into the forest, occasionally stopping to turn and fire at the arachnid.

"Let's get the hell out of here," Ted told the sharpshooter.

"I'm hit," the sharpshooter groaned, grasping his thigh and wincing in pain. The seal was on his back, a large gash on his inner thigh spurting blood.

Ted took out a knife and cut one of the sleeves off of the sharpshooter's shirt. He quickly wrapped the sleeve around the upper thigh and tied it tight to form a tourniquet to stem the bleeding. "That should hold it. You think you can walk?"

"No, I think my leg is broken," the man replied through grunts of pain.

Grabbing the soldier by his shoulders, Ted dragged him through the grass as he heard the rumble of tanks barreling single file down the path and into the clearing.

The tanks, their pleated tracks churning up dirt, separated as they entered the clearing and took position side-by-side in front of the arachnid. The creature redirected all of its firepower at the tanks, which allowed time for the surviving Seals to escape. The front armor of the tanks was hit with multiple airfoil strikes, none of which penetrated the thick steel plating.

The left tank loaded an explosive round into its main canon and aimed it at the arachnid. "Fire!" its commander ordered, and the projectile blasted out of the long brown barrel, hitting the creature squarely on the front of its carapace and exploded in an orange fireball. The force of the blast lifted the arachnid several yards into the air and threw it backwards, its carapace tilted at a forty-degree angle. The creature crashed through the white tree behind, shattering it into thousands of pieces. Its momentum caused it to tumble into the forest behind, knocking down trees in its path.

"Direct hit!" Porter shouted as he watched from the feed of Ted's helmet cam. "Die, you bastard!"

As it landed feet first, the arachnid's weight caused it to sink several feet into some loosely packed soil upon landing. Its legs flexed, searching for solid ground. It was the first time it had demonstrated any vulnerability whatsoever.

"Yes!" Vinod cried. "It's not impervious to weapons."

Joshua shook his head. "I think you spoke too soon."

Righting itself by extending its legs to their farthest reach and pressing them against the ground, the arachnid lifted itself from the earth and scrambled at high speed towards the tanks, its legs undamaged as it repositioned its tentacles. The right tank, which had loaded an armor-piercing shell, fired at the charging creature, but the round missed its mark, landing in a large cloud of dirt next to the arachnid.

The creature advanced to the middle of the clearing and stood still, its tentacles focused on the tanks, which were reloading their canons with exploding rounds. The creature aimed four tentacles at each of the two canons, the slits in each of its eyes opening wider. Hundreds of airfoils flew through the air and entered the canons' openings, jamming the newly-loaded ordnance, a fact that the operators of the tanks couldn't recognize from their internal positions.

In quick succession, each tank exploded in large fireballs as their commanders gave the order to fire. The jammed shells had exploded inside their canons, setting off chain reactions in the remaining ammunition, destroying the tanks and killing their occupants. They lay in hundreds of pieces on the ground, burning and belching thick black smoke into the air. To the observers in Moe and on the carrier, it looked as if the machines had been disassembled and incinerated. They were barely recognizable as tanks.

The shockwave of the exploding tanks hit Ted, who was lifted off the ground and knocked backwards violently. He landed on the grass, unconscious, as his helmet flew off and rolled through the grass.

"It even knows how to destroy non-biological organisms," Liz stated as the gravity of the images in front of her sunk in. "This is not going to end well."

*   *   *

Williams, Langdon, and Pierce watched the unfolding events on the video feeds from the command center of the carrier.

"The area is taking heavy fire," a technician said. "The mission to capture the arachnid is definitely off-script."

"My God," Williams said in a whisper. "It's a virtual slaughter."

"It's murdering Seals and making our tanks look like playthings," Langdon said. "This is horrific."

Pierce immediately turned to the XO. "Scramble the fighters," he ordered. "My orders are to destroy the arachnid."

He glanced at Williams, who nodded.

"Annihilate it," she said coldly.

Warning horns and sirens sounded on the flight deck, dozens of men running to their launch stations as pilots climbed into F-18 cockpits.

*   *   *

Lieutenant Santiago Perez, codenamed Cobra, climbed into the cockpit of his F-18 Hornet. The jet's canopy was quickly closed, his copilot seated behind him giving a thumbs-up that he was ready. "Punch it," the copilot said.

Perez glanced at the fly-by-wire display. Everything—engines, weapons, targeting, communications, and tactical status—used touchscreen interface and LCD display. The pilot had the option of overriding the electronics in order to manually control the plane, and Perez had done so on several occasions. But the fighter had been battle-tested for years, and the fly-by-wire system was as reliable as they came. Perez looked sideways as the flight deck manager, down on one knee, held out his arm and pointed to the end of the carrier. It was a "go."

Perez fired the engines as the plane was catapulted from the carrier, adding thrust as the tail cleared the end of the flight deck. He went into a sharp climb and circled in a holding pattern as he waited for the three other jets in his squadron to launch. As squadron commander, he would fly point. It was only a matter of minutes before he'd be joined by the other F-18s; the squadron headed for North Korea.

"Afterburners," Perez ordered.

The jets acquired additional thrust, speeding towards the forested area where the complex was located. His orders from Pierce earlier that morning had been unambiguous: destroy the creature if launch became necessary.

Moments later, the lieutenant radioed the carrier.

"Coastline in sight, Ford. Moving to designated coordinates two hundred miles northeast of Pyongyang."

"Roger that, Cobra," the flight controller on the carrier said. "Happy hunting."

The squadron was supersonic as it crossed into North Korean airspace. Perez gave the order to descend. Somewhere below there was a giant spider he meant to obliterate. The jets raced low past the landscape. The last known coordinates of the arachnid had been fed into the onboard computer, but Perez would obtain visual confirmation after engaging the LCD weapons display before turning over the controls to the targeting pod that would unleash the awesome fury of the AMRAAMS. The plan was for all four fighter jets to unload their weapons in rapid succession. It was a solid example of overkill, but those were his orders. If successful, his squadron would leave nothing but a crater on the ground. The immediate area would be as dead as the moon for years.

Chapter Nineteen
The White Flash

Several moments elapsed before the scientific team assimilated the destruction in the North Korean forest, which had been transformed from a scene of tranquility to a battle zone. The arachnid stood tall and triumphant in the clearing, having routed the mission's special forces. Despite being upended by a canon blast, it had sustained no damage at all.

"We're fucked!" Vinod said as he saw images of the burning tanks. "Totally fucked!"

"Maybe not," Porter replied. "The fighters should be here soon."

Porter monitored the conversation of the fighter jets that had been scrambled from the carrier and were now supersonic. "It's out of our hands," Porter stated. "Let's hope the Navy can bail us out."

"Distance to weapons range, ninety seconds," Lieutenant Perez said. His voice had an electronic quality to it, and it was obvious to Porter that his mouth was covered by a mask that contained both oxygen and a radio feed.

The arachnid moved into view on the screen on a feed seen by the helmet cam of a fallen soldier. Porter enlarged the feed.

The arachnid had stopped firing and was inspecting one of the dead bodies with a single tentacle that circled the air above the corpse.

"What's it doing?" Rachael asked with tears in her eyes as she thought of the fallen soldiers.

"Don't know," Joshua answered somberly. "Maybe inspecting the body. It's downright morbid."

"It's a malevolent bastard," Vinod said, a sullen look on his face.

They watched as the tentacle picked up something from the fallen seal much as an elephant would pick up a banana from the ground.

"Damn peculiar," Liz said. "What did its tentacle just retrieve?"

Porter zoomed the feed on the screen.

"It looks like the soldier's communications device," Vinod answered. "The electronics that transmit the video feed from the camera."

The group watched as the creature tossed the device onto its carapace, where it fell into one of the gill slots.

"Is it eating it?" Vinod asked.

"I don't think so," Joshua answered. "It doesn't need a simple communications device for energy."

The creature stood motionless for a few seconds, then crouched on the grass of the clearing and formed a tight ball, its legs surrounding its carapace. To the team, it appeared to have formed a protective cage for itself.

"Thirty seconds to weapons range." Perez's voice now came through the speaker in Moe for all to hear.

The tips of the arachnid's legs changed color, glowing a dull white.

"What's it doing?" Liz asked.

"Preparing," Rachael theorized. "Maybe it's not taking its victory for granted."

"Preparing for *what*?" Vinod asked.

"Perhaps it somehow senses that the fighters are nearby," Liz said. "Maybe the insects spotted them."

The white glow grew brighter and started moving higher up its legs. By the time the color had nearly reached the top of its legs, they glowed white-hot. When the color had ascended all the way, a brilliant white flash—an explosion of energy—emanated from the arachnid.

The lobby of Moe went dark, the lights and LCD screens completely dead. The occupants felt tiny pricks, similar to small electrical charges, dancing across their skin.

"Everything's out," Vinod said in the darkness. "We've lost all the feeds!"

"Remain at your stations," Porter ordered. "Maybe they'll come back on."

"Joshua?" Rachael's voice was fearful, tentative.

Her husband reached out and squeezed her hand. "Right here, Rach."

*   *   *

Perez had led the squadron to within a mile of the arachnid. Using his main touchscreen, he positioned the targeting indicators over the creature, which he could now see using the cockpit's enhanced imaging systems. The squadron would be over the target within a matter of seconds.

"Lock and load, gentlemen," he said over his radio. "I'll fire and peel away. Assume attack pattern delta and fire in sequence before reclaiming formation. We'll confirm destruction before heading back to the mother ship, but I doubt if that will be necessary. Let's make this one-stop shopping."

"Roger, Cobra," came three voices representing the other pilots.

Perez was set to fire his AMRAAM when a cockpit alarm sounded.

"What's up, Cobra?" his copilot asked. "Are we still go?"

Perez didn't have time to answer. A bright white flash radiated from his target, and the controls and screens in his cockpit went blank. Nothing worked at all. He lost control of his aircraft as it started to veer off track. "Shit! We've lost all controls. I've got nothing!"

The fighter pin-wheeled in the air, careening out of control. Perez pulled the ejection handle, and he and his copilot blasted out of the jet, the canopy having been released by an explosive charge as the fighter spun like a toy airplane. From his parachute, the lieutenant saw his spinning fighter crash in a fireball near the clearing.

*　　　　*　　　　*

Ted awoke to the sound of an explosion in the forest. The pain in his eardrums was sharp as he experienced a brief moment of deafness. After getting his bearings, he looked beside him and saw the sharpshooter, his eyes closed, and checked for a pulse. There was none.

He retrieved his helmet and put it on. Looking at the clearing, Ted saw the arachnid in a crouched position, its tentacles curled on its carapace. Spotting an armored quad a few feet away, he wondered if it were a possible means of escape, but he dared not break into a run since the creature was far too observant.

After surveying the destruction in and around the clearing, Ted moved slowly towards the vehicle, but the creature didn't move. He climbed gingerly into the seat and tried to start the engine. It wouldn't turn over. He hit the ignition again, and the motor roared to life.

No, he thought. *Not escape. I'm going to fulfill the mission.*

The arachnid's tentacles uncoiled, pointing directly at him.

"Why am I not surprised?" Ted mumbled.

Ted gunned the engine and headed towards the path next to the remnants of the still burning tanks. The vehicle moved slowly since it rolled over patches of grass, dirt, and weeds. A barrage of airfoils hit the right-side metal shielding of the vehicle as it finally rumbled onto the path. The attack stopped as he accelerated to full speed down the dirt road. He could see in a rearview mirror attached to the left handle of the quad that the arachnid was giving chase, a cloud of dust trailing behind as it moved at high speed. With the dirt road having been badly cratered, the quad lost its normal handling because the metal plates, as feared, occasionally bit into the dirt and sand, sending the vehicle skidding left and right. Ted compensated quickly each time to keep the four-wheeler on course.

The handling only grew worse. The path veered left, and the quad made a wide turn, almost spinning into the forest. Ted turned the handle hard and kept the quad on the hard-packed dirt, squeezing the throttle.

Was the creature gaining on him? He couldn't tell, but it definitely seemed that Vinod had been correct in his assessment that the arachnid couldn't fire while moving since his vehicle wasn't getting hit.

"I'm heading down the path!" he shouted into his microphone. "The arachnid's chasing me!" There was no response from the team. "Come in," he said. "Do you copy?" There was still no answer.

The path now veered right, snaking past a cluster of trees.

"Shit!" Ted screamed as he felt the quad skidding to the left.

He eased up on the gas, waited, and then squeezed the throttle. The creature was only fifteen yards behind him.

He heard the sound of airfoils hitting the back shielding of the quad and saw that the creature had ceased its pursuit. The shots only lasted for a few seconds before the arachnid resumed the chase.

The vehicle bounced wildly along the uneven surface, at moments becoming airborne as it hit large bumps. Ted kept the throttle wide open as he fought to control the quad. With the metal side-plating still digging into dirt, the quad was in danger of going into a roll. His destination, however, was the pit trap since luring the monster into the cage was his only hope of survival, and he didn't have far to go.

The quad slowed as the metal plating dug more deeply into the dirt. As the creature drew closer, Ted fed the vehicle gas in short bursts as he rapidly turned the handle left and right to help jar the quad loose. It worked. The quad accelerated to full speed as it continued along the path.

As he navigated a bend, he recognized the camouflaged trap just ahead. He had sketched the entire scene on a legal pad, and he recognized landmarks on either side of the trap. With the throttle still wide open, the quad flew over the trap, bouncing over the false lid. Two of the vehicle's plates had been jarred loose by the rough ride and rattled against the quad's metal frame.

"Don't quit on me now, baby," Ted said to the four-wheeler as the handle began to vibrate in his hands.

Holding his breath, Ted watched in the rearview mirror as the creature ran onto the lid, its tentacles raised high in the air, poised to strike. With a loud crashing sound, the false lid collapsed, causing the arachnid to drop in a cloud of dust into the trap. The explosive charges went off, forcing the lid to swing up and over, slamming shut with a tremendous *bang*.

Ted braked hard and exited the vehicle since he had a limited view of the trap. He could hear the creature struggling to get out of the cage—the sound of its legs furiously clawing against metal—but the loud metallic scratching eventually stopped.

"Got you, you bastard!" he exclaimed as he got back on the quad and rode back to the complex.

Chapter Twenty
Fried

"What the hell's going on?" Porter shouted in the darkened lobby of Moe. "We've got nothing, nothing at all! No power, no video feeds. I need to know what's happening to my men! Bhakti, get out there and see if you can get the power restored."

"You want *me* to go out *there* with that thing running around?" Vinod asked in the darkness. His voice expressed disbelief bordering on defiance. "Hell no, Porter!"

"Jesus, Bhakti!" Porter exclaimed, pulling his revolver from his belt. "I'll go with you. You're the electronics expert, and we need to get the power back on. I have to communicate with my men!" He produced a pocket flashlight that had a powerful narrow beam and aimed it at the front doors.

Vinod followed Porter out the doorway towards the solar panels and battery packs. In the distance, smoke from the burning tanks curled into the air, staining the blue sky with large patches of gray.

"Damn," Vinod said. "That's a lot of smoke."

Porter admonished his companion. "Save the sightseeing for later."

Fortunately, the solar panels, glistening in the sun, had suffered no damage.

Inside Moe, Rachael sat next to Joshua, distraught. "I can't believe it! All those men . . . dead. Everything was planned down to the last detail."

Joshua embraced Rachael tightly as he saw Liz sobbing. "Liz, come here," he said.

Liz knelt by the couple, the open front doors allowing weak sunlight to seep into the lobby. Joshua included her in his embrace as he reflected on the tragedy of the last several minutes.

*   *   *

Joshua found his thoughts drifting, and whether it was because his mind had partially shut down or whether it was due to the sudden silence after the thunderous battle, he was nevertheless caught up in reflections of his work three years earlier. He had trusted Seth and the petrins from the earliest days of first contact using quantum entanglement. He regarded it as axiomatic that any advanced civilization—certainly one billions of years beyond Earth's technology and using primordial spookyons to reach across vast distances to contact new civilizations—would be peaceful. His reasoning had been aligned with many great philosophers and scientists who believed that any extraterrestrial culture able to survive its nuclear age would progress towards becoming a peaceful species that used its advanced technology wisely. The movie stereotypes were wrong. There would never be an *Independence Day* scenario in which ET would seek to wipe out and colonize a planet. How could any civilization in the cosmos thrive for millions of years unless it had learned not to misuse scientific advancements?

To Joshua's thinking, the petrins had validated such faith in species that were far beyond Earth's fledgling steps in reaching for the stars—Earth, which had only ushered in the Industrial Revolution two centuries earlier. Seth's race had rapidly gained the trust of the scientific team, which even then consisted of himself, Rachael, and Vinod. Their alien friend, for that is exactly how they regarded him, had spoken to them of strict ethical and moral codes both for themselves and species throughout the universe, of which there were many. Protocols were in place to prevent any interference by the petrins so that a species could never harm itself using alien technology, a classic science fiction concept called the prime directive: never alter the evolution of an alien society.

But petrin technology was back on Earth, and Seth was nowhere to be found. Indeed, Rodrigo's video log had shown that Joshua's former assistant had asked to speak to him personally but had been told that he was busy on "another project." Rodrigo had definitely contacted the petrins as evidenced by a DNA code that was adequate to grow an arachnid similar to the one he had encountered on New Eden, but that technology was now in the process of causing great violence and destruction on Earth. Could Joshua have misjudged Seth and the petrins? So much information originally requested by the scientific team three years earlier had been denied, the alien response consisting of the dreaded word "redacted." There were simply some things that humans were not allowed to know. Had Seth lied to the team? Had they been naïve? Had Porter been right all along in his overtly military assessment that the petrins would one day seek to rule the Earth? Had redacted information disguised a hidden agenda beneath the allegedly peaceful petrin profile of peace and cooperation?

At recent briefings, Joshua and the team had defended Seth and his home world. After all, the petrins were their parents. They'd seeded the entire universe with life and had even cured Earth of the deadly Ebola pandemic. But on this particular day, Joshua entertained doubts, for an arachnid in North Korea had destroyed many lives. Soldiers were dead, and the military was under attack even though the original mission called for establishing contact and communication if at all possible.

Maybe humans are simply too ignorant, Joshua thought. *Maybe they were in no position to begin to understand a species billions of years ahead of them or to comprehend the nature of existence.*

Joshua thought of *The Day the Earth Stood Still.* A peaceful alien race had sent an ambassador to Earth for the purpose of issuing a warning: join the cosmic assembly of peaceful species or face annihilation by a harsh robotic police force lest earthly violence contaminate the galactic neighborhood. Had the petrins, drawing on the wisdom and intelligence of the collective, used raw data and computing power to decide that human impulses toward violence simply couldn't be checked? Was the arachnid in North Korea a robotic police officer?

The petrins had total control of their technology. Nothing was haphazard. Joshua felt a sinking feeling. Maybe his planet had not passed muster. He had no other explanation for what was happening in the forest of North Korea. And yet, deep down, he still trusted Seth. There had to be a reasonable explanation for what was happening.

"Josh, you okay?"

It was Rachael, who was kneeling beside him—Rachael, who herself was now the one offering comfort. She and Liz looked with concern at the scientist from Berkeley who hadn't spoken for several minutes.

"Yeah, I'm okay."

But he wasn't. His thinking was conflicted.

*   *   *

Vinod and Porter reached the solar panel and battery array. A total of sixteen panels fed the complex. On one knee, Vinod inspected the maze of wiring between the panels and the batteries. "The wiring between the panels and the batteries looks intact," he said.

Vinod next opened the gray breaker box that interfaced the battery array with the power lines to the complex. "Looks like all the breakers are tripped. Must have been one mother of a power surge."

Vinod methodically flipped the breaker switches back to their ON positions and glanced over his shoulder to verify that the lights inside Moe were on. "Power's back up—for now."

"What's that odor?" Porter asked.

"Yeah, I smell it too." Vinod turned his gaze to the twelve-foot satellite dish a few yards away and noticed that a small wisp of white smoke was rising from its gray communications panel. The two men walked to the panel, which Vinod opened and inspected.

"This thing's fried," Vinod said. "You're smelling burning plastic."

"Can you get it fixed?"

"Are you kidding me? Look at this thing. All the circuit boards are melted. There's no repairing this." Vinod pointed in the general direction of the arachnid. "Call it collateral damage, and don't ask me how or why. This wasn't done by airfoils."

"Our communications with the carrier may be out," Porter said, "but maybe we can still pick up the video feeds from the men." They hurried back to Moe to see if the general was correct.

"I see you got the power back on," Joshua said as the two entered the lobby.

"Yeah, all the breakers were tripped," Vinod said, "but satellite communications are down." He described the damage he'd found during his brief foray outside of Moe before approaching the LCD screens. "I'm going to see if I can get these things working so we can restore the feeds."

Vinod pushed the power button on the first screen and then the second. Nothing happened—they were still dead. "These are getting power, so why aren't they turning on?" He pressed the buttons again, but the screens remained dark.

"Do you think they have an internal breaker that may have tripped?" Joshua asked.

"Maybe. Help me get the back panel off of one. I need to look inside."

"Hurry, you two," Porter said with urgency. "I need to know what's happening in the clearing. For all we know, the arachnid may be on the move."

Joshua and Vinod removed the rear panel by releasing the latches that held it in place. The two men worked quickly.

"Shit!" Vinod exclaimed as he peered inside. "The electronics in here are completely fried, just like the com panel. There's no fixing this either.

We're screwed." He stepped away and wiped sweat from his forehead with his shirtsleeve.

"How's that possible?" Rachael asked. "Was it some kind of massive power surge?"

"That's my guess," Vinod said, "but I've never seen one that could melt plastic."

Joshua inspected the electronic circuit board of the LCD screen. The wiring and capacitors seemed intact, but anything that contained silicon, such as the integrated circuits and the microprocessors, had burn marks.

"Can't be a power surge," he concluded. "Whatever fried this panel targeted only semiconductors and components made of silicon."

"Targeted?" Liz said.

"Exactly," Joshua said. "Targeted."

"What the hell could cause that?" Porter asked.

"It must have been some kind of EMP," Joshua speculated.

"What's that?" Liz asked.

"Electromagnetic pulse," Joshua answered. "It's a large power surge in the electromagnetic spectrum. It's kinda like a bomb, but it doesn't damage material, only electrical systems. This one must have been designed to specifically destroy components based on silicon."

"Designed," Rachael repeated. "We're talking about the arachnid, right?"

Liz nodded. "More premeditation on its part."

"The military has been working on such a device for years," Porter stated. "It's still in development though, and not ready for use."

"Well, apparently this arachnid has perfected it," Joshua said. "An EMP is the only thing that can cause the damage I'm seeing here. Liz is right. It apparently knows how to use an EMP with the same surgical precision as it uses airfoils."

"Josh," Vinod said, "if that's the case, then anything that contains silicon—anything with a semiconductor within range of the EMP—is completely useless."

"I'm afraid so."

Vinod put his hands on his hips and lowered his head in exasperation. "Is there anything this monster *can't* do? It checkmates us at every move."

"Wait," Rachael said, alarmed. "*All* of our technology is silicon-based. If none of our electronics work, then we're practically back to the Stone Age. What do you think the range of the EMP is?"

"Hard to tell," Joshua replied. "It's not unlimited since an EMP requires vast amounts of energy. The range of the pulse would depend on how much energy was used."

"How about the fighters?" Porter asked. "Would they have been affected?"

"If they were within range of the EMP," Vinod replied, "they'd become incapable of flight. All modern aircraft are fly-by-wire. Their guidance and control systems are based on electronics and computers that, in turn, control all actuators on the plane."

"Goddamn it!" Porter shouted as he pounded his fist on a table in the room. "I'm not accepting a no-win scenario."

"And I've got even worse news," Vinod continued. "You can forget about any weapons the fighters carry, or *any* modern weapon systems, like the ones on drones. They all contain semiconductors and electronics. They'd be completely useless. And judging from the smell of burning jet fuel outside, my guess is that at least one fighter went down."

"Josh," Rachael said, "how'd the creature know to do this?"

"I have a possible explanation," Liz offered. "It may have gotten the idea from the fallen seal's communication device."

"What do you mean?" Joshua asked.

"The EMP happened after the creature took the communications device and ingested it," Liz explained. "Maybe by internalizing it, it figured out how it worked. It somehow scanned it and figured out that our technology is based on silicon and therefore modulated the EMP to target specifically for that."

"Do you really think it's smart enough to figure out how our technology works that quickly?" Rachael asked.

"It doesn't need to understand how it works," Vinod replied. "It only needs to know what it's made of. That electronic device is mostly just metal and plastic—pretty simple material. The microprocessor and integrated circuits are where the real action is. Using Seth's definition of life, those are the components that contain the most information, the most life. It may have scanned the items in the device that contained the most information, which in this case was encoded on silicon."

"It always comes back to information when we're dealing with petrin technology," Joshua said.

"The peaceful petrins," Porter remarked sarcastically.

The general's comment was not lost on the scientist, who remained conflicted on his estimation of petrin behavior.

"I guess it's plausible," Rachael said. "Information is at the heart of everything they do." She paused and turned her head as she heard the sound of a motor. "I think I hear something."

The noise grew louder and closer.

"It's an engine," Joshua said.

The motor stopped, and a few seconds later Ted stumbled through the door, breathing heavily. He was covered in dirt, but he was grinning from ear to ear.

"I got the som' bitch!"

Chapter Twenty-One
Survivors

Porter and the team gathered around Ted and ushered him to the nearest chair. He was bruised, and his uniform was torn in several places. Ash covered his sleeves, and his skin had numerous abrasions.

"What do you mean you got it?" Vinod asked.

"I mean I got the arachnid into the trap," Ted replied, still gasping for air.

"How?" Porter asked, eyes wide.

"The thing chased me down the trail on my quad," Ted explained. "Pretty much the way we had it planned. I led it to the trap and the damn thing fell in. The explosives went off and sealed the bastard inside."

"It's still in there?" Joshua asked excitedly. "Is it trapped?"

"Yeah," Ted replied. "I waited for a while, but it couldn't get out. It's was thrashing around pretty good at the beginning, but the thrashing eventually stopped."

"Goddamn, Tabasco!" Vinod exclaimed as he gave Ted a bear hug. "You da man!"

"Great job, soldier!" Porter said with a smile while patting him on the back.

"Where are the other Seals?" Ted asked, searching the faces of the team.

"You're the first one back," Rachael replied.

"What about the feeds?" Ted asked.

Vinod explained how the EMP had fried all electronics.

"Then we need to look for survivors," Ted said, heading for the door. "We don't leave men behind."

"Hold up a second," Porter said, adopting a somber tone. "We lost a lot of men out there, but it doesn't make sense to randomly search the forest, especially without any communications or equipment. I know your men are well trained, and I'm sure they'll be searching for survivors before returning to the complex. The last thing we need is to become separated. The carrier will send a rescue team for us. The best course of action is to wait here for survivors to make their way back."

Ted's voice was weary but displayed considerable frustration. "You want me to just wait when I know there are injured men out there?" Ted asked. "*My* men?"

"*Our* men," Porter corrected. "You've neutralized the threat, and we're all grateful for that. It was a hell of a job. But the Seals are not in immediate danger if the arachnid is in the cage. We need to wait for reinforcements. Once that comes, I assure you that we'll go after them if they haven't reported in."

Ted didn't agree with Porter, but he wasn't going to go against the orders of a superior. He sat, too tired to speak further.

"Can I examine your radio, Ted?" Vinod asked. "I need to see the damage inside it."

Without looking up, Ted handed it to Vinod, who began disassembling it.

"What're you looking for?" Joshua asked Vinod after he had taken the cover off of the device.

"I want to see how much damage was done to its components. This device was much closer to the source of the EMP compared to the electronics here at the complex. I want to find out if there's a significant difference in the amount of damage between the two."

"For what purpose?" Joshua asked.

"So I can figure out the range of the EMP. If the two have a similar amount of damage, then the range would be quite far, maybe extending to the carrier. But if Ted's radio has more damage than the components in the complex, we can assume the carrier was unaffected."

"If the carrier *was* affected," Liz said, "then . . .."

She didn't need to finish her sentence. Everyone knew the ramifications of the nearby naval vessels' communications being compromised, including the carrier. The team at the complex would be helpless, plus the destructive power of the arachnid might be far more deadly than they had imagined. Just how far did its reach extend?

Vinod looked at the radio's components for several seconds, his thumb moving over the circuitry.

"What'd you find?" Joshua asked.

"Definitely a big difference," Vinod responded. "Ted's radio has much more damage. I think we can assume that the carrier was unaffected by the EMP."

"That's a relief," Joshua said, exhaling.

It wasn't long afterwards that the first survivors started returning to the complex, a group of seven men: three uninjured and four injured, one in critical condition. Liz took the Seals to the lab to treat them as best she could given the limited medical supplies available. The soldiers had numerous wounds from the airfoils, broken bones, burns, and some had internal bleeding.

Soon, another group of six Seals returned, all with only minor injuries. Ted asked one of the men about any injured still in the forest. The seal stated that they had conducted an extensive search for survivors, but all of the men they had encountered were dead, shredded by airfoils.

Ted was heartbroken. There were forty-eight Seals under his command, as well as six Army personnel who had operated the tanks. All that were left were himself and thirteen others. His team had been decimated by the arachnid. He sat in a chair, his head resting on his hands as Rachael approached.

"You and your men did a great job out there," she said, sitting next to him with her hand on his shoulder. "Extremely brave. True heroes in every sense of the word. The world is in your debt."

Ted didn't speak for a while. "Thanks" was all he could muster.

Liz returned from the lab several minutes later, a worried look on her face.

"How are my men?" Ted asked.

"Most are stable," Liz replied, "but there's one who's lost a lot of blood, and he's going into shock. I don't think he's going to make it unless he gets blood soon."

"The carrier rescue may arrive at any minute," Porter said.

"The soldier is critical," Liz said. "Even if they get here soon, I'm not sure he'll survive the flight back to the carrier."

"I'm O negative," Vinod stated.

"You're a universal donor?" Liz said. "Are you sure?"

"Yes, definitely O negative. You have the IV stuff you need for a transfusion?"

"Yeah, let's go."

Liz and Vinod headed for the door.

"Vinod?"

Vinod turned to see Porter addressing him.

"Thank you, son."

Vinod smiled at Porter and gave him a fake salute before leaving.

The final group of survivors, six pilots from three fighters, arrived twenty minutes later.

"What happened up there?" Porter asked.

"There was a blinding flash, and my entire squadron lost control of our fighters," the pilot said. "I'm Lieutenant Santiago Perez." The squadron leader extended his hand, taken firmly by Porter. "What happened, sir? We acquired the target and were about to fire."

"It's a long story," Joshua said, "but you were hit by an electromagnetic pulse that fried your fly-by-wire instrumentation. The arachnid caused it."

"I believe there were four fighters in your squadron," Porter said.

"That's correct, general. The two pilots in the fourth jet didn't get a chance to eject."

"I'm sorry, lieutenant," Porter said. "We've lost men down here too."

"By the way, what happened to the cage?" Perez asked. "My squadron was briefed on its presence and your overall mission objectives."

"What do you mean *what happened to the cage*?" Porter asked, blood draining from his face.

"We saw it on our way here," Perez said. "It looked like it was destroyed. The lid was shredded and there were thousands of those airfoils everywhere."

"The arachnid wasn't inside?" Porter asked with dread in his heart.

"No, sir."

*   *   *

"What the hell just happened?" Langdon shouted in the command center of the carrier as all video feeds from the Seals turned to static. They had heard the fighters getting ready to launch their weapons when the feeds all stopped.

"I don't know," Captain Pierce said. He turned to one of the communications specialists.

"We've lost all coms from the area," the technician replied, "including coms with our fighters. We have no visual whatsoever of the complex."

"What about the drones?" Williams asked.

"Nothing from them either."

"We've got to get those people out," Williams said emphatically. "They may still be under attack. Captain, launch some rescue copters, and I want air support to go with them."

Chapter Twenty-Two
The Rescue

Vinod walked into the lobby of Moe with a bandage around his left elbow. "Don't worry, guys. Mission accomplished. Liz says the soldier is stable for now."

"That's great, Vinod," Rachael said as she gave Vinod a hug. "That was very generous of you. How're you feeling?"

"I'm fine, but I didn't get a cookie." Vinod sensed the concern of the others in the room, his demeanor turning serious again. "What's wrong?"

"Bad news, I'm afraid," Joshua answered. "The pilots that just returned informed us that the arachnid has escaped the cage."

"You mean that thing's still running around out there?"

"Seems that way," Joshua said. "This creature's unbelievable. It seems to be defying the laws of physics."

"How so?" Rachael asked.

Joshua explained his reasoning. "How is it that the arachnid seems to have unlimited ammunition? I've been going over this in my mind. It used an incredible amount of ammo fighting the Seals and the tanks. The pilots said that the bottom of the cage was filled with airfoils, but how is it creating them? After all, it only has a limited storage capacity in its body, and as Rachael pointed out, it can't be filled with an unlimited amount of ammunition. There has to be room for other essential organs. Where the hell does all the metal for this ammo come from?"

"Who knows, man?" Vinod replied. "But if that rescue doesn't get here soon, we won't be alive to find out."

"I think I hear something," Rachael said a few minutes later. "Copters!"

The distant sound of gyrating chopper rotors grew louder and higher in pitch by the second.

The group ran outside and saw two ospreys accompanied by three helicopter gunships. The air vibrated with the spinning of the rotors as they descended, the five aircraft darkening the sky above the complex.

"They sent three apaches with the ospreys," Porter remarked. "Commander, tell Dr. Yang and the other soldiers in the lab to prepare for immediate evac."

Ted hurried to the lab as the group watched the ospreys land in the field next to the lab. The apaches veered off and flew low, patrolling the tree line at the edge of the field. One of the ospreys carried medics with additional supplies.

"I want the wounded, the remaining soldiers, and the pilots loaded onto the first osprey," Porter commanded. "Once they're on board, the commander, the scientific team, and I will board the second one."

The ospreys kept their rotors running, ready for immediate take-off as Porter's order was carried out. As soon as the first osprey was loaded, Porter commanded to its pilot, "Go, go, go!" The osprey's engines roared as it started to lift off of the ground. "Come on!" he shouted to the others through the rotor blast. "We need to get on the other one."

As the group ran to the second osprey, bodies leaning forward to avoid the rotor wash, an explosion knocked them to the ground. One of the apaches was on fire and spinning wildly as its rotors were mangled by airfoils emanating from the forest. With fire spitting from its engine, the apache rolled on its side, hovered unevenly, and crashed onto the ground in an orange fireball.

"We've got to get the hell out of here!" Vinod cried as he climbed aboard the osprey.

The two remaining apaches flew to the spot where the first had gone down. They fired their guns and rockets into the forest in a continuous barrage, causing bright orange explosions. The arachnid burst from the tree line, smashing tall pines like matchsticks, its tentacles focused on the two apaches. A torrent of airfoils tore open the bodies and rotors of the copters, which wobbled and then fell rapidly, creating two additional fireballs. Acrid smoke drifted across the field and into the forest.

The first osprey was high in the air and had already rotated it engines for horizontal flight. The arachnid focused its tentacles on the departing aircraft but didn't fire. Instead, it ran full speed towards the osprey still on the ground.

Porter was the last to board. "Let's get the hell out of here!" he shouted.

The pilot revved the engines, and the machine lifted off the ground, grass whipping wildly from air currents created by the rotors. The charging arachnid stopped its advance and unleashed a volley of airfoils at the osprey's engines and rotors. The aircraft had only risen a few yards when its left rotor exploded in fragments, one of which crashed through the roof above the pilot and penetrated his chest. He slumped in a pool of blood as the osprey fell to the ground with a hard thump, rocking left and right before stopping, leaning on its right wing. Clouds of black smoke surrounded the crippled aircraft and sent searing waves of heat in every direction. The arachnid advanced, its tentacles aimed at the downed aircraft.

"Back to the building!" Porter shouted over the din of airfoils hitting the exterior of the craft.

The group jumped out of the burning osprey and ran towards Moe, covering their mouths to avoid inhaling smoke. They had almost made it to the door when they turned and saw the osprey's destroyed fuel tanks explode, sending more fire and smoke into the air. A thunderous shockwave swept over the complex, blowing out several windows.

They ran in horror as the arachnid ceased firing and scrambled directly towards them, its articulated legs moving quickly across the complex with perfect coordination. The group rushed into the building, latched the doors, and huddled at the rear of the lobby.

"If that thing can destroy tanks," Joshua said, "it's going to get in here in a matter of seconds."

With a loud crack, a single tentacle broke through the doors and scanned the room with an ominous eye, the arachnid too large to fit through the doorway.

"Retreat into the halls!" Ted shouted.

They ran deep into the interior of Moe and stopped, their hearts pounding as the terror of the situation engulfed them. No one made a sound as they listened for a few minutes, but there was only silence.

"Do you think it's gone?" Rachael whispered.

"Don't know," Joshua replied, "but I wouldn't count on it. It knows we're in here."

"It's so methodical in everything it does," Liz said.

"I'm going to take a look," Ted said as he moved cautiously down the hallway. He returned a few moments later. "It's not in the lobby, nor did I see any tentacles."

"We need to seal the building," Porter said.

"Oh, shit!" Vinod exclaimed as he thought of something. "I noticed that the garage door was open when we got into the osprey. I'm sure the arachnid could fit through there."

"Come on, Ted," Joshua said. "You and me."

Ted and Joshua headed for the garage. They got to an interior door that led to the garage, one with a window in its upper portion. The garage was empty, but its rolling metal door was indeed open. Joshua's heart sank as he noted that the arachnid was standing outside the two-story opening, its tentacles examining every inch of the doorframe.

"The damn thing's sitting right outside," Joshua whispered.

"Is it coming in?"

"No. Seems like it's inspecting the opening."

Pushing his face sideways against the glass, Joshua glanced at the wall on the other side of the door. On the wall was a protruding red pushbutton that activated the garage door motor. It was only a few feet away, but he knew that a tentacle would spot him if he tried to enter.

"What do you want to do?" Ted asked.

"Nothing right now," Joshua said, observing the creature.

After a few moments, the arachnid crawled away from the opening, making its way methodically across the field between Moe and the forest.

Seeing his chance, Joshua pushed the door open and hit the close button. The motors of the garage door whirred to life, and it started closing with loud, metallic, creaking noises. Two tentacles turned towards the closing door, but the arachnid continued its march to the field. The garage door finished closing without incident.

"Why didn't it come in when it had the chance?" Ted asked, standing beside Joshua.

"I'm wondering that myself," Joshua replied. "Strange. Let's get back to the others."

"You go," Ted responded. "I'm going to the roof to use the telescope to see where that thing goes."

"Be careful," Joshua said. "It can backtrack awfully fast if it spies you."

"I'm a backwoodsman. I'm stealthy by nature."

Chapter Twenty-Three
Survival Mode

Ted returned to the lobby to find the rest seated in chairs. The doors hung crookedly on broken hinges as evening sunlight streamed in.

"Where'd it go?" Joshua asked.

Ted took a seat with the others. "It did a couple of circles around the complex, looking at everything with its tentacles. Then it hunkered down in the field close to this building and is sitting there now."

"Are its tentacles curled up?" Liz asked.

"No, they're all pointed directly at this building," Ted replied.

"Oh, Fuck!" Vinod replied slowly turning his head left to right with his eyes closed. "We're completely screwed! We're never going to get out of here." Vinod opened his eyes and stared at the ceiling, his head leaned back. "I knew it man. I knew I should've never agreed to come on this mission."

"Settle down, Vinod," Joshua said. "It's not going to help if we panic. We'll just have to wait for another rescue from the carrier."

The rest nodded in agreement. The consensus was that there was little they could do. They had little equipment at their disposal, and the remaining Seals had been evacuated to the carrier.

"I don't think there's going to be another rescue," Porter said solemnly, his head slumped.

"What? Why?" Rachael asked.

Porter looked up and scanned the faces staring back at him. "Because I wouldn't send one if I was in charge."

"Why?" Liz asked. "Doesn't the military have a saying about not leaving any man behind?"

"Look," Porter explained, "the main purpose of this mission was to capture or kill the arachnid—period. We knew that this creature couldn't be allowed to roam free. The risks were too great. We also knew that this was a dangerous mission with many unknowns. There was the possibility of loss of life, but this is the case with any military operation. The original goal of trying to communicate or capture the arachnid was considered because if these *were* possible, we could study the creature, discover why it's here, and learn its weaknesses. On the other hand, there was much discussion at the higher levels about not conducting the mission at all. Many advocated blowing this thing to bits with aerial weapons, but then we'd lose the opportunity to study it. So it was decided, with my approval, to try this mission first. At this point we have to consider the mission a failure.

"The military has already lost a lot of men. This recent rescue attempt cost the lives of all the apache pilots as well as the pilot of the osprey. They're not going to risk more loss of life just to save the six of us. They're going to move on to the next phase." Porter lowered his head again before he spoke. "I know that if I were in charge, that's the decision I would make."

Vinod glared at Porter. "You son of a bitch! You wouldn't try to save us? Our lives mean that little to you?"

"No," Porter said with a faltering voice.

Was this genuine emotion from the unflappable General Porter? Rachael wondered. He looked resigned and not at all like the man who had declared only a few hours earlier that he wasn't going to accept a no-win situation.

Porter raised his head. "I respect you and value all of your lives. But with leadership comes great responsibility. Sometimes you have to sacrifice something that's dear for the greater good." Porter turned to Joshua. "I believe that's what you did when you decided to break the sphere in the lab even though you knew it would be the end of Rachael. You were sacrificing something dear for the greater good."

Joshua slowly nodded.

Vinod, however, was not swayed. "Cut the bullshit, Porter. You knew you were taking us on a suicide mission, but you brought us anyway. That's on you."

"I brought myself too," Porter said defensively. "I knew it would be dangerous. We all did. But saying it was a suicide mission is going too far. None of us thought that or we wouldn't be here. The mission goals were considered to be attainable."

"He's right," Joshua added. "The military wouldn't have gone through the motions without the possibility of some kind of payoff. We were simply outmaneuvered by a creature with superior weaponry."

"General," Liz said, "you mentioned something about the next phase.

What exactly is that?"

Porter crossed his arms and looked at those around the table. "Aerial bombardment."

"A cruise missile or carpet bombing?" Rachael asked.

"Possibly both," Porter replied.

A terrifying thought occurred to Joshua. "What about nuclear?"

Porter paused before responding. "Yes. It was discussed."

"Discussed?" Vinod said. "Why weren't we told about these options? We had a right to know."

"Nuclear would be the final option," Porter replied. "We never envisioned a scenario where we would have to use a nuclear weapon while we still had some people here, but I believe this is the scenario that the military is stuck with now."

"General," Rachael said, shocked at what she was hearing, "are you telling us the U.S. government would nuke this place? The blast radius would be huge, and there may still be quite a few people in the surrounding area. The collateral damage could be enormous."

"I'm aware of that," Porter said. "All I know is that the nuclear option was discussed, but they wouldn't do it haphazardly. They'd do their best to warn and evacuate any people in the vicinity, and they'd probably use a limited tactical nuclear device."

"Limited," Joshua said. "You don't know that for sure."

"No," Porter admitted. "I don't."

"Oh, man," Vinod said, agitated and shaking his head. "I can't believe this! Josh, you said don't panic. Do you think it's time to panic *now*? There's not going to be a rescue mission, and we're fucked regardless of the method the military decides to use for this aerial bombardment. With that arachnid sitting right outside our door, they're going to kill us all along with it."

Vinod turned to Porter. "I don't know what's worse—the thought of getting ripped to shreds by airfoils or getting killed by my own government. There's no way out of this. We've got nothing. No coms, no weapons—nothing!"

"There has to be a way out," Rachael said emphatically. "There just *has* to be. We can't just sit here waiting to be killed."

Porter was silent.

"How about if we try to escape?" Liz offered. "We run into the forest and get as far away from this place as we can. Maybe we'll escape the blast radius if a limited tactical nuclear weapon is used."

Ted shook his head. "That's not going to work. I analyzed the arachnid's movements from the roof. When it circled the buildings, I think it was looking for all openings in the complex. It has line of sight to any exits that would offer escape."

"Besides," Joshua added, "we're forgetting the arachnid's insect surveillance system. That would definitely spot us if we left the building."

"Unbelievable," Vinod lamented. "Just unbelievable."

"How about if we try to sneak out after dark?" Liz suggested. "Maybe the insects won't see us."

"I don't think that's a good idea," Joshua replied. "This is an advanced creature with advanced biology. We have to assume that its eyes, and probably the eyes of the insects, can see in the infrared spectrum. It wouldn't matter whether its light or dark outside."

The group was at a loss when it came to finding a way to escape or effectively deal with the arachnid. None of the suggestions tendered by team members seemed to have any probability of success, and with aerial bombardment a likely scenario, the situation appeared hopeless. They got up and paced nervously around the room, racking their brains to see if there was anything they had missed—any possible escape from their impossible situation. Vinod was the exception, choosing to remain seated as he nursed his anger and regret at joining what had become, in his estimation, a suicide mission. Slowly, team members drifted back to their seats.

"General, how much time do you think we have before this bombardment starts?" Joshua asked.

"It's past sunset and getting darker outside," Porter said. "I'm sure they'd want a visual on the target before launching any kind of attack. I'd think they'll wait until daybreak. They'll need to verify that the arachnid is still in the same position, so my best guess is that it will begin a few hours after daybreak."

"So we have until then to figure out how to kill this thing," Joshua stated, unwilling to give up.

"Kill this thing?" Vinod said, still agitated. "Josh, you're dreaming. A whole fucking army and a couple of tanks, along with fighters and helicopter gunships, couldn't kill it. How the hell are the six of us—with no weapons, communications, or electronics, for that matter—going to kill the arachnid? It's hopeless."

"We have to try!" Joshua shouted, angry at Vinod's sense of futility. "I'm not going to just sit here and wait to be killed. We have some of the best scientific and military minds sitting in this room. We have to come up with something, no matter how crazy it is. What do we have to lose?" Joshua stood and faced Vinod. "You can either be part of the problem or part of the solution. Which one is it going to be?"

Vinod wasn't satisfied with the notion that a solution could be manufactured out of thin air. "What are we going to do? MacGyver a weapon from paper clips and rubber bands?"

Joshua ignored the sarcasm.

Porter sat straight, cleared his throat, and sounded once again like a man in command. "Okay then. What do we have at our disposal? Let's brainstorm—let's work the problem."

"We still have some C-4 left," Ted said optimistically.

"Well, at least that's a start," Joshua said, taking a seat. "But we can't just throw C-4 at it. I don't think a simple explosion is going to kill it. It wasn't affected by the exploding tank shells or the rockets."

"What about formaldehyde?" Liz offered. "The Koreans have a couple of barrels of it in the lab."

"Formaldehyde?" Rachael said. "Is that some kind of poison?"

"Yes," Liz replied. "It would be deadly to any living organism."

"But Liz," Joshua interjected, "this creature may have completely different chemistry than any creature on Earth. Why do you think formaldehyde will affect the arachnid?"

"Because of the way formaldehyde works," Liz said. "This creature may be alien, but it's still biological—still based on DNA. The way biological systems work is that DNA is used as an information-carrying molecule whose eventual purpose is the production of proteins synthesized from amino acids. I'm sure the proteins found in this creature are quite different than those on Earth, but they're proteins nonetheless and are surely made from amino acids. Formaldehyde works by cross-linking proteins. It's like a glue that doesn't allow them to move or decay, rendering them ineffective. That's why the cadavers we dissected in med school were preserved with formaldehyde."

Rachael understood what Liz was getting at. "So what you're saying is that if we could inject this thing with formaldehyde, it would essentially be like pickling the creature alive."

"Exactly."

"That's good," Joshua said. "Very good. What if we could somehow blow a hole in the creature with the C-4 and then spear it with a hollow pipe to inject the formaldehyde into it? This, at least, seems to have a possibility of working."

"It's a good thought," Ted remarked, "but the C-4 isn't going to work unless it's placed directly on the creature—right on one of its weak points. That's the only way I can see it punching a hole in that armor, and I don't think that thing's going to let us get close enough, or stand still long enough, to slap some C-4 on its weakest point."

Joshua rested his hand on his chin and thought of the challenge posed by Ted. Slowly, a grin spread across his face. "We could freeze it first."

"Freeze it?" Liz asked. "How?"

"Hear me out." Joshua sat forward and spoke, his tone more optimistic. "This facility has a tokamak, and a tokamak needs superconducting coils to create the magnetic field to contain plasma in its chamber. In order to get the coils to become a superconductor, they need to be cooled to near absolute zero. This tokamak here, just like ours in Berkeley, uses liquid helium to cool the coils. There are a couple of tanks for liquid helium in the basement. I saw them when I was inspecting the tokamak." Joshua paused and scanned the faces looking back at him. "They're still full."

Vinod, seeing a glimmer of hope, spoke more positively. "Josh, let me get this straight. You want to pour liquid helium on the arachnid to freeze it."

"Yes, but just as a first step. I'm not sure this alone will kill it."

"I get it," Vinod said. "While it's in the frozen state, you attach the C-4 to the creature at its weakest point, maybe at the junction of one of the tentacles and the carapace."

"Yes, go on," Joshua replied with a grin.

"You blow a hole in the creature by exploding the C-4," Vinod continued. "Then you jam a spear into the hole and fill the bastard up with formaldehyde."

"You got it," Joshua said as he looked around the room for a response.

Team members shifted in their seats. They'd been resigned to defeat, but Joshua's plan, as technically difficult as it sounded, gave them renewed hope. They leaned forward, all eyes on the young scientist who was offering a fighting chance to stay alive.

"Well hell," Ted said, breaking the silence. "Sounds crazy, but it's worth a try. I've built a lot of gator traps in my time, and some involved chicken wire and duct tape."

"Let's do it," Rachael said enthusiastically. "It's better than sitting around waiting to be sliced and diced or blown up."

"It's a plausible plan, Dr. Andrews," Porter said, "but I have a couple of questions. Where does the arachnid need to be in order for you to spray the liquid helium on it? I'm assuming that with something that cold, you can't just run an ordinary hose to it. What's your delivery system?"

"That's true," Joshua said. "Liquid helium needs to flow in specially designed piping that can withstand extremely cold temperatures. Also, it can only be pumped using a special pump, but both are in the basement. We have access to that type of equipment. I don't see the creature being able to be lured to the basement though because the arachnid's too big to fit into the stairwells. I see this operation happening in the garage because it's the only place big enough to hold the creature with room to spare. If we can lure it there, I'm sure we can route the liquid helium piping to a point in the ceiling and douse the thing."

"We also need another pump," Liz said. "One that can pump liquid so that, in turn, we can pump the formaldehyde into the creature."

"I saw a sump pump in the basement," Vinod said. "It's normally used to pump water out if a basement floods. I'd work great for pumping any kind of liquid."

"Are the pumps or any other necessary equipment susceptible to an EMP pulse?" Ted asked.

"No," Joshua replied. "These are simple electrical devices. No silicon involved."

The mood in the room continued to improve. The thought of having *some* chance of survival, even though the odds were slim, was better than a posture of resignation. Even Vinod seemed hopeful as exhibited by the smile on his face, not unlike the one people saw when he was hatching plans for a party.

"Hey," Rachael said, looking around the lobby, "is it just me or do the lights in here seem to be getting dimmer?"

Vinod scanned the incandescent lights of the room. "Oh, shit!" He got up and ran out of the room.

"Where's he going?" Ted asked.

A few moments later, the lights went out completely. The room was now lit only by the waning light of dusk streaming through the broken doors.

"Damn," Ted remarked. "Do you think the arachnid cut the power somehow?"

Vinod ran back into the room, breathing heavily, before anyone could answer.

"What happened?" Joshua asked.

"I forgot something," Vinod answered, taking a seat. "So stupid on my part. I should've thought about it sooner."

"What?" Rachael asked.

Vinod explained his rapid departure. "The solar panels that provide power to this complex are silicon-based. They haven't been recharging the batteries since the EMP. The batteries have been draining since then and are almost fully depleted. That's why the lights started to dim. I cut the connection from the batteries to the complex to prevent them from draining completely."

Joshua thought about the implications of the power loss. "Well, that's a problem. We need power to run the pumps for both the helium and the formaldehyde. Do we have enough to run those?"

"I doubt it," Vinod said. "I don't think the batteries have enough amps left."

"We need a way to charge the batteries before tomorrow," Porter said. "Any ideas? At this point, nothing is too outrageous to consider."

"We have some gas left in the garage," Ted said. "Can the pumps run on gas somehow?"

"No," Joshua replied. "That's not how they work."

"I think I can convert the gas into electricity though," Vinod said, no longer the defeatist. "Ted, you still have the quad?"

"Yeah, it's in the garage."

"It has a headlight, so it must have an alternator," Vinod said. "We can run the engine on the quad and use its alternator to charge the battery." Vinod mentally calculated the energy requirements for the pumps. "We'd have to run it for a few hours, but I think it'll work."

"Looks like we have a plan," Porter said. "There's a lot of work to do, and everyone's going to have to pitch in. Any final questions before we start?"

"I have one," Rachael said. "How're we going to lure the arachnid into the garage?"

"That's a good question," Joshua said. "I watched the arachnid when it approached the opening of the garage. It seemed hesitant to enter."

"Maybe it's claustrophobic," Liz remarked.

"Right," Vinod said with a chuckle.

"No, I'm being serious," Liz insisted. "The arachnid was trapped for a while in that cage. It probably took time for it to blast its way out. I'm sure that being in the cage, even for a limited time, was uncomfortable. It may be reluctant to go into another enclosed space."

"Makes sense," Rachael said, "but claustrophobia is linked to an emotion—fear. Are you saying that this thing has emotions?"

"Why not?" Liz asked. "Most upper-level creatures on Earth display some type of emotion. The arachnid displayed protective behavior towards that white tree when Ted approached it. It also seemed to show anger when it was hit by the tank's projectile and when the tree was destroyed. And it was probably angry when it chased Ted down that trail. Think of a dog.

You can sense its emotions simply by observing what it's doing with its tail."

"Even if you're right," Rachael said, "fear is a strong emotion, one that's hard to overcome."

"Then you have to use another strong emotion to overcome it," Liz said. "Something like anger."

"Leave that to me," Ted said with a smile. "I know how to piss that thing off. I'm sure it's still angry at the guy who led it into a trap. It'll want revenge, another strong emotion. I'll let it chase me on the quad into the garage. I'm the mouse, and it's the cat chasing the mouse, like Tom and Jerry."

"I hope it's going to turn out like Tom and Jerry," Vinod remarked. "Tom never won."

Chapter Twenty-Four
The Long Night

The team got busy with the work required for the plan. The biggest task involved rerouting the liquid helium piping from the tokamak to a point near the ceiling above the garage. Joshua, Rachael, and Porter volunteered for the job. It was difficult work, and they used flashlights since the sun had set. They couldn't afford to waste any power for the lights inside Moe.

They began by dismantling some of the piping around the tokamak. Fortunately, the pipes were somewhat flexible and could be bent without kinking. They had to connect multiple sections of pipe end to end, but this presented no problem. The sections were threaded with a male end on one side and a female on the other, which meant they could be screwed together.

They ran the piping up the stairwell from the basement to the third floor. From there, the pipe had to run across the ceiling and then be pointed downward.

"How are we going to get the pipe across the ceiling?" Rachael asked. "It's sixty feet above the garage floor."

"Someone's going to have to climb across those steel support structures," Joshua replied, pointing to a network of horizontal beams near the ceiling. "Fortunately, I've done some rock climbing."

The ceiling of Moe was supported by numerous, primary, parallel steel I-beams on which the ceiling rested. A few feet below the primary beams were secondary I-beams that ran parallel to the primary beams that were placed between the primary beams. The primary and secondary beams were connected with large steel rods welded to both sets of beams. The result was triangular-shaped parallel structures that supported the weight of the ceiling.

Joshua would have to climb up to one of the lower secondary beams using a vertical service ladder that ran from the garage floor to ceiling, with access points adjacent to the railings on each floor. He would then crawl along the top of one of the lower beams to a position over the center of the garage floor three stories below. The area he would have to crawl along was narrow, and there was a significant risk of falling.

"Be careful," Rachael said.

"I've got this," he said, with a wink.

Joshua wore Ted's helmet on his head. He wore this not so much for the protection it offered, but for the light it provided from its built-in light source. He needed to be able to see in the darkness while still leaving his hands free.

Starting from the third floor, Joshua climbed the ladder, the end of the pipe clamped securely to a utility belt he wore. The belt also held a large roll of duct tape as well as a section of rope. Hand over hand, he ascended the rungs until the he was near the ceiling. The trailing pipe rattled against the metal ladder, and he paused several times to make sure that the pipe wasn't damaged since he couldn't afford to have any leaks in the conduit for the liquid helium. Finally, he reached one of the lower beams of the ceiling support.

Joshua removed the rope from his utility belt and fashioned a rope harness by tying the rope around his waist and threading it around each thigh and then up and around his waist again. He then tied the other end of the rope around one of the lower beams he would be crawling on top of. If he slipped, the rope would catch him even though he might fall several feet.

The beam was even narrower than it looked from below. It was only a foot wide, and he carefully shifted his weight as he lifted his left knee and then his right onto the support. The length of pipe was heavy since it ran a considerable length now that he had pulled it so high into the air, and it threatened to pull him off balance, so he compensated by leaning to his left since the pipe was clamped to the right side of the utility belt. Joshua wasn't afraid of heights, but he'd always had the benefit of having his ropes staked hard into solid rock when climbing, and the leather harness he used on outings was a great deal more sophisticated than the loops he'd made in the rope.

Joshua carefully inched along the top of the steel beam, keeping his eyes focused on the steel directly in front of him as he dragged the pipe behind him. If he looked left or right, he knew there was a possibility that he would grow dizzy and fall. He was sweating and breathing hard from the exertion, and the beam was barely wide enough for both of his knees as they moved forward in a slow crawling motion. If either knee slipped so much as an inch to the left or right, he would almost surely slip from the beam, and he wasn't interested in testing the strength of the harness.

When he reached the point over the center of the garage, he used his right hand to unclamp the piping from his utility belt and pointed the end downwards towards the floor. Now came the trickiest part of all. He needed to affix the pipe to the beam so that the force of the liquid helium wouldn't cause the pipe to spray the liquid in all directions, like a garden hose snaking across a driveway when a spigot is opened.

Joshua slowly laid down flat on top of the beam, face down. He then retrieved the duct tape from his utility belt and, using both hands, wrapped the tape numerous times around both the beam and the downward pointed pipe. He had used almost all of the tape when he finally grasped the end of the pipe and shook it to make sure that it was secure and wouldn't move when the force of the expelled liquid helium was applied. Rather than reattaching the duct tape to his utility belt, Joshua simply let it fall the sixty feet to the garage floor below. He got back up from his prone position and knelt on top of the beam again.

Joshua was breathing hard, and the exertion was making him tired. His joints ached from holding them in cramped positions. Next came a task that he hadn't prepared for: he had to back up. This wasn't going to be easy since the space afforded on top of the beam was now reduced further by the pipe that laid on top of it. He'd have to place his hands and knees on either side of the pipe. Blindly, he inched backwards, unable to see the beam behind him. He had to trust that he was moving backwards in a straight line. He turned his head to the rear, but he couldn't see the beam behind him.

"Josh!" Rachael screamed.

Joshua's right knee had slipped from the beam, causing his body to collapse onto its surface, arms and legs draped over the steel.

"I'm okay," he called in a hoarse voice.

Slowly, he raised his body back onto the beam, hands and knees squarely on the structure. With only a few feet to go, he backed up until he reached the ladder. He crawled one foot past the rungs so that he could reach out and take hold of the ladder's side with his right hand and swing his right foot onto the nearest rung. Then he took hold of the ladder with his left hand and brought his left leg next to his right. He was back on the ladder. Joshua disconnected the safety rope from his waist and thighs, and let it dangle from the ceiling. Before descending, he closed his eyes and took several deep breaths. He was exhausted. He climbed back down to the third floor.

"Great job, Dr. Andrews," Porter remarked after Joshua's return. "I felt like I was watching a circus act."

"Believe me," Joshua said, starting to feel energy returning to his limbs, "I think I'll stick to research. The big top is no place for yours truly."

The next job for Joshua, Rachael, and Porter was to find a way to remotely turn on the pump in the basement so that the liquid helium could be pumped through the positioned pipe. Without any way to communicate verbally once the plan was implemented, Joshua felt that the pump needed to be turned on from a point where someone could visually see when the arachnid had entered the garage.

They scavenged wiring from the tokamak coils—miles of it ran around the torus—and ran it from the helium pump in the basement up the stairwell to the railing on the second floor. Since the railing overlooked the garage floor, this location would provide the optimal place from which to activate the pump. With the wiring in place, they attached a switch to the end of the wires that, when flipped, would cause a wide stream of liquid helium to douse the garage via the piping. According to Joshua's calculations, the quantity would be sufficient enough to achieve their purpose.

*   *   *

Vinod had multiple tasks to perform. First, he and Ted connected the alternator of the quad to the battery connection of the complex. Ted fired up the engine, and electricity flowed into the batteries. Ted noted that the quad was in an enclosed space since the garage door was closed.

"What about carbon monoxide?" he asked.

Vinod looked around the garage. "It's a fairly small engine, and this is a pretty large space. There'll be some carbon monoxide build-up, but I don't think it'll reach dangerous levels."

Vinod calculated that the engine would have to run for four hours to supply enough energy to the batteries to power the two pumps. Ted stood vigil by the quad, filling its tank with gas as needed.

Between gas fill-ups, Ted was in charge of getting the C-4 ready. He gathered the remaining plastic explosive and molded it into a single unit, guessing he had about twenty pounds worth. He then sank a detonator into the clay-textured mass and ran a length of dual wires from the detonator to the actuator switch, making sure the actuator had its safety on before connecting the wires to it. The wires themselves had to be sufficiently long so that when the explosive blew, the operator of the actuator would be at a safe distance so as not to be harmed by the explosion.

His makeshift generator now running, Vinod helped Liz with the formaldehyde setup. He scavenged the sump pump from the basement and positioned it near the railing on the third floor. He made the electrical connections to the pump and also attached a switch in order to turn the pump on.

He and Liz next needed to travel to Larry to connect the pump via flexible tubing to the barrels of formaldehyde. This meant that the couple would have to leave the relative safety of Moe and venture outside. Fortunately, the arachnid had positioned itself so that Larry was partially hidden from its view. There was a door from which they could exit Moe without being seen. Vinod cautiously opened it and peered outside.

"Looks like the coast is clear," he said as he looked towards the sky. "I don't see any of those insects flying around either."

They ventured outside, glancing quickly in the direction of the arachnid. They spotted the edge of its carapace, but no tentacles were visible. The clearing and the forest seemed unnaturally quiet given the explosions that had filled the air during the arachnid's attack.

He and Liz ran the short distance to Larry and entered without being noticed.

Now in Larry, Liz and Vinod found a long section of large-bore flexible tubing. They attached a Y connector to one end of the tubing, and from each end of the Y they attached two short segments of tubing, which they placed into the two barrels of formaldehyde. Vinod grabbed the other end of the tubing and the couple went back to the exit of Larry. Vinod once again searched for any insects before they began their sprint back to Moe.

During their run, Liz tripped and fell, landing face-down on the grass. Vinod dropped the tubing and threw himself on top of the exobiologist, his hand swiftly wrapping around her head and covering her mouth.

"Don't take this personally," he whispered into her ear. "I had to make sure you didn't instinctively cry out. That bastard and its tentacles are pretty close by."

She nodded, and the two climbed to their feet, Vinod again taking hold of the tubing. They silently resumed their sprint.

Once back in Moe, they ran the end of the tubing up a stairwell to the pump on the third floor. The positioning of the pump on the third floor was planned. The arachnid stood almost two stories tall, and the junction between the carapace and its tentacle, if successfully penetrated by the C-4, would be well off the ground. The only way to access it, therefore, would be from above. Someone would have to jump from the third floor onto the arachnid's carapace in order to jam the formaldehyde-carrying tube and its needle into the creature.

"I think we made a mistake here," Vinod stated as he was about to connect the tubing to the pump.

"What?"

"This pump is on the third floor, but the source of the formaldehyde is on the ground floor."

"So?"

"There's not going to be enough suctioning power on the pump to pull the fluid this high up."

"Can we get a stronger pump somehow?"

"Doesn't matter how strong the pump is," Vinod said. "Pumps that suction fluid use a vacuum but they don't actually pull the fluid. It's the differential between atmospheric pressure and the vacuum that allows the fluid to rise. There's a limit to the height a pump can suck fluid that's dependent on the atmospheric pressure. I believe it's somewhere around thirty feet for a fluid like water. There's no way this set up could work."

"What do you want to do then?"

"We need to move the pump to the ground floor so that it's pushing fluid and not sucking it."

"But the pump needs to be activated from the third floor so that we can see when the formaldehyde spear is in place."

"That's true," Vinod responded as he thought about a solution. "We'll have to get a long length of wire and route the switch on the third floor to the pump on the ground floor."

Liz and Vinod got busy changing the location of the pump to the ground floor and then ran tubing and wiring from the pump to a switch located on the third floor.

Forming a needle at the end of the tubing was the next project. Liz and Vinod found a straight section of pipe six feet long that Vinod cut at an angle at one end with a hacksaw. The cut formed a sharp point at the end. It was, in effect, the world's largest hypodermic needle. They squeezed the end of the tubing that came from the formaldehyde pump over the blunt end of the needle.

"There," Vinod announced. "The formaldehyde IV system is all set. Let's go and see how Ted's progressing on the battery charging."

Liz and Vinod entered the garage floor and saw Ted kneeling next to the still running quad with a welder in his hand.

"What're you doing?" Liz asked.

"Some of the plating on the quad got loose on my last ride. I'm going to re-weld it."

"Need some help?" Liz asked.

"Sure. I could use an extra pair of hands."

Liz knelt next to Ted as Vinod started to walk away. "Where you going?" Liz asked.

"Gotta do something," Vinod replied. "I got my own special project to work on."

Chapter Twenty-Five
The Missile

At 0500, Joshua and Rachael sat in the lobby of Moe, waiting for the rest of the team to finish their tasks. Porter had gone to check on the C-4 setup since he would be the one to set off the actuator.

Rachael sat next to Joshua, her head on his shoulder. "Josh, do you think this is going to work? It's ingenious but complex."

"Do you want an honest answer?"

Rachael thought for a moment before answering. "Not really."

"Then of course it's going to work," he said with a smile.

Rachael put her arm around Joshua and gave him a hug. "You know there's a real chance we may not survive the next few hours. Are you afraid?"

"Of course I'm afraid. I'd be crazy if I wasn't, but it comforts me to be with you," Joshua said turning to Rachael with a smile. "You remember the day we first met, and I asked you if you considered yourself to be a lucky person?"

"Yes, I remember that. I think I said that I'm fairly lucky."

"Well, I don't really believe in luck . . . most of the time. I believe for the most part that we make our own luck. Most of the time we're in control of our own destiny. But there are times when things are outside our control, and in these circumstances, luck can't hurt."

Rachael gazed into Joshua's eyes and gave him a kiss.

"But Josh, whether it was luck or not, I cheated death and always assumed that we'd be a normal couple and grow old together. There's still so much life ahead for us. It would be a tragedy if we didn't get to experience it. Have we come this far to see everything end?"

Joshua kissed Rachael. "Our lives together have not been wasted."

"But—"

"I know what you're saying, but still, we were the first humans to speak to alien intelligence, and we're the only humans to visit another planet. Much more fortunate than most, I'd think. For me, the glass is half full."

Joshua was trying to be optimistic. He knew they were faced with an almost impossible situation. They had come up with a possible solution, but he knew this was a Hail Mary at best.

"But there's still so much we haven't done, and there are so many places I want to visit," Rachael said. "I've never been to Africa or South America." Rachael paused and lowered her head. "And I'd love to raise some children someday. Maybe that more than anything else."

"You're right," Joshua said resolutely. "There's much we still need to do. That's why we're going to take that arachnid out today. I just feel it."

Rachael removed her necklace from inside her blouse. It had a cross on it that she brought to her mouth and kissed. "I hope you're right."

Joshua eyed the cross. "Me too."

The remaining members of the team joined Rachael and Joshua in the lobby when they'd finished their respective jobs. None of them had gotten any rest since they had worked through the night.

"Looks like everything's all set," Joshua stated after the others had taken their seats. "I want to go over the steps of the plan so that everyone's on the same page. There's going to be a lot of communication in rapid succession, some of it nonverbal."

Joshua went over the ambitious steps in detail. First, everyone had to be in their proper places. On the quad, Ted would start out in the garage and then ride out in plain sight of the creature. As before, he would let it chase him. The quad would be used to lure the arachnid into the garage.

Porter would be on the ground floor of the garage. He had three jobs. The first was to operate the garage door. He would open it when everyone was set in order to allow Ted to exit and engage the arachnid. Once the arachnid was in the garage, Porter would have to close the door quickly. Joshua had been worried that if the door wasn't closed, the arachnid would simply run out when hit with the liquid helium given its speed and dexterity. It would take several seconds for the door to close, during which time they would be at greatest risk. The arachnid could fire its airfoils at will. Everyone would stay hidden, out of the line of sight of the arachnid if at all possible. The group was keenly aware that airfoils could travel around corners.

Rachael would be positioned on the second floor next to the switch that operated the pump for the liquid helium. As soon as the door was closed, she would activate the pump and douse the creature with the freezing liquid.

Liz, Vinod, and Joshua would be positioned on the third floor close to the railing overlooking the garage floor. After the arachnid had been frozen by the liquid helium, Vinod would jump from the railing onto the carapace of the creature. It would be a long drop, but this was something that couldn't be avoided. From the second floor, the top of the carapace of the creature would have been higher than the second floor which would have made it impossible to get on top of the creature.

Once Vinod was on the carapace, Porter would toss up to him the C-4, which Vinod would pack tightly around the base of the nearest tentacle. Vinod would then climb down from the creature and join Porter, who would be a safe distance away to avoid the explosion. With Vinod at his side, Porter would detonate the explosive and hopefully blow a hole in the armor.

Joshua would then jump from the third floor with the formaldehyde spear onto the arachnid and plunge it into the hole created by the C-4. When the spear was correctly positioned, Liz would enact the final step, which would be to turn on the pump for the formaldehyde, hopefully killing the arachnid.

"That was a very thorough description of the plan, Dr. Andrews," Porter stated. "I think we all know our duties."

The first rays of daybreak slanted through the broken doors of the building. It was early, but the air was already warm and humid.

Vinod glanced outside and asked, "When do you want to start?"

"I want everyone to be set to go in thirty minutes," Joshua replied.

"I have to reconnect the batteries to the complex before we start," Vinod stated.

"I want to take a look from the roof to make sure the thing didn't move overnight," Ted stated. "I need to know where to drive the quad."

"Good idea," Joshua stated. "I'll go with you."

*　　　　　*　　　　　*

Joshua and Ted climbed up the stairwell to the door that led to the roof. They cautiously opened it and looked outside. The roof of the building had a four-foot-high retaining wall surrounding its edges. The two men bent low and walked to one of the walls, which was in disrepair, with numerous cracks and holes in its concrete.

Ted positioned himself close to one of the holes while Joshua found another and peered through it.

"It's still in the same position," Ted said in a hushed voice. "Hasn't moved an inch."

The creature had all of its tentacles pointed at the building as if waiting for the slightest motivation to fire.

"What's that behind it?" Ted asked.

Joshua saw a small white object a foot high next to the creature. It looked like the sapling of a tree.

"It looks like it's trying to grow another one of those white trees," Joshua remarked. "I wonder what they do. The arachnid seems to place a lot of importance on them."

"Well, at least now I know how to piss it off," Ted said. "Mess with the tree."

As they watched, the creature suddenly shifted all of its tentacles to a direction one hundred degrees away from where it was previously looking.

"Whoa," Ted whispered. "What's it looking at?"

Joshua scanned the horizon and spotted a fast-moving object skimming the tree line—headed directly towards them. "It's a cruise missile! The arachnid's insects must have spotted it. Porter's timetable for aerial bombardment was correct. They're not wasting any time."

"We're screwed!" Ted exclaimed. "If the missile hits anywhere close to the arachnid, the blast will destroy this complex."

The duo watched in horror as the missile advanced at supersonic speed. When it was half a kilometer away, the arachnid opened fire, spewing airfoils at the weapon. Ted and Joshua watched as the stream of airfoils and the missile came into contact. The missile exploded in midair with a massive fireball and fell into the forest below. A few seconds later, the shockwave from the explosion hit the complex, which shook but was otherwise unaffected.

The two men watched the arachnid through the retaining wall as it continued looking in the direction of the missile for a full minute before turning its tentacles back towards Moe.

"That thing just saved our lives," Joshua said.

"Let's not return the favor," Ted replied as they made their way back to the stairwell.

Chapter Twenty-Six
Battle

Vinod returned to the lobby of Moe after reconnecting the power supply to the complex when Ted and Joshua walked in.

"What the hell was that explosion?" Vinod asked. "It nearly knocked me on my ass."

"A cruise missile," Joshua answered. "The arachnid attacked it, and it blew up in midair before reaching its target."

"That target being us?" Rachael asked.

"That target being the arachnid," Joshua said. "It was headed straight for it. But you're right. If it had hit the arachnid, we surely would've been collateral damage."

Porter contemplated their situation. "Since the missile attack failed, I'm sure that either carpet bombing or a nuclear attack is imminent. The president, Williams, and the joint chiefs aren't going to wait. We don't have much time."

"Then let's do this," Vinod said.

*   *   *

Everyone was in position to execute the plan. Ted was on the quad, the engine revving. He gave a thumbs-up to Porter, who pushed the button to open the garage door. The plan was in motion.

The door rattled open slowly as Ted looked outside. He couldn't see the arachnid since it was on a side of the building not facing the garage. He throttled the engine, drove outside, and turned left. As he rounded the corner, he saw the arachnid, which immediately repositioned its tentacles in his direction.

"It's a patient son of a bitch," Ted mumbled.

Ted turned the quad hard so that the metal shielding would protect him from any airfoils, which came in a torrent and bounced off the shielding. When he had re-welded the plating on the quad, he had raised it so that it wouldn't dig into the dirt again. He sped towards the garage, but the arachnid didn't follow. It stood still, continuing its barrage. *Damn it! Come after me, you bastard,* he thought as he put his quad in reverse and backed up towards the creature. He was close enough so that the dark gray mottling on the carapace could be seen in the rearview mirror.

The noise of the airfoils hitting the shielding was deafening. Ted wondered how much longer the plates could hold out against the onslaught. When he had gotten sufficiently close to the creature, he stopped the quad and retrieved a grenade from his belt. He pulled the pin and lobbed it backwards over the shielding. The grenade exploded close to the small white tree and blasted it to pieces. The explosion lifted the quad a few inches off the ground, and it bounced unevenly for the next several yards as Ted started to drive forward. A cloud of dust and smoke drifted over the area, partially obscuring the arachnid. As the cloud cleared, the creature was in plain view, but the airfoils ceased their strafing of the quad as the arachnid charged directly at him. Ted gunned the engine and raced ahead, the arachnid in rapid pursuit.

The quad suddenly slowed, the motor making a grinding sound, its RPMs slowing.

"Not now, for God's sake!" Ted groaned.

He threw the vehicle into neutral, pumped the accelerator, opened the throttle, and gave the quad gas before putting it back into drive. It sputtered, lurched forward, and gained traction as it sped off.

Ted depressed the accelerator, rounded the corner of the building, entered the garage, and slammed on the brakes, causing the vehicle to skid on the oil-slick floor and crash into the far wall. Ted was thrown forward but snapped back hard against the thinly padded seat, his head bouncing off the steel plate behind him.

The arachnid bounded into the garage, stopped, and opened fire with four tentacles directed towards the quad while the other four surveyed its surroundings. It was searching for additional threats. Porter pounded the switch before him and hid behind some metal equipment in the garage. The garage door started to close.

While still firing with four of its tentacles directed at the quad, the arachnid let loose with its other four tentacles. It fired at random objects in the garage, causing sparks to fly as airfoils ricocheted off metal objects. The noise was deafening.

The garage door was halfway closed when a portion of the quad's rear shielding finally gave way. The creature had created a small hole in the back shielding through which it now directed its airfoils.

Ted felt a searing pain in his left shoulder. "I'm hit!" he screamed.

Rachael, knowing that Ted wouldn't be able to hold out much longer, activated the switch for the liquid helium pump. A massive stream of liquid helium flowed from the hanging tube and landed on the arachnid, creating a white mist caused by the condensation of the ambient water vapor in the air. The arachnid stopped firing and moved its tentacles wildly about like whips as it tried to back out of the garage. It was blocked, however, by the closing door. It shrieked, producing the sound of a cricket at ear-piercing decibels. Its tentacles flailed, hitting the sides of the garage and aluminum barrels stacked against its walls. It was definitely demonstrating an emotion: panic.

"Gotcha, you bastard!" Porter cried triumphantly as the door reached the cement floor.

Liquid helium continued to rain down, which stopped the arachnid's cry. The creature's wild movements slowed, and its tentacles fell limp against its carapace and froze in place as liquid helium dripped off of their ends. The arachnid was completely frozen, and Rachael turned off the pump.

"Go, Vinod!" Joshua shouted.

Vinod ran to the third-floor railing, climbed over, and jumped. He landed feet first on the arachnid, which was covered in a layer of ice. He wavered precariously, arms extended like a surfer trying to maintain his balance on a surf board. His feet slipped, and he fell sideways, sliding off the carapace. His hands reached for one of the frozen tentacles which he was able to grasp, ending his slide. Pulling himself, he climbed back on top of the carapace.

Vinod winced as he felt a searing pain in his hands. He could still move his fingers but had almost no sensation left in his hands. His hands were numbed by the extreme cold they were exposed to when he'd grasped the tentacle.

Porter ran directly beneath Vinod.

"Catch!" he shouted as he tossed the C-4 into the air, the detonator and wires attached.

Vinod caught the explosive with cupped, frozen hands and started packing it at the base of the nearest tentacle.

Liz, Joshua, and Rachael watched from the railings above as Vinod worked to place the explosive in an optimal location. His numb right hand pushed the clay as far as it would go into the joint where tentacle met carapace.

"Hurry, Vinod!" Joshua shouted. "We don't know how long this thing's going to stay frozen."

"Almost done!" Vinod replied.

He finished surrounding the base of the tentacle with C-4 and started to climb down by stepping onto the arachnid's legs. His foot slipped on the icy surface, and he tumbled, landing with a bone-jarring thud on his back. Groaning from the pain in his lower back, he rolled onto his side.

Porter ran over to Vinod and grabbed him by his shirt and dragged him across the floor away from the arachnid. Vinod got up with difficulty, his joints and muscles sore, and crouched next to Porter. "Thanks," he managed to say through waves of pain. He flexed and extended his fingers as sensation slowly returned to his fingers.

Porter held the actuator for the detonator in his hands. "Let's hope this works," he said as he disengaged the safety and turned the handle of the actuator.

Everyone held their breath, their hearts racing as they waited for the explosion . . . but there was none.

"What the hell!" Porter exclaimed as he twisted the handle of the actuator a second time. Still nothing.

Porter and Vinod simultaneously spotted the problem. One of the two wires leading from the actuator had been cut, probably by a stray airfoil.

"Shit, one of the wires is cut!" Vinod exclaimed.

Porter and Vinod raced to the broken wire with the actuator. Vinod quickly disconnected the broken wire from the actuator while Porter, using his teeth, stripped the end of the wire still connected to the detonator of its insulation. Vinod quickly reattached the stripped wire to the actuator. The men stared at each other as something instantaneously dawned on them. With the now shortened wire, whoever activated the actuator would not be a safe distance from the C-4 explosion.

Porter grabbed the actuator from Vinod and shouted, "Get back, Bhakti!"

"But Porter . . .."

"Get the fuck back!"

Vinod scrambled to a safe distance and turned towards Porter, who was kneeling with his back to the creature. Porter looked up from the actuator and gazed into Vinod's eyes.

"Porter!" Vinod screamed.

Still staring at Vinod, Porter turned the handle on the actuator. An explosion rocked the garage as the C-4 blew, knocking the general to the floor. His body lay unmoving, sprawled face-down on the ground.

"Porter!" Vinod shouted, but he received no response.

The explosion severed the tentacle from the arachnid, which landed next to Porter's right arm, but no blood flowed from the creature's wound. Instead, a blast of blue-green flames shot three feet from the hole in the carapace.

"Damn!" Vinod shouted as he saw the flames jetting out from the arachnid. The fire filled the garage with acrid-smelling fumes, causing team members to cough and cover their mouths.

Vinod covered his face with his arm and scrambled to the switch that would open the garage door and vent the fumes. The door rose and the fumes drifted into the clearing.

Joshua climbed over the third-floor railing with the formaldehyde spear in his right hand. He suddenly felt lightheaded. He leapt from the railing and landed feet first on the carapace and managed to stay upright despite his disorientation. He moved to the fire-breathing hole in the carapace and plunged the spear deep inside. Because of the flames, he stood to the side of the hole and held the makeshift syringe obliquely, arching his back to distance his face from the searing heat.

"Now, Liz!" he shouted.

No fluid flowed through the tubing connected to the spear, and Joshua's eyes opened wide as he struggled to maintain his balance, coughing to expel the noxious fumes from his lungs.

"Liz!" he shouted, looking towards the ceiling, but there was no response.

Rachael watched in horror from the second-floor railing as one of the arachnid's tentacles started to move slowly. "Josh!" she screamed. "Look out! It's moving again!"

Vinod watched horrified from the garage floor as Joshua avoided the slowly moving tentacles while trying to keep the spear in place. He noticed that the tips of the arachnid's legs were starting to glow a dull white. The whiteness was growing brighter and started climbing up the legs of the arachnid.

"Josh!" he shouted. "The thing's trying to put out another EMP pulse!"

Vinod's heart sank as he thought of the implications of a potential EMP pulse. If the creature was able to let off another pulse, it would trip the breakers again cutting power to the complex. If that happened, the formaldehyde pump wouldn't work.

Joshua bent low to avoid being hit by the tentacle, his hands still holding the spear in place. *What happened to Liz?* he wondered as he looked to the ceiling. *Helium!* Joshua realized that the third floor was filled with helium. When the liquid helium evaporated, it was lighter than air and therefore had displaced all air from the third floor, causing a lack of oxygen. The helium wasn't toxic, but Liz had likely passed out.

"Rachael!" Joshua shouted, "go upstairs and throw the pump switch, but don't stay there too long! That floor's filled with helium!"

Rachael raced upstairs and saw Liz lying on the floor unconscious. She ran to the switch and flipped it on. The pump whirred to life. Rachael took a breath and shouted, "It's on!" Her cry came out in a high-pitched voice secondary to the lower density helium that filled her lungs. She knew she didn't have much time. Feeling lightheaded, Rachael grabbed Liz by the feet and dragged her to the stairwell. She seized Liz's limp body around the waist and carefully lowered her, step by step, to the second floor. Gasping, she released the body and, hands braced against her thighs, coughed before inhaling, filling her lungs with oxygen.

Standing to the side of the opening produced by the C-4, Joshua held the spear in place as the formaldehyde was injected into the arachnid. Its tentacles had come to life again and moved slowly but in no particular direction as flames continued to blast sporadically from the hole. The spear was becoming uncomfortably hot, and he didn't know how much longer he could hold it.

Vinod noted that the white color of the arachnid's legs had disappeared. The creature suddenly slumped to the ground as its legs collapsed, producing the sound of dozens of metal rods breaking and crashing together.

"Got you, you monster!" Vinod shouted at the immobile creature.

Joshua released his hold on the spear and waited to see if there was any more movement from the arachnid, but there was none. He climbed down on the twisted legs of the creature and collapsed next to Vinod, exhausted. The flames abated, leaving a smoldering hole.

"Is it dead?" Joshua asked Vinod, out of breath.

"I think so."

"Wait," Joshua stated with a look of concern. "I think I see something moving."

The duo watched as small pieces of the undersurface of the carapace popped open like small trap doors. Through the openings, seven baby arachnids, a foot in diameter, emerged and scurried out of the garage and into the forest beyond the clearing.

"There are more of those bastards out there now!" Vinod exclaimed.

"They're still babies," Joshua said. "They won't be lethal for a while. At least we have some time now."

"Josh, you check on the others," Vinod said. "I have to do something." He ran into the building.

"Rachael, are you okay?" Joshua shouted.

"Yes," Rachael called from the second floor. "And Liz is starting to come around."

Ted appeared from behind the quad, holding his left shoulder, which was covered in blood.

"You okay?" Joshua asked.

"Hit, but okay. Is it dead?"

"I think so."

Joshua ran over to Porter, rolled his body over, and felt for a carotid pulse. "He's unconscious but alive. Rachael, is Liz awake?"

"Yes!" Liz shouted. "I'm okay."

"I need you down here!" Joshua shouted. "Porter's hurt. He's unconscious." Joshua turned to Ted, "We did it! We're all alive."

"Hopefully we stay that way," Ted said. "We have to get a message to the carrier before they carpet bomb us."

*   *   *

Fifteen minutes earlier, Williams, Langdon, and Captain Pierce sat in the command center on board the USS Gerald R. Ford, watching multiple video feeds on the monitors in front of them. One of the feeds was from a cruise missile launched from the carrier and showed a rapidly moving landscape of forest and clearings as it moved at near supersonic speed towards its target. Another feed was a live satellite image of the complex and the surroundings, the arachnid positioned at the center of the frame and close to the largest building.

"One minute to target," a voice announced over the speakers.

"That thing's not even moving," Langdon said. "It's just sitting in the field."

"You spoke too soon," Williams said as they saw the tentacles of the arachnid point in a different direction.

The video feed from the cruise missile went blank as an explosion was seen on the satellite image.

"What happened?" Captain Pierce asked.

"The missile was destroyed before hitting its target," a technician said, sitting at one of the consoles.

"Was it airfoils or an EMP pulse?" Pierce asked.

"Unknown," the technician responded.

"How far away are the bombers?" Williams asked.

"About thirteen minutes to the drop zone," the technician replied.

"Captain, at what altitude are the bombers flying?" Langdon asked.

"Forty thousand feet," Pierce answered. "That should be high enough to be out of range of any EMP pulses. Our technicians estimated that the range of the previous pulse was eight kilometers, so at forty thousand feet they're over twelve kilometers high."

"Dina," Langdon asked, "are you sure there's no other option? There may still be people alive in the complex."

"We've been through this before, Robert," Williams replied without emotion. "We can't risk another rescue mission, and we have to destroy this arachnid while we have the opportunity. We know its exact position and can direct our firepower at it. If it runs into the woods, it'll be tougher for us to kill it."

"I know," Langdon said with resignation.

"I realize the ramifications of what we're doing," Williams said. "I don't take this decision lightly."

"Look!" Langdon said as a quad emerged from one side of the building.

All eyes were glued to the satellite feed and watched as the quad approached the creature. The arachnid fired on the quad, which backed up towards it before moving forward again. An explosion appeared next to the arachnid, which ran after the four-wheeler.

"They're still alive!" Langdon shouted.

The group watched intently as the quad rounded the side of the building and entered the garage, followed by the arachnid.

"They may not be alive for long," Williams replied. "They're trapped in there with that thing."

A full ten minutes passed with no motion evident on the screen.

"Two minutes to bombing range," the commander of a B2 bomber announced.

"Captain," Williams said, "make sure those B2s center their targeting run over the largest building. We know the arachnid's in there now."

"Affirmative," Pierce replied.

"One minute until bombing range," the commander announced a short time later.

"Goddamn it!" Langdon shouted as he thought of the imminent death of his colleagues trapped in the building.

"Wait!" a technician shouted as he ran towards the others with a piece of paper in his hand. "I've got something. It's a Morse-coded message I picked up on the AM band."

The technician handed the paper to Williams, who read it. "Call off the attack, captain!" she shouted.

Langdon hurried to Williams' side and read the paper. ARACHNID DEAD. SIX SURVIVORS.

Chapter Twenty-Seven
Sick Bay

Vinod, Liz, Joshua, and Rachael sat at a table in one of the dining halls on the USS Gerald R. Ford. The hall was cramped but more modern and well-equipped than the dining area in Curly.

"Man," Vinod remarked as he took a bite of fried chicken. "So nice to have some normal food."

"And it's nice to decompress," Liz said. "North Korea was pretty intense. As much as I want to study extraterrestrial biology, I don't want to do it while dodging airfoils."

"I wasn't really worried," Vinod proclaimed. "Rum, classic rock, and science can handle anything."

Liz slapped the table, almost choking on her food, and everyone at the table laughed.

"Oh, right," Joshua said. "This from a guy whose mantra was . . .." Joshua mimicked Vinod's voice, "'Man, we're totally screwed. We gotta get out of here now! We're totally fucked!'"

"Just a few speed bumps," Vinod said casually. "And hey, is this any way to thank the man who saved your lives using Morse code."

Joshua nevertheless continued his impression. "I should never have come on this mission, man. I want to get the hell out of—"

An announcement came over the ship's speakers, interrupting Joshua's spot-on impersonation. "Dr. Andrews, Ms. Miller, Dr. Yang, and Mr. Bhakti, report to sick bay immediately."

"Shit," Vinod said, dropping a piece of chicken. "I only took one bite of my food."

The foursome dropped their eating utensils and were escorted to a lower deck. They entered the sick bay to see Ted and Porter on beds adjacent to each other. It was a clean, modern medical facility with vital signs displayed on LCD screens next to the beds.

Williams and Langdon stood next to Porter while a doctor studied his chart. Ted had a sling on his left arm, a wide bandage on his shoulder.

"How're y'all doing?" Ted asked matter-of-factly.

"We're good, Ted," Liz answered. "How's the shoulder?"

"Aw, just a flesh wound."

"It's more than a flesh wound, commander," the doctor commented as he put a stethoscope on his ears and listened to Porter's chest.

"He just woke up," Williams said, referring to Porter. "We haven't told him anything yet."

"The blast really rang his bell," Langdon said.

Porter looked around the room, still groggy.

The doctor took off his stethoscope, looped it around his neck, and said, "He has a concussion and a pulmonary contusion, but he's going to be okay."

"Damn, Porter," Vinod said, walking up to Porter's bed. "You're one tough cookie."

"I'm military, Bhakti," Porter said in a hoarse voice. "We're *all* tough." Porter looked at the people in sick bay. "So the plan worked? The arachnid's dead?"

"It worked," Joshua replied with a grin, "although not quite as we envisioned. We had to play a few things by ear."

"I know," Porter said. "The pain in my chest is evidence of that. But is the damn thing dead?"

"Yeah," Vinod remarked. "That thing's as dead as a doorknob. They transported it to the ship. It's locked up in a hold somewhere down below."

"Mission accomplished," Porter said with a weak smile.

"Unfortunately, the danger has not completely passed, general," Langdon said. "The arachnid spawned seven more juvenile arachnids after it died, and all escaped into the forest. We have no idea where they are."

Porter appeared disheartened and shook his head. The team had worked hard and had succeeded in killing the arachnid, but perhaps a new mission would be required, one more difficult than the first.

"Seven?" Porter said. "We'll need more troops and firepower."

"General, they're quite small," Joshua said. "Maybe a foot across. I don't think they're dangerous yet, but obviously we don't want them to become full-grown."

"Then we still have work to do," Porter said, looking resolute despite his condition. "Maybe we can convene an emergency meeting right here in sick bay."

"You get some rest, Mitchell," Williams said. "We're formulating the next steps even as we speak. Frankly, we can't commit more troops or firepower until we've studied the dead arachnid further."

"I don't rest on a mission," Porter said, attempting to get up by propping himself on his elbows. He immediately became dizzy and lay back down.

"Jesus, Porter," Vinod replied. "Take it easy. You've done enough soldier shit for one day. That was very brave of you, by the way—exploding the C-4 so close to the arachnid."

"Just part of the job." Porter closed his eyes to reduce the spinning sensation he felt from his sudden movement. "How'd we get back on the ship? I thought for sure that we'd be bombed."

He glanced at Williams, who nodded, indicating that the order had indeed been given.

"That was Vinod's doing," Rachael piped in. "It was brilliant really. He was able to send a message to the ship in Morse code that we were alive and that the arachnid was dead. He did it with only a minute to spare."

"Message?" Porter asked. "How? I thought all of the electronics were fried by the EMP."

"Not *all* the electronics," Joshua replied. "The EMP affected all silicon-based semiconductors and electronics, but if you recall, the Koreans had vacuum tube radios and transmitters stored at the complex. They weren't affected by the EMP, so Vinod used them to rig up an AM transmitter."

Porter smiled at Vinod. "Nice thinking, Bhakti."

"I didn't have time to rig up a full audio transmitter, but I could send pings on the AM band. I knew all that electronics shit I learned at Berkeley would come in handy someday."

"Commander Johnson," Porter said, tilting his head, "you showed exceptional bravery out there. I'll personally see to it that you get the appropriate commendation for this."

"Appreciate it, general, but I'd like to make a request."

"What is it?"

"I'd like a team to retrieve my fallen men. We don't leave anyone behind."

"No we don't," Porter replied. "I'll look into that personally. Dr. Andrews, do you think a team sent in to retrieve the fallen would be in harm's way?"

"I don't think so. The juvenile arachnids are too small to be any real threat. But the team retrieving the Seals needs to be fully armed. They should try to destroy any juveniles they encounter."

"I'll get a team together right away," Williams stated.

"So, what's the plan for dealing with the juveniles?" Porter asked looking at Williams.

"You really won't take it easy, will you?" Williams asked.

"It's not in my nature."

"Okay," Williams said with a sigh. "Here's what we have so far. Commander Johnson is going to recuperate on the ship for a few days and will eventually rejoin his Seals in Virginia. We're going to airlift the rest of you back to Berkeley tomorrow. General, you can go with them if the docs think you're okay to travel."

"Screw the docs," Porter said. "I'll be ready."

The doctor rolled his eyes and frowned as he left sick bay.

"Dr. Langdon and Dr. Yang are going to be tasked with assembling a scientific team to study the dead arachnid in order to see how it works and to discover any weaknesses—assuming it has any—that we can use against the juvenile arachnids in North Korea. It will take a few days for the carrier to get back to the San Francisco Bay area to deliver the arachnid to the lab. What we do from there depends on what the scientific team learns about the creature."

"Sounds like a logical course of action," Porter said, "but we should leave men behind to monitor the arachnid's offspring."

"We're using surveillance drones for that," Williams explained. "It's safer. The drones haven't spotted anything yet."

Porter nodded his approval.

Vinod walked over to Ted's bed and whispered into his ear. "Hey, Tabasco, are the docs going to let you out of here today?"

"Possibly. Why?"

"Party in Rachael and Liz's room tonight," Vinod whispered. "I got the captain to get us a couple of bottles of Gray Goose he had stashed."

"I heard that, Mr. Bhakti," Williams stated with a stern face.

Vinod looked like a kid caught with his hand in the cookie jar. Williams was the only person who intimidated him, the only person he never talked back to. But he respected her because she was always willing to listen to both sides of an issue.

Williams stared at Vinod, a smile slowly crossing her face. "I'll have some ice and snacks sent to their room tonight. You all deserve a celebration. The country—in fact, the whole world—is in your debt."

"Oh, it's on, baby," Vinod said.

"I'll make it," Ted said. "Glad I got hit in my left shoulder. My right arm's still good for bouncing quarters."

*   *   *

The gathering was tame considering that it was one of Vinod's parties. The scientific team and Ted sat around a table drinking Grey Goose with various mixers. There was, of course, the constant blast of classic rock coming from Vinod's Bluetooth speaker, which played "More Than a Feeling" by Boston.

The group was physically and emotionally exhausted from the events of the past several days and was in a reflective but celebratory mood.

"I can't believe we beat that thing," Ted said, his right hand holding a bloody Mary with Tabasco.

"It was a group effort," Joshua said. "We couldn't have done it without everyone's help. But Ted, you got the ball rolling by getting that thing to chase you into the garage. That's courage with a capital C."

"I've outrun a lot of wildlife in my days," Ted said with a laugh. "Mostly gators, plus a few nutria and wild hogs. And I didn't want to waste all the money the Navy invested in my training."

Liz looked down at the table, a somber expression on her face. "Well, I didn't do much of anything. I wish I'd realized that the helium was filling the third floor before I passed out."

"Come on, Liz," Vinod said, holding her hand. "You kidding me? You were a huge help. If it wasn't for you coming up with that formaldehyde idea, that thing would still be alive. Everything we did was because of you."

"Besides," Joshua added, "your most important contribution may be yet to come. Looks like you're going to be in charge of studying the dead arachnid. There are still seven more of those things running around, and *you* have to find out what makes them tick. Can you imagine trying to do what we did seven more times?"

Vinod shook his head. "Jesus, Josh, you really are a buzz kill sometimes. Can't we just have one night to celebrate still being alive? Come on, man. We did a fucking unbelievable job. All of us, including Porter."

"I'll drink to that," Rachael said, raising her glass.

The others clinked their glasses against hers and drank.

"Hey, I have another toast," Ted said. "To all my brothers that paid the ultimate sacrifice." His voice cracked with emotion as he thought of all the men he had lost. "We're all indebted to them."

Tears formed in Rachael's eyes as she thought of the fallen soldiers. She raised her glass a second time. "To the Seals."

The group sat in silence as they contemplated those who had not been as lucky as they. They all knew they were fortunate to be alive since killing the arachnid had entailed far more danger than they had anticipated.

"I'm going to call it a night," Ted said. "My shoulder's still pretty sore, and I'm tired."

"Gonna miss you, Tabasco," Vinod said. "We're flying to Berkeley tomorrow, and you're going to be on the other side of the country."

"Same here," Ted replied. "Y'all my people. Make sure you keep in touch. I want to know what you find out about the arachnid."

"Absolutely," Joshua said. "You do the same." He yawned and stretched his arms wide. "I think we should call it an evening too."

Rachael glanced at Vinod's hand, which was still folded around Liz's. "Vinod, you want me to find somewhere else to stay tonight so that you and Liz can be together?"

Liz and Vinod looked at each other and burst out laughing.

"What's so funny?" Rachael asked.

"Should we let her off the hook?" Liz asked Vinod.

"Sure. She's suffered long enough."

"Rach, you've been played," Liz said. "Vinod and I have been putting on a show for you. I *know* that Vinod's gay. There was never anything going on between us."

Joshua remembered the night Rachael had him down the Tabasco-laden drink. "*They* played *you*, Rachael?"

Rachael looked annoyed. "Why would you two lead me on like that?"

"Oh, Rach," Vinod answered, still laughing, "it was fair play after what you pulled on the two of us. You know—how you thought Liz was interested in me and yet you never bothered to tell her I was gay. You were setting us up, and you know it."

"Nice!" Joshua said with a chuckle. "You two had us both going pretty good, especially Rachael. Vinod, I think she was actually a bit jealous of Liz."

"You need to stop," Rachael said to Joshua, her cheeks flush with embarrassment.

"What did Porter say earlier today?" Vinod asked. "Mission accomplished."

Rachael rolled her eyes. "You two are hilarious," she said with sarcasm.

Chapter Twenty-Eight
Uncontrolled Reproduction

Later that evening, Rachael and Liz cleaned up from the party and packed their belongings.

"I hope you're not angry that Vinod and I played a prank on you," Liz said.

Rachael smiled good-naturedly. "No, it's fine. I guess I had it coming."

Rachael picked up her duffel bag from the floor and lifted it onto the dresser. A photograph fell out of the bag and landed by Liz's feet. Liz reached down and picked up the photograph, which was a picture of a very young Rachael with her arm around a boy of about ten years old.

"Here, you dropped this," Liz said.

"Thanks."

"Who's the boy in the picture?"

"My twin brother Richard."

"I didn't know you have a brother," Liz commented.

"Richard passed away when we were kids. I keep this picture as a memento."

Liz gently touched Rachael's arm. "I'm sorry. I'm sure that must have been very traumatic."

"Yes, it was. We were best buddies. I still miss him at times."

"What happened to him?"

"He died from cancer," Rachael said, tears welling up in her eyes. "Ewing's sarcoma, to be exact. We tried everything to save him, but it was unsuccessful."

Liz let go of Rachael's hand and sat on the lower bunk, her head lowered.

"What's wrong?" Rachael said, sitting next to Liz.

When they'd talked on their first night on the carrier, Liz had felt that their relationship was too new to tell Rachael about the details of her engagement to Bojing, and why it had ended. She knew they had more of a connection now, a connection solidified by a perilous experience they'd shared at the complex. Rachael had, in fact, saved her life by carrying her down from the third floor of Moe. She was now a friend—no, a sister— who she felt comfortable speaking to.

It took Liz a few moments to compose herself. "You remember when I told you the other night that I had been engaged and that it hadn't worked out?"

"Yes."

"I wasn't being completely honest with you. Our engagement didn't end as a result of some incompatibility between us. My fiancé, Bojing, was diagnosed with colon cancer a few months after our engagement. He died a month before we were to be married."

"I'm sorry," Rachael said as she gave Liz a hug. "I guess we both know what it's like to lose someone close at such a young age." Rachael released Liz from her embrace. "Damn cancer! It's such a horrible disease."

The women sat in silence for a few moments.

"Yes, it is," Liz agreed. "You remember when we were looking at the cell from the surveillance insect in the lab? You asked me if I thought the cell knew that it was part of a larger organism."

"I remember."

"For some reason, my thoughts turned to Bojing then. What if the cell on the monitor had been a cancer cell? Cancer starts off as a single cell, the result of the same force that drives evolution—mutation. But a cancer cell has no real purpose. Its only function is to reproduce and replicate at any cost. Unlike an ordinary cell, it serves no constructive purpose for the larger organism. In fact, its limitless reproduction usurps resources from the larger organism, eventually killing the organism and itself in the process. What's the point of its existence?" Liz paused and looked at Rachael. "You're a religious person who believes in a creator. What need does a creator have for creating cancer?"

Rachael always found it hard to answer questions about her faith or why, as the proverb went, bad things happened to good people. But as a believer in science, her faith was informed by reason, and she had a specific answer for Liz.

"I've received similar questions over the years. I don't view cancer as God's creation. You're right. It serves no purpose. I view it as a side-effect of the force needed to create life. Life requires reproduction and mutation in order to evolve. It needs these two in order to become a more complex version of itself, but mutation that leads to replication *without* differentiation is detrimental to life. That's the essence of cancer. Seth said something to this effect when we were interviewing him at Berkeley."

"I wish I'd had the opportunity to meet Seth," Liz said wistfully. "He may have been right. At its core, cancer leads to the de-differentiation of an organism. It causes it to become more random, and randomness *is* the petrin definition of death."

"You're right. Maybe someday we'll find a cure for cancer. I'm sure the petrins have already figured that out—probably eons ago. Their genetic engineering methods are too sophisticated to allow for mutations that cause cancer."

Liz regarded Rachael as an enigma, a person well-grounded in science but one who also believed in a creator. She wondered how Rachael regarded Richard's death in the context of her religious views.

"Do you believe that you'll see Richard again in an afterlife?"

"Yes, that's exactly what I believe, but—"

"But what?"

Rachael didn't answer. Something had gnawed at her ever since she'd been on New Eden. Was Richard already in heaven? She had always assumed so from the moment he passed away, but when she had awakened on New Eden, and Joshua told her that she had died, she realized that *she* hadn't gone to heaven. There was simply nothing—no notion of the passage of time. She shared this seeming gap in logic with Liz.

"But you weren't actually dead according to the petrin definition of death," Liz countered. "The information that was you was never lost. You were cryogenically frozen. Maybe you don't go to heaven until your last copy is erased from the universe."

"That's exactly what Joshua said to me in New Eden—that my last copy was still part of the universe."

"It makes sense. If you're tethered to this universe because your information—your life—is still here and there's the possibility of your being revived, then going to an afterlife makes no sense."

"That's what I've come to believe," Rachael said. "It's the only way the concept of an afterlife makes sense to me after what I've been through. But there's a consequence to this belief as it pertains to Richard. Like me, Richard was frozen in a cryo facility after his death."

Liz now better understood Rachael's dilemma. "Oh, I see. You're worried that if Richard is still frozen—if his life is still a part of the universe—then he may be unable to go to heaven."

"Exactly," Rachael said, crying.

"Are you thinking of taking Richard out of the cryo facility and letting him go?"

Rachael sobbed even harder. Liz had gotten to the crux of her conflicted feelings, feelings she had not expressed to anyone, not even Joshua.

"I don't know what to think," Rachael said. "Part of me wants to do exactly that—release his information from the burden of this universe so that he can attain the afterlife—but wouldn't that also be like murder? Would allowing his frozen body to be removed from the cryo facility randomize the information which defined him? Would I be killing him? Knowing what I know now and what I myself have gone through, should I end any chance of *him* being alive again? Should I deprive him of what I *myself* have benefitted from? It's an impossible choice for me."

Liz put her arm around Rachael's shoulder. "It's not something you need to decide now. You told me that when you were in that state, it was like nothing—there was no consciousness or passage of time. Richard's not in any pain, and he's not being tortured. He's just . . . suspended. It seems to me that there's no pressure on you to make such an important decision at this time. But I know you'll make the right choice if it ever comes to that."

Rachael wiped away her tears and composed herself. "I guess you're right. I'll make the choice if and when the time comes." Rachael turned to Liz. "Thanks for talking with me about this. It means so much to me. This is difficult for me to discuss. I haven't even spoken with Josh about it."

"Anything for a friend, but speaking of Joshua, what does he think of your religious views? I know more than one couple that's separated or divorced because of their differing viewpoints about religious beliefs, or the lack thereof."

A smile returned to Rachael's face.

"Actually, he's pretty tolerant about my beliefs. As I've told most of my friends, our mutual respect helps us navigate any differences of opinion."

"You've never argued over religion or the concept of God?"

"Never, although we've had some healthy debates."

"Hmmm. What's *that* like?"

"Well, Josh says that life is possible because it obeys the natural laws of the universe. But who made the laws of chemistry and physics—who made the universe operate according to those laws? And Joshua always says that we make our own luck. Me? I think providence—call it God if you want—has a subtle hand in events. That's my intuition, and Josh is okay with that."

"In other words, he likes you for yourself—for your individuality."

"Yeah, that's as good a way to put it as any. He lets me be who I am. I'm Rachael, and Josh is Josh."

*   *   *

The team was flown in a C-130 cargo transport to Hawaii on the first leg of their journey back to Berkeley. Joshua and Rachael sat in the seats lining the drab green interior of the fuselage as the others dozed off, read, or typed on their laptops. Joshua decided to share with Rachael his latest thoughts on the petrins, those he had harbored after so many men had been lost in the battle against the arachnid. He summarized his thinking that maybe Seth and the petrins had decided that Earth couldn't be trusted to use its emerging technology wisely.

Rachael was caught off guard. "I can't believe you're saying this," she said in a low voice so the others wouldn't be privy to their conversation. "We've always trusted Seth implicitly. We said as much in our briefings before going to North Korea."

"I know," Joshua said, talking just above a whisper, "but the arachnid *is* petrin technology. There's no way around that fact."

"But Rodrigo didn't talk to Seth."

"That doesn't change things. The petrins are a collective, and Rodrigo was talking to their hive mentality, and they gave him the DNA code that enabled the arachnid to grow in the North Korean lab. I just can't understand why. The petrins are too far advanced to unleash technology haphazardly."

"But maybe they thought they were doing it for a good cause, in this case to cure cancer, and messed up somehow."

Joshua shook his head in frustration. "That's my point. They wouldn't have created the arachnid accidentally in an effort cure the Korean dictator's disease. As masters of genetic engineering, they couldn't have inadvertently sent the wrong code. They had to have known what they were doing."

Rachael leaned back against the headrest and closed her eyes as she considered Joshua's words.

"I know what you're saying," she said, "but everything they did three years ago demonstrated the highest regard for life and ethical behavior. I find it hard to believe that they would hurt anyone."

"I do as well, but I have to go by the facts. While they shared much of their culture with humans, they redacted a great deal of information. Who's to say that much of what they withheld was connected to ideas of which civilizations should be allowed to continue and which had to be eliminated?"

"Eliminated? Josh, you're really reaching. You're forgetting the fact that they left us a cure for the virus and saved humanity."

Joshua took a deep breath. "You could be right. In fact, I *hope* you're right. But the petrins have had three years to evaluate our species. We rejected their offer to relocate humanity on New Eden, and because Seth toured the world in android form, he got to see some of us at our worst."

"But he said that humans would be allowed to develop on their own without petrin interference. In essence, he said they would stand aside, just as parents must watch their children make mistakes."

Joshua sat straighter in his seat. "And that's my point exactly. Remember that he said that, in their estimation, humans stood little chance of survival."

"So what? They could just wait for us to destroy ourselves. There would be no need to send an arachnid to accomplish the task."

"What if the petrins have decided they want to use Earth as a node after all, a node to disseminate more primordial cells through the universe? They have a grand scheme to seed life throughout the cosmos, and as Seth said, not all of their cells land on habitable planets. If they decided that we will *definitely* destroy ourselves, maybe they don't want to waste valuable galactic real estate."

Rachael seemed frustrated with Joshua's line of reasoning. "Then they could wait for us to finish ourselves off. What's a few hundred or even a few thousand years on the cosmic timescale? It's the blink of an eye. You're sounding like General Porter."

"Maybe you're right," he conceded. "I'm just unsettled by what I've seen. It's as if there's a missing variable in this equation. I'm telling you, Rachael, that there's something the petrins haven't told us, something that would explain the awful events we've witnessed."

A troubled look crossed Rachael's face as she turned to face Joshua.

"They've no doubt kept a great many things from us in order to adhere to their prime directive of noninterference, but . . .."

"But what?"

"I think you're right. Something in the mountain of redacted information three years ago would almost surely be able to explain the militaristic arachnid in North Korea, one totally different from the ones we rode and flew on New Eden."

Joshua looked at his wife's eyes and squeezed her hand.

"They held something back," he said. "Something very important."

Rachael nodded. She didn't necessarily agree with all of Joshua's reasoning—she didn't believe the petrins would be heartless enough to arbitrarily eradicate Earth to gain a new node so quickly, but when evaluating all known facts of the situation in North Korea, one thing seemed certain: the universe might not be nearly as friendly as they'd assumed after contacting the benign yet advanced race called the petrins.

The aliens were definitely harboring a secret.

Chapter Twenty-Nine
The Black Sphere

Dr. Elizabeth Yang wheeled a metal cart through the corridors of the Bowman Particle Research Center. It had been two weeks since the military had delivered the arachnid to the center for detailed scientific analysis. The creature had been airlifted to the particle center in the dead of night in a large steel-reinforced crate using a heavy-lift helicopter.

Williams and Porter were in Washington D.C. but would be joining the team via video conference. This was to be the second weekly meeting since the arachnid had been delivered to the center. The first meeting had been a disappointment to team members since not much information about the arachnid had been obtained during the first week. The dearth of information was not from a lack of trying, however. The armor of the arachnid had proven extremely difficult to cut through. Regular saws had been unable to penetrate it. Without gaining entrance to the inside of the arachnid, there could be no progress on finding out how it worked, let alone discovering some operational or biological weakness that could be used to eliminate its offspring.

Liz rolled her cart into one of the conference rooms. The scientific team and Langdon were already seated at the table. Porter and Williams' video images were displayed split-screen on an LCD panel on a wall of the room.

"Looks like we're all here," Williams said through the video interface as Liz took a seat at the table. "Dr. Yang, I hope your team has made some progress in your examination of the arachnid. As you know, we view your research as critical to the eradication of the remaining arachnids in Korea."

"Yes," Liz said. "Actually, we *have* made progress this week on researching the creature. I have a few things to show you today."

Liz stood, retrieved a piece of large, dark-grey material from the middle shelf of the cart, and placed it on the table. The object was rectangular in shape and had a slightly curved surface. More than anything, it resembled a shin guard worn by a soccer player, only much bigger. It was an inch thick and measured one-by-one-and-a-half feet.

"This is a piece of the arachnid's exoskeleton. We cut it from one of the legs."

Joshua picked up the object from the table. "It's much lighter than it looks," he remarked as he turned it over in his hands.

"Yes," Liz said. "This piece weighs only seven hundred grams."

"It's hard to think that this can repel artillery shells," Joshua said, handing the object to Vinod.

"What's it made of?" Vinod asked, trying unsuccessfully to bend it. "It's very stiff."

"We've been able to analyze its internal structure," Liz answered. "It's made of about a thousand layers of woven fabric. The layers are oriented in varying degrees of rotation relative to each other and are embedded in some type of extremely tough excreted resin."

"What are the fibers of the fabric made of?" Langdon asked as he handled the object.

"Carbon nanotubules," Liz answered. "They're what's giving this object and the exterior of the arachnid it's dark grey color."

"Woven carbon nanotubules?" Joshua said with surprise. "That's incredible. No wonder you had difficulty cutting through it."

"We finally managed to penetrate it with a plasma cutter," Liz said.

Frustrated, Porter addressed the meeting. "Do one of you scientists want to tell me in English what you're talking about. What are carbon nanotubules?"

Joshua explained the structures to the group. "Carbon nanotubules are made from pure carbon, which has unique properties that allow it to bond with other carbon atoms to form high-strength bonds. Each carbon atom can bond with either three or four other carbon atoms. If it binds with four carbon atoms, it does so in a three-dimensional structure. The result is an extremely rigid crystalline lattice that is one of the hardest substances known. We commonly refer to this material as diamond."

"Diamond?" Williams said. "You mean like in jewelry?"

"Exactly," Joshua replied. "Diamonds are pure carbon in a three-dimensional lattice. The strength of the carbon-to-carbon bonds in diamonds makes them extremely hard. As I said, carbon can also form bonds with just two other carbon atoms. In this configuration, the resulting structure is a flat sheet of carbon only a single atom thick. Imagine a single layer of carbon atoms in a pattern consisting of adjacent hexagons. Each vertex of the hexagon would represent one carbon atom, which is then bonded to three others. The result of this configuration is a substance called graphene."

"I think I've heard of graphene," Vinod replied. "Didn't some guys get the Nobel Prize for making graphene from graphite using scotch tape?"

"Correct," Joshua answered. "Graphite, like in pencil lead, is just stacks of flat sheets of graphene. Those researchers were able to get a single layer of graphene by repeatedly peeling off layers of graphite using scotch tape."

"There's a lot of research being done on graphene," Langdon added. "It's strength and electrical properties are incredible. The research is in its preliminary stages since we haven't been able to artificially produce graphene in any significant quantity."

"That brings us to carbon nanotubules," Joshua continued. "Carbon nanotubules are essentially sheets of graphene rolled into a tube, with the sides attached to each other using carbon-to-carbon bonds to form long threads of a pure carbon structure that is extremely strong and light. Also, graphene and carbon nanotubules are some of the best electrical conductors around. I have no doubt that they have something to do with the arachnid's ability to produce an EMP. If you recall, the pulse started glowing in its legs and then ascended."

"We've been researching carbon nanotubules for some time at NASA," Langdon added. "Because of their extreme tensile strength and light weight, they would make an ideal material for a tether that would run from the surface of the Earth to space. The tether would be used as an elevator for transporting objects into space and would alleviate the need for rockets. The problem is that no one has figured out how to create long segments of nanotubules yet." Langdon turned to Liz. "You say the arachnid can weave these nanotubules into a fabric?"

"Yes. We believe the arachnid has cells that actually excrete carbon nanotubules. These cells shift position slightly as the tubules are excreted, creating a woven fabric, the threads of which are nanotubules. Multiple layers are then stacked at different angles to each other and embedded in a resin matrix."

"It's like rebar and concrete," Joshua replied. "The nanotubules provide the tensile strength, and the resin provides its compressive strength. No wonder our weapons couldn't penetrate it."

Porter was restless. "Not what I want to hear. We need weapons that can kill these bastards. I don't want to hear about how tough it is."

"What about combustion?" Langdon asked. "Carbon nanotubules, just like diamonds, are made of pure carbon, which means they can definitely be oxidized. They can burn."

"Diamonds can burn?" Rachael said. "I didn't know that."

"Yes," Langdon said. "Given a high enough temperature and an oxygen-rich atmosphere, diamonds burn completely into carbon dioxide."

"We tried burning this structure," Liz said. "No go. The resin in which the tubules are embedded is completely fireproof. We still haven't figured out what the resin is made of, but it doesn't burn. In fact, we tried subjecting the resin to various conditions, such as extreme heat and strong acid. Nothing seems to have any effect. Like I said, the only way we were able to cut through it was using a plasma cutter with a very concentrated stream of high energy plasma."

"What else have you found out?" Williams asked. "There's a lot more to this creature than armor. We need to know how it operates."

"Exactly," Porter said. "We need actionable information."

"We had a lot of difficulty getting to the internals of the arachnid even after we successfully cut through the armor. Every time we made a cut in its exterior, flames shot out just as they did when we blew a hole in it with C-4. It's as if its blood spontaneously combusts. We finally drained all the fluid from its circulatory system. What we found was that it has two circulatory systems that are completely independent from each other. There's no centralized pumping system like a human heart for either system. The arachnid seems to use a form of peristalsis to move fluid through its body."

"What is peristalsis?" Porter asked.

"It's how the gut works in humans," Liz explained. "The muscles surrounding our intestines contract intermittently to push food through. The blood vessels in this creature have contracting elements that push fluid forward, so there's no need for a heart."

"I'm sure that's a tactical advantage for the creature," Porter stated. "No single point of weakness that we can target."

Liz retrieved two glass vials containing opaque fluids, along with an empty beaker, from the bottom shelf of the cart and placed them on the table. The fluid in one vial was light blue in color, while the other was orange.

"These vials contain fluids from the two circulatory systems," she said. "The fluids are its blood, so to speak. In the arachnid, they only mix at the capillary level. That means its circulatory system is designed to deliver these fluids directly to the cells of the creature, but separately."

Liz opened the cap on the vial of the blue liquid and poured its contents into the beaker. "Watch what happens when the two fluids mix."

Liz then poured the orange fluid into the beaker. There was an immediate reaction in the beaker, with flames and smoke shooting from the top. Everyone instinctively rolled their chairs back from the table, startled by the reaction.

"What the hell was that?" Vinod asked, wide-eyed.

The flames slowly died down, leaving only wisps of smoke emanating from the beaker.

"The two fluids are hypergolic," Liz explained.

"Hypergolic?" Williams said.

Langdon explained the term. "Hypergolic refers to two fluids that explode or burn as soon as they make contact with each other. NASA is very familiar with hypergolic fluids. We've used them often as fuel for rocket engines. In fact, the rockets that allowed the Apollo astronauts to lift off from the lunar surface and return to the command module used hypergolic propellants. NASA needed a failsafe rocket that would ignite in the vacuum of space. Otherwise, the astronauts would have been stranded on the moon. When the two fluids were pumped into the reaction chamber of the rocket, there was immediate combustion, firing the engine."

"Let me get this straight," Porter said. "You're telling me that this creature internally pumps liquids that explode if they make contact with each other?"

"That's essentially correct," Liz said.

"Problem solved," Porter said confidently. "We just need to find something that can shoot through its armor, and the arachnid will automatically explode from within."

"It's not that simple, general," Liz said. "First, finding something that can reliably penetrate the armor might be difficult, if not impossible. Second, even if a projectile could penetrate the armor, the creature wouldn't explode. Mixing the hypergolic fluids would cause a fire, but it would cauterize the vessels from which they were leaking, essentially sealing them off. A single projectile that could penetrate its armor would damage the arachnid, but it wouldn't kill it."

"But it still seems like a disadvantage for the creature to me," Rachael said. "What's the advantage of having hypergolic fluids for the circulatory system? The risks are obvious."

"The advantage is energy density," Joshua answered. "The more energy you can pack into a smaller space, the more efficient the organism becomes. I believe it's this energy density that allows the creature to move that massive frame so quickly. It can utilize a large amount of energy very quickly if needed. The trade off as any material gets more energy dense is that it gets more explosive, but the arachnid has its seemingly impenetrable armor to protect it against this."

"What have you found out about its internal organs?" Langdon asked.

Liz continued her report. "What's important is what we *haven't* found. There are no discernible respiratory or digestive systems. However, we did find an organ that seems to secrete iron into a specified shape. It's the organ that creates the airfoils. It seems to be able to extract iron from its bloodstream and secrete it into the shape of airfoils. As far as the airfoils themselves are concerned, we found thousands of them in some type of storage organ. Joshua was correct in his analysis that these airfoils are generic in shape. They're not modified to fly a specific path."

"Then how is the creature able to shape these at will when it wants to hit a target?" Vinod asked.

"That's where the tentacles come in," Liz answered. "The airfoils slide through a slot that travels down the length of a tentacle before being shot. It's like the barrel of a rifle. The slot is lined with an abrasive substance, underneath which, is a muscular layer. We believe the creature is dynamically shaping the airfoils as they're being fired."

"Wait," Joshua said. "You mean to tell me that the arachnid is changing the shape of each airfoil while it's traveling through its tentacle? It's rapidly modulating the musculature inside its tentacles to shape the airfoil while it's being fired?"

"That's what we believe based on our current analysis. This is why it's able to fire so many targeted airfoils so rapidly. They're actually programmed, or shaped in this case, while they're in the act of being fired."

"Amazing," Joshua remarked as he thought of the efficiency of the design.

"We also found eight highly-muscular, thick-walled organs connected to each tentacle," Liz stated, continuing her analysis. "We believe that these organs compress air to an extreme pressure, which accounts for the propulsion of the airfoils."

"Are you telling me that this thing can't run out of ammo since it's constantly making more?" Vinod asked.

"I'm not sure. We don't know at what rate the airfoils are produced. Although it's possible that it can make them as fast as it fires them, that would require an enormous supply of iron, which is the main element that makes up the airfoils."

"The arachnid seems to have an unusual relationship with iron," Joshua said. "It seems to obtain it at will."

"Speaking of iron," Liz remarked, "we found some of those iron balls we saw in Korea inside the creature."

"So it must be eating the iron balls to get its iron supply," Rachael speculated.

"That's where things get even stranger," Liz said. "The iron balls were in a portion of the creature that was a long tube, with the balls getting bigger as they approached the end of the tube, which was connected to a small opening at the back of the carapace."

"It sounds like a digestive tract," Langdon said. "Maybe it's collecting the iron balls, whatever their source, from the forest and somehow digesting them."

"That's exactly what we thought too," Liz said. "But when we analyzed the musculature of the tract where the iron balls were located, it was going in the opposite direction. It was built to *push* the iron balls out, not pull them in."

"Are you saying that this thing shits iron?" Vinod asked.

Liz grinned at Vinod's crude interpretation of the process. "That's what we believe from our analysis."

"Where the hell is all this iron coming from?" Joshua asked, frustrated. "It's got so much iron that it becomes a waste product. Makes no sense. It can't just conjure up iron out of thin air. No matter how advanced it is, it has to operate according to the laws of physics."

"We're still analyzing the contents of the hypergolic fluids," Liz said. "There's definitely a high concentration of dissolved iron in one of the fluids, but as to the ultimate source of the iron, we don't know where it comes from. We did, however, find that its central nervous system has a brain located just below the center of the carapace. It's composed of three segments. One is similar to our cerebellum. It's relatively large and seems to be responsible for automated movements and calculations. It's the part that allows the creature to shape and target the airfoils. There's a large amount of neural processing power there. The second segment of its brain is like our cerebrum and is used for higher-level thinking. It's not much larger than the cerebrum of a typical animal on Earth. Therefore, we don't believe the arachnid is capable of higher-level thought. It's simply an animal, albeit a very dangerous one. The final segment is also fairly large, but we haven't figured out what its purpose is. It's not connected by any neural pathways to other parts of its body."

"If it's not intelligent, at least that's a strategic advantage," Porter said, looking for any positive news from the scientific team. "We outthought it once, and we can do so against its offspring if it comes to that. These things may seem invincible, but they're not. We've proven that."

"The next thing I have to report is that we found a dead juvenile arachnid inside the carapace."

"A baby arachnid?" Vinod said, surprised.

"Yes. The arachnid contains eight areas for reproduction—eight wombs, so to speak. One contained the juvenile, and the other seven were empty. I'm sure that's where the ones that escaped came from. The one we found, which was close to the area of formaldehyde injection, was killed by the chemical. I doubt that the ones that escaped were affected."

"So obviously the arachnid can reproduce," Langdon observed.

"I'm not sure I'd call it reproduction," Liz said. "We're running preliminary studies on the juvenile, but I have a feeling that it has the exact same DNA sequence as the adult. It's just a hunch, but I think the juvenile is a clone."

"Goddamn thing can clone itself?" Porter said. "More bad news."

"You said earlier that the arachnid had no respiratory or digestive systems that you could find," Rachael said. "Then what does it eat? Where does it get its energy? All living creatures on Earth either consume or absorb energy."

"Another mystery," Liz said. "We don't know, but it may have something to do with an object just we discovered last night. It's the final object I have to show you—and the strangest yet."

Liz lifted a cloth covering the top of the cart. Beneath it was a spherical black object slightly larger than a golf ball. The rest of the group got up and gathered around the cart.

"What is it?" Joshua asked.

"I was hoping *you* could tell *me*," Liz said. "We have no idea what it is. We found thirty-two of these spheres just beneath the carapace near its gill-like openings. They were suspended by thin cables made from carbon nanotubes. We don't think they're cellular, and we couldn't cut them using any method. Even the plasma cutter couldn't scratch the surface of these objects."

Joshua leaned close to what seemed to be a perfect black sphere except that it had small holes along its surface. "What are the holes for?"

"Unknown," Liz answered. "We scanned the contours of the sphere with a laser scanner and discovered that the holes are conical in shape and meet at a single point at the center of the sphere. There are sixty-four holes, all evenly spaced."

"Can I touch it?" Vinod asked.

"Yes."

Vinod ran his fingers over the surface of the sphere. "It's warm," he said. "Almost hot."

"We noticed that too," Liz said.

"Heat?" Joshua asked surprised. "Has it cooled at all since you first measured its temperature?" Joshua asked.

"No. Its temperature has been a constant forty degrees Celsius."

"How can that be?" Joshua asked. "For it to be giving off heat, it must also be giving off energy. Unless it has a constant energy supply, it has to cool." Joshua thought of other materials that gave off large amounts of heat over extended periods of time. "Is it radioactive?"

"Nope. No radioactivity at all."

"Damn strange," Joshua said, his hand on his chin.

"Can I pick it up?" Vinod asked.

"Go ahead," Liz replied with a curious grin.

Vinod grasped the object with his right hand and tried to lift it, but the object didn't budge. "I can't." Vinod peered under the shelf. "Is it magnetic?"

"No, not magnetic."

"There has to be *some* force acting on it," Vinod said after unsuccessfully trying to lift the sphere a second time.

"Oh, there's a force acting on it alright," Liz said, "but it's not magnetism. It's gravity."

"Gravity?" Vinod asked puzzled, peering closely at the golf-ball sized sphere.

"The object is really heavy. About forty pounds. Try lifting it with two hands, but be careful. Don't let your fingers get trapped under it or drop it. It might crack the floor."

Vinod grabbed the object with both hands. Straining, he lifted it a few inches before slowly returning it to the cart. "Goddamn thing is heavy!"

Joshua stared in amazement at the object. "For the sphere to weigh forty pounds, it must be incredibly dense."

"Absolutely correct," Liz said. "That object and the other spheres we found in the arachnid are by far the densest objects we've ever measured. In fact, they're almost seventeen times denser than the densest element on Earth—osmium."

"How could it be that dense?" Rachael asked. "Isn't that physically impossible?"

"No, not impossible," Joshua said, stroking his chin. "Atoms on Earth are mostly empty space. The nucleus and electrons take up just a small fraction of the total volume of an atom, but this space can be compressed.

The cores of stars are highly dense because extreme gravity and pressure causes atoms to become compressed and therefore much denser, even denser than this object. But for the sphere to hold this density on the surface of the Earth requires a continuous flow of energy. Energy must be expended in order to keep the atoms in this sphere so tightly packed."

"It gets even more bizarre," Liz said. "We analyzed its density distribution this morning. It gets denser as you go deeper into the sphere. In fact, ninety percent of its mass is contained in the central ten percent of its volume."

"Remarkable," Joshua said under his breath.

"I think I've done as much as a biologist can do with this sphere," Liz said. "Joshua, I was hoping you and your team of physicists could analyze it further. This is well outside the realm of biology."

"Absolutely," Joshua responded with excitement. "I'll get started on it right away."

"Josh," Vinod said, "I'd like to watch you test the sphere."

"Me too," Rachael said.

"Sure," Joshua said. "The more minds working on this, the better. We have to figure out how it works and what its purpose is."

Chapter Thirty
Star Child

Rachael and Vinod entered one of the physics laboratories of the research center the next morning. Joshua was already there and had spent the remainder of the previous day and most of the night helping technicians set up the equipment needed for running experiments on the enigmatic black sphere.

"You ready to get started, doc?" Vinod asked. "You ready to solve the mysteries of the universe?"

"Almost," Joshua replied as he adjusted a setting on one of the instruments. "I'm doing some final calibrations on the equipment."

The black sphere was located in a large glass chamber on top of a table with a thick surface. The chamber was a cylinder two feet in diameter and had a dome-shaped top into which multiple tubes and wires entered. The chamber rested on a flat bottom, the composition of which Rachael and Vinod couldn't identify. Around the glass chamber were numerous laboratory instruments that would be used to measure various properties of the sphere as well as the atmosphere inside the chamber.

"Man, you've got a shit ton of equipment here," Vinod remarked. "Looks like Dr. Frankenstein's laboratory."

"I want to measure as many properties as I can," Joshua said. "The instruments measure multiple properties of the sphere simultaneously including temperature, mass, volume, and radioactivity. Those are recorded on that computer terminal." Joshua pointed to a terminal on a desk to the left of the setup. "Vinod, I'd like you to sit there and report any changes on the sphere."

"Yes, sir," Vinod responded with his now-signature fake salute.

Joshua pointed to a second computer terminal on the opposite side of the room.

"That terminal records the atmospheric conditions inside the test chamber—everything from pressure and temperature to the composition of the molecules that're in the atmosphere in the chamber. Some readings are measured continuously, like temperature and pressure, but others, such as the composition of the atmosphere, take time to run, so we'll make those measurements as needed. Rachael, I'd like you to sit there and monitor those readings."

"Yes, sir," Rachael responded with a grin, mimicking Vinod's earlier gesture.

Joshua continued his explanation of how the experiment would work. "I'll handle the equipment that manipulates the various conditions in the chamber. We're going to subject the sphere to different atmospheric changes and see what responses we get."

He continued setting up the laboratory equipment, his hands moving carefully and with precision.

"There," he finally said, hands on his hips as he took one last glance at the plethora of instruments. "I think I'm ready to start. Vinod? Rachael?"

"Ready," they said simultaneously.

A computer terminal that would be used to control the test chamber was located between the other two. Using this terminal, Joshua could manipulate the atmosphere and other physical conditions in the chamber.

"Let's get started," he said, taking a seat in front of the terminal. "Everyone please announce your baseline values."

Vinod went first and relayed the measurements from the sphere. "Temperature 40.12 degrees Celsius, volume 48.07 cubic centimeters, mass 18,522 grams, and no radioactivity."

Rachael relayed the readings on her terminal. "Pressure in the chamber is 754 millimeters of mercury, with a temperature of 25.2 degrees Celsius."

"Rachael, run an atmospheric composition check of the air in the chamber," Joshua instructed. "I want a baseline for that as well."

Rachael entered the command on her terminal. The check would take a minute to complete and would sample the air in the chamber and display its composition.

After a minute, Rachael announced, "Check complete. Composition is nitrogen 78.08 percent, oxygen 20.95 percent, argon 0.93 percent, carbon dioxide 0.04 percent, and humidity 19 percent."

"Good," Joshua said. "That's the typical composition of the atmosphere on Earth. There are no contaminants. Now that we have baseline values, let's start by increasing the temperature in the chamber." Joshua typed a command into his terminal.

"Atmospheric temperature rising," Rachael announced after a few seconds. "Now reading 29.2 degrees Celsius. Pressure is also rising. Now at 770 millimeters of mercury."

"It's expected that the pressure in the sealed test chamber will rise with the temperature," Joshua said. "That's related to Boyles law. As the temperature of a gas is increased in a closed space, the pressure has to increase. What about the sphere, Vinod?"

"The sphere's temperature is also rising. Now passing 42.8 degrees Celsius." Vinod paused and looked at his screen with a shocked expression. "The volume of the sphere is shrinking! Volume is now reading 47.98 cubic centimeters."

"Are you sure?" Joshua asked, surprised.

"Yes," Vinod replied defensively. "I know how to read numbers from a terminal. The sphere is definitely shrinking in size."

Joshua and Rachael looked at the sphere, which didn't appear different, but they knew that such a small change in size would be imperceptible to the human eye. Only the highly-calibrated laser measuring instruments in the lab could pick up such a small variation.

"What about the mass?" Joshua asked.

"Mass is stable," Vinod replied. "Unchanged from its original value."

"Incredible," Joshua commented. "The sphere is smaller in volume, but the mass has remained constant. That means it's actually getting *denser* than it was."

Joshua scratched his chin, thinking about what could make the sphere denser. The atoms in the sphere had to be getting closer together, but to Joshua this meant that it had to be expending more energy. But what was the source of this energy?

"I'm going to reduce the temperature back to baseline to see what happens."

Joshua typed the commands into his terminal. The temperature in the chamber immediately started to drop, and the team recorded the changes associated with the reduction in temperature: the sphere cooled, and its density dropped. All of the values returned to their baseline readings.

"Damn strange object," Joshua muttered, looking at the results as he contemplated his next change. "I'm going to evacuate the air from the chamber. Let's see what the sphere does in a vacuum."

Joshua typed commands on his terminal activating a vacuum pump that whirred to life and started sucking air from the chamber.

"My God, it's getting larger!" Rachael cried, looking directly at the sphere. "*Much* larger."

Joshua, Vinod, and Rachael stared wide-eyed at the expanding sphere. Its color remained unchanged, however, as Vinod glanced at the readouts on his terminal.

"The volume's really increasing now," Vinod said. "Shit, it's going to break through that glass if it gets much larger."

"Almost a complete vacuum now," Rachael said, checking her screen. "The pressure is reading 4 millimeters of mercury."

A few seconds later, the chamber was a complete vacuum, and the expansion of the sphere stopped well before it contacted the glass walls.

"The sphere's volume is huge now," Vinod said. "It's about seventeen times larger than it was before. It's also much cooler—slightly lower than room temperature. Its mass, though, is exactly the same."

Joshua was unsure as to what could be causing such drastic changes in the sphere's density. Its mass hadn't changed, but its volume, and therefore its density, had changed radically depending on the atmosphere in the chamber.

"Josh," Rachael said, "there are many materials that expand with less pressure. Think of a sealed plastic water bottle on an airplane. As the plane climbs in altitude and the pressure drops, the bottle becomes bigger. Shouldn't we have expected this?"

"Expansion due to lower pressure usually happens with gases, not solids." Joshua leaned back in his chair and stared at the ceiling. "Some objects expand with less pressure, but I don't think that's the reason *this* sphere is expanding. Remember what I said yesterday. In order for the sphere to be as dense as it is, it must be using energy to hold its atoms close together. I still think this phenomenon of density change has something to do with energy. If the sphere can't produce energy, then it can't hold its atoms close to each other, so it expands. Somehow, removing all of the air in the chamber caused it to lose its energy source. There must be something in the atmosphere that the sphere is using to create energy."

"Yeah, that makes sense," Vinod said. "But what could it be? The atmosphere is made up of nitrogen, oxygen, argon, carbon dioxide, and water vapor. How could it create energy from that?"

"I don't know," Joshua replied, deep in thought. "But it must be doing it. That's the only thing that makes sense. Its density is now the density of any ordinary metal on Earth, which means that there's no force on the atomic nuclei to pull them closer—no force making the sphere dense. They've reverted to their normal state. The sphere *had* to have been using energy to contract the spacing between its atoms while in its denser state. I can see no other explanation."

The room was silent as Joshua lifted his right index finger.

"I have an idea," he said. "Let's fill the chamber with helium to atmospheric pressure and see what happens." Joshua turned back to his terminal and quickly typed the appropriate commands, causing the chamber to begin filling with helium.

"Pressure rising," Rachael announced. "Now reading 130 millimeters of mercury."

"What are you thinking?" Vinod asked. "Why helium?"

"Helium is a noble gas," Joshua answered. "It's highly inert. Its electron shells are full, so it doesn't chemically react with anything. I want to see what the sphere does in an inert atmosphere."

As the chamber filled with helium, the sphere started shrinking.

"It's also getting hotter," Vinod noted glancing at his terminal.

"Pressure is at atmospheric," Rachael said. "Now reading 754 millimeters of mercury."

"What's happening with the sphere?" Joshua asked.

"It's almost back to its baseline volume and temperature," Vinod replied, "but not quite. It's slightly larger and cooler than baseline."

Joshua got up and studied the readouts from Vinod's terminal.

"Unbelievable," he muttered. "The sphere must somehow be obtaining energy from pure helium. Otherwise it wouldn't have been able to get denser and hotter from when it was in a vacuum."

"Josh, how is that possible?" Rachael asked. "How can it get energy from helium when helium doesn't react with anything else?"

Joshua sat and stared at the ceiling again, hands laced behind his head. *How can something obtain energy from a completely inert substance like helium? How can a creature obtain large amounts of iron when there are no natural sources of iron?* The arachnid was an enigma, but the answer lay with the sphere. His mind sifted through years of learning—through years of experience in physics and science. There *had* to be an answer, one that aligned with the laws of physics. *Iron and energy, how are they related?* An idea formed in Joshua's mind, one he almost dismissed because it was so radical. Joshua snapped his head down and stared straight at the sphere. *Could it be true? Was it crazy? Was this what was actually happening inside the sphere?*

"Rachael," Joshua said excitedly, "run the diagnostic test on the atmosphere in the chamber. I want to see what the composition of the air is."

"Why?" Rachael asked as she started the test. "Shouldn't it be 100 percent helium? That's what you filled it with. What're you looking for?"

213

Joshua got up and stood behind Rachael. "I have an idea—a crazy idea, but it could explain everything."

Rachael awaited the results of the analysis as she stared at her terminal. "It says it will take another forty-five seconds," she said. She turned to Joshua and repeated her previous question, "Josh, what are you looking for?"

"Yeah," Vinod said. "I'd kinda like to know myself. You're pushing the envelope on the mad scientist routine. What gives?"

Joshua was silent. He walked away from Rachael, pacing with his arms folded; his mind reeled with the ramifications of his epiphany. He remembered what Seth had said about the nature of life and how it was pure information. He now knew how this statement could be related to what was happening in the sphere recovered from a creature not of this world.

"I'll explain . . . after you give me the results," Joshua replied, his voice tremulous.

"Josh, you're frightening me," Rachael said.

"I'm okay," Joshua responded trying to remain calm. "Just give me the results when they're ready."

Vinod got up from his seat and walked over to Rachael's terminal to view the results. He knew that the usually stoic Dr. Joshua Andrews was not one for theatrics. Whatever he was thinking, the implications were obviously huge.

The test finished, and Rachael read the results. "The atmosphere in the chamber is 99.99 percent helium, but there *is* a trace amount of another element."

Joshua stopped pacing, his pulse quickening, his back turned to the others. "Is it carbon?"

"Yes!" Rachael gasped. "How'd you know?"

Joshua dropped to his knees, overcome with emotion. "My God . . .."

Rachael raced to his side. "Josh, what's the matter?"

Joshua stood up and slowly walked to the chair in front of his terminal and slumped, his knees weak. His mind raced with the implication of the new findings. It took him some time to get his bearings and pull himself back into reality. He saw the faces of Rachael and Vinod looking down at him.

"What is it Josh?" Rachael asked with growing concern. "What's going on?"

Joshua finally managed to get some words out . . . .. "It's a star. . . .. The sphere's a miniature star!"

Chapter Thirty-One
The Atomic Organizer

"What do you mean it's a star?" Vinod asked. "It's not a ball of glowing gas out in space."

"Why don't you two grab a seat," Joshua said. The young scientist clasped his hands as he took deep breaths.

Rachael and Vinod dragged their chairs closer and sat facing Joshua, who was pale, perspiration beading on his forehead. Joshua grabbed a bottle of water from his desk, took a swig, and composed himself.

"We've been wondering for quite some time what the energy source for the arachnid is. We've also been wondering how it was able to obtain iron when there was no source of iron in the North Korean forest. I remember Liz saying something while we were in Korea—that it can't just make iron out of thin air. Well, that's exactly what the arachnid's doing. It's making iron out of thin air."

Vinod was shocked. "How? That would violate the laws of physics."

"Remember when we speculated that the arachnid's energy source might be nuclear?" Joshua said.

"Yes," Rachael replied, "but we discounted that since we measured no radiation in the area."

"There's no radiation, but its energy source *is* nuclear," Joshua stated. "But it's not nuclear *fission*, like in a reactor. It's nuclear *fusion*, like in stars."

Vinod and Rachael stared at Joshua, trying to understand what he was getting at.

"Nuclear fusion?" Rachael asked incredulously. "Are you sure?"

"It's the only thing that would explain the readings," Joshua replied. "It explains everything."

"In what way?" Vinod asked.

Joshua explained his reasoning after taking another sip of water.

"You both know that the sun and other stars like it fuse hydrogen into helium, releasing vast amounts of energy. But billions of years in the future, the sun will run out of hydrogen. At that point, the core of the sun will get denser and hotter as it succumbs to gravitational pressure. As its core gets hotter, the sun will start fusing atoms of helium together. The usual product of helium fusion, which fuses three helium nuclei together into a single nucleus, is carbon. Just as with hydrogen fusion, helium fusion releases a large amount of energy, but not quite as much as hydrogen fusion. In stars more massive than the sun, when the helium runs out, the core of the star will get even hotter and denser. The fusion process in the core progresses to form larger and larger elements. The fusion of larger and larger nuclei releases less and less energy. But elements can still fuse and release *some* energy all the way up the periodic table until you get to iron. According to the laws of physics, you can't fuse beyond iron and get energy. Iron is the final product. It's the nuclear ash of stellar fusion.

"I believe this sphere is a nuclear fusion device. It fuses elements smaller than iron into larger ones creating energy. It uses some of this energy to maintain its density by pulling the nuclei of its matter closer together. Maybe this density is what enables the sphere to enact nuclear fusion. This use of energy, because it's not a completely efficient process, releases heat. That's why the sphere is warmer than room temperature. The more energy it's able to generate, the denser and hotter it gets. When it was in a vacuum and had no fuel to work with, its density and temperature were that of any ordinary metal in a vacuum. But when it has fuel—when there are elements smaller than iron—it fuses them to create energy and elements with larger nuclei. That's why the arachnid is dumping the excess iron in the form of those balls we found in Korea. Iron is the ultimate waste product of nuclear fusion."

Vinod and Rachael contemplated the revolutionary concept Joshua had proposed. Nuclear fusion from a sphere the size of a golf ball? How advanced was the technology used by the arachnid?

"That's incredible," Vinod murmured. "Nuclear fusion outside of a star. It's hard to believe Josh, but if it's true, it definitely explains a lot."

"Yes," Joshua said. "It answers all of the questions we had about the arachnid. It explains its power source and how it grows without taking in nutrition."

"What do you think the arachnid was using in the atmosphere for fusion?" Rachael asked.

"I don't really know," Joshua answered. "If it could fuse any atom smaller than iron, it could use almost anything. All of the elements that make up the atmosphere are smaller than iron but remember that there's plenty of hydrogen in Earth's atmosphere. Hydrogen is bound to oxygen in the form of water molecules. There's water vapor in the atmosphere. The arachnid could use a simple process like electrolysis to split water molecules and obtain pure hydrogen. It could then fuse the hydrogen into helium to get vast amounts of energy."

Joshua's explanation had focused his mind, and he was now calm. He stood and paced, his eyes looking at the floor as his mind continued to process his revelation. He spoke each word deliberately, knowing that what he was proposing would have been regarded as fringe science at best, but he was convinced that he was correct. In fact, the corollary of what he proposed was even more astounding.

"Just think about it, Rachael. The arachnid can start out with pure hydrogen and use nuclear fusion to create heavier elements like carbon, nitrogen, and oxygen. These elements are the building blocks of life. It can then use these elements to create complex molecules like amino acids and proteins. The arachnid can not only create iron out of thin air—it can actually create *life*! The only thing it needs is information. That information would be the pattern in which to arrange molecules to create any organism it chooses."

Vinod understood the implications of Joshua's words. "Information is—"

"Everything," Joshua said. "Remember Seth's entire definition of life? He said life is the specific arrangement of molecules for a defined purpose. Life is just information at its most basic level. The petrins, or whoever created this arachnid, have discovered how to create life from nothing but protons, neutrons, and electrons. It's that elementary. They've figured out how to manipulate atoms at the nuclear level to first create the atoms they need and then to use them to create complex molecules, which are then arranged in a specific order to create life."

Rachael's mind reeled at the thought. "Life from nothing but information and hydrogen. It reminds me of something you said on New Eden. 'Such a vast universe with incredible energy and matter, but the only thing that counts is how that matter and energy are arranged.' This goes way beyond anything our scientists have ever thought of. In fact, it seems to be beyond the realm of science fiction."

"But it *is* science, not science fiction," Joshua replied. "Nothing I told you violates any laws of physics, and I know of a way to test my theory."

Joshua sat back in front of his terminal and started typing, fingers playing over the keys at incredible speed.

"What are you going to do?" Vinod asked.

"I'm evacuating the chamber," Joshua replied. "I'm going to expose the sphere to a complete vacuum again."

The pump sprang to life, and the chamber soon became a complete vacuum. Vinod noted on his terminal that the sphere became larger and cooler, having the density of any ordinary metal on Earth.

"It's what you expected, right?" Vinod said.

"Yes," Joshua replied as he entered a new command on his terminal. "I'm now filling the chamber with xenon gas to atmospheric pressure. Xenon is also a noble gas, but with atomic number fifty-four, which is larger than iron's atomic number of twenty-six. You can't fuse xenon nuclei and get energy."

"The pressure in the chamber is atmospheric," Rachael said moments later.

They all noted that the sphere was at a normal density, size, and temperature as any ordinary metal. It hadn't changed from the values it had in a vacuum.

"So this proves that the sphere can't obtain energy from xenon," Rachael noted. "You were right. The sphere *is* a miniature nuclear fusion device."

Vinod reflected further on the discovery. "I understand now what happened. The Koreans captured a primordial spookyon that was used to transmit the DNA—the information for the arachnid. They used the DNA sequence to start growing an arachnid, which escaped and grew into an adult." Vinod paused. "Then that means that this sphere was actually manufactured by the arachnid. It had to have been according to this scenario."

"Yes," Joshua said. "That's the only way this could work."

"A biological process that can create a fusion device," Rachael said with astonishment. "But the reverse is true as well. A fusion device can initiate a biological process. Josh, we marveled at how the petrins were able to create an entire ecosystem on New Eden using only DNA, but this is next-level science. They can manipulate atoms—even the nuclei of atoms—using just information."

"Yes," Joshua said, reflective. "It's elegant in its simplicity."

He remembered the time many years ago on the stage of Wheeler auditorium at Berkeley when he was a PhD student. He thought of the presentation about spookyons and how he and Henry Bowman had manipulated the Mars rover in real time using entangled spookyons. And he vividly recalled kneeling over the face of his mentor, Dr. Henry Bowman, in his final moments of life at the end of the presentation. The last words Henry had uttered to Joshua before his death seemed even more profound now: *Everything is information.*

*　　　*　　　*

Rachael was awed by what Joshua had discovered, but she also assumed that what her husband had learned had been known and practiced by the petrins for millions of years. But had Seth hinted at Joshua's discovery three years earlier? Granted, much had been redacted in their interviews with the alien, but had Seth dropped even the slightest clue about the ability to harness nuclear fusion at a smaller scale? She knew Joshua was correct in his assertions, but she was determined to verify the astonishing claims he had made by looking through the archived transcripts conducted in the bat cave in the months following first contact. She needed to refresh her mind as to what Seth had told the team and, perhaps more importantly, what he had *not* told them. Her journalistic instincts were still strong—to research and track down facts—and she was determined to find out if Seth had dropped even the smallest clue about energy production from atmospheric atoms using nuclear fusion.

Rachael took the elevator to the basement level of the complex. The particle center was heavily guarded since the arachnid was stored there, and uniformed Marine guards stood at the entrances and exits of all corridors on each floor. Rachael, however, had clearance to go anywhere in the expansive facility, and she merely showed her ID badge as she walked past various checkpoints within the building.

The basement used to archive research was only protected by a single private security guard, and she smiled and walked past him into a room with numerous shelves filled with thousands of boxes of files. From memory, Rachael knew that the transcripts of interviews with Seth were kept in a separate room at the end of the archives. She placed her right thumb on a sensor and was given access to the room. She walked in and looked at several dozen more shelves holding transcripts, as well as audio and video, of the famous sessions with Seth. All sessions, of course, were also stored in digital form on servers in the facility's computer network, but those files were encrypted. The same files were also on servers at the NSA and the Pentagon. Accessing them anywhere would alert anyone at the other locations that someone was reviewing the sessions, and she'd decided that she'd rather not have to explain why she wanted to look at the files. Joshua would tell the government soon enough what he had learned, but she was looking for clues that would enlighten her about the possible utilization of fusion as the petrins pursued their ambitious and longstanding plan to seed the universe with cells. That was a different area of investigation altogether, one that might be related to what she and Joshua had discussed on the C-130 while en route to California. Just how eager were the petrins to spread their nodes across the universe? Was Joshua correct that the aliens might terminate species that were on the brink of exterminating themselves despite their otherwise benevolent intentions? The arachnid in Korea was hostile, but it was definitely petrin technology, and Joshua was correct: the petrins were hiding something—or perhaps some other species was capitalizing on petrin science. Whatever that "something" was might possibly be related to the capabilities of the black sphere. Exactly how far did petrin technology extend? Joshua's discovery about the nature of the sphere painted the petrins or their equivalents as nothing less than alchemists, creatures who could make something from nothing or transmute one element into another. If they could manufacture energy at will, for what purpose was that energy used? In North Korea, it had decimated the government's troop deployments. Perhaps the biggest question was why Rodrigo had been denied access to Seth, who had been assigned as ambassador to Earth.

Fortunately, the importance of the material gleaned from interviews with Seth had been deemed important enough to warrant redundant storage, with multiple copies of all sessions stored in different formats and at different locations.

Rachael ran her index finger across labels on stacks of brown cartons as she silently read dates and session numbers. Below the dates were further tags indicating what had been discussed in the various sessions, such as NUMBER OF ALIEN SPECIES, PETRIN MORALS AND ETHICS, PETRIN TECHNOLOGY, NATURE OF THE COLLECTIVE, NONINTERFERENCE, and many more. Rachael decided to narrow her search to cartons dealing with petrin technology. Straight ahead were cartons representing sessions 109-118, and their labels indicated that some of the discussions with Seth had revolved around petrin energy production.

Rachael removed four cartons from the gray metal shelves and stacked them by a table in the far-right corner of the room. For the next hour, she sat and sifted through the transcripts, each bringing back memories of the exhilaration the team had felt as they collected data from an alien species for the first time in human history.

It was a section of session 112 that caught her attention. Seth had been articulate and had moved, with some exceptions, beyond the vernacular of the urban dictionary he'd accessed from Vinod's algorithm, but he had also been more evasive than usual. Rachael carefully read the exchange the team had had with Seth that day.

*   *   *

Joshua: So Seth, are there any limits to what petrins can do technologically? You are, after all, billions of years more advanced than humans.

Seth: Limits? Yes, of course we have limits. We don't pretend to be what you call God or gods.

Vinod: What kind of limits?

Seth: We, just like you, are limited by the natural laws. Those we cannot alter.

Joshua: Let me come at this differently, Seth. Are petrins continuing to evolve?

Seth: Yes. I think your own scientists can see the process of evolution taking place across the universe. For example, you now know how solar systems form from accretion discs of dust caused by supernovas. That's evolution. And your biologists can see that life is always becoming more complex and evolving into higher life forms.

Rachael: How far can we evolve as a species?

Seth: That's redacted.

Joshua: What about petrins? You're continuing to evolve, so how far can *you* go?

Seth: That's also redacted.

Vinod: But you said you have limits? Are you implying that one day you might *not* have limits because you'll continue evolving into ever more complex beings?

Seth: I'm not trying to imply *anything*. I simply can't answer your question in a way that you could understand.

Joshua: What about your technology? Can that evolve indefinitely?

Seth: Good question, but I'm afraid the answer is redacted.

Vinod: But technology, like life, is a matter of information. *Everything* is information. Is there a limit to the information that can be discovered and used technologically?

Seth: I think I just answered that. You simply changed the terminology of the question.

Joshua: Alright, Seth. I get it. The answers to those questions might influence how we conduct our research and what goals we might pursue. Correct?

Seth: Correct. There are some answers that humans will have to discover on their own.

Joshua: Got it, so let me ask something more rudimentary. You passed through a nuclear age—survived what humanity is struggling through now. Right?

Seth: I think that's self-evident.

Joshua: And you harnessed energy that wouldn't destroy or pollute your planet, right?

Seth: Obviously.

Joshua: For us, that seems to be nuclear fusion, which we can't even begin to accomplish on a massive scale, but which would solve the energy requirements for our entire planet.

Seth: What's your question?

Vinod: He's trying to ask if petrins use nuclear fusion.

Seth: Yes, we do. You know about fusion, so that's a question I can safely answer.

Joshua: How far advanced is Petri in using fusion?

Seth: That, I'm afraid, is redacted.

Joshua: Okay, forget about how advanced you are in fusion technology. What are its applications?

Seth: As you know, one application is to produce energy.

Rachael: But on what scale?

THREE MINUTE PAUSE BEFORE REPLY.

Seth: Redacted.

Vinod: Come on, dude. Just tell us how much energy can be produced.

Seth: Your own scientists can crunch the numbers, bro.

Vinod: Yeah, but what are its practical applications? Fusion produces energy, but energy can be used in a gazillion ways. You said energy production was *one* of its applications. That means there are others.

ONE MINUTE PAUSE BEFORE REPLY.

Seth: Redacted.

Vinod: So you're really telling us that petrins can do some heavy-duty shit with fusion.

Seth: Still redacted, bro.

Joshua: Is fusion somehow related to the evolution of life into greater and greater complexity?

Seth: Redacted, Josh.

Vinod: Is fusion the ultimate source of energy in the universe?

Seth: Redacted.

Rachael: Humans currently believe that fusion, if used on a massive scale, might bring peace to the Earth. There would be no more fighting for energy sources. It would be virtually free and abundant. But can it be misused?

Seth: All technology can be misused. I think the history of your planet unfortunately demonstrates your point. Fusion, for example, is the second phase in the detonation of what you call your hydrogen bomb.

Rachael: True, but I'm specifically asking what kind of danger fusion might pose, if any, discounting the hydrogen bomb.

Seth: That's redacted. You're really asking me about applications again.

Joshua: You're tipping your hand, Seth. It sounds like some applications might be good, while others might be bad.

Seth: Any power source can be used for either good or bad. That seems obvious.

Joshua: You said petrins are still evolving. Did you mean technologically or biologically—as a species. I'm simply asking you to qualify your answer.

Seth: Life and technology are both a matter of information, so you're making an arbitrary distinction.

Joshua: I'm not referring to biological information. I'm talking about technology as humans use the term.

Seth: I understand.

Joshua: So is petrin technology still evolving?

Seth: The entire universe is evolving, Josh. Everything is information constantly seeking greater complexity.

Joshua: That means your fusion technology is still evolving.

ONE MINUTE PAUSE BEFORE REPLY.

Seth: Yes.

Vinod: But in what way?

Seth: Redacted.

Vinod: Is fusion the key to unlocking other technologies or applications?

Seth: Also redacted.

Vinod: That's as good as a yes.

Seth: I would have to disagree. You're still asking about applications, and we can't share advanced technologies with you.

Joshua: Seth, fission is splitting the atom. Fusion, on the other hand, combines atoms and releases energy in the process. You've often spoken about life—information, if you will—combining to achieve greater complexity. This idea of combination . . . well, I'm wondering if fusion, since it combines elements, is an integral part to how petrins see the universe evolving.

Seth: Redacted.

Joshua: Fusion occurs within stars as they collapse, correct?

Seth: Of course.

Joshua: It's how heavier elements are created and then released in supernovas.

Seth: Your scientists are certainly aware of this.

Joshua: Are petrins able to replicate this process artificially? Perhaps using sophisticated fusion reactors that we can't imagine?

FOUR MINUTE PAUSE BEFORE REPLY.

Seth: We have created fusion reactors, but I can't tell you any details about them. I can appreciate your curiosity about such matters, but so many of your questions today are seeking specific answers that would compromise our basic directive not to divulge information that you must learn for yourself.

Joshua: You can't blame a guy for trying.

Seth: No, and I appreciate the insatiable curiosity of your species.

*   *   *

Rachael had found what she was looking for. Seth had not spoken directly of any kind of black sphere or making molecules and elements from atmospheric gases, but he had been especially evasive about fusion technology. While it was understandable that petrins wouldn't divulge any advanced applications of their technology, he had never been more reticent than when questioned about fusion. But certain exchanges stood out in her mind. He wouldn't answer whether or not fusion was the ultimate source of energy in the universe. He admitted that fusion technology was still evolving inasmuch as all petrin technology in its broadest sense was always evolving. More importantly, he wouldn't answer *how* it was evolving—that response was expected—but he did say certain types of fusion applications might be harmful or pose a danger to an advanced civilization. And Seth had paused to confer with the collective far more than usual, and in a short space of time. In retrospect, it was obvious to Rachael that the team had touched a nerve when they started talking about fusion and energy production. In Joshua's words, Seth had in all likelihood tipped his hand.

Perhaps the most meaningful redaction, however, was when he refused to answer Vinod's question as to whether fusion was the key to unlocking all other technologies. In light of Joshua's discovery about the black sphere—that it acted as a miniature star that had the power to create life itself—Rachael suspected that the answer to Vinod's question was a resounding "yes."

And then there was Joshua's question: *Are petrins able to replicate this process artificially? Perhaps using sophisticated fusion reactors that we can't imagine?* Without knowing it, Joshua had alluded to the kind of technology they'd been studying in the lab. Whether or not Seth knew about the black sphere, he had delayed in answering the question, and there were many possibilities for the delay. Maybe the petrins possessed the technology or were pursuing it. Then again, perhaps another highly evolved civilization—another child of the petrin seeding process—had developed such technology. Whatever the case, Joshua's question had been on the mark without his knowing it.

Rachael removed her cell phone from her jeans pocket and snapped pictures of the transcripts. She would show them to Joshua and ask his opinion to see if he reached the same conclusions as she had. She didn't feel she was being paranoid. Indeed, the journalist in her knew that she had come across meaningful information. If Joshua agreed, he would know how to proceed—how and when to share the insights provided by the transcripts with the government.

*   *   *

Rachael found Joshua in his office as he combed through reams of data on his desk.

"Got a minute?" she asked.

"For you, always."

Rachael entered, closed the door, and sat.

"What's up?" Joshua asked. "You look worried."

"Is it that obvious?" she asked, handing Joshua her phone. "I went into the archives in the basement and took some pics of the transcripts of our sessions with Seth, but I'll give you the short version of what I found."

Joshua leaned forward, curious as to why Rachael had come to his office.

For the next ten minutes, Rachael shared what she had read in the basement.

"I think Seth was hiding something about petrin developments in

225

nuclear fusion," she said. "Tell me if you think I'm reading too much into our conversation back then, but Seth seemed particularly evasive on the topic. It might explain a lot."

Joshua swiped through the picture files on Rachael's phone until he found the photos of the transcripts. He spent the next several minutes reading the excerpts Rachael had transferred to her cell.

"Wow," he said before letting out a low whistle. "At the time, this seemed par for the course. Judging from his comments, we never gave this exchange a second thought given all the redactions Seth injected into almost every session. We did push him a bit on certain points, but we *always* did that. How did you possibly remember this?"

Rachael frowned at Joshua. "I was a journalist long before I was a PR director for NASA. Journalists have good memories." She winked at Joshua. "Especially this one, Dr. Andrews. So what do you think?"

Joshua leaned back and wiped his face with both of his hands before looking at his wife.

"I think we were onto a line of questions that the petrins were quite eager to avoid."

"More than most issues that we brought up? Be honest with me."

"Definitely. I even asked them if there was an artificial means of replicating heavier elements through fusion. The phrasing of our questioning unintentionally stumbled onto something that Seth had to continually communicate about with the collective, and it all had to do with nuclear fusion."

"Coincidence?"

Joshua shook his head. "I doubt it. A star the size of a golf ball would have knocked our socks off. Hell, it did when I myself discovered it. But Seth still managed to play it close to the vest. We still don't know the ramifications of how this kind of fusion technology might be used on a *planetary* scale. We know that the arachnid in North Korea used it for deadly effect, but that's really the extent of what we know. I now think it goes much deeper."

"But Josh, the petrins have the ability to make life from almost nothing—from some of the simplest elements in the periodic table. That would make them almost omnipotent."

Rachael ceased talking. The ramification of her statement was far-reaching.

"Does this shake your faith?" Joshua asked.

"No. The petrins apparently learned how to do this, but who made the petrins? I still believe in a creator, if that's what you're getting at."

Joshua reflected on how to respond to his wife's discovery in the archives. The transcript raised several issues.

"Well, I think fusion technology holds some special importance to petrin civilization, and we have to consider what's at the very heart of their reason for existence. What is their primary goal as a species?"

"To seed the universe with cells in order to spread life," Rachael answered.

"That's right."

"And you therefore believe that fusion is somehow related to this grand design they have?"

"Impossible to say at this point, but what piques my curiosity most is the implication by Seth, even though it's between the lines and redacted, that this technology might be dangerous depending on its—"

"Application," Rachael said, finishing Joshua's thought. "Yeah, that's what the whole session boils down to for me. It was certainly dangerous—possibly misused—in North Korea."

"But we don't have proof it was the petrins," Joshua countered.

"It's a smoking gun, Josh, even if we don't have the specifics. We have an evasive petrin ambassador on the one hand, and wholesale slaughter in North Korea on the other. We're connecting a lot of dots, but I'm sure they form a picture."

"And we have a sphere the size of a golf ball that uses nuclear fusion like a star. That's a really big dot."

"Where does that leave us?" Rachael asked.

"With confirmation."

"I'm not following."

"We now know for certain that Seth is hiding something big, and I'll bet money that it has to do with fusion and their grand design to create nodes throughout the universe."

"And?"

"And sometimes, their plans go horribly wrong."

Chapter Thirty-Two
The Nuclear Option

The next day, Joshua called an emergency meeting of the entire team. He felt that his discovery couldn't wait for their normally scheduled weekly meeting given the startling nature of his experiments with the sphere. Porter and Williams flew to Berkeley from D.C. to be there in person. They knew that if Joshua was calling an emergency meeting, it had to be extremely important. It was known among the team and top military brass that the president was extremely concerned about recent developments in North Korea and the presence of seven juvenile arachnids. He wanted his advisors physically present if any new development demanded a briefing.

When the entire team was gathered in a conference room at the particle center, Joshua methodically explained to the group what they had found out about the sphere. He told them about its ability to fuse smaller atoms into larger ones, releasing energy in the process. He also described to them his theory about how the arachnid was using the sphere to create life from simple elements.

The group listened intently to his findings without interruption. When Joshua had finished, Langdon was the first to speak.

"A nuclear fusion device. That's mind-boggling! Dr. Andrews, what do you think would happen if the sphere were placed in a pressurized environment?"

Joshua was puzzled by the question. "A pressurized environment? What do you mean?"

"What if the sphere were exposed to a gas such as pure hydrogen, but at many times normal atmospheric pressure. What would happen?"

"I'd expect that the rate of fusion would increase. The sphere would get denser but would also release much more energy in the form of heat."

"What are you getting at, Dr. Langdon?" Williams asked.

"Dina, we've been trying for decades to build a nuclear fusion reactor. Even now, the ITER Project in France is spending billions of dollars trying to get nuclear fusion to work efficiently, but they may not have a prototype for years. If we could subject these spheres to the proper environment, we could have unlimited energy on Earth. It could go a long way to solving the global warming problem because fossil fuels could gradually be phased out. Attaining nuclear fusion has been the Holy Grail of energy production for decades. Humanity would never lack for energy again if nuclear fusion was safely and efficiently harnessed to power homes, factories, and virtually every industry on the planet."

Porter perked up at the comment. As usual, his mind thought in purely military terms. "Our own nuclear fusion reactor. That would be very strategic for the United States."

Liz shook her head, and Vinod sighed deeply and audibly. With Porter, everything always came down to a military application.

"But should we be using alien technology for our own benefit?" Rachael asked. "We don't know what the long-term effects would be. There are both ethical and practical issues to be considered."

"I know, I know," Langdon answered. "I'm getting way ahead of myself. There would be a lot of technical and moral hurdles to get through. I was just brainstorming one of the possibilities."

Porter, however, didn't want to let go of the idea. "Imagine an entire submarine or aircraft carrier powered by a sphere. Imagine what kind of advantage that would give us."

Rachael glanced at Joshua, waiting to see if he would disclose the content of their recent private conversations about the petrins.

"As Rachael pointed out," Joshua continued, "there could be quite a few things we need to consider before trying to apply the technology of these spheres. I'm all for considering the possibility but trying to utilize their technology comes with a huge caveat."

"Explain," Williams requested.

Joshua related how he and Rachael had been having misgivings about the long-term motivation of the petrins. Had Seth been completely honest with them? Had they changed their attitude about humans and decided to use Earth as a new node for spreading intelligence through the cosmos since humanity had declined their offer to relocate to New Eden?

"I'm shocked," Langdon said. "At earlier briefings you spoke quite passionately about Seth's honesty and how the petrins could be trusted implicitly—that they could never be behind any trickery."

Vinod glared at Joshua, feeling betrayed. "Thanks for keeping me in the loop, guys," he said sarcastically.

"I'm sorry, Vinod, but Rachael and I were just thinking out loud, so to speak. We have no hard and fast evidence, although Rachael has uncovered some revealing clues originating from Seth himself."

"What the hell are you babbling about?" Porter asked.

Everyone at the meeting was genuinely confused.

Joshua summarized the portion of the session in which the team had questioned Seth about nuclear fusion.

"Doesn't surprise me," Porter said. "He redacted what would have amounted to volumes of data."

"So the guy was evasive," Vinod said. "He was on hundreds of occasions. Maybe thousands."

It was Williams who understood clearly what Joshua was saying.

"Seth was certainly hiding many things from us," she said, "but the conclusion you're drawing is that there is an aspect of petrin fusion technology that could be very dangerous. Events in North Korea validate such concerns. What Seth doesn't say in the transcript is as telling as what he *does* say."

Joshua nodded. "We've been looking at the petrins as a species so advanced that they would never harm anyone, and although I had begun to doubt that assumption, I don't think they ever would, at least not knowingly. I would have to speak to Seth before drawing any final conclusions. But the import of what I'm saying is that the petrins themselves may have experienced moments when their technology, as advanced as it is, has gotten away from them—has turned dangerous, perhaps even lethal. That would explain events in North Korea."

"It makes sense," Langdon said.

Porter seemed unsettled. "The fact of the matter is that we ourselves now have the technology, or at least know the theory behind it. I think we should explore how to use it. They sent it to Earth for reasons unknown, but we're now in possession of it."

Joshua leaned back and folded his arms. "I admit it's tempting, general, although I'm not advocating a military application for it. Just the opposite, in fact. Unlimited energy that's produced safely might change the geopolitical climate forever. How many wars have been fought over natural resources, oil, and land that's energy-rich?"

"You're a starry-eyed optimist," Porter said. "We'll always need a strong military with both offensive and defensive capabilities, and the kind of energy production you're alluding to could give us a weapons superiority that the Pentagon has never dreamed of.'"

"For non-military applications, it would certainly be safer than nuclear power plants," Rachael said.

"It would indeed," Joshua said.

"I sense there's a 'but' coming," Williams said.

"Indeed there is," Joshua said. "We'd be using technology that is millennia beyond anything we now envision for nuclear fusion. As with the ITER Project, humans have justifiably been searching for a way to harness the power of fusion, but the spheres go far beyond that. It's a formula for creating life itself. I don't know if mankind is ready to wisely exercise such responsibility. If the petrins or other aliens utilizing this kind of technology have misused it, do we really think that humans can handle the power of creation?"

Porter returned to his original point. "For God's sake, we have the technology sitting right here in the lab, and we should use it! The first use should be geared towards protecting ourselves from more of those damn creatures that killed our men in uniform. And we should use it to defend our planet. *They* sent the technology here—it sure as hell wasn't a cure for cancer—and maybe this is a case where we fight fire with fire."

"Are you kidding me?" Vinod asked angrily. "You want to use the sphere for military applications? The technology would have to be shared with the world. It wouldn't be the exclusive property of the United States or the military." He paused and shot an angry glance at Porter. "Why not just breed arachnids and then harvest more spheres from them? Let's weaponize our own enemy."

Williams knew that Vinod was being sarcastic, but she responded to his statement anyway.

"We need to get back on topic," she said. "There's absolutely no way we want the arachnids to reproduce. In fact, our immediate goal is to destroy those that are in Korea. We can't allow the juveniles to grow to adulthood for obvious reasons. They themselves would eventually reproduce, and that would endanger the safety of the entire world. As for the sphere and fusion technology, that's a discussion for another day. It may be months or years before a decision can be reached on what to do with the spheres."

"I wholeheartedly agree," Langdon said.

"Speaking of the juveniles," Liz added, "I have more findings to report. We were able to dissect and study the dead juvenile arachnid. It doesn't contain any metal, so therefore it had no airfoils or fusion spheres. It does, however, have a large yolk sac. I think the creatures grow using the energy and proteins in the sac. At some later stage of development, the creatures may grow the spheres to start the fusion process, but at present they don't seem to have that capability."

"So they're not lethal?" Porter asked.

"I don't believe so."

"Not yet," Porter said, "but they'll eventually have the capability to be as destructive as the arachnid that produced them. After all, we believe they're clones, so there's no reason to think they would be any less hostile or destructive after maturing."

"A valid point," Williams said.

"If they're not lethal, then maybe we can send another military team in to finish these things off," Porter suggested confidently.

"Maybe," Liz said, "but the armor in the juvenile is still very tough. Recall that we had to cut pieces with a plasma cutter. I don't think conventional weapons will have much of an effect."

"I don't think it's a good idea, general," Langdon added. "These juveniles are fairly small. It'd be difficult to locate all of them if they're hiding in the forest. We have to make sure that all seven of them are killed so that they can't reproduce."

"We have to do something," Porter stated. "We don't know how long it'll be before the juveniles become lethal."

"I don't think another military mission is what the president wants," Williams said. "He doesn't wish to put more men in harm's way, but I do have a question for you all directly from the president. You've had over two weeks to study the arachnid. You've discovered what it's made of and how it works, but have you identified any weaknesses that we can exploit to kill the remaining arachnids in Korea? That's the task at hand."

Williams glanced around the room, but no one said a word.

"I'll take that as a no," she said. "I know that everyone here is under the opinion that the arachnids must be eradicated. There's no dissension on that point, so I have another question, and it's also straight from the president. You've told us about the strengths of this creature and its shielding and weapons capability. Is there anything you've discovered about the arachnid that leads you to believe that the juveniles could survive a thermonuclear explosion?"

All heads immediately turned towards Williams.

"Thermonuclear?" Joshua asked. "Like a hydrogen bomb?"

"Yes."

"Their armor is extremely strong," Liz said, "but I don't think even *they* could survive the extreme heat and force of an event that powerful."

"Dr. Andrews?" Williams said.

"I don't know if the spheres inside the creatures, assuming there *are* any in these juvenile arachnids, would survive or not. Liz didn't detect one in the dead juvenile, but the other seven are alive and have been growing for the past two weeks. But the spheres in themselves are not immediately harmful. They're just energy sources. The arachnid, in the end, is biological." He inhaled deeply before rendering his final opinion. "I don't think the arachnids could survive a thermonuclear attack."

Vinod was shocked. "You're going to drop a hydrogen bomb on North Korea? That would be murder!"

"We've already informed the North Koreans. They're still not responding to our messages, but we know they're getting through just as before. They've already evacuated the area for many additional miles around the complex. It's our belief that they themselves were preparing to nuke the area, but their weapons don't have anywhere near the yield that we can generate."

"What's the weapon and its yield?" Joshua asked.

"Five megatons," Williams replied.

"Are you mad?" Vinod asked.

"That's over three hundred times the bomb dropped on Hiroshima!" Joshua exclaimed.

"We need to sterilize the area," Williams replied. "We want to eradicate those creatures from the face of this planet. But still, it's not the largest thermonuclear explosion ever recorded. The Russians exploded a device in 1961 that was close to fifty megatons. Look, this plan has been in motion for a while. It was the final option. The device has been under construction for a few weeks. We were hoping not to use it, but there's nothing your scientific team has found out about the arachnid that's an actionable weakness. You've all said so yourselves today. We're out of options, and we don't want to waste any more time since we don't know how fast these creatures grow. At this point, it's almost riskier *not* to do this than to postpone it. The president was waiting until after this meeting to make his final decision. I'm going to recommend that we proceed. The bomb is scheduled to be dropped at seven a.m. Korean time tomorrow, which will be three p.m. here."

"We should discuss this," Joshua said.

"It's a political decision made at the highest levels," Williams said. "It's out of your hands."

"I'm in complete agreement," Porter said smugly. "It's our best option at this point. Halfhearted measures are a waste of time."

"How far into the ground will such an explosion penetrate?" Rachael asked.

"Why?" Williams asked.

"The juvenile arachnids are nowhere near as powerful as the adult. These are instinctual creatures, and they may try to protect themselves. Many species in the animal kingdom do so when they're not fully-grown. If they bury themselves underground, or somehow find a cave to hide in, the bomb may not affect them. The arachnids could possibly survive if they were deep enough underground."

"It's a salient point," Williams agreed, "one that we'll have to take our chances with. Our satellites and drones will be continuously monitoring the area for months after the explosion to check for the creatures." She paused as she closed a leather briefing binder on the table. "I'm going to adjourn this meeting at this point. General Porter and I have to travel back to D.C. in a few hours. I have to brief the president on our meeting today. I want the rest of you back in this conference room at two-thirty tomorrow afternoon to observe the detonation."

"Count me out," Vinod said.

"Attendance isn't optional," Williams said.

"Whatever," Vinod said dismissively.

The group got up from the table and started to exit the conference room.

"Dr. Andrews and Dr. Langdon," Williams said, "I need you two to stay for a moment."

The rest of the group exited the conference room, Joshua and Langdon sitting at the table next to Williams.

"The president has a special project for you," Williams said. "We know there's a possibility that the bomb may not accomplish our goal. Rachael was correct in her assessment that if the creatures are deep enough underground, the explosion may not affect them. The president wants to have options on what to do if our plan doesn't work. We're at the limits of our technology at this point, and there's nothing else we can think of doing if we're unsuccessful." Williams appeared disturbed. "That's why the president has told me to authorize you to capture a primordial spookyon."

Joshua stared at Williams, mouth open. He immediately realized the implications of what she was saying. "You want to reconnect with the petrins?"

"Yes. We don't know if they're directly behind the creation of the arachnid or not, but at the very least we may be able to get *some* answers from them—why the arachnid is here and what its purpose is. Our UN ambassador has secretly asked for a reprieve from the moratorium on primordial spookyon collection, and the UN has agreed. But I want to make something very clear. We just want to establish a communication channel—that's it. We don't want you to have any communications with the petrins. We simply want to have that option ready if the need arises."

"Establish a channel," Joshua said. "That will mean not only trying to capture a primordial spookyon in a Bowman sphere, but also making sure it's connected to the petrins. Dina, I want to use the security key that Seth provided to make sure we do just that."

"You may use the key to verify communications, but nothing more. Just establish a channel to the petrins, verify the connection, and then wait for further instructions. Are we clear on this?"

"Crystal clear," Langdon said.

"Yes," Joshua said.

"How long do you think it will take to establish this channel, Dr. Andrews?" Williams asked.

"I don't know. We've gotten better with spookyon technology over the past few years, but primordial spookyons are a different story. If I were to hazard a guess, it may take a couple of months."

"Then I want you to get started on this project right away." Williams said. "Give it top priority."

Joshua was relieved and hopeful. If he could speak to Seth after opening a channel of communication using entangled spookyons—assuming permission was granted to use the open channel—not only might the alien be able to clear up the mystery of why the arachnid had been grown in North Korea, but perhaps Seth would be able to allay the misgivings he and Rachael had recently harbored. Joshua was doubtful, however, as to whether Seth would go into more detail about petrin use of fusion since it would still violate the petrin prime directive of not influencing the technological advancement of another species. On the other hand, what would be the point of redacting information on a process that humans were now aware of? Either way, it would be interesting to see what Seth's response might be once he learned that humans knew of the capability of the black sphere.

Joshua knew that he was getting ahead of himself. Opening a channel of communication with the petrins using Seth's security key was one thing. Being allowed to communicate once again with the petrins was another. That decision lay with the president. For now, he would try to capture the primordial spookyon and see how the politics of the situation played out.

Chapter Thirty-Three
Science Has Known Evil

The next afternoon, Joshua, Rachael, Vinod, Liz, and Langdon gathered in the same conference room at the research center. Vinod had calmed down and begrudgingly acknowledged that he saw no other way to eradicate the juveniles other than a nuclear detonation. On the LCD panel were multiple satellite video feeds focused on the area of North Korea where the complex was located. Another feed originated from a ground-level angle aboard a ship positioned in the Sea of Japan. The final feed came from the bomber that would deliver the thermonuclear device. It was a B2 stealth bomber flying at forty thousand feet, its feed showing the slow-moving surface of the Earth below. It currently displayed ocean, but near the top of the image, a coastline was slowly coming into view.

"Five minutes to drop zone," the commander of the B2 announced over the speaker in the conference room. "Altitude forty thousand."

It was a cloudless morning over North Korea, and the drop zone would be clearly visible to the B2.

The group in the conference room sat in silence, watching the video feeds.

"Forty thousand feet," Vinod said. "That bomb's got a long way to fall."

"They wanted to make sure the bomber was high enough to be out of range of any potential airfoils or EMP pulses," Joshua said, "but I doubt the juvenile arachnids are capable of producing either at this point."

"Josh, the bomb doesn't actually hit the ground when it explodes does it?" Rachael asked.

"No. Unlike conventional bombs, nuclear bombs are set to explode in the atmosphere for maximum effect. I believe this one is programmed to detonate when it reaches four thousand meters. The resulting fireball and shockwave will affect a large area from that altitude."

"I read that a thermonuclear bomb is actually two bombs in one," Liz stated.

"That's true," Joshua said. "There are two stages to the explosion. First, a conventional fission bomb is detonated, creating the incredible heat needed to start the fusion process. The heat generated is similar to the temperatures at the center of the sun. Then, within milliseconds, the heat from the first explosion causes the secondary explosion, which is a fusion reaction. Fission causes hydrogen isotopes in the bomb to undergo nuclear fusion to form helium, which releases vast amounts of energy. The fusion energy is the truly destructive power of a hydrogen bomb."

Vinod folded his arms and stared at the screen. While he had reluctantly agreed with other team members that the forthcoming action was necessary, he knew that no one, not even those in the government, could accurately foresee the ramifications of what was about to happen.

"Nuclear fusion," Rachael remarked in a somber tone. "The same process that's going on in the black spheres. It seems ironic that the arachnid was using fusion for a constructive process in that it was beginning the organization of elements and molecules into life itself, albeit a form of life that is destructive to humans. We're now using the same process for a destructive purpose—to kill the arachnids."

Liz knew about Rachael's religious and moral convictions and wanted to press her on the subject. "So who's using fusion in the better way, Rachael? Us or the arachnids?"

"That's really a moral question, one that maybe only God knows the answer to." Rachael paused as she considered a more in-depth answer. "Humans are the result of evolution, which is predicated on the concept of survival of the fittest. Isn't that also what the arachnids are trying to do? Survive and replicate? From a purely evolutionary standpoint, there's only one right answer—whichever species survives. I guess the answer to who is doing it for a better purpose depends on what the ultimate goal is for either species."

"Are you insinuating that we shouldn't be doing this?" Vinod asked. "We shouldn't be bombing the arachnids? I'm the first to have reservations about this course of action, but we wanted to peacefully communicate with the arachnid if at all possible. It didn't even give us a chance."

"Absolutely not. The arachnids, even though they're just trying to survive and replicate, are very destructive. They kill indiscriminately and cannot be allowed to roam the Earth. We all agree on that point."

"Kill indiscriminately," Liz echoed. "I'm not sure that humans haven't done the same at multiple points throughout history."

"What are you saying, Liz?" Joshua asked. "Do you think we're no better than the arachnids?"

"No. I'm actually advancing the opposite argument. Despite our capability to destroy life indiscriminately, humans have one characteristic that the arachnids haven't shown—empathy. Despite our checkered past, I believe that humans are on a path to preservation. Even though we may have evolved because of survival of the fittest, I don't believe we're on a path of existence or reproduction at any cost. We're growing morally as a species. When we feel that our survival isn't threatened, we have the capacity to help species that are. I think that's what separates us from the arachnids—what we do when allowed to thrive or when our own survival is not in doubt."

"Morally, we were deceived by whatever alien species sent us the information to create the arachnid," Vinod said. "It was supposed to be a medical cure. You can't separate the creature from the malevolent intent of its designers."

"Point well taken," Langdon said.

"One minute to drop zone," the commander announced.

The group watched in silence as the video from the bomber showed the forested landscape below. The outline of the complex they'd inhabited for over a week came into view and was centered in the frame.

"My God," Rachael said.

"It's hard to think we were just there," Joshua commented.

"It's hard to think—period," Vinod said.

"Payload deployed," the commander announced.

The B2 turned hard away from the site after the bomb had been released and flew away at full speed. It took a full two minutes for the device to reach the designated altitude, at which time its internal electronics started the detonation process. Suddenly, all feeds on the LCD became a brilliant white. The intense glow slowly faded to bright orange and, after a few seconds, an enormous mushroom cloud appeared on the screen from multiple angles.

"Now science has known evil," Joshua said in a whisper.

"What'd you say?" Vinod asked, transfixed by the images of the expanding mushroom cloud.

"Now science has known evil," Joshua repeated. "It's what Robert Oppenheimer, the physicist who led the Manhattan project, said as he watched the first nuclear explosion on Earth."

*   *   *

After the thermonuclear detonation in North Korea, the scientific team was partially disbanded. Vinod went back to his work as the CTO of his AI firm, and Rachael, returned to her much-neglected duties as the PR director for NASA. Over the next few weeks, many press conferences were held at the center. The public had been informed of the nuclear detonation as well as the reasons it had become necessary. Rachael, as the PR director, gave frequent news conferences to provide updates.

It had been a few weeks since the explosion, but there was still nothing to report. Spy satellites had scoured the area of the detonation but had not picked up anything unusual. This meant that the news conferences focused on questions about what had happened in the past. How had the military operation gone? Why had the Koreans broken the moratorium on primordial spookyons? How had the scientific team been able to kill the arachnid? Were there new developments on the research being conducted on the dead arachnid? Were the petrins responsible for the presence of the arachnid on Earth?

Rachael, Langdon, and Liz, who jointly conducted these press conferences, were free to tell reporters anything they wanted regarding the mission and subsequent ongoing research on the dead arachnid. There was one topic, however, that the president had decided should be off-limits, that topic being the existence of the nuclear fusion-generating spheres. He felt that public knowledge about a nuclear device as small as a golf ball that could create unlimited energy under the correct conditions would be unwarranted given that nations would almost certainly seek to weaponize such power, much as General Porter had wished to do for the United States. The existence of the spheres and their capabilities would be classified as Top Secret.

The scientific team had collected thirty-two spheres from the arachnid, each having the capability for immense power or destruction in the wrong hands. The spheres couldn't be destroyed. Nothing the scientific team subjected them to seemed to affect them physically. In the end, it was decided to put them into safe, well-guarded storage. They were sealed in an airtight metal container filled with xenon gas. The xenon prevented them from having fuel for nuclear fusion, rendering them inert. The container was stored in a specially-designed safe in the bat cave.

Over the next few months, the press conferences became less frequent as the amount of new information dwindled. Rachael could give no further updates since the existence of the spheres and Seth's digital key for reconnection were classified at the highest levels. Otherwise, she had very little to offer in the way of ongoing research into the arachnid, and details on the mission in North Korea had been completely covered. As for whether the petrins had been responsible for the arachnid as opposed to another alien race, the answer remained elusive.

A month into the research, Liz's team started the process of trying to sequence the DNA of the arachnid. They had difficulty with this in that the results seemed to be error-prone, but they later realized that what they thought were errors in the sequencing process were not errors at all. They'd discovered that the arachnid was a mosaic. Unlike humans, who have the same DNA in every nucleated cell, the arachnid was actually four genetically separate entities that had grown together into one creature. Liz theorized that instead of starting from a single cell, arachnids grew from four separate progenitor cells. Each cell line divided and formed different biological systems for the arachnid. Liz and her assistants had no idea which cell line developed into which organ system, but the arachnid was genetically like four creatures in one, intermixed at the cellular level.

Joshua, as instructed, had gotten to work trying to capture a primordial spookyon connected to the petrins. This meant long hours of work with the tokamak and testing whatever spookyons he and his team were able to capture. As before, the vast majority of tests were negative. There was no entanglement with any other spookyon.

In the second month of his research, however, Joshua managed to capture two primordial spookyons that were entangled. These, like the spookyon that he and Rachael had found three years earlier, had a mathematical carrier signal. It was the same square root signal Rodrigo had indicated in his logs, but when Joshua tried to verify a connection with the petrins using the security key that Seth had left, he failed. These spookyons, whatever intelligence they were connected to, were not connected to the petrins.

Joshua began entertaining the idea far more seriously that Rodrigo may have indeed contacted an entirely different alien species, albeit one that had used petrin technology. The square root wasn't establishing contact with the petrins, but there was no doubt that Rodrigo had contacted *someone*—some alien intelligence—in the universe.

Seth isn't available. He's been assigned to a different project.

Joshua was convinced that this explanation had been an outright lie. Seth had insisted on using a specific code so that humans could reestablish contact with the petrins, and Seth had always been Petri's ambassador to Earth. Who else was out there?

Finally, in month three, Joshua was able to capture a third primordial spookyon that was entangled and transmitted a mathematical carrier signal. He was more hopeful this time since the carrier was pi, the same that he and Rachael had discovered in the bat cave years ago. He went through the process of verifying the connection using the security key. Joshua was surprised but pleased to see the words VERIFICATION PASSED on his computer terminal.

Joshua stared at the glowing green sphere in the spookyon detector. "Hello, Seth. Nice to connect with you again, my friend."

Chapter Thirty-Four
Reconnection

Having exited the research center, Joshua jumped on his Harley and rode to the condominium he and Rachael shared. He knew that Rachael would be excited to hear about how he had finally been able to reestablish contact with the petrins, and he wanted to tell her in person.

Joshua parked the motorcycle in the garage next to Rachael's Tesla, dismounted, and hung his helmet over the left handlebar. He had been working late, and Rachael had been home for a few hours. He found her busy in the kitchen.

"Hey, what's for dinner? Smells good."

"Meatloaf," Rachael answered with a grin.

"Very funny," Joshua replied.

He knew that Rachael was kidding. She had known since their first meeting that he was a vegetarian.

"We're having green chili and cheese enchiladas," Rachael said as Joshua kissed her on the cheek. "Anything new at work?" she asked, taking the enchiladas from the oven.

"Maybe," Joshua said with a sly grin.

Rachael had known him long enough to gauge when he was hiding something from her.

"Maybe? Come on—what is it?"

Joshua didn't respond, but continued grinning.

"What?" Rachael repeated.

"I've reestablished contact."

"With the petrins?" she said excitedly. "With Seth?"

"I ran the security protocol that Seth left for us on a new spookyon that we captured today. It checks out. We have a connection with the petrins, but I haven't talked with Seth yet. As you know, it's only an open channel."

"Are you sure?"

"Yes. The carrier was what we saw the first time—pi—not what Rodrigo stumbled on."

"Oh, Josh!" Rachael said as she gave him a hug. "Congratulations!"

Joshua had known that Rachael would be happy about the news. Seth was, after all, the reason she was alive, but he pressed her on the issue. "We've had a big change of heart, haven't we?"

"What do you mean?"

"You vehemently tried to convince me to end our connection with the petrins on our last night on New Eden. Now you're happy to be reconnected? What gives?"

Rachael knew that Joshua was half-kidding, but their last night on New Eden had been one of the most gut-wrenching evenings of her life. She didn't appreciate the fact that Joshua was bringing it up in such a nonchalant manner and abruptly withdrew her arms from around his waist.

"Are you really going there?" she asked, hands on her hips.

Joshua was caught off guard by her reaction. "Um . . . I was just kidding Rachael, but you're right. I shouldn't have brought it up like that. I'm sorry."

Rachael's glare softened a bit, and she resumed preparations for dinner.

"Seriously though," Joshua said, "how're you feeling about reconnecting with the petrins?"

"I'm at peace with it. I know that I was the one who convinced you to break the sphere, but the situation and circumstances have changed in many ways. Things are different now."

"In what way?"

"First, I don't have the fear of all humanity being transported to an alien planet under the control of the petrins. Second, if the arachnids survived the nuclear blast, I'm happy to speak with the petrins and get their explanation on why their technology is here—to know the secret that Seth has been hiding. And just speaking with Seth doesn't put us in any immediate danger." Rachael paused and looked down. "Finally, I miss Seth. I never got a chance to thank him for what he did—saving my life—saving *all* of our lives. So yes, I'm happy that you've reconnected with the petrins."

"I knew you would be," Joshua said, embracing Rachael. "I just had to know your reasons. But who knows if we'll ever get to use the connection? Williams told me that it would be used only as a last resort—only if the hydrogen bomb didn't eradicate the juvenile arachnids."

Rachael was conflicted. "I don't know if I'd be happy or sad if we got to use the connection. It would be great to speak with Seth again, but that would mean we hadn't eliminated the arachnids."

Joshua nodded. "I also have mixed emotions about the opportunity to speak with Seth again since he might be upset with me about breaking the sphere. On the other hand, I believe he owes us an explanation—probably several."

Rachael understood Joshua's concern. He had told Rachael many years ago about how he had broken the sphere. Seth had had no warning. Joshua had inactivated him using his Apple watch while he was walking behind him. He had extracted the Bowman sphere from Seth while he was in his inactivated state and had ruptured the sphere. Had he betrayed Seth's trust?

"Josh," Rachael said as she grasped his hand, "we both know Seth and regard him as a close friend. I'm confident that he would be forgiving of your action."

"I appreciate you saying that. It gives me some degree of solace, but I wonder how he'll feel if we press him for answers about fusion and, well . . . everything that's happened."

"I think he'll understand, but we deserve to know the truth. Being a member of an advanced species doesn't mean he can do whatever he wants."

"Totally agree. He's not—"

"Omnipotent?"

Joshua couldn't refrain from laughing at the religious reference.

As Joshua and Rachael sat for dinner, Rachael's phone rang, and she recognized the caller.

"It's Ted," she said in an excited voice, putting the phone on speaker. "Hello, Tabasco. You're on speaker with me and Josh. How're you doing?"

"Hey, y'all," Ted said. "I'm doing okay. How're things with you? Y'all slice and dice that arachnid in the lab?"

"We're good," Joshua responded. "Yeah, we sliced that sucker up, and we've learned some valuable information, but Liz is still doing research. How's that shoulder of yours?"

"It's getting better. I'm out of the sling, but I got some bad news from the docs."

Rachael and Joshua glanced at each other.

"What kind of bad news?" Rachael asked.

"They told me the airfoil went through my shoulder joint. It messed up some of my cartilage, so there's permanent damage. It'll be okay for doing most stuff. I can still be involved with the Seals, but they told me they won't release me for any type of combat duty anymore."

Rachael looked at Joshua with a sullen expression. "So sorry to hear that, Ted. Are you okay with that?"

"It is what it is," Ted said with resignation. "Guess I'm going to be a pencil pusher from now on."

"That's too bad," Joshua replied.

The team had formed a strong bond with Ted. They had survived an incredible life-threatening situation together, and he was definitely one of their group now.

Rachael thought of a way to cheer him up. "Hey, you still got some time off?"

"Yeah, still on medical leave."

"Why don't you come to Berkeley?" Rachael asked. "We'd love to get together."

"Great idea," Joshua said. "You're welcome here anytime. I can show you around the lab."

There was a pause on the line before Ted answered. "I might just do that. It may cheer me up a bit, seeing y'all. Maybe I'll bring along some Louisiana moonshine for Vinod."

"I'm sure he'd love that," Rachael said. "He'll have a party planned, complete with songs to fit the occasion, before you land."

"Okay, let me think about it. I'll catch y'all later."

Rachael touched the screen and ended the call.

"I miss Ted," she said. "He's such a great guy, but I feel that he's putting on a brave face about his shoulder. It must be killing him inside not to be able to perform his combat duties as a seal."

"I'm sure you're right. For someone who has gone through that much training over the years, this must be very disappointing. Still, it would be great to see him. Hope he decides to come out."

*   *   *

Two weeks later, Joshua and Rachael were summoned to Robert Langdon's office at the research center. They noticed that Liz was already seated on the couch, and Williams and Porter were split-screen on a video conference on the wall-mounted monitor. They took a seat next to Liz as Langdon, who was seated behind his desk, said, "Looks like we're all here, Dina. What do you want to talk about?"

"I'm switching my video feed to my laptop," Williams replied.

The monitor now showed an image of Williams' desktop from her computer. The group watched as Williams moved her mouse and opened a folder filled with jpeg files. She double-clicked on one, which opened full-screen and revealed two arachnids standing next to each other. They were in a clearing surrounded by a forest of tall trees.

Everyone knew the implication of what they saw on the screen.

"When was this taken?" Joshua asked.

"About five hours ago," Williams said.

As a reporter, Rachael had always been good at picking up details that others didn't notice. "Why are there trees surrounding the clearing they're in?"

"Why are you asking?" Williams asked.

"We bombed that area with a five-megaton thermonuclear device," Rachael said. "There shouldn't be any standing trees, let alone ones with green pine needles."

"Very observant of you," Williams said. "This image was taken south of the blast zone—about a hundred miles from the DMZ. We hadn't noticed anything for a few weeks in or around the blast zone, so we decided to expand our sweeps. This was the result."

"How do you think they survived?" Liz asked. "Were they underground, or do you think they moved far away from the complex before the detonation?"

"That's unknown," Williams said. "All we know is there are two arachnids close to South Korea. We've already informed both North and South Korea of our findings. They told us they're taking defensive actions, although they haven't specified what those might be."

"Are these two the only ones you've found?" Langdon asked.

"So far," Williams replied, "but we're still scanning the surrounding area."

"Have you had a chance to analyze the size of the arachnids?" Liz asked. "How do they compare to the one we killed?"

"Using the perspective of the surrounding trees, we have a good idea of their size. We don't believe there're fully grown. We estimate that their measurements are about seventy-five percent as large as the original arachnid, but we feel that they'll reach adulthood fairly soon. But they're already lethal."

"In what way?" Langdon asked.

"We've tried to destroy them with firepower from predator drones. We were unsuccessful. In fact, the drones didn't even have a chance to fire their weapons. They were spotted by the arachnid's insect surveillance system and were destroyed by EMP pulses before they could fire."

"Then obviously the information from the first arachnid—that our technology is silicon-based—must have been transmitted to the juveniles,"

Joshua stated.

"It was hard enough dealing with *one* of those creatures," Porter said, his voice devoid of his usual bluster. "How the hell do we deal with more of them?"

There was silence as Williams removed the image of the arachnids from the screen and reverted to her webcam feed.

"At this point, we've exhausted all of our options," she said with a sigh. "We can't keep unleashing nuclear detonations on wider and wider areas. We'd just be chasing our tail, and radiation levels would be unacceptable in surrounding countries. At this point we have no other choice except to ask Seth and the petrins how to deal with them."

"The petrins?" Porter said. "Those bastards are the probably ones behind these arachnids."

"We've surmised as much from the outset, general. If they're behind this, we'll at least get an idea as to why, but we have to face the fact that we're in over our heads. We have to contact Seth unless someone has a better idea."

There was silence in the room. No one had any suggestions.

"Okay," Williams said. "Robert, I want you to come up with a plan on how to proceed. We need to fire up our android alien. I only hope he can offer some help."

"I want it noted on the record that I'm against this," Porter stated. "We don't know if contacting Seth will help us or hurt us."

"Duly noted, general, but this comes from the president. We'll take all necessary precautions," the White House Chief of Staff said as she ended the call.

"Dr. Andrews," Langdon said, "I may need your help with the reactivation process. Can you stay for a few moments?"

"Sure."

Rachael and Liz got up to leave.

Joshua took Rachael's hand in his. "Looks like you'll get to thank Seth in person after all."

*　　　*　　　*

Vinod rejoined the group for the reactivation of Seth. He didn't want to miss the chance of greeting his old friend. He was, after all, a member of the 103 Club. He'd also made it clear that he'd advocated connecting with the petrins from the moment he'd learned that an arachnid had been detected in North Korea.

"I have just one thing to say," Vinod declared.

"Yes, which is 'I told you so,'" Rachael said with a sneer.

"That's right. I deal in information. Seth was the dude with the answers all along, but better late than never."

They gathered around the motionless form of the android on his pedestal in the bat cave. His android body had been in storage since Joshua had ruptured the sphere inside his chest cavity after returning from New Eden. He resembled a figure on exhibit at a wax museum or Disneyworld. His likeness to a human was eerie, but the android that had once traveled the world to visit heads of state and scientists was lifeless.

Langdon had had his scientists test and refurbish any non-working parts of the android, and he was now in pristine condition. The security protocols for Seth were the same as before, which included Bluetooth tethers to Apple watches. Each member of the scientific team, which now included Liz, was issued a watch.

Rachael had strong, conflicting emotions when she saw Seth's android body. It reminded her of the self-sacrifice she made that final night on New Eden. She remembered crying next to the lifeless body of Joshua after he had been transported to Earth. The first time she died had been the result of a car accident, and it had been a sudden event as she, Joshua, and Vinod had driven into the mountains on a rainy day. The night on New Eden was different. She had chosen self-sacrifice and had awaited her fate. She remembered the agonizing minutes during which she'd embraced Joshua's body, wondering what his ultimate decision would be. She'd wanted the sphere broken so that humanity would be forced to forge its own destiny rather than be kept in perpetual comfort on New Eden. Would Joshua decide to break the sphere and end her life, or would the inanimate body she was lying next to come back to life at some point in the future to live with her on New Eden? A few minutes later her vision had gone blank, but she never lost consciousness, only the sensation of being in her body. This feeling quickly abated as her vision returned. She felt a prickly sensation in her scalp as the biograins exited her skull. When she opened her eyes, she was in the bat cave, although she didn't recognize it immediately. There was a lot of laboratory equipment present which hadn't been there before, equipment Seth had used to manufacture a cure for the viral outbreak and also to start growing petrins should humanity choose to be relocated to New Eden, making Earth available as a new node for petrin civilization. She'd gotten up from the table she was lying on and pulled back the cloth screen that surrounded her. She saw Joshua, tears on his face, staring at the image of Seth frozen on a projector screen.

Now she was seeing Seth again. Those old feelings suddenly reemerged from the recesses of her mind. Here was an android—no, a person whose conversations with Joshua she had wished terminated. In the end, he was someone who had shown his generosity by saving her life, not once, but twice. Rachael waited with trepidation for Seth to be activated.

Joshua had installed the new Bowman sphere inside of Seth's back. Vinod's algorithm for communication had not been used since the petrins were already fluent in the English language. Joshua had simply verified the connection using the security code and then installed the sphere in Seth.

With everyone gathered in front of android Seth, as he'd come to be known, Joshua and Langdon entered the activation signal on their watches.

Seth opened his eyes, turned his head, and looked at the faces around him. A broad smile appeared on his face. "'Sup, humans?"

"Seth!" Vinod exclaimed, rushing toward him.

Seth got down from the pedestal to greet his friend.

"What's up, bro?" Seth asked as he gave Vinod a high five and then embraced him. "Long time no see." Seth glanced at Vinod's tee shirt du jour, which was a cover of the *Paranoid* album by Black Sabbath. "Iron man?"

Vinod grinned at Seth. "You know it, man. In your honor."

The reference to the song escaped the others in the room.

Rachael and Joshua lined up behind Vinod to greet Seth. Overcome with emotion, Rachael was speechless. Tears rolled down her cheeks as she gave Seth a hug.

"I've wanted to say this to you for such a long time," she said, sobbing. She stepped back and looked at Seth. "Thank you for saving my life."

Seth smiled. "Anything for a friend. I wouldn't have had it any other way."

Rachael wiped the tears from her face and embraced Seth again.

Seth's expression turned suddenly solemn as he faced Joshua, who looked at Seth with trepidation. "Et tu, Joshua?" Seth said, staring stone-faced at Joshua.

Joshua didn't know how to respond. He recognized the phrase as a quote from Shakespeare's *Julius Caesar*. They were the words Caesar had uttered to Brutus, his close friend, when Brutus had betrayed him and stabbed him in the back.

A smile slowly reappeared on Seth's face. "Just kidding, bro." Seth approached a relieved Joshua and gave him a hug. "No hard feelings. I know you were just doing what you thought was right."

Seth looked around the room and greeted Langdon and Porter with an informal "'sup."

He then saw Liz and walked up to her. "I haven't met you before. I'm Seth," he said with an outstretched hand.

Liz was speechless. This was the first time she had met Seth in person. He was like a guru for her since, like Vinod, she was a member of the 103 Club. She had read everything written about him and had assiduously studied his comments and travels after his initial activation. Seeing him in person proved to be overwhelming.

"Uh . . . hello. I mean . . . welcome . . . or . . .."

"Sorry, Seth," Joshua said. "We should've introduced you two earlier. This is Dr. Elizabeth Yang. She's a physician and an exobiologist." Joshua turned to Liz. "Liz, this is Seth."

"Nice to meet you, Dr. Yang," Seth said as Liz shook his hand.

Liz was surprised by the cold, plastic feel of Seth's hand. "Hello Seth. I've heard a lot about you. You can call me Liz, by the way."

"An exobiologist, huh?" Seth remarked.

"Yup."

"Hmmm. What need would the Bowman Particle Research Center have for an exobiologist?" he asked rhetorically.

Liz laughed at Seth's wry humor as she continued staring at him in awe.

Dina Williams was the last to greet Seth. She clasped his hand with both of hers, and her voice had an uncharacteristic emotional quality. "Seth, I want to thank you on behalf of all of us here, as well as all of humanity, for leaving us a cure for our viral outbreak years ago. You showed unbelievable compassion for a species that is much less developed than the petrins. We can't thank you enough."

Seth had known Williams well enough to know that she was sincere in her gratitude. "As I told Josh, we consider humans to be our children. Parents always want their children to grow and succeed. We had the best of intentions for humanity when we wanted to transport you to New Eden."

"I'm sure you did," Williams said, letting go of Seth's hand.

"We had anticipated the possibility that you would terminate your connection to us, but if you did, I wanted to make sure you were taken care of. The collective agreed that I could manufacture the cure as long as we didn't share the technology behind the process."

Vinod was still beaming at the sight of Seth, who had always been receptive to his unorthodox speech and mannerisms.

"Who'd have thought that we could capture another primordial spookyon connected to Petri," Vinod said.

"My connection to you is not through Petri this time," Seth said. "You are connected to one of our petrin nodes on another planet, and your signal is being relayed through our spookyon network back to Petri. We knew as soon as your security key was used that humans had reconnected with us. I was waiting anxiously for some data to be transmitted on the connection, and I'm happy to see you *all* again." Seth looked with curiosity at the faces around the room. "So why the reconnection? Somehow I feel it wasn't just to catch up. Everyone appears to be greatly concerned about something."

"You're right, Seth," Williams said. "There's a specific reason we reconnected with you. Instead of telling you, however, I'd like to show you."

"Ah yes," Seth said. "I believe the correct phrase is 'a picture is worth a thousand words.'"

A short time later, the group and Seth were seated in a conference room.

Joshua had been carefully watching Seth's every movement and reaction since he had been reactivated. He was looking for any sign that would reveal that Seth had already known about the arachnids that were now on Earth. He knew that if Seth had already known about their presence, then the petrins were somehow involved in the process. But despite careful observation, he noted no evidence of any such knowledge. The true test, however, would come when he was presented with the pictures of the arachnid.

"Seth," Williams began. "We have another biologic infestation on our planet, but this time the infestation is not natural to Earth. We would like your opinion on it and possible help in eradicating it."

"I can't violate our prime directive, but I'll certainly listen to whatever you have to say and keep an open mind."

"I understand," Williams said as she produced the latest satellite photograph of the two arachnids and slid it over to Seth, "but circumstances are rather different this time. The infestation appears to be petrin technology."

Seth picked up the photo and examined it, his features displaying great concern. Seth became frozen. He didn't move any part of his body as he stared at the photograph.

Joshua looked at the motionless android and could see the expression of shock that occupied his face—one that further allayed his fear that somehow the petrins were behind the arachnid coming to Earth. When he had captured the two primordial spookyons with the square-root-of-two carrier signal that the security key could not be verified with, he had begun to doubt that the petrins had anything to do with the arachnid even though it was definitely petrin technology. The shocked look on Seth's frozen face confirmed for him that the petrins had no knowledge that an arachnid was on Earth.

Seth remained motionless for a full minute, and Joshua theorized that he must have been having a protracted discussion with the collective. He surmised that the presence of the arachnid on Earth was as troubling to the petrins as it was to humans.

"Do you recognize it?" Langdon finally asked. "Is it petrin technology?"

Seth snapped out of his trance.

"Yes, I recognize it, and it *is* petrin technology. But the collective didn't create it." Seth looked at the faces around the table. "This is a creation of Medusa."

Chapter Thirty-Five
The Mad Scientist

"Who or what is Medusa?" Langdon asked.

"I don't know if you'd consider Medusa a who or a what," Seth replied. "I guess she's a little of both."

"She?" Rachael asked.

"It's an arbitrary gender I've assigned her, as well as her name. As you know, petrins don't have genders like humans, and our names are digital. I chose a male gender for myself and picked the name Seth from the literature that was provided by Vinod's algorithm that taught us English. I've done the same for Medusa. Her gender and name are arbitrary, but something you can easily identify with."

"Buy why Medusa?" Rachael asked. "Medusa is a figure from Greek mythology, a demon with serpents for hair who was so hideous that simply looking at her would turn a person to stone."

"We view Medusa as a demon," Seth replied.

"Why?" Rachael asked. She felt that Seth was being evasive. Would information about Medusa be redacted? If so, why had he mentioned the name? Surely the collective had an obligation to explain the havoc caused by whomever or whatever Medusa was.

Joshua's eyes caught Rachael's, and the couple knew they were both thinking the same thing. Medusa had been the secret Seth had been hiding—or possibly one of many secrets. Would he now divulge what the petrins had been withholding and explain what had been redacted in the session Rachael had researched and shared with Joshua?

Seth paused for a moment. He was apparently conferring with the collective about how much to tell humans about Medusa and what the implications would be. The rest in the room stared at him, waiting for an answer. In the end, the collective gave Seth permission to tell her story.

"Medusa is not easy to explain," Seth replied. "It's a long and ancient tale, so bear with me. Josh, you remember the conversation we had before I transported you to New Eden, the one about the origin of the cell and how one of our most brilliant scientists created it to spread life throughout the universe?"

"Yes, and everyone here's familiar with it."

"Good. That will make my explanation a great deal easier. The petrin scientist, the one who created the cell eventually became Medusa. After we created the cell and exploded our solar system's ice planet that we had seeded with cells, we transformed ourselves into cell-based organisms. As you know, we believe that at its core, life is just information. It doesn't matter what the substrate of that information is. Information can be stored electronically on a hard drive, for example, or it can be stored in DNA. It's still the same information and represents the same lifeform. Shortly after the creation of the cell, we took our own information—the life that defined ourselves and transformed ourselves into cell-based creatures. Petrins as you know them today are based on DNA and biology. During that early time, we were not a collective. We were individuals much like yourselves, but we could communicate with each other, but only intermittently, like humans currently do.

"Medusa was a brilliant scientist, the most intelligent, creative, and, unfortunately, arrogant of our race. She figured out a way to interface biology directly with spookyons. Using this technology, we became a collective that operated more as a large unified organism with a common purpose rather than as individuals. This unification caused our intellect and efficiency as a species to grow exponentially. This all happened before our first cells had reached distant planets and started to grow.

"Shortly after we had become a collective, a debate sprang up in the collective. Keeping in mind that we had previously found no other life in the universe, our main goal for releasing cells was to expand our society to multiple solar systems and establish petrin nodes on other worlds in order to seed life throughout the universe. The debate was about what to do with indigenous life forms that evolved on those worlds and that would achieve enough intelligence to capture primordial spookyons and contact us. The vast majority of us felt that even though they were rudimentary creatures compared to ourselves, they should somehow be preserved and allowed to continue living and evolving. But a small number of petrins, led by Medusa, didn't subscribe to this notion. They felt, much as humans do when they breed animals as livestock or plant rows of corn, that they could be sacrificed for the greater good of the collective. They believed that since we were their creators, we had the right to use them or destroy them as we saw fit after we had established their world as a new node for petrins. This was, and still is, a moral argument.

"As I've mentioned before, any member of the collective can disconnect from the group, but only for short periods of time. This was not originally the case. Early on, there was no restriction on disconnection. Petrins were allowed to disconnect and go their own way if they chose to do so. Medusa, therefore, disconnected herself from the collective over this debate. She felt she was superior in intellect and ability to all other petrins. She ultimately decided to create her own collective, but this new collective, instead of being a collection of individual petrins like ourselves, would be solely comprised of clones of herself because of her alleged superiority. Medusa grew her collective. She transformed herself into a separate collective of clones of herself approaching the size of our collective, exponentially increasing her intellect. She started collecting primordial spookyons and sending a carrier signal with them, like we do, in order to establish first contact with any intelligent species that had developed as a result of the cells we sent out billions of years earlier. Her only motivation is to expand her collective—to grow at the fastest rate possible in order to create more copies of herself and thereby become even more intelligent. In the process, she destroys all societies created by the cells because she feels they are lowly creatures not worthy of her effort. They are simply a means to an end.

"The petrins and Medusa have been competing for our children, for the fruits of the cells we had seeded throughout the cosmos. At the beginning, the petrin collective was much larger and more widespread than Medusa, but over the countless millennia she has become our equal, if not our superior at this point." Seth picked up the photograph from the table. "These arachnids were designed by Medusa. Somehow she has made contact with Earth and transmitted the information needed to create them here. Her arachnids are called infiltrators. They are the first step in making a planet into a node for Medusa. They have only one goal—to destroy the indigenous population. They are the tip of the spear of evil."

For several moments after Seth had finished speaking, the group sat in shocked silence as they pondered his incredible story. Liz thought about the discussion she and Rachael had had about the cell of an individual organism and how it performed a specific task without knowing what the ultimate function of the organism was.

"She's a cancer," Liz finally said, breaking the silence in the room. "Medusa is a cancer."

"Yes!" Seth replied excitedly, knowing that at least one person had understood the deeper meaning of what he'd said. "Medusa *is* a cancer."

"In what way?" Langdon asked. "I'm not following."

"I'll try to explain," Liz said. "When we were in Korea, Rachael and I looked at an individual cell under a microscope. It was designed for a specific purpose and performed a specific function. But this cell was just part of a more complex organism made of millions of cells, each with a specific task that was required for the overall functioning of the organism. If one of the cells of the organism gave up its specialized function—gave up its cooperative nature—and started reproducing or cloning itself indiscriminately, then it degraded the functioning of the organism that it was a part of. This is exactly what we consider to be a cancer: a single cell that reproduces without limit and usurps the resources needed for other cells as well as dedifferentiates the organism as a whole. This unrestricted reproduction causes the organism to lose some of its order, or life as petrins define life. This loss of organization eventually leads to the death of the organism. As the cancer grows, the organism that it's part of becomes so dedifferentiated that it eventually ceases to function. It dies. Medusa is acting like a cancer. She's reproducing and taking up resources and habitable planets that could be used by other societies. She is therefore dedifferentiating the universe itself. She is a cancer on the cosmos."

"Exactly," Seth said. "I couldn't have said it better myself. We consider anything that undergoes unrestricted reproduction to be a cancer. For us, there is no difference between a virus or a cancer cell. A virus is simply a cancer that can be transmitted between people. We view anything that reproduces without purpose as a cancer. It's detrimental to life as a whole. For example, we considered your recent viral outbreak that would have wiped out humanity to be a cancer. It's the unrestricted reproduction of a single entity, a simple virus in the case of your recent viral outbreak, that causes the loss of differentiation that defines humanity as a whole. This is one of the reasons we left you the cure for the virus. In our minds, we were curing a cancer that was afflicting humanity.

"After Medusa's rebellion, the petrins enacted laws to prevent this from ever happening again. One law was the one I've already mentioned. No petrin can permanently disconnect from the collective. No petrin can go rogue. The second law is that there can be no cloning of sentient entities. I mentioned this to you during my previous visit, although I didn't explain that this was the result of what Medusa did to herself. It's permissible to make backup copies of sentient entities, but only one copy of a sentient entity is allowed to function at a time—only one copy is allowed to be living."

For the scientists in the group, the discussion of Medusa was both profound and frightening. For Porter and Williams, who lacked the scientific insight of the others, it was terrifying.

Seth again looked at the photograph of the arachnids. "How did this happen? How did Medusa make contact with Earth? This is exactly what we wanted to prevent. That's why I left the security key—to make sure you were indeed connected to the petrins if you attempted communication using primordial spookyons."

The group was silent. Seth had indeed left such a safeguard, but humanity, given its competitive nature, had not disseminated this information globally. It had been selfish, and this was now costing them dearly.

Joshua turned to Porter and Williams with a look of "I told you so" on his face. Williams bowed her head, knowing that she had made the final decision to keep Seth's security code a secret, a decision she now deeply regretted.

"We made a mistake," Williams said. "Humans are not as cohesive a species as we'd like to be. As you know, we've divided ourselves into countries, which are competitive and adversarial towards each other. It was in this environment of competition that we decided not to disseminate your security code to other countries. We kept it for ourselves. I realize now that this was a mistake, a mistake with enormous consequences. Your intentions were to protect humanity, but our shortcomings as a species failed you. I'm truly sorry for this."

"I understand," Seth said solemnly. "What's done is done. We'll just have to move forward from here."

"Seth," Williams said, "if these arachnids are a cancer on humanity, how do we get rid of them? Will you help us?"

Seth's response was more measured than usual. "These infiltrators are definitely the work of Medusa, but they have subtle differences from the last infiltrators we witnessed decades ago."

"Decades ago?" Joshua asked. He was surprised it had been so long since petrins had encountered Medusa.

"Yes. It has been decades since petrins have come face-to-face with one of Medusa's infiltrators. Ordinarily, petrins have no direct conflict with Medusa. When societies become intelligent and discover spookyons, they eventually make contact with either us or Medusa. Those that contact us first become one of our nodes, and they are afforded the protection of the collective. We try to nurture their growth and prevent their self-destruction by moving them to a new planet under petrin guidance. This is what I was trying to accomplish by transporting humanity to New Eden. Unfortunately, some societies make contact with Medusa first. She takes over their home planet as a new node for herself killing the indigenous population in the process. There is normally not much opportunity for confrontation between the petrins and Medusa. Occasionally a society will make contact with Medusa first and become infected with infiltrators. In an attempt to save themselves from Medusa, they look for other intelligent species using spookyons and eventually contact us. But these occasions are rare. The last time we had to deal with this was decades ago."

"Were you successful in ridding that society of Medusa?" Rachael asked.

"No," Seth replied. "We're almost never successful in ridding a planet infected with infiltrators and Medusa. The best we're usually able to accomplish is to save the society by moving it to a new home world. Their original planet either becomes destroyed by war between the petrins and Medusa or becomes a node for Medusa if we lose the war."

Porter was red-faced with anger. "I was against establishing any kind of rapport with the petrins from the very beginning—three years ago, when Dr. Andrews accidentally made his connection. I tried to warn everyone at the time that the project involved too many unknowns—that the entire endeavor would come back to haunt us. But I was dismissed and overruled—told that I was ridiculous for thinking that we'd one day be attacked by an advanced species. All advanced cultures, I was told, would be peaceful. And now—"

"General," Joshua interrupted, "we—"

"Let me finish, Andrews. We've been attacked, and which part of the petrin collective is responsible doesn't make a damn bit of difference to me. The reality is that it *did* happen, but we don't have just *any* ordinary invasion. Earth is threatened by a megalomaniac who wants to take over the entire universe! This Medusa creature is someone or some . . . *thing* that even the petrins haven't had much success in dealing with, so what the living hell are we supposed to do—humans who are hopelessly behind Petri in technological sophistication. The one thing I'm not convinced of is that we should trust Seth a second time. He lied to us once and may be doing so again."

"I understand your distress, general," Seth said, "but I didn't lie to you. Information was redacted."

"Same difference!" Porter shot back.

"He cured the virus!" Rachael said.

"And he left us a security key to protect us from Medusa," Joshua pointed out.

"And we're still in this mess anyway," Porter said. "From the outset, I said we couldn't account for all the variables, and I was right."

"Wait a minute," Vinod said angrily. "*You* were the one who decided to keep that security key from other countries. We wouldn't be in this mess if it wasn't for that."

"Enough!" Williams said, ending the heated exchange. "Mitchell, I am forced to agree with your logic. Seth, you should have provided a reason for giving us a security key. You were aware that humans are comprised of nation-states that do not always get along."

Seth was silent for a minute while he communicated with the collective.

"We did what we thought was best," he said when he was finished conferring with his fellow aliens. "We saved humanity from the virus and left you a safeguard against connecting with Medusa. Even though we knew that you had divided yourselves into countries, we didn't realize the extent to which this division existed. It really comes as a surprise to us that you distributed the cure for the virus to other countries, but not the security key. Your division into countries is much more complex and nuanced than we envisioned. However, you must have known that it was our intention when we left you the key, that it was meant for all humanity just like the viral cure was."

"Yes," Joshua said somberly looking at the others around the room. "We definitely knew that was your intension."

"You contacted us," Seth said. "We were just listening. Once you successfully made a connection with us, you became part of community of advanced civilizations whether you liked it or not."

It was Langdon who spoke next. "Seth is correct. Humans have an insatiable curiosity to explore, which is what NASA is all about. Admittedly, we had the opportunity not to pursue the original connection with the petrins, just as General Porter has pointed out. Nor did we have to grant Seth the request that we construct an android body for him. But I submit that humans have dreamt of exploring space for a very long time, and if we had passed on the chance three years ago, we would have eventually established contact with the petrins or Medusa because it's who we are. The quest for knowledge is in our DNA. In fact, we were lucky to have made contact with Seth first rather than Medusa. At least our viral outbreak was cured, and if we'd contacted Medusa, we'd all be dead and wouldn't be alive to be having this conversation about humanity's survival."

"There are valid points on both sides of the argument," Williams said.

"It would have been nice to live in blissful ignorance and to have been left on our own for an indefinite period of time. In the end, however, the virus might have wiped us out before space exploration could continue since only a few humans were predicted to survive."

"And just maybe it was providence that we contacted Seth when we did," Rachael said. She spoke tentatively, hesitant to inject her beliefs into the conversation.

"That may be true as well," Williams said, "but the bottom line is that we'll never know for sure about any of this. We're where we are."

"If I may interject," Seth said, "all civilizations face crises as they become more developed. Your struggle with nuclear weapons is a prime example. It has been our experience that sooner or later, advanced cultures develop spookyon technology. That, in fact, was our goal when we disseminated the cells in the first place. When that happens, a species must face many difficult decisions, and you're facing those at this moment of your history. It was inevitable."

"And this was a discussion worth having," Williams said. "In fact, it was unavoidable. If we move forward, we have to be able to trust Seth."

Joshua knew the time had come to voice his recent musings.

"Seth," he said, "Rachael and I recently went back over the transcripts of our original interviews with you. It was obvious that you were hiding more than just technological information in order to conform to your prime directive. We knew that you were holding back something quite important. I realize now that *something* had to do with Medusa. How would we have felt if we knew that the entity that had created biological life, the entity that was the most responsible for our existence, regarded us as expendable? That's a hard pill to swallow. I, for one, feel very fortunate that there exists individuals such as yourself that value all forms of life. By redacting the information about Medusa, you were just trying to protect us . . . I realize that now. Given these revelations, I want you to know something . . .."

Joshua glanced at Rachael who gave him a knowing nod. "I trust you. You've been forthcoming about Medusa, and I for one believe that humanity's fate is in your hands, just as it was with our previous viral pandemic."

"I thank you for your confidence," Seth said.

Joshua looked at those present. Everyone seemed in agreement, surprisingly even Porter. They all knew they were in a dire situation, a situation that only Seth and the petrins had any possibility of remedying.

"Very well," Williams said. "I thank you for clearing the air, Mitchell. Is there anything further you'd like to add?"

"Yes," Porter answered. "Seth, are you saying that there's nothing we can do to get rid of these arachnids. It sounds like you're laying out a no-win situation, a doomsday scenario."

"I'm not saying that," Seth responded. "It's possible to defeat Medusa, but it's highly unlikely. Infiltrators are not immortal. They can be destroyed, but the problem is that if one is killed, it automatically releases eight more offspring that are even better than the original. By killing one, you create more, which makes them extremely hard to eliminate. Like a cancer, they replicate indiscriminately."

Joshua thought of the hard work that had gone into the mission in North Korea. Had they made matters worse by killing the original infiltrator? Many men had died, and he hoped that they had not done so in vain.

"Seth," Liz asked. "You said that the offspring of the infiltrators are better than the original. In what way are they better?"

"Each generation is better because of information transfer. When an infiltrator dies, it transmits the information it has learned during its existence to its offspring. It also transmits information about *how* it died. The offspring adjust their activities according to this information. Each successive generation of infiltrators is smarter and better-adapted to its environment than the previous generation."

"So in essence what you're saying is that they evolve generation by generation," Liz said. "Each generation learns from the previous generation through information transfer."

"Yes."

Williams took another photograph from her briefcase. It was a screen capture from one of the video feeds from the Seals when they had first encountered the arachnid. It showed the infiltrator in the clearing with the white tree behind it. "Can you tell me what this white tree-like structure is?" she asked.

"It's a spookyon collector," Seth replied with a look of surprise. "It's actually a good sign. The infiltrator is trying to establish a primordial spookyon connection to Medusa. The fact that it was growing one of these means that it has no data link to Medusa but was attempting to create one. Primordial spookyons were produced by the Big Bang and can no longer be created. The leaf-like structures on this tree are spookyon collectors. The collectors filter particles hitting them and search for primordial spookyons that are connected to Medusa. This is definitely an advantage for us. It means that the infiltrators are operating on instinct only. They don't have the benefit of Medusa's considerable intellect to aid them. The color of a leaf on the tree turns red when it establishes a connection to Medusa."

"That explains a lot," Joshua said. "It explains the protective behavior that the infiltrator in Korea was showing towards the white tree and why it placed so much importance on it."

"Yea," Vinod replied. "It was like ET. It was trying to phone home."

Porter spoke up, a note of hope in his voice. "Since they're not connected to Medusa, do you think we can eradicate the infiltrators?"

"Possibly," Seth replied. "I'll need more information. The first photo you showed me had a picture of two infiltrators nearing adulthood. That means they have had at least one reproductive cycle. This usually happens when an infiltrator dies. What happened to the first infiltrator?"

"We killed it," Vinod stated. "We have it here in the lab."

Seth looked at Vinod with shock. "You managed to kill an infiltrator and keep its body intact?"

"Yes," Liz replied. "It's more or less intact."

"That's amazing. How did you manage to do that? These creatures are almost impossible to kill without using a highly-destructive device such as a nuclear weapon that would vaporize them and not leave any remnants."

"It's a long story," Vinod said, "but let me tell you—it wasn't easy, bro."

"I'd love to get the opportunity to inspect the dead infiltrator," Seth said.

"I'm sure that can be arranged," Williams said, "but I don't understand why a society with the intelligence of the petrins still has so much difficulty killing these things. Can't you simply create a virus that attacks them?"

Seth chuckled at the notion. "You forget, Miss Williams, that we have waged many wars with Medusa over the millennia. Such simple methods are useless now. The arachnid has an intelligent immune system. It's not like the human immune system, which randomly produces different antibodies to see what fits a particular pathogen. This would take way too much time. In fact, the infiltrator's brain has a separate lobe just for this function."

Liz recalled the third lobe of the brain from the infiltrator that her team had dissected.

"This segment of their brain searches for any signs of foreign DNA and automatically builds an immune response specific to it," Seth continued. "There's no virus or any such entity that can affect it. What else have you used to try to kill the infiltrators?"

"Just about everything," Porter said. "Conventional weapons don't seem to penetrate its armor. We recently tried a thermonuclear bomb, but the picture of the two arachnids was taken after we did so."

"They were probably underground," Seth theorized. "That's what they do instinctively when they're still young. An infiltrator, even an adult, can't survive a nuclear blast, so they try to hide from it. How long ago was your last detonation?"

"About three months ago," Porter replied.

"Then I suggest you release another device immediately."

"Why?" Williams asked.

"For a couple of reasons. First, it will kill any infiltrators that are on the surface, so it has a good chance of reducing the total number of infiltrators present. But you're right. There's only a minimal chance of eradicating them completely. Second, and probably most importantly, it will wipe out any of the spookyon collectors that are present. Once a connection with Medusa is made, all bets are off. There's nothing we can do at that point. The balance of power will have irreversibly tipped in Medusa's favor. It's imperative that we periodically bombard the infected area with nuclear detonations to wipe out any spookyon collectors they may have built."

"But what if the spookyon collectors are underground?" Vinod asked. "They wouldn't be affected by our nuclear blasts."

"They don't work underground. Their filtering paddles, or leaves as you'd call them, need a constant flow of new material hitting them. An underground cave has no airflow, so the paddles would be ineffective. They need the wind."

"How do we know they haven't already connected to Medusa?" Joshua asked. "It's already been three months since the last detonation."

"A good point," Seth replied. "The juveniles take some time to grow, and they don't start creating the spookyon detectors until they have the ability to protect them. Have you seen any collectors in your recent surveillance of the area? If the collectors are present, they're still searching for a connection and haven't connected to Medusa."

Williams reached into her briefcase and sifted through the satellite photos. She found the one she was looking for and dropped it on the table for everyone to see. "This was taken a couple of hours ago." The photo was a picture of a spookyon collector being guarded by a single infiltrator.

"Nice!" Vinod said. "They haven't made a connection yet."

"Very fortunate," Seth said.

"I'll tell the president to order another nuclear strike immediately," Williams said. "But we can't keep dropping nuclear weapons. They destroy a significant amount of landscape, not to mention the houses and infrastructures of the humans. Also, there's nuclear fallout, which can travel long distances. This isn't a permanent solution."

"It's exactly like cancer," Liz said. "We use chemotherapy and radiation to kill cancer cells, but in the process these modalities also kill healthy cells. The infiltrators are the cancer, and nuclear weapons are the chemotherapy. In the end, if a patient dies, it may be from the cancer or the therapy."

"An apt analogy," Seth said. "No, nuclear bombardment can't be a permanent solution. Over time, it would render your world uninhabitable. But it will give us time to come up with a permanent solution. I'll need specifications on your military capabilities to work out a plan."

"We can provide you with that," Porter said.

"I also need to know more about this particular version of the infiltrators that Medusa is using," Seth said, examining the latest photograph. "As I've said, this one is different from previous versions. I don't see an orifice from which it takes in nutrition, and these slots on top of the carapace are something I haven't seen before."

Joshua was somewhat confused by the statement. "It doesn't need an orifice for nutrition."

"Why?" Seth asked.

Joshua was still confused. Did Seth not know about the fusion spheres? "Because it gets its energy from nuclear fusion spheres."

Seth looked at Joshua with a shocked expression. "Fusion spheres?"

"Yes. When we dissected the dead infiltrator, we found thirty-two black spheres of very high density. We tested them in our lab and realized that they fuse smaller atoms into larger ones to create both energy and larger elements."

Seth stared ahead, his mouth slightly agape. His eyes slowly closed, and he lay his head on the table.

"What's wrong with him?" Rachael asked.

"I think I know," Joshua said. "He was obviously shocked by the revelation that the infiltrator contains these spheres. Petrin fusion technology was the other secret Seth was hiding as evidenced by the sessions we've told you about. It may have something to do with Medusa or perhaps the petrins' agenda to seed cells throughout the universe."

The group waited for a response from Seth for a full minute before Langdon said, "Josh, maybe there's something wrong with his connection. Maybe you should check it."

Joshua walked over to Seth and lifted his shirt to expose the door to the compartment in his back that held his Bowman sphere. He used his thumbprint to unlock the compartment, opened the door, and saw the sphere glowing a bright green.

"The connection is fine," he reported. "It's using a tremendous amount of bandwidth though. Maybe the petrins are having a collective-wide discussion." Joshua closed the compartment and returned to his seat.

A few moments later, Seth opened his eyes and sat up straight, a forlorn look on his face. "She's finally done it."

"Who's done what?" Rachael asked.

Seth didn't respond, looking straight ahead at no one in particular. He was trying to get his bearings. He finally saw the group staring at him, waiting for a response. Seth clasped his hands on the table before speaking. "I need to explain the purpose of the universe."

Chapter Thirty-Six
Gita – Part Two

Explaining the purpose of the universe? This was a bold undertaking, even for a petrin. Could Seth really explain the ultimate question—the reason why all life exists? The reason why the universe itself exists? This had been the subject of much discussion between Joshua and Rachael, and Rachael had been of the firm opinion that the petrins, as advanced as they were, had not figured out "the big picture."

No one dared utter a word as Seth began his explanation.

"Billions of years ago, when we were alone in this vast universe—when we had found the primordial spookyons created by the Big Bang—we endeavored for thousands of years to use them to find other life—other purposeful matter such as ourselves—but we found none. As far as we could tell, we were alone.

"There was no purpose to the universe. Why this vast cosmos filled with matter and energy arranged according to the laws of physics, but only a small fraction organized for a specific purpose? Why was only a small fraction of the universe life? We decided that the universe beyond Petri was without purpose, slowly going from the present to the future according to the natural laws resulting from the Big Bang. There was no substance to it, no order, no meaning—no life like us. We were a tiny island of organized information in a vast sea of randomly organized matter and energy.

"We concluded that it didn't have to remain this way. We could provide some order to this chaos. We had the means to spread life, something meaningful we could imprint onto this blank canvas. So we came up with a plan to use seeds to spread life and make the universe more ordered—more purposeful. The seed we created was the cell. It was a single unit of information that could replicate, grow, and evolve given the right

266

climate. Medusa created the cell with the intention that it would eventually make the universe more meaningful—more ordered. We therefore assigned a new purpose to the universe. We didn't know who created it, but we felt that we had realized its purpose. The purpose of the universe was to become more complex, to reorganize itself into more purposeful structures that would serve a higher purpose. We realized that the entire cosmos could become a living entity. We still don't know the *ultimate purpose* of the universe or what the ultimate purpose of life is. We only surmised that the universe was created to grow and evolve, eventually becoming a single organism composed of billions of individual living societies, each society serving a specific function without knowing the ultimate purpose of the larger organism of which it was a part. These societies were meant to be connected to each other via an information conduit—the spookyons that were created at the moment of the Big Bang. We suspected that we had found the meaning of life, the reason we all exist. The meaning and purpose of life is . . . *life itself.* Life is meant to grow and evolve. It's meant to make itself more complex. It's meant to transform the universe into a single, connected living entity. All of us, including petrins and humans, are just nodes in the fabric of a single living entity that the universe was destined to become."

The group's attention was fixated on Seth, and no one interrupted his train of thought. He was their immediate creator revealing the purpose for which they had been created. Perhaps much of what Seth had redacted in his earlier interviews would now be revealed, although Joshua suspected that the petrins were so far advanced that they would never be able to reveal the extent of their technology. But to reveal the very meaning of life? Everyone assembled waited for knowledge that might change the course of history. Seth had conferred with the collective, and it appeared from his demeanor that his species felt that it had no choice but to reveal secrets that normally would not be shared with a civilization at Earth's present level of scientific knowledge.

"The seeds we had created—the cells we blasted into space—were only the beginning. They were the starting point that would allow the universe to achieve its ultimate purpose, but there was a problem with our plan—a limitation to our seeds. They could only survive in a specific environment, one that could support organic life. This meant that the vast majority of our seeds would land on worlds that couldn't support their existence, worlds that were devoid of the materials and the environment needed to support organic life: oxygen, carbon, and a source of energy such as a nearby star to produce temperatures that would allow for liquid water. After we exploded our ice world filled with seeds, we wondered if we could seed life on *barren* worlds. Could life be created out of nothing but matter or energy? We knew that life at its core was just information, the specific arrangement of atoms that served a higher purpose. Could we create a cell, a single microscopic entity, that could transform a barren planet into one capable of sustaining life with nothing but the resources it found there?

"At first we thought this impossible, but with the enhanced thought processes of the collective, we realized it *was* possible. The universe is simply matter and energy that arranges itself according to the laws of physics. Matter and energy can be transformed from one to the other. Matter can become energy, and energy can become matter. Your own Einstein showed this with his $E = mc^2$ formula.

"We realized that the universe had the building blocks needed to create life, but we needed to find a way to reorganize matter and energy into a more purposeful form. If a cell fell on a barren planet, one that couldn't naturally support life, it would need to transform the planet into something that could. It would need to change the atomic makeup of the planet—would need the ability to transform one atomic element to another. But changing the elements—changing actual atoms from one element to another on a barren world—how could this be accomplished? We knew that nuclear fusion could be the answer."

Joshua knew from his experiments on the sphere at the particle center where Seth was headed with his explanation, if only in broad strokes. He realized more than ever that Rachael had been right to search the archives for information that might indicate what Seth had previously redacted. It was all about fusion, but he would soon learn that the application of the sphere's technology was much broader than he had envisioned.

"Fusion is the process that makes stars shine," Seth continued, "but it's also a process that creates more complex elements from simple ones. At that time, we already had nuclear fusion reactors on Petri. They were massive structures that held a miniature sun that allowed elements smaller than iron to fuse in order to create energy. But these fusion reactors couldn't be contained in the microscopic structures of a cell, nor could they be replicated by a cell. We realized that there was nothing about the laws of physics that prevented nuclear fusion from happening on a microscopic scale, but we simply didn't have the technology to accomplish this. If somehow we could miniaturize the process of nuclear fusion and place this process inside of a cell—make fusion a biological process—then a single cell could be created with the means to transform an entire planet—no matter its composition and no matter its distance from an energy source like a star—into a living entity. It would have the means to transform matter into whatever elements were needed for life, and also contain the information to dictate the structure of the newly-created mater into a purposeful entity. Imagine a single microscopic cell that could transform an entire lifeless planet into . . . *life*. The life that resulted from this process would be solely dependent on the information that the original cell contained within itself: the information contained in its DNA."

"So you *do* regard yourselves as gods," Porter interjected. "Beings who have the awesome power of creation. I, for one, find the notion offensive. Technology doesn't equal the divine."

"No, general, we do not think of ourselves as gods. As I've already said, we don't know who or what made the universe, but the cosmos has the ability I'm describing built into its fabric, its natural laws. It's been intrinsic to the universe since its creation—since the Big Bang. We merely *discovered* this potential, nothing more. We do not pretend to know *why* it exists in the first place."

"Proceed," Williams said. "This is not the time for a metaphysical discussion. We have a common enemy to fight."

"Until today, neither the petrins nor Medusa has had such technology, but we knew that the first of us that could create such technology had the ability to transform the universe in their own image. They would have the ability to dictate what the ultimate purpose and structure of the universe will be."

Seth turned to Joshua. "If what you're saying about these fusion spheres is correct, Medusa may have taken the first step in creating this technology. She has been able to miniaturize the process of nuclear fusion to the size of a small sphere. Although it's still not in the realm of the microscopic size of a cell, it's on the path towards such a development. If Medusa succeeds in making nuclear fusion a biologic process that can be replicated, all of us, humans and petrins, are in peril. The universe, instead of being comprised of life made up of diverse societies, will be filled with cancer—endless copies of a single entity. The universe will become the domain of Medusa."

The group was dumbstruck at Seth's explanation. Had the petrins found the purpose of the universe? Was the universe destined to become a single living entity comprised of individual societies interconnected by primordial spookyons? Rachael was aware because of her scientific knowledge and religious beliefs that great thinkers—scientists, philosophers, and theologians—had posited something called the Omega Point, a moment in time far in the future when all intelligence operated as a single entity as a result of biological evolution. Was Seth now revealing a similar notion?

As for Liz, she thought of her discussion with Rachael in the North Korean lab. They had wondered if an individual cell that performed a specific function had any knowledge as to the ultimate purpose of the organism which it served. Was this the case with humanity? Was human society simply a cell, a node that performed its function without knowing the ultimate purpose of the organism of which it was a part?

For Joshua, the notion of using the laws of physics to reorder matter and energy into a living entity on a planetary scale was a profound revelation, and he was overcome with emotion. He stared at Seth, stunned and speechless, as a tear rolled from the corner of his eye.

"Is this even possible?" Rachael asked. "Can you transform an entire planet using only a single cell?"

"Yes, it's possible," Seth replied in a measured tone. "You may not have realized it yet, but the combination of life—purposeful complexity, and the replication of life—reproduction, is *the* most powerful force in the universe. Nothing can stop it. This combination has the potential to transform all matter and energy in the cosmos."

"How is that possible?" Langdon asked. "Life as we know it is but a small speck in the vast amounts of matter and energy that make up the universe. How can something so small effect so much change on something so vast?"

"I assure you, Dr. Langdon, that there's nothing about this notion that goes against the laws of nature or physics. Let's consider a planet in your own solar system, such as Saturn. Organic life as you know it is not possible at present on Saturn. It's ninety-four percent hydrogen, has no significant quantity of water, and is much too cold, on its surface anyway, to support organic life. Wouldn't you agree?"

"Yes," Langdon replied. "Saturn can't support organic life."

"Let's suppose that a single microscopic cell with the ability of biologic nuclear fusion and with DNA that contained the blueprint for a living planet was dropped into Saturn's atmosphere. The process would then begin. The cell would start fusing the hydrogen of Saturn inside itself at a microscopic level into the larger elements needed for life such as carbon, nitrogen, oxygen, and others. This process would also yield energy and heat. The cell would use this heat to raise the temperature inside itself to the level at which biological processes could take place. The cell would then use the atoms it created during the fusion process to create more complex molecules like water, amino acids, and proteins. Once it had accomplished this, the cell would use these materials to make a copy of itself. It would replicate.

This new cell would undergo the same process as the original cell and, in turn, replicate itself. Through a few doubling cycles of these cells, all of Saturn would be transformed into an organic soup of cells with all of the elements needed for life: water, heat, and organic molecules. This soup could later reorder itself into a more complex entity made of more specialized cells that have a specific function that serve the larger organism. A single cell dropped on Saturn, with the ability of nuclear fusion and the genetic information of the structure of the final entity, can transform the entire planet into a living organism. This process would not take centuries or even decades. Because of the power of exponential growth afforded by reproduction, it could happen in days."

"All of Saturn can be turned into living cells in days?" Vinod asked, shocked by the idea.

"Yes. If you take the mass of an average cell that can divide and replicate once per day, the entire mass of Saturn would be transformed in approximately one-hundred-and-thirty doubling periods, or one-hundred-and-thirty days."

No one said a word for a few moments as they let Seth's explanation sink in.

"My God," Joshua said under his breath. "All of Saturn transformed into life in less than four months. That cell would be the ultimate von Neumann probe, but even von Neumann didn't have the foresight to imagine that a probe, instead of simply replicating itself, could transform an entire planet. He was missing the component of information, a blueprint of what the planet could transformed into. The process is ingenious. There's no need for complex machinery or years of terraforming. A single microscopic cell can transform an entire planet. Information and the replication of this information is all that's required. There's even no need for a sun. The cells use fusion as their energy source and could use any leftover hydrogen for fusion energy for the completed structure."

"Exactly," Seth said. "And this energy source for the planet could be located at its core. This would ensure that any energy and heat created would be fully-utilized by the planet—used by this single organism. There would be no waste of energy. On the contrary, it would be highly efficient. Imagine an entire planet as a single living entity with an internal energy source."

Joshua's mind reeled at the implications of such a process. It was a completely new outlook on the universe. For Joshua, it was a profound revelation that bordered on a religious experience. He thought of the long-term ramifications of the process.

"The planet would be akin to a living Dyson sphere," he said under his breath.

"What's a Dyson sphere?" Liz asked.

Joshua turned to Liz. "It's a concept described by Freeman Dyson in the 1960s. Dyson imagined the energy requirements of a highly-advanced civilization. His solution was to build a superstructure completely surrounding a star in order to capture its total energy output. But Dyson spoke of the highly complex engineering and vast material resources needed to build such a sphere. With the process that Seth has described, none of these are necessary. A single cell with the correct information can construct the equivalent of a living Dyson sphere in a matter of days. It would simply organize organic matter as a shell surrounding a central nuclear fusion reactor. The concept is mind-boggling and would change the course of the universe."

"Precisely," Seth said.

As Joshua pondered the process Seth had described, a doubt entered his mind, a doubt that could have only been recognized by a physicist.

"I have a question," Joshua said. "If you were indeed able to implement this process—if you were able to transform the hydrogen of Saturn into larger elements which, in turn, would be reorganized into more purposeful structures in a matter of days—it seems to me you'd have a problem with *too much energy* being produced."

"Too much energy?" Langdon asked.

Joshua explained his thought. "If you transformed that much matter using nuclear fusion over that short a period of time, you would release an enormous amount of energy. Our own sun converts only a minuscule fraction of its mass from hydrogen to helium over the course of a year but releases vast amounts of heat and energy. In the process Seth describes, an enormous amount of energy would be released over a very short period of time. I would think that the heat alone released by that much fusion would simply vaporize the planet."

"Truly brilliant, Dr. Andrews," Seth responded. "You are, of course, correct. There's definitely an issue with too much energy being created, but there's also a solution to this problem—two possible solutions actually. Remember that fusing atoms smaller than iron *releases* energy, but fusing smaller atoms into atoms larger than iron *absorbs* energy—a tremendous amount of energy. In space, these heavier elements are created almost instantaneously in giant bursts of energy called supernovas. The biologic process of nuclear fusion we envisioned doesn't have to stop at iron. This same process, if *fed* with energy, could create the heavier elements and absorb any excess energy in the process. We would simply need to achieve the correct balance of fusion before and after iron in order to maintain the correct temperature for the resulting living planet."

Joshua was impressed with the elegance of the process. "You could literally create any element you wanted in the periodic table, even those with an atomic number larger than iron."

"Yes."

"You said there were two possible solutions to excess heat production," Joshua stated. "What's the other?"

"The other is how all of the matter in the universe was originally created by the Big Bang," Seth explained. "Pure energy can be transformed into matter itself."

"Matter from only energy," Rachael said. "And even *that* matter could be reorganized into purposeful structures. You could create life from pure energy."

"Now you better understand why we define life as purposeful information. We can take pure energy and derive life from it. The only thing needed is the information for the pattern of the resultant entity. This information, by our definition, is life."

Seth paused for a moment before continuing, looking at the faces of those assembled to gauge their reaction. They were mesmerized by his presentation.

Rachael had studied Seth's features as he spoke. Although he was an android, he seemed to be displaying a level of emotion that she'd never witnessed before. He had adopted many human mannerisms when they'd first made contact with him, and even more when he had assumed the form of android Seth after a Bowman sphere had been placed in his chest cavity. Break dancing, after all, was not something anyone expected an advanced alien to engage in. But despite all of his human-like behaviors three years earlier thanks to Vinod's algorithm that had taught him how to mimic certain gestures and idioms, Rachael had never before seen Seth exhibit such deep human feelings. His body language, facial expressions, and tone of voice revealed someone who was deeply troubled and concerned about Medusa and the challenge facing both their cultures, Terran and petrin. Rachael felt more than ever that Seth and the petrins truly cared about humans, their children, as well as the fate of all cultures that had evolved as a result of the petrin seeding process performed billions of years ago.

By the same token, Rachael also observed Seth as being quite vulnerable for the first time she'd known him. He was not an omnipotent creature even though mankind and the 103 Club had regarded him with awe after his appearance on Earth. Whatever he was now revealing—and would reveal in the course of their meeting—Rachael saw someone who represented a race that, despite learning knowledge related to the very existence of the universe, nevertheless had limitations. She knew that she and Joshua would be discussing Seth's presentation in the near future. She continued to study the android as he continued his presentation, which continued to amaze his listeners.

"We don't feel that we have invented life or evolution," Seth stated. "These are processes that have been happening since the Big Bang. Shortly after the Big Bang, almost all matter was hydrogen and helium. The universe has been in the process of becoming more complex by creating larger elements and more complex molecules since its inception. We have simply harnessed these processes and made them more efficient and directed. Now you can better understand why we feel that the universe was created to become a living entity—why life and its processes can transform the cosmos."

Rachael contemplated what was being discussed as it related to her religious beliefs. Had the creator made the universe for a higher purpose? Was life just a means to create a living entity that encompassed the cosmos? The thought was both awe-inspiring and humbling.

"You're attempting to understand the purpose of the creator," she said. "You're trying to know the mind of God."

Seth turned to Rachael. "Isn't that what all scientists are trying to do?"

Smiling, Rachael didn't reply. She had always felt that science, instead of disproving religion or a creator, would eventually find evidence for one.

The religious undertones of the discussion were not so easy for Joshua to ascribe to. His mind operated on a more concrete level and was still racing as it realized more of the incredible physical ramifications of the process Seth had described.

"My God," he said. "This has the potential to extend the life of the universe exponentially."

"How?" Vinod asked.

Joshua composed himself and turned to Vinod. "Seth is right. The universe has been becoming more complex from its inception. It started out as just hydrogen and helium, but it's been on the path of creating larger atoms and more complex molecules. Some of these molecules became even more complex—they became alive. But this process is not infinite. The base elements like hydrogen and helium can't last forever. Stars created more complex atoms from the hydrogen and helium created shortly after the Big Bang. But stars can't shine forever. Eventually, trillions of years in the future, the hydrogen fuel needed for nuclear fusion in stars will eventually run out. The universe will eventually become dark and cold when this happens. But present-day stars are not using the vast amounts of energy they create for any specific purpose. They simply spew this energy into the cosmos. For example, only a tiny fraction of the energy created by our own sun lands on Earth. The rest is wasted. If this process of reorganizing hydrogen into living planets can be used in nebulas where stars are formed, hydrogen can be used to form a mini-sun at the *center* of a planet instead of an external sun that simply spews energy into empty space. This is the Dyson sphere concept I've mentioned. The hydrogen would last much longer and extend the potential life of the universe."

Joshua paused as his mind considered the implications of his own revelations. He had always felt that physics would explain the course of the cosmos as it moved from present to future, but he now realized this was not the case.

"The ultimate destiny of the cosmos is not in the hands of natural laws as we have always thought," he said. "The ultimate destiny of the cosmos is dependent on information and is in the hands of living organisms."

The ultimate destiny of the cosmos is in the hands of living organisms. Seth had not been sure he would be able to convey to humans the transformative power that life had over the cosmos as understood by the petrins—why life and its replication were the most powerful forces in the universe—but Joshua's last statement assured him that he had.

"What do you mean, Josh?" Liz asked. "How is the destiny of the cosmos in the hands of living organisms?"

"Einstein showed us the relationship between matter and energy," Joshua said, "but the petrins have taken it to another level. There is a third element to this equation—information. Matter and energy are interchangeable, but it's how that matter and energy are arranged that will determine the fate of the universe. If there was no life in the universe—no purposeful information—then the universe would simply move from the present to the future according to the laws of physics. But life, as we've learned today, given the right circumstances, has the ability to radically reorganize the substance of the cosmos. Life has the ability to change the destiny of vast quantities of matter. Just think of what Earth would be like if a petrin seed hadn't landed here. Our planet would be much different. There would be no oxygen in our atmosphere. Instead it would be filled with carbon dioxide and methane belched out from volcanoes. It's life using photosynthesis that rid our early planet of these greenhouse gasses and released oxygen into the atmosphere. If it wasn't for that seed from Petri landing on Earth, our planet would be more like Venus. A super-heated wasteland devoid of any beauty and complexity. Life in the form of purposeful information that the petrins created that landed on our planet billions of years ago had a profound effect.

"It took billions of years on Earth to enact this change, but this idea of nuclear fusion as a biologic process accelerates this process exponentially. Before this discussion, we couldn't fathom transforming a planet the size of Saturn into a living entity in a matter of days because we were too nearsighted, but because of the processes of life that Seth described, it's definitely possible. Just think of what's needed to begin this process. We wouldn't need vast amounts of energy or matter since it already exists on Saturn. The only thing required is information—information on how to make fusion a biologic process and then information on how to structure the results of that fusion process into a living entity. This information, as Seth puts it, is *purposeful* information. It's *life*."

Porter was having difficulty with the highly-scientific discussion. "I'm finding it hard to believe that a single microscopic cell can transform an entire planet. It seems too unbelievable. It sounds like you're dealing in the theoretical. In my line of work, we deal in the tangible."

"General, it's the process of life itself on a much larger scale," Liz said, now also understanding the implications of Seth's revelations. "All of us started out as a single microscopic cell, but in just nine months, that cell rearranged matter billions of times its own mass into a complex living entity—a baby. As another example, think of an oak tree. It starts out as a small acorn, but over years it rearranges water from the ground and carbon dioxide from the atmosphere into a complex living entity exponentially larger—an oak tree. But the entire information for the construction of the baby or the tree was contained in the original cell that started the process. Over varying periods of time, information alone was able to reorder and control matter many times its original mass into a purposeful entity."

Liz paused as she contemplated a succinct way to express her thoughts. "Matter is a slave to information," she finally stated. "This process is not limited to an entity on the size of a human or an oak tree. A planet would operate on a much larger scale, but depending on the doubling time of the cells, there's no reason it can't be possible. An entire planet as a single living organism . . . it's a quantum leap of scientific technology."

Seth, knowing that at least some in the group had understood his goal in revealing this information, steered the conversation towards more immediate concerns. "All of this speculation is moot. If Medusa has the power to use nuclear fusion as a biologic process, then *she* would be in control of how matter is rearranged. All of us, including the petrins, would be laid waste. The universe, instead of becoming a diverse entity, would revert to a cancer-like state—endless clones of Medusa."

"Battling Medusa is something I can get behind," Porter proclaimed. "Surely we can strategize a way to defeat her even if she has the edge right now."

"It seems to me that she doesn't have an advantage anymore," Liz said turning to Seth. "We have the fusion spheres for you to study. We also have the DNA from which the spheres were created. If you decode the DNA, you'll find the instructions for creating the spheres, and the petrins would also have this technology, thus leveling the playing field."

"It's not that simple," Seth stated. "I'm sure the DNA of the infiltrator is encrypted."

"Encrypted?" Vinod asked. "How?"

"Remember that we've been at war with Medusa for quite some time. These wars are genetically-based. The DNA of our combatants is encrypted at the molecular level such that if any of our assets fall into the wrong hands, they can't steal our technology. However, I'm sure we can glean *some* valuable information from studying the spheres themselves, but that would have to happen here on Earth, where the spheres are located. They can't be transported to a petrin node since we explore via spookyon transmission, not conventional space travel."

Williams looked at Seth. "We can give you whatever resources you need to study the spheres, but I'm hoping you can help us eradicate the infiltrators."

"We'll try our best," Seth stated emphatically. "Our fates are now interlinked. You need to preserve Earth because it's your home planet. We need Earth in order to find the secret of the fusion spheres. I'll need to see what you've found out about the infiltrator, and I'd also like to examine one of the spheres. Then I'll need some time to confer with the collective about a plan of action. Can we meet again tomorrow morning?"

"Of course," Williams replied. "Dr. Andrews and Dr. Yang will show you the infiltrator and the spheres, and we'll meet again in the morning." Williams got up from her chair. "I have a nuclear strike to order."

Chapter Thirty-Seven
Infoplosion

Joshua and Rachael escorted Seth to the lab to show him the fusion spheres. Vinod and Liz took a break before Liz was scheduled to escort Seth to show him the infiltrator. They sat on a bench in the garden behind the lab, the sun bathing them in its noonday warmth.

"What do you think of all this?" Liz asked.

Vinod inhaled deeply and shook his head. "It's a mind-bender alright. In one sense, it reframes everything, and I could see that Joshua was really blown away. As for me, I'm an information theorist, and a part of me isn't surprised that the universe depends solely on information to become meaningful and purposeful. We've known since Darwin that life was becoming ever more complex, and what is genetics but massive amounts of information in the form of DNA? The universe has always been growing more complex—Seth said so—but we already knew that even on our own limited human scale. It all makes perfect sense to me. Name one thing in the world or in the universe that isn't information."

Liz stared at the gardens and shrubbery and thought.

"I can't," she said. "Everything can be broken down into bits of quantifiable data, whether it biological, chemical, or physical. We may not have the equipment to measure everything as accurately as we'd like—or at all—but everything is information. I've never doubted that part at all."

Vinod nodded. "So for me, this is kinda cool. The revelations that Seth has told us today leads me to believe that the cosmos is a vast computer system. It manipulates data at the atomic level using the instruction set created during the Big Bang."

"What instruction set?"

"The four fundament forces of nature: gravity, the strong and weak nuclear forces, and electromagnetism. Data is useless unless there is some way to read and manipulate that data. There are two basic components to a computer: memory to store data, and a microprocessor that manipulates that data. Matter and energy, which are interchangeable, are the storage medium for data and the four forces are the instruction set of the microprocessor of universe. The universe is acting exactly like a computer. It validates my life's work in information theory."

"So you're saying the purpose of the universe is to be a computer of sorts?"

"No, I'm saying that the *function* of the universe is to be a computer of sorts, but like any computer, its purpose depends on its programming."

"So what is the universe programmed to do?"

Vinod shrugged. "Who knows? I don't have an answer for that. According to Seth, neither do the petrins. Why? Do you have some insight into its programming?"

"Maybe," Liz answered. "Maybe the universe was meant to be *self-programming*. Think about it. The petrins acknowledge that they didn't create the universe. They don't even know if the universe *was* created. It may have just emerged via random happenstance which allowed for the presence of life. Whether it was created or not, the universe is definitely on a path of ever-increasing complexity. If it was created, however, whoever created it didn't need to program the ultimate purpose—an ultimate fate. Maybe life is destined to find its own purpose—life could be self-programming."

"You may be right," Vinod said. "Maybe there is no grand ultimate purpose. Maybe the only purpose is to simply just exist. That's too esoteric for me to comprehend. I'm happy viewing the universe as a computer and all matter and energy as data. Even classic rock is data." Vinod grinned from ear to ear. "But really *good* data, mind you."

"And why do you like that data so much?" The look on Liz's face indicated that she was challenging Vinod.

"Because it speaks to me."

"In a quantifiable way?"

"Well . . . not exactly."

"I'm going to give you a music quiz."

Vinod sat up straight and folded his arms. "You're wasting your time, but go ahead."

Liz rubbed her hands together and ran her tongue along her lips. "Ever hear of Peggy Lee?"

"Yeah, but I don't know her music."

"She was a blues singer, and one of her most famous songs was 'Is That All There Is?' It's a song about life, love, and death, and the chorus asks the same question over and over: is that all there is?"

"What's your point?"

"Seth told us what fusion can do at a microscopic, cellular level—make Saturn or *any* planet into a living entity. It made me wonder—is that all there is?"

"My God, isn't that enough? I don't know if anyone can answer that."

Liz touched Vinod's chest with her index finger. "Maybe in a few trillion years, when the universe has reached its potential for life and all societies are connected, somebody will come up with the answer."

"Some great thinker? An alien collective?"

"No, the universe itself. If its purpose is to become alive and aware of itself, perhaps it will finally have the ability to answer its own question. Maybe everything Seth described is only the first step in something much grander."

"Holy shit, Liz. Do you know what you're saying?"

"Just brainstorming, but once the universe is wholly sentient, maybe that's the just the beginning of things."

For one of the few times in his life, Vinod was speechless.

*   *   *

Later that evening, Joshua and Rachael drove home in silence from the research center in Rachael's Tesla. Rachael drove as Joshua stared straight ahead; his mind preoccupied as it realigned itself with the new information it had received during the day. Joshua was playing multiple "what if" scenarios in his mind of the ramifications given the new revelations that Seth had provided. His mind had taken years to learn the intricacies of science. He had resigned himself to the fact that the planets orbited around the sun essentially unchanged in both their orbits and composition for millions of years, and this would not change for millions more. He had always thought that the solar system, and even the universe was static in the timescale of his lifetime. Nothing really significant would happen to it since it simply moved from the present to the future according to the natural laws, but this was no longer the case. He now knew that there was a force that science had not contemplated—the force of information—that had the ability to make drastic physical changes over very short periods of time.

Rachael glanced over at Joshua and contemplated asking what he was thinking about but relented. She knew that disturbing him while deep in thought would only provide inattentive responses.

After they arrived home, Joshua poured a single-malt scotch into a tumbler of ice and sat facing Rachael at their kitchen table. Rachael cradled a glass of red wine in her hand. They were both physically and emotionally exhausted due to the events of the day. They had stayed late at the research center showing Seth the fusion spheres and the infiltrator. Seth reviewed all of the information that Liz's team had learned from their studies on the infiltrator, and Joshua showed him his research on the spheres.

"Amazing little device," Seth had said after seeing the capabilities of the sphere.

After Seth had been given all of the research they had gleaned, he had been inactivated and plugged in to charge in the bat cave. His mind on Petri would confer with the collective on a plan to deal with the infiltrators left on Earth. They would reactivate him in the morning and hope that the collective had come up with a plausible plan—some way out of their self-imposed peril.

"What an unbelievable day," Joshua stated. "I was remembering the other day how I looked into Henry's eyes on the stage in Wheeler as he took his last breath. I remembered the last words he spoke to me—everything is information. I don't think even he knew how profound that statement would be. Just think of it, Rachael—being able to transform an entire planet, even the entire cosmos—by using the right information. Life and ordered structures can replace the disorder of the cosmos. We used to think of exploring other planets and solar systems to see what's out there, but the petrins are right. What's out there is simply the result of the interactions of energy and matter obeying natural laws. It doesn't have a purpose. Life and the information that underlies it *are* its purpose. Information and its replication have enormous physical power that we've never contemplated."

"Physical power? Care to explain?"

Joshua looked up at Rachael and thought of how to best explain what he had been ruminating over for the past couple of hours. "Saturn has been orbiting our sun for millions of years essentially unchanged. We have no other expectation than to believe that it will continue to do so for the next million years. You agree?"

"Yes."

"What if Saturn were to suddenly explode in a flash of energy and be vaporized? What would we have thought before today as to what could have caused such a drastic event?"

Rachael contemplated the question for a while before answering. "I don't think we'd have any explanation. However, we'd feel that whatever the reason for the explosion, it would have to obey the physical laws, but we wouldn't know why it had exploded."

"Correct," Joshua replied. "Now try to think of a plausible reason, one that's still within the realm of the physical laws, of why Saturn could vaporize so suddenly given the revelations that Seth has given us today."

Joshua took a sip of his scotch as Rachael once again took some time to think about the question. "I guess it could be because of something you mentioned earlier today. You were discussing with Seth the possibility of the fusion process of the cell dropped on Saturn creating too much energy and vaporizing the planet. Maybe something like that could be the cause."

A smile grew on Joshua's face. "You're absolutely correct. That could be the exact reason. Maybe a cell that has harnessed nuclear fusion as a biologic process that could also replicate, and in doing so, could amplify this process exponentially would create so much energy and heat so quickly that the planet would simply vaporize. But what was actually introduced onto Saturn to cause this explosion? There was no massive collision with another object, there was no massive exertion of the four known physical forces that could cause this. The cause of this explosion on a mass many times the mass of the Earth was simply information. It's not really an explosion at all if you think about it. It's . . . .." Joshua paused as he tried to think of the correct word to describe the event. "It's an . . . infoplosion," he finally stated. "It's pure information enacting its purpose on physical matter, but on a grand scale."

"An infoplosion?"

"Yes. It's information and its replication making massive physical changes on matter many times its original size. Like Seth said, information and its replication have the potential to be the largest agents of change in the universe. What occurred to me on our drive home is that this infoplosion, the exponential replication of cells, is not so different than a chain reaction that causes other explosions like nuclear fission explosions. In these explosions, the chain reaction happens because of the replication of neutrons. When a neutron hits a heavy element like uranium, it causes the atom to split and release energy, but it also releases more neutrons in the process which continue the reaction. This is the definition of a chain reaction. But isn't life doing the same thing? One cell splits into two, which split into four, which split into eight, and so on. But unlike nuclear explosions which is a run-away replication of neutrons, an infoplosion is the exponential replication of information—of life itself."

"You may be correct," Rachael replied as she let the concept sink in. "By your logic then what Liz described today could also be considered an infoplosion. How a baby grows from a single cell, or how an oak tree forms from a single acorn. These events could also be thought of as an infoplosion."

"Absolutely. The ramifications are huge. We've never really realized it before, but information and its replication can make rapid and drastic changes on the physical world. It really changes the way we think about the future for humanity. I feel that we've been looking at the universe in the wrong way."

"What do you mean?"

Joshua took a sip of scotch before continuing. "It's as if we were an artist that was given a grand, blank canvas, but instead of painting some incredible masterpiece, we spent our time examining the canvas itself. We poked and prodded it to figure out how its burlap was arranged and how it may have been made. In the process, we learned much about its construction, but ignored the purpose for which it exists."

"I see," Rachael replied. "In your analogy, the universe is the canvas. You feel that humanity has spent its time figuring out *how* it came to be without much examination of *why* it came to be."

"That's *exactly* how I feel after the revelations that Seth gave us today," Joshua said disconsolately.

Rachael put down her glass of wine and rested her chin on her hands, her elbows on the table. "It's always seemed like a dichotomy for me why scientists when presented with something like a leaf from a tree, they eagerly search for the *why* questions. Why do the chloroplasts exist? Why do the stomata exist? What are their functions? But when presented with something as grand as the universe, they don't ask why, only how. How was the universe formed? How did the planets and solar systems come into existence? Scientists seem to have had a blind spot for the why questions as they pertain to the universe."

Joshua smiled as he realized the hidden purpose of Rachael's musings. "I see where you're going with this. In order for scientists to apply a why question to the universe, they must assume that the universe *has* a purpose, a reason for existence. You can't ask why something happens unless that something has a purpose."

"Yes."

"And in order for it to have a purpose," Joshua said, "then it must have been *purposefully* created. There must have been a creator."

Rachael didn't reply, but a broad grin appeared on her face. She took another sip of wine before speaking.

"The petrins asked the why questions regarding the universe millennia ago and came up with their own answer—life," she said. "No one, not even the petrins, knows if life is indeed the reason why the universe was created, but they were unafraid to ask the question. They saw the blank canvas and realized what it was and started the process of creating an incredible painting on it, one made of the beauty and complexity of life."

"I suppose you're right. In order for the petrins to do what they've done, they had to have postulated some purpose behind the existence of the cosmos. But like you said, they're *assuming* this purpose. They don't know for sure. I guess you would consider them agnostic, much like I am."

Rachael was enjoying the erudite back and forth discussion and was reminded of their conversation over their first dinner at Angelino's three years earlier. "I'm never going to convince you of a creator, am I?"

"I wouldn't say never. Just not yet. But you're right about one thing. The petrins *were* unafraid of trying to ascribe a purpose to the universe. Humans, on the other hand, have been narrow-minded in their thinking. I feel like a lot has changed today for mankind. We used to think of humanity venturing into space to colonize other planets. It's seems meaningless now."

"I disagree," Rachael said. "Like Robert Langdon said, it's in our nature to explore. We have the drive to do so, and as President Kennedy said, space is the next frontier. We shouldn't berate ourselves just because we don't have the same knowledge as the petrins. It took them billions of years to acquire the abilities and insight they have."

Joshua remained unconvinced. "The whole idea of traditional space exploration seems juvenile to me now. Just think about it. We had dreams of one day colonizing Mars, but knowing what we found out today, why would we want to live on some barren, lifeless rock like Mars? Humans would have to be completely enclosed in some protective shelter at all times due to conditions there. Mars is a harsh environment, one that's lethal to human life. There would be no simple pleasure such as taking a walk through a forest surrounded by the grandeur of life. Why would we want to spend the effort or the resources to colonize a planet that's hostile to life when there's a better alternative to terraforming? With cellular fusion, we could make a planet as hospitable as Earth."

"But petrins had to explore space with spookyon technology to reach the conclusion that there was no other intelligent life but themselves. That didn't happen overnight. Seth is condensing billions of years of petrin history into a brief explanation. And his society was not without hardship or conflict. It had disagreements and ultimately wars with Medusa."

"I know that, Rachael. But Seth has nevertheless advanced human understanding billions of years in the space of a day. Here's the bottom line. Instead of colonizing Mars, what if we designed a paradise world with the perfect physical conditions needed to support human life, or *any* biologic life for that matter—a warm world with liquid water and all of the other conditions perfect for life. Once we designed such a world, the blueprints for it could be encased in the DNA of a single cell, a cell with the capability of biologic nuclear fusion and replication. This cell would then be sent to another planet in our solar system, and as Seth explained, it would transform that planet into exactly what we had designed within only a few months. How many humans wouldn't want to move to a paradise world rather than a barren rock like Mars?"

"A paradise world," Rachael repeated. "Don't you think that was what the petrins were trying to create for us on New Eden? Yet we both decided that it wasn't what humanity wanted."

"That's true, but that was because of the situation we were given. All of humanity was going to be relocated to New Eden and be under the governance of the petrins. Those are the things that bothered us, not the planet itself. Think about it—if New Eden was a planet in our own solar system without any petrin involvement, do you think humanity would have any qualms about colonizing it?"

"I suppose not," Rachael answered after some thought.

"I feel like I'm living in a new era," Joshua stated. "Everything has changed. Our *futures* have changed. All that humanity has been striving towards for decades seems like a waste of time."

Rachael saw something in Joshua's face that she had not seen before—resignation.

"Not that much has changed," she said. "You're still you, and I'm still me. We're still in our condo having a drink together. We'll still go to sleep tonight and wake up tomorrow."

Joshua was frustrated with Rachael's line of reasoning. How could she be so dismissive about what they had learned? For him, the entire nature of existence had been altered.

"You don't think that what Seth told us changes everything?" he asked. "He redefined our place and purpose in the universe. Just a few years ago we thought we were the only life in the universe. Humanity was the pearl in the oyster of the cosmos. Now we're just an afterthought, another inconspicuous piece of what the universe will eventually become."

Rachael shook her head vehemently. "An afterthought? Are you serious? What about art, literature, and music? Don't they constitute evolving purpose and complexity? These things matter. They give us dignity no matter how small we are in comparison to the size and age of the universe. Besides, petrins don't want clones. They sent out cells to create diversity, and humanity displays diversity in billions of ways every day. Isn't mankind's creativity and drive fulfilling the reason that petrins sent out their cells in the first place? Cellular fusion technology gives a species everything it wants. After all these years, I still don't believe that's healthy, and it's why you broke the Bowman sphere. You're losing your perspective, Josh."

"*I'm* losing *my* perspective?" Joshua said defensively.

"Look, I understand that humanity's place in the universe may have changed, but it's only changed on the timescale of the universe. Your idea of creating a paradise world in our own solar system is millennia away. Even at this point, neither the petrins nor Medusa have figured out how to accomplish it. They simply realized that it was possible. Not much has changed for you and me. We'll still experience life together, and we'll go about our days doing what humans do. We'll grow old together, hopefully raise children together, and eventually die. Biologic fusion technology is far in the future, so is mankind supposed to stagnate for a billion years until all the things Seth theoretically described becomes reality? It's not who we are as a species."

Joshua looked at Rachael inquisitively. He thought that maybe her religious beliefs were affecting her ability to process the information Seth had provided, beliefs helping her through a time of uncertainty. She had always believed that there was a higher purpose to the universe, one determined by a creator. Maybe learning more about how that process would happen wasn't as jarring to her as it was for himself. He'd always believed that science would reveal the ultimate truth, but science and what it had predicted had changed for him in a radical way. His view of his place in the cosmos had changed irreversibly, and he envied Rachael's ability to put things into a perspective that didn't affect her outlook for mankind.

"Do you think God created Medusa?" he asked.

"I think God created the *universe*, of which Medusa is a part," Rachael replied without hesitation. "He created it in order for life to exist. Life can be both constructive and destructive. For that matter, *humans* can be both constructive and destructive. It's up to the life of the universe to determine its own way. Its *own* way, Josh. God gave us self-determination, and that hasn't changed. It's up to us to determine our own path. Medusa wasn't predestined to become evil. She made a conscious choice."

Joshua was amazed at how Rachael was able to reduce the complex ideas that they had learned into a simple but compelling response. He reached out and covered Rachael's hand with his.

"There are times, like this one, when I wish I had your faith. I respect that about you."

"I appreciate that Josh, but my faith isn't *blind* faith. Remember that Seth admitted that the petrins don't know who or what created the universe. They may have indeed discovered startling technology, but that doesn't mean they've found all truth. Don't forget that it was petrins who *assigned a new meaning* to the universe. They *surmised* it, to use Seth's own language. And remember that Seth has reiterated several times that petrins don't know the ultimate purpose of the cosmos. Once the universe is alive, if it ever gets to that point, can anyone predict what it might say, think, or do? Perhaps, like Seth earlier today, it might tell us new revelations. We simply can't think that far ahead."

Joshua nodded. He knew the strength of his wife's beliefs, and he'd learned to respect them, although at the present he was suffering from information overload.

"We still have to do whatever we can to eliminate the infiltrators and end the influence that Medusa has on our planet," Rachael said. "That's going to take science, Josh. We're all lucky to have someone with your knowledge helping us."

"*I* appreciate *that*."

Rachael withdrew her hand and took another sip of wine. "Hey, I have a bit of good news. Ted texted me and said that he's decided to visit. His flight arrives at noon tomorrow."

Joshua's demeanor brightened. "It's going to be great to see him again. Maybe we should offer him our spare bedroom."

"I already did. But apparently he's made plans to stay with Vinod."

Joshua chuckled as he took a sip of scotch. "I should've seen that coming."

Chapter Thirty-Eight
The Petrin Plan

The next morning, the group reassembled with Seth in the conference room. A second hydrogen bomb had already been detonated over the infiltrators' location in Korea, and the reaction of world governments was becoming more alarmist. Radiation from the detonations had begun to spread across parts of the Asian rim because of prevailing upper steering currents, and people in general were nervous and afraid. Visceral fear was manifesting itself throughout all cultures of the world. Many religious sects were proclaiming apocalyptic doom, while most scientists were pleading for calmer heads to prevail.

The information that humans had reconnected with Seth and the petrins had been made public and had dominated all news coverage worldwide. It was the hiding of information regarding the security key that had landed humanity in its current predicament, and there was little desire in the upper echelons of the U.S. government to repeat this mistake. This release of information, and the resulting worldwide anxiety, made this meeting with Seth critical in the eyes of the world. Every occupant of the conference room felt the weight of the pressure to come up with some plausible solution to their current predicament.

"Plans are underway to evacuate a major portion of the Korean peninsula," Williams told the group at the start of their meeting. "Between the radiation from the bombing and the proximity of the infiltrators, a large swath of the area has become uninhabitable. Last night there were several EMP pulses that knocked out the power grid in localized areas. Even vehicles such as cars and trucks near the pulses ceased functioning, making the evacuation difficult."

"Electronic ignition," Vinod said as a means of explanation. "Most vehicles don't have a distributer anymore. They have electronic ignition that relies on silicon."

Williams turned to Seth. "Has the collective been able to analyze our current situation?"

"Yes," Seth replied, looking down at his hands, "and I'm afraid the analysis is not positive."

"What do you mean 'not positive?'" Porter asked.

"The collective has taken the information you gave me about your military resources, most of which are dependent on silicon-based electronics, thus rendering them of limited use. We've made a list of areas in which we would have an advantage and those where Medusa would have an advantage and then played out our best-case scenario. The possibility of defeating Medusa has only a very small chance of success—only a small probability of eradicating the infiltrators from the Earth."

The group's hearts sank at Seth's last statement. Was there no hope for Earth? Had it been infected beyond repair?

"What are the reasons for the pessimism?" Langdon asked. "We did a pretty good job in North Korea, and that was before we had your help and the assistance of the collective."

"The reasons are multiple and complex," Seth replied, "and remember that what I'm telling you is the result of consultation among the vast network of those comprising the collective. It's our belief that in order to completely eradicate the infection, every single infiltrator must be killed. Even if only one is left, it can reproduce. We estimate that most of the juveniles escaped your first nuclear detonation by hiding underground. We also believe that those that survived have had enough time to grow and undergo another reproductive cycle. Our current estimates of how many infiltrators, including those that are close to adulthood, and those that are now still juvenile is around forty. Since most of your weapons are ineffective, we have determined the best way to find and kill the remaining infiltrators is by creating our own arachnids to hunt and destroy them. The infiltrators are in a highly radioactive area, which means that using human armies is out of the question. The arachnids' armor protects them from radiation.

"Medusa's infiltrators are more advanced than the ones we could create. First, they have the fusion spheres, which means they don't have a need to eat or reload ammunition like ours would. They create energy and metal at will. Also, its insect surveillance system is an enhancement we haven't encountered. It wouldn't be difficult for the petrins to reproduce it, but it would take time, something which is in short supply. The more time we let pass, the more the number of infiltrators continues to grow. This surveillance advantage, however, is mitigated by the fact that you have satellites in space that we could use for surveillance, but the visual resolution is not as granular as that of the insects.

"Our arachnids would nevertheless have one big advantage over the infiltrators—intelligence. As long as the infiltrators don't have a spookyon connection to Medusa, they operate on instinct only. They cannot use higher-level thinking and strategy. We have a connection to the petrins and the collective through the spookyon in me. We could use this connection to allow individual petrins to remote control the arachnids we create, making our arachnids highly intelligent, but there's a limitation due to the bandwidth constraints of my spookyon as it pertains to the number of arachnids we would be able to control simultaneously. We estimate that number to be five."

"Are you saying that five arachnids are the maximum number you can create to go after the infiltrators?" Joshua asked. "You've already stated that there are more infiltrators than that. You'd be outnumbered."

"I'm not saying that five is the maximum number we can *create*," Seth replied. "That's the maximum number we can *control* at any given time. If we simply gave them an automated, animal-like brain, they would lose their advantage and would easily be wiped out. This would therefore be a poor use of our resources."

"What do you estimate our chances of success to be?" Langdon asked. "What is the probability of us being able to eradicate the infiltrators given the analysis you've done?"

"We estimate chances of success to be less than four percent, and even this estimate is based on the fact that the infiltrators don't have a connection to Medusa. If they connect, the probability of success would be zero."

No one responded as the direness of the situation sank in. They had put themselves in a position where there was little hope, and much of the blame had to lay with humanity itself and its failure to become a more cohesive society.

"The best I think we can do at this point is to buy time," Seth said. "The possibility of eradicating the infiltrators is remote."

"Buy time for what?" Porter said tersely. "If what you're saying is true, we're all doomed."

"Buy time for the evacuation of the planet," Seth replied calmly. "Buy time to be able to move humanity to New Eden."

The group stared in shock at Seth. Was this their only alternative?

Would they have to leave their home planet, the cradle of their civilization? "New Eden?" Rachael said. The very name of the planet had sparked strong emotions in Rachael's memory.

"Yes. We've finished terraforming the planet. The dome that you and Joshua encountered has been removed, and the entire planet would belong to humanity. We had no anticipation of humans contacting us so quickly after you disconnected. We had continued terraforming the planet in anticipation of moving another intelligent species there that had made contact with us. Their planet would have been a new node for Petri, and they would have been relocated to New Eden. But the collective has decided that New Eden could be yours if you wish. Remember, we would never force any species to do anything against its will. The decision to evacuate would be completely up to you. Our original reason for wanting to move humanity to New Eden was preservation—to prevent your self-destruction. The circumstances have changed, but the goal is still the same— preservation. We would still be preserving humanity, but now for different reasons. The petrins are willing to arrange the relocation any way you deem fit. We could still transport humanity and all of its data to New Eden as before, but what we do from there would be completely up to you. If you wanted to disconnect completely from the collective and be on your own, with no influence from us, that could be arranged. If, however, you wanted to have some level of supervision from Petri so that your odds of survival as a species would be enhanced, that would also be possible. You are free to make your own choices."

"We're not going to just surrender without a fight!" Porter exclaimed. "You expect us to just give up on Earth and evacuate? That's out of the question!"

"We don't expect you to give up, general," Seth said calmly. "We're not saying that no effort should be made to eradicate the infiltrators. Quite the opposite. We should do everything we can to achieve that goal, but there needs to be a contingency plan in the likely case that the eradication fails. We also have selfish reasons for wanting to delay Medusa's grip on Earth. It will give us time to study the fusion spheres and attempt to reproduce its technology. As I've told you before, the spheres can't be transported to a petrin node. For petrins, our very survival is linked to being able to create these spheres for ourselves. This will rebalance the power struggle between us and Medusa."

Williams looked directly at Seth. "Your struggle is our struggle," she said. "We will do whatever we can to help you in that endeavor."

"Your help would be most welcomed. I just hope we have enough time to discover how Medusa is creating the spheres using biology."

Rachael remembered her time on New Eden and how her waking up there had been seamless despite the fact that her mind was on Earth.

"Maybe we can expand that time," she said. "Maybe we can improve our odds of success."

"How?" Seth asked.

"You said earlier that you could create more arachnids, but the petrins wouldn't be able to control them due to the bandwidth limitation of the spookyon inside you."

"Correct."

"What if humans, not the petrins, controlled the additional arachnids that you're able to create?"

"How could they do so?"

"When I was on New Eden," Rachael replied, "you used biograins to interface with my brain to allow me to control my body. Couldn't we use a similar process to allow humans to control an arachnid? There would be no primordial spookyons needed, only the non-primordial type that we can create here on Earth. You can use the biograins and a spookyon pair to interface a human brain to an arachnid, thus allowing a human to control the arachnid."

Seth stared straight into space, obviously conferring with the collective.

"We're not sure if it would work," Seth finally said. "The arachnid's physical structure is completely different than a human's. The experience for a human would be completely foreign and overwhelming, something we feel you wouldn't be able to handle."

"Maybe you could make some modifications to the interface," Vinod suggested. "You know, make it easier for a human to control an arachnid— try to make it a more human-like experience. I can definitely help with the interface design. If you can build it, then I can help program it."

Seth paused again before he replied. "We still don't know if it will work, but we feel that it's at least worth a try. We'd like to test this idea first before we allocate resources to create a large number of arachnids that could be human-controlled. We can build a test arachnid with a human interface along with the five others that we would control. We would need a human test subject to interface with the specially-modified arachnid, preferably someone with military and combat experience."

Joshua and Rachael looked at each other.

"I have the perfect person for that job," Joshua said. "He's on a flight to Berkeley as we speak."

Chapter Thirty-Nine
The Test Subject

Five months had passed since the meeting with Seth during which he had told the scientific team, Williams, Porter, and Langdon of their limited chances of success in eradicating the infiltrators from Earth, but much had happened during that time. The nuclear bombing of the Korean peninsula had continued on a regular basis as dictated by the constant stream of satellite images received by the U.S. government and its spy satellites. As war waged between Medusa and Earth, the infiltrators had expanded their territory far beyond the area surrounding the complex used by the scientific team and the Navy Seals. The entirety of the Korean peninsula, as well as a portion of eastern China, was now evacuated. The only solace for the scientific and military teams was the fact that the latest satellite images revealed that the infiltrators continued growing the white spookyon collector trees, which meant that the infiltrators had been unsuccessful in connecting with Medusa. While nuclear bombardment had had only limited success in halting the spread of the infiltrators, preventing a connection to Medusa was a major win.

Using the tokamak in the lab, Joshua found another primordial spookyon connected to the petrins, and he had succeeded in creating another Bowman Sphere for a connection. This meant that up to ten arachnids at a time could be controlled by the petrins, but Seth didn't want to waste the bandwidth afforded by the new Bowman sphere during the time before the arachnids growing in the lab became fully mature. He had insisted that the bandwidth of the second sphere be used to start transmitting data that would be archived in order for humanity to be evacuated if the need arose. To accomplish this, Vinod had built an interface between the second sphere and the Internet. The petrins were now downloading the content of the global Internet to one of their data nodes.

The bat cave was once again a biological laboratory used by Seth. He had started growing embryonic arachnids, six in all, in small tanks located in the bat cave. The DNA for five out of the six arachnids was identical; the sixth, however, was different. Seth had modified the interface for this arachnid according to a design created jointly by himself and Vinod which would hopefully allow for a human to control it. When the arachnids had outgrown their initial incubation tanks in the bat cave, they were transplanted to six two-story tall aquariums located in one of the above-ground storage areas of the lab.

Seth had also been conducting extensive examination of the fusion spheres. He had made considerable progress in learning how they worked but still didn't understand how they had been created by a biologic process. The petrins therefore couldn't produce the spheres themselves. To Joshua's dismay, any research and information gleaned from examining the spheres was redacted from scientists at the particle center. The petrins felt that the knowledge of such technology was not something that humans were ready for. Joshua had protested, pointing out that his own research had already discovered much of the spheres' capabilities. The prime directive, therefore, shouldn't apply.

"Seth, we didn't have to reveal the presence of the spheres on Earth," Joshua said.

"That would've been a foolish choice," Seth said. "You realized that it was important for the collective to know that Medusa had gotten this far in miniaturizing the fusion process. This revelation is why the collective thought it necessary to reveal the purpose of the universe and ultimately to show you that fighting Medusa might be futile. And all of these details were necessary to show you how imperative evacuation to New Eden might become."

"That may be true, but my point is that the spheres were in *our* possession, and I was able to figure out their purpose and how they worked."

"You wouldn't have been able to duplicate the technology."

"But neither can you."

Seth folded his arms as the two men stood in the bat cave.

"Josh, you're a clever man and a fine scientist, but that doesn't mean your species is ready to handle the awesome kind of power that comes with such technology. It is, after all, the power of creation from virtually nothing but simple atmospheric molecules. Given your military and political history, do you really think humanity could responsibly apply such technology even if you were able to harness it?"

Joshua ran his hand through his hair. "I don't know the answer to that. Perhaps not, but we know the technology exists. You know that we'll pursue it on our own even if you don't share your research on the spheres. There are many peaceful applications of this advanced fusion technology."

Seth appeared sympathetic to Joshua's argument.

"I understand your position as a scientist, and it's regrettable that we've been forced to reveal so much to you given that humanity is still in its infancy as far as technology is concerned. However, you haven't done very well with fission, now have you?"

"No, we haven't, but I always thought that we could overcome our faults as a species."

Seth nodded. "And perhaps you will, but we can't be a part of your research. You still have a long way to go, and the prime directive is still in force. In fact, it will remain so even if you relocate to New Eden. This decision of the collective is final."

Joshua remained silent for several seconds as he stared at his friend. His face was expressionless. Then a smile crossed his face. "Hey, I had to try," he said.

"I would have expected nothing less," Seth replied.

*   *   *

Joshua, Liz, Rachael, Vinod, Ted, and Seth stood in front of six enormous glass aquariums in a storage area of the Bowman Particle Research Center. The rectangular-shaped containers were two stories tall and were filled with the clear gelatinous material Joshua had first seen in the bat cave the night he had been transported to New Eden. Three years earlier, the gelatin had contained embryonic petrins. The contents were now something much different. Each tank contained an almost fully-grown arachnid.

"They'll be ready to go tomorrow," Seth said to the others while he inspected one of the arachnids growing in the tank. The group had labeled the new arachnids as defenders. They looked similar to Medusa's infiltrators with a few minor exceptions. The color of their armor was a deep blue instead of dark gray due to a slight change in composition of the resin used for their armor. The defenders used cobalt in their resin, cobalt being an element with an atomic number greater than iron. Seth's study of the fusion spheres revealed that they could create any element up to and including iron, but not beyond. The cobalt, which was provided by humans, made the defenders' armor slightly stronger than the infiltrators'.

The carapace of the defenders was also different. It didn't have gill slots on top, and there was no hole for an insect surveillance system. It did, however, have an orifice on its front so it could obtain nutrition. There was no chance of growing nectar trees on Earth, and it had been decided that some form of human nutrition would have to suffice. They decided on Ensure, which was a balanced nutritional drink that contained protein, sugars, and water. Given the size of the defenders, large quantities of the drink had been produced and stockpiled.

The ammunition that the defenders would use would also be slightly different. The defenders wouldn't be able to create their own airfoils and would have to be reloaded with them periodically. The airfoils themselves would be manufactured by humans. The leading edge of the projectiles would still be razor-sharp, but they would be made of a harder metal and could inflict more damage to the infiltrators' armor. The airfoils were generic, with none of the subtle shaping needed to fly a curved path. But as with the infiltrators, defenders could shape the airfoils while they were being fired.

Liz marveled at the creatures they were standing in front of. They had started life as four progenitor cells encoded with DNA which contained the information that had allowed them to grow into their current form. As a biologist, she was curious as to how the petrins created such a creature. "Seth, how does the process work? How do you design something like these creatures and create progenitor cells that grow into them?"

Seth paused before answering. He was conferring with the collective on how much he should reveal. Humans had not yet learned the secrets of DNA. They hadn't learned why a certain sequence of DNA would grow into a tree, and why another, utilizing the exact same processes, would grow into something entirely different like an elephant.

"It's very similar to a process that humans already employ." Seth turned to Vinod. "Vinod, I know that you're a programmer. You write code for an application to allow it to perform whatever function you decide. I know that the code for your computer applications are written in binary—in sequences of ones and zeros, but you don't directly write ones and zeros, do you?"

"Of course not," Vinod replied. "That'd be incredibly difficult. When programmers write code, we program in a higher-level language like Java, C, or Swift. Then there's a program called a compiler that takes the higher-level code and translates it into machine language. Machine language is the binary series of ones and zeros that's read and executed by the microprocessor when the app is running."

"We use an entirely similar process," Seth said. "Except the machine language for our application, so to speak, is DNA. When we design a living entity, we simply design its structure and the materials from which those structures are constructed. Then we have something like your compiler that translates that design into DNA."

"I'd love to have *your* compiler," Vinod stated.

"I'm sure you would," Seth replied with a smile.

"The cell is really a computer of sorts," Liz said. "The microprocessor in a normal computer executes the binary code of an application. I guess the analog in a cell would be the messenger RNA and the ribosomes. They read and translate the DNA and build proteins made up of a specific sequence of amino acids as dictated by the DNA."

"An apt analogy," Seth remarked.

Vinod completely understood the process that Seth had described. "You're really just programmers just like me. Except you program in a biologic language and your applications are living entities."

"Yes, we *are* programmers. But we feel that *anyone* that creates new life is also a programmer. Since we feel that anything that contains purposeful complexity is life, then an author, an artist, an architect, or even a chef we would consider to be a programmer. They all create new life."

Liz was awed by the simplicity of the explanation. "So do you have a computer of sorts that you use to design these living entities?"

"Yes," Seth answered. "It's called the collective."

Vinod grinned at the response. Of course the collective was akin to a computer—possibly the most advanced computer system contained in the universe. It was a grand machine on a cosmic scale that processed vast amounts of information and could create entirely new information—new life. The only other computer that may be more powerful was Medusa. These two computer systems were locked in a battle that had spanned millennia that would determine the fate of the universe. Their next conflict would soon happen on Earth.

"You all set for your VR experience, Tabasco?" Vinod asked Ted with a slap on his back.

Vinod was referring to the testing of the human-to-defender interface that Ted would initiate the next day on the specially modified defender. This defender had an extra lobe on its cerebellum that would act as a translator for the interface between human and arachnid.

"Good to go," Ted responded. "I'm looking forward to it. It'll be like playing a video game. And I'm not just a seal, but a Cajun. I've battled my share of critters in the bayou. This one's just a little bigger."

"What kind of critter?" Vinod asked.

"Blue crabs two feet long. Not all that different from infiltrators really except in size. They look like the juveniles. And of course there's the Manchac swamp monster and the Loup Garou. That's a werewolf of sorts."

Vinod shook his head. "Not buying, Tabasco."

"Google it."

Vinod looked up the references on his phone, his mouth hanging open.

"Those creatures actually have a Wikipedia page. Are you telling me that . . .."

Ted laughed. "Had you goin', Vinod. Those are legends." Ted's face suddenly turned serious. "That's not to say that there aren't some dangerous animals back home. I've seen gators take off people's limbs. And some snakes thirty feet long can unhinge their jaws and eat a wild pig whole."

"Seriously?"

"Just give me a crack at those infiltrators. I'll show you who's serious."

*   *   *

The next morning, the group met in the bat cave with Williams, Langdon, and Porter. Ted lay on a table with Seth looking over him, a beaker with biograins in his hand. The others sat in front of the split-screen projector. The left side of the image was a simulcast video feed of the visual interface in the defender that Ted would control, and it would show exactly what Ted was seeing. The right side of the image was a video connected to a camera on a drone that would follow the defender. At present, it showed the specially-modified defender standing motionless in the clearing of a forest near Berkeley. The defender had been transported to the forest for Ted's training session.

"This will tingle a little," Seth announced as he poured the strange blue biograins over Ted's head.

The biograins flowed over Ted's skull and penetrated his skin, and his vision went blank as he lost all sensation of his body for a few moments. His senses returned shortly, and when he opened his eyes he was in a crouched position, knees bent, in the forest clearing. Ted stood, and the observers in the lab noted that the defender also stood as it mirrored Ted's movements. Ted felt completely normal—completely human. He noticed that his physical makeup was unchanged: he had two arms and two legs. His perspective, though, had changed dramatically. The trees of the forest seemed miniaturized, much smaller than normal trees. He turned his head to look around, and the left image on the projector panned to follow his movement, but the external view of the defender showed that its tentacles had rotated only slightly.

One of the biggest obstacles in developing the human-to-defender interface had been the fact that humans only had two eyes, while the defender had eight, one on the end of each tentacle. The human brain could therefore process visual information from only two tentacles at a time. Additionally, the defender had no head. It was therefore decided that if Ted turned his head, the two tentacles that he was currently using to see would only rotate through a small arc of motion. If he turned his head farther than the arc limit, the visual interface to Ted's brain would automatically switch to the next pair of tentacles. This transition would be completely seamless. To Ted, it would feel like he was looking around, but in reality the biologic translator was interpreting his intentions into actual physical movements in the defender.

"Whoa, this is weird," Ted said. His voice output from his brain was interfaced via the biograins with the speakers in the bat cave since the defender didn't speak. When Ted spoke, only other defenders and the people monitoring the interface could hear him. "I feel like a giant human in a forest."

"You *are* bigger," Seth explained. "The defender is much larger than you are. You're seeing the translation of that size difference as you being a very large human. It'll make it much easier to control the defender if you have the correct perspective."

The image displayed on the screen in the bat cave was two-dimensional, but the image Ted saw was in vivid 3D. As he focused on objects at various distances from him, they became more defined.

"This is freaky," he said. "Kinda surreal."

"What's freaky?" Seth asked.

"I feel like I can almost sense the distance to an object. It's strange."

"Your depth perception has been enhanced significantly," Seth said. "Humans' depth perception is caused by the presence of two separate eyes that are a fixed distance apart. This distance causes each eye to have a slightly different perspective on what each is seeing. This difference, or what's called parallax, is automatically interpreted by your brain as depth. The defender has a variable distance between the two eyes that you're using since they're on the ends of mobile tentacles. The farther apart they move, the better depth perception you have because of increased parallax. When you focus on an object close to you, the tentacles automatically move closer together. When you focus on something farther away, the tentacles move farther apart, giving you excellent depth perception even for distant objects."

"Damn cool," Ted said as he practiced focusing on near and distant objects in order to understand how this enhanced visual sense worked.

Next, Ted looked down at his hands. Each one held a weapon, a gun with a trigger. Although he could feel the guns in his hands, he couldn't let go of them. It was as if they were literally attached to his hands. The interface had been designed this way since human hands were versatile, and people did almost everything with their hands. There was no real analog for hands on the defenders, however. Seth wanted to make the interface with the defenders as human-like as possible, but since there was no comparable action to picking something up, it had been decided that the operator's hands would be used to control the defender's weapons.

Ted aimed the gun in his right hand at a tree trunk in front of him. In his vision, a horizontal bright red slit appeared on the trunk. As he moved his weapon, the slit followed.

"The red line you're seeing is a targeting marker," Seth explained. "When you fire your gun, that's where the airfoils will hit."

"Can I shoot?" Ted asked.

"Go ahead," Seth answered.

Ted pulled the trigger on the right gun, and a stream of airfoils blasted the target area on the tree trunk.

"Holy shit!" Ted exclaimed. "This thing is powerful!"

Ted realized he was using a variable-speed trigger. The deeper he pressed it, the faster the rate at which ammunition flowed. When he depressed the trigger all the way, large chips of wood blasted off the tree trunk as a stream of airfoils cut through it. Ted let go of the trigger.

"Damn!" he cried. "The Seals need something like this."

Porter looked at Williams as if to ask *Can you ask Seth for some of these for the military?* The military applications for such a weapon even in the absence of an alien threat were enormous, and the capabilities of the defender were not lost on Porter. It would be far more versatile and maneuverable than a tank.

Williams looked at Porter and simply shook her head "no."

Ted pointed his left gun at the tree trunk. There were now two targeting slits superimposed on the trunk as he fired both weapons. The tree trunk exploded, large chunks of wood flying through the air in all directions. In a matter of seconds, the trunk destabilized, and the tree started to topple towards him.

"Look out, Ted!" Rachael shouted.

Ted stepped to his left, but it was too late. The tree fell right on top of him. Ted could feel the impact of the tree on his shoulder and back, but it didn't affect him. It was as though the tree was made of a super-light material like paper mâché. He simply moved farther left, and the tree fell to the ground.

"I'm fine," Ted announced. "I hardly felt it."

"Remember, you're much denser and stronger than a human body," Seth explained. "Objects that would normally harm a human won't affect you as much. You can definitely be killed, but it'd take a much larger force."

"I think I'm going to like this shit," Ted said enthusiastically. "I feel like some kind of superhero."

"Right," Vinod replied. "Tabasco Man."

"Try moving around the forest," Seth suggested.

For Ted, walking was completely natural, but as they watched the viewing screen, the observers noted that the defender was moving on all eight legs in a coordinated fashion. The brain in the defender was translating Ted's intended movements into corresponding movements for the defender.

"I'm gonna try running," Ted said.

The arachnid moved faster, running between trees and breaking the lower branches as if they were made of balsa wood. Ted, however, barely felt the contact with the branches. To him, he might as well have been moving through tall grass instead of breaking branches extending far from their trunks.

Ted started running even faster, juking left and right with ease to avoid trees in his immediate path.

"He's really good," Seth remarked to the group in the bat cave. "I thought it would take him days to get used to the interface."

"He's a seal," Joshua remarked. "One of the most highly trained humans on the planet."

The defender suddenly stopped, its legs tilting left then right. "I feel kinda dizzy," Ted remarked.

"Hold on," Seth said. "I'm recalibrating the connection to your inner ear."

"That's better," Ted said a few moments later. "Hey, how do I shoot around things? You know, like those infiltrators can."

"I was going to save that for tomorrow's training session," Seth replied. "I didn't want to overwhelm you."

"Hell no," Ted said obstinately. "I'm good with it now."

"Okay," Seth said with a shrug. "Try targeting a tree trunk with your right hand."

Ted did as he was told, and the red targeting line again appeared on a trunk directly in front of him.

"Feel for a button on the gun near your right thumb."

"Got it."

"Now hold down the button."

Ted depressed the button, and the targeting line changed to the red image of an airfoil. Next to the airfoil was a number that currently read 10.3.

"The number represents the current distance to the target in meters," Seth said. "With the button held down, try turning your wrist towards the left."

The airfoil target indicator changed its orientation so that it was pointed to the left. As Ted moved his wrist further left, the airfoil indicator also turned further left. As Ted turned his wrist back towards the front, the airfoil indicator did as well. When his wrist was pointing directly in front of him, the indicator was just the narrow line that he had seen before. Ted pointed his wrist, and therefore his gun, to the right. The indicator now pointed to the right.

"Try moving your hand farther away and then closer."

As Ted moved his hand farther from his body, the airfoil became slightly smaller, but the numbers displayed next to it started increasing. The opposite happened when he brought his hand closer. The airfoil got slightly larger, and the numbers started decreasing.

"I get it," Ted said. "I bend my wrist to set which direction the ammo comes from, and I move my hand forewords and backwards to set the distance."

"He's a fast learner," Seth commented.

"Lemme try this thing out," Ted said before targeting various tree trunks.

He blasted airfoils in all directions and at all distances by moving and repositioning his hand. He started with the right hand and then incorporated his left.

"Damn, this is the real deal!" Ted exclaimed as he stopped shooting.

"Got one more control to tell you about," Seth said. "When you're fighting an infiltrator, you can't randomly shoot airfoils at it. You have to find a spot on the infiltrator, hopefully a weak point on its armor, and bombard that point with airfoils to weaken that area and eventually penetrate it."

"Got it."

"I'd like you to aim your right gun at a point on a tree trunk," Seth requested, "and then fire, but keep firing only at that spot."

The spot on the trunk was blasted with airfoils.

"Now push forward on the button that your right thumb is on."

Ted pushed the button forward, and the stream of airfoils hitting the target increased significantly. Within seconds, a narrow hole had been drilled through the trunk.

Ted suddenly stopped firing. "Hey, what was that?" he asked.

"Remember that the defender has eight tentacles—eight sources to shoot airfoils from," Seth explained. "When you're shooting with your right gun, only one tentacle is firing. When you push the thumb button forward, it recruits the other three tentacles on that side to also fire at the target you've set."

"Shit! That's sweet," Ted said. "So if I have both my guns pointed at the same place and I've got both thumb buttons pushed forward, all eight tentacles will fire at one spot."

"Exactly."

"That's some serious firepower," Ted said. "I'm definitely gonna blow some holes in those bastards. Let's see what this thing's capable of. I'm goin' full out."

Ted started running and juking through the forest, hitting various targets along the way. Branches fell to the ground like wooden rain as he targeted the intersections with their trunks.

"He can fire while running!" Vinod exclaimed. "That'll be a definite advantage. The infiltrators can't do that."

"We left that option open," Seth said. "The defenders being controlled by the petrins will also have this advantage, but I wasn't sure how accurate a human-controlled defender was going to be while moving. Let's test the accuracy."

Ted stopped firing. "Okay."

"I want you to target a branch on one of the trees," Seth instructed. "Pick one about the diameter of an infiltrator's tentacle. Then while running and moving, I want you to try to cut it off."

"Got it."

The targeting indicator lights focused on a tree branch. Ted ran and avoided trees, keeping the indicators on the branch. During his run, he pulled both triggers, and the branch was instantly severed with surgical precision from the point where it was connected to the tree.

"Tentacle off," Ted said.

"Incredible," Seth remarked. "I'm amazed at how adaptable the human cerebellum is. It takes an extreme amount of information-processing to keep locked on a moving target like that."

"It's not *any* human who can do that," Liz said. "He's been training for years for movement and targeting. His cerebellum is a lot more programmed than ours."

"Yeah," Vinod said. "Ted's the man. None of us could do what he's doing."

Ted noticed a small bar at the bottom of his visual field. It seemed to be an indicator of some type that was half full.

"Hey, Seth? What's that bar at the bottom?"

"That's your ammo indicator. You've got about half your ammo left."

"How will I know about energy? How will I know when I need to drink some of that Ensure stuff?"

"That's simple," Seth answered. "You'll feel thirsty."

*   *   *

The scientific team took a break with Ted while Seth nourished the defender and replenished its ammo. They ate dinner in one of the cafeterias at the research center.

"What was it like, dude?" Vinod asked. "Must have been unreal controlling that thing."

"It was kinda unreal and real all at the same time," Ted answered. "It was unreal in that I was a lot larger and stronger than I normally am, but it was real in that it didn't seem like I was playing a video game, even a VR game. It was like I was actually there."

"Not surprised by that," Joshua commented. "Rachael and I had the same experience on New Eden. We couldn't distinguish it from Earth except for the environment."

"Could you see your legs?" Liz asked.

"Yeah. I was in some kind of white, skin-tight outfit that went all the way to my feet, which were covered with shoes and padded with soles."

"That's the exact same outfit Josh and I wore on New Eden," Rachael said. "We need to teach Seth and the petrins about fashion. Seems their outfits are very utilitarian."

"We can't let Vinod in on that," Ted remarked, looking at Vinod's tee shirt, which today was the cover of the debut album from Asia. "We'd all be wearing rock tee shirts."

"Good one, Tabasco," Joshua said with a chuckle while giving him a

304

high five.

"I get it," Vinod said defensively. "Roast on Vinod time."

"Don't take it so hard, Vinod," Rachael said, putting a hand on his shoulder. "They wouldn't be joking about you if they didn't consider you their close friend. Besides, none of this would've been possible without your help. I know you collaborated with Seth on the user interface for the defender. From Ted's performance so far, it looks like you did an incredible job."

"Gotta hand it to you, bro," Ted said. "That's one sweet interface."

"Guess all those hours of playing first person shooters came in handy after all," Vinod remarked, perking up.

Ted's next session was held after sunset. The sky was moonless and therefore afforded optimal conditions for night training. The eyes of the defender, in addition to being more light-sensitive than human eyes, could see in the infrared spectrum, allowing it to pick up heat signatures. The defender, having been serviced by Seth, was back in the forest, with Ted again interfaced with the arachnid. Porter and Williams had gone back to D.C., but the others were gathered in the bat cave to continue observing the training.

The image displayed on the projector was virtually devoid of color. It was a black and white image of the forest but had high definition, and objects could be discerned easily.

"Are you sure it's dark outside?" Ted asked. "I can see perfectly fine."

"Definitely dark," Seth replied. "There are a couple of stationary targets that I want you to find and destroy. The targets are warm and give off heat, but you should be able to see them with your infrared vision."

Ted crouched low and started his patrol through the forest. As he crouched, the observers in the bat cave saw the defender also lower its posture. In every way, it matched Ted's movements thanks to the enhanced interface created by Vinod. After Ted had walked for a minute, he saw a red indicator light on the left side of his visual field. A high-pitched beeping sound also came from his left side. He turned and saw a box glowing red. He aimed his weapons and destroyed the box, its glow fading.

"What was that sound I heard?" Ted asked.

"It's a directional indicator," Seth replied. "The defender has eight tentacles and therefore eight eyes. You can only see through two eyes at a time, but the others are still receiving a visual input. If one of them sees a heat signature or an unusual motion, an indicator will be displayed in your visual field to show you in what direction to turn in order to see the disturbance. You'll also hear a beeping sound that will seem to come from the area of the disturbance. Obviously, the disturbance is not producing the sound. The sound will be injected into your auditory nerves with varying amplitudes and with a slight variation in timing that will allow your brain to determine the direction of the disturbance from your current field of view."

"So essentially he's got eyes in the back of his head," Rachael said.

"Colloquially put, but correct," Seth said.

Ted saw and heard an indicator to his right. He rapidly turned, guns drawn, and spied a quickly-moving heat signature. He fired and destroyed the target.

"Whoops," Ted said. "A squirrel."

"That thing's a goner," Vinod remarked.

"Not part of the training," Seth said, "but a good segue to the next part of the exercise. Multiple motorized remote-controlled cars have been positioned throughout the forest. The cars are toy 4x4s, each one foot long. When I activate them, they're going to dart between the trees. I want you to find and destroy them."

"I'm on it," Ted said.

Seth activated the vehicles, and over the next few minutes the defender ran quickly and efficiently as it destroyed multiple targets. Ted moved at an incredible pace, firing at targets simultaneously with each of his guns. The observers stared in awe at how fast the defender was running, turning, sighting, and destroying the targets. It seemed as if Ted was in a fast-paced video game, but for the seal, he was simply engaged in target practice.

"Blasted all those suckas," Ted announced as he finished hunting the designated targets.

"I'm going to take it up a notch," Seth said. "I'm increasing the number of targets."

"We need some mood music," Vinod stated. His phone was connected via Bluetooth to the audio system in the bat cave. "Welcome to the Jungle" from Guns N' Roses played over the speakers.

"Oh, it's on now," Ted said enthusiastically as he heard the music.

Seth released a new wave of targets. The group watched as Ted blasted targets attacking from all directions, their plastic components exploding as airfoils easily sliced them to shreds. Next, without informing Ted, Seth released a group of aerial drones into the forest. The drones approached the seal's location and were sensed by the defender's rear tentacles. The defender rolled onto its carapace, its legs and tentacles pointed in the air. While still on his back, Ted destroyed the drones without a moment's hesitation and rolled back onto his feet.

"Amazing," Seth remarked, his mouth agape. "I'd planned for another whole day of training, but I don't think it's going to be necessary. He's good to go."

Chapter Forty
Land of the Free

Ted pressed his thumb against the fingerprint reader that allowed him entrance into the newly-constructed Defender Control Facility at the Bowman Particle Research Center. It had been six months since he had first remote-controlled a defender using the biograin interface.

The Defender Control Facility was a new building at the complex that housed both the biological laboratory where defenders were grown as well as the facility where the Seals and other special operations combatants were interfaced with biograins in order to control defenders that were deployed in the battlefield.

"Commander Theodore Johnson. Access granted," a computerized female voice announced as the doors opened.

Ted walked into the building and down a hallway that led to the remote-control ward. The ward was a gymnasium-sized room with over a hundred cots organized into four rows, and Ted saw that most of the cots were full of military combatants, both male and female, seemingly asleep. Ted, of course, knew they weren't sleeping. Each combatant, a member of the special forces, was remote controlling a defender in the battlefield.

Ted lay down on the nearest empty cot. A technician in a white lab coat approached his cot with a beaker of biograins.

"Welcome back, commander. What's your assignment today?"

"Hey, Maurice. I'm going with a group of four to patrol the northern perimeter," Ted said.

"Good luck," the technician said, holding the beaker of biograins above Ted's skull. "Are you all set?"

"Yes."

The technician poured the biograins onto Ted's head, and they entered his skull. He had rejoined the battle.

The war with the infiltrators had been grueling. The defenders had been successful in halting the progress of the infiltrators, and they had pushed them back onto the Korean peninsula, which is where the battles were currently being fought. The biggest issue for the defenders was that whenever an infiltrator was killed, it spawned eight juveniles which were immediately targeted next by the defenders. A few of the juveniles would occasionally escape which meant that the total number of infiltrators was never significantly lessened. One soldier had likened the operation to whack-a-mole. If you killed one, others automatically appeared.

The bombing of the Korean peninsula had continued, successfully preventing the infiltrators from contacting Medusa, but it had left the Korean peninsula a nuclear wasteland. The radiation had also affected the surrounding areas of China and Japan, and radiation levels had risen across the Pacific rim.

The war, at this point, was essentially a stalemate. Both the defenders and the infiltrators had their strengths and weaknesses, which canceled any advantage the other had. Unlike the defenders, the infiltrators had the ability to create energy and ammunition at will. The biggest advantage for the defenders was that they were remote-controlled by either petrins or humans, which gave them superior intellect. This strategic advantage usually caused any one-on-one battle between an infiltrator and a defender to end with the defender gaining the upper hand, but there were heavy losses on both sides. The rotting corpses of dead defenders and infiltrators dotted the Korean landscape, which no longer resembled the pristine pine forest where the scientific and military teams had encountered the first arachnid.

The nutrition and ammunition replacement for the defenders was accomplished via high-altitude bombers dropping caches of both ammo and Ensure in areas controlled by the defenders. Radiation prevented ground-based resupply of the defenders.

The insect surveillance system of the infiltrators had initially been an advantage because they had advanced knowledge of any defenders in the area. But the defenders soon learned that the insects gave away the location of the infiltrators. Since the insects had to return periodically to their infiltrators to refuel, defenders could simply follow an insect back to its source and attack it. The infiltrators, due to their rudimentary, animal-like brains, couldn't learn that the insects had become a liability. There was no doubt, however, that if they managed to connect with Medusa, this advantage would be lost. One of the key objectives for the defenders, therefore, was to locate and destroy any spookyon collector trees they found. Unfortunately, all spookyon collectors couldn't be found by the defenders alone because of their increasing numbers, so nuclear bombing continued relentlessly, poisoning more of the atmosphere. The bombing itself had to be well-coordinated since defenders in the area of the drop zone needed to be evacuated before bombs could be dropped.

Even though the petrins had the ability to incorporate the spawning of juveniles into the defenders, this wasn't done. Any juvenile spawned by a defender would need nutrition, which was in short supply in the battlefield despite airdrops. It was therefore decided that is was safer and more prudent to grow the defenders at the lab and then transport them to the combat zone. To date, the lab had produced over two-hundred-and-fifty defenders, but many of these had already been killed. Approximately one hundred defenders were currently in the field, but new ones were being grown at the lab. It took a great deal of time to transport mature defenders to the battlefield, which was a further setback for Earth's defenses. It also entailed considerable risk since moving the defenders into a radioactive hot zone was a risk for cargo transport planes, which landed on the periphery of the Korean peninsula and took off in as short a time as possible. Remote controllers then maneuvered them into battle.

Joshua had managed to capture two additional primordial spookyons connected to the petrins over the last six months. This meant that petrins could control twenty defenders. The remaining defenders were controlled by special operations military combatants. Even though the human-controlled defenders performed exceptionally well, they were no match for the petrin-controlled defenders. The petrins had brains that were significantly more advanced than human brains, and they could therefore recruit more computing power throughout the collective. This advantage for the petrin-controlled defenders readily showed on the battlefield. These defenders were extremely difficult for the infiltrators to kill, and their destruction was only accomplished if infiltrators outnumbered the defender. It was for this reason that each group of defenders was led by a single petrin-controlled commander.

Even though the defenders managed to stop the advance of the infiltrators, the defenders were nevertheless outnumbered by Medusa's arachnids due to the infiltrators' ability to spawn when killed. Many juvenile infiltrators went into hiding and grew to maturity before rejoining the battle.

*   *   *

Joshua, Rachael, Vinod, and Liz were summoned to a meeting in Langdon's office. Seth was already in the office when the four walked in. Porter and Williams joined via video conference as usual.

"Seth has called this meeting," Langdon informed the group. "He wants an update on how we think the war is going and what our plan of action is from this point on. Mitchell, I'd like you to begin with an assessment of the conflict."

"There hasn't been much progress in eliminating the infiltrators over the last month," Porter said. "We've held our lines and have prevented the infiltrators from expanding their area of influence, but it's requiring more and more defenders to accomplish this. It's also our assessment that the total number of infiltrators is increasing, evenly matching the number of defenders we have in the field."

"That's an untenable situation, general," Williams interjected. "The more time that passes, the more nuclear weapons have to be dropped, which not only renders the immediate area uninhabitable, but also affects the surrounding areas with higher and higher levels of radiation. We received reports today that the radiation levels in parts of western Japan are at critical levels. The Japanese are starting to evacuate these areas. Additionally, radiation levels in the atmosphere are climbing over North America and Europe because of prevailing upper-level steering currents."

"Goddamn it!" Porter exclaimed, frustrated. "I realize it's untenable! We're throwing everything we can at those bastards, and we've succeeded in stopping their advance, but we can't eliminate them. Their ability to replicate is astounding."

"This is a war of attrition," Langdon said somberly. "In my opinion, we'll have to up our firepower to have any chance of eliminating the infiltrators."

"That's also my opinion," Williams said. "We can't keep up this stalemate much longer. We need more defenders. Seth, is there any way you can increase the rate of defender production?"

"We're making them as fast as we can," Seth replied. "Each defender has a growing time of three months. The only way to increase the production would be to build additional labs, preferably at other locations around the globe."

"That can be arranged," Williams said.

"There's still a problem," Joshua said. "It takes three months to grow a defender, and I'm guessing that it will take at least two months to build these additional labs. That's five more months of additional nuclear bombardment. Much larger parts of our planet will become uninhabitable from radiation during that time."

"I realize the implications," Williams said. "This war is turning large portions of our world into a nuclear wasteland, but at this point there are no other options. If we want to keep our planet, we have to eradicate the infiltrators. Like it or not, this is the only viable plan—a surge in defenders."

"I concur," Porter added. "We simply have to outnumber the enemy. It may sound like oversimplification, but it's been a sound tactic in war for thousands of years."

The group was silent as they thought of what would happen over the next few months even with a surge in defender production. The outlook was not encouraging. They knew that the prospect of escalating the war against the infiltrators might result in the eventual goal of eliminating them from the Earth, but what would be left of mankind's home world? Even if the infiltrators could be eliminated, the planet would be permanently altered by radiation, a poisoned shell of its former self.

"I know it's not what you want to hear," Seth said, "but this is why the petrins' analysis of your situation was so dire—why we gave you only a very limited chance of success. Our analysis hasn't changed much. We believe your chances of success are now are still less than ten percent. Our estimates of success are higher than what I told you originally since we can now employ human-controlled defenders, but the odds are still slim. Again, these odds are dependent on the infiltrators not being able to connect with Medusa. If that happens, there's no chance of success."

"Are you trying to pour salt on our wounds?" Porter asked. "Maybe you didn't download enough information about human determination and resolve."

"Not at all general," Seth said. "You've done an amazing job really. However, I am saying that you have to start considering more seriously the need to evacuate your planet. You're lucky in a way. Most societies that Medusa infects don't enjoy the benefit of having contacted us first. Most cultures get wiped out without ever knowing what happened to them or why it was happening. I know that leaving your home world is a last resort but think of other worlds that Medusa has destroyed. They had no options—no escape. We're offering you an alternative, one that you need to take more seriously given the way the war is going."

There was more silence before Rachael spoke up.

"He's right," she said. "We need to prepare for that possibility. Seth is offering us a way out. We'd be derelict in ignoring it. Do we really wish our culture to become extinct? Did humanity toil and evolve for a hundred thousand years to be eradicated from the universe? Do we want the last copy of all life on Earth to be lost forever? If the universe has a destiny, I believe we should be part of it."

All eyes turned to Rachael at her statement.

"Miss Miller," Williams said, "all of us are acutely aware that it was you who vehemently argued for disconnection from the petrins during our first encounter with them. You felt that humanity wouldn't be free to chart its own course on New Eden. I remember from your report that you felt that New Eden was akin to a zoo. What's changed?"

Joshua looked at Rachael. He considered speaking up for her but thought better of it. It was Rachael's question to answer.

"This situation is different," Rachael replied. "The last time we were in New Eden, a large portion of humanity was facing death from a viral outbreak, but humanity wouldn't have become extinct. Humanity still had a future on Earth. But what future is there if Medusa takes over this planet? What future is there if we turn our paradise into a nuclear wasteland? My main reservation with having humanity go to New Eden was that it wouldn't be free. We would have been under the control of the petrins, but Seth has told us that we are free to choose how much influence the petrins have over us. That would be *our* choice now." Rachael turned to Seth. "Am I correct, Seth?"

"Yes. We would transport humanity and the data that represents humanity to New Eden. How much influence we have over you from that point on will be up to you. We can completely disconnect if you wish. Our only goal has always been to preserve your species. I hope that I've been able to convey our vision of what we wish the universe to become—an interconnected network of diverse societies where each has its own individual strengths. Saving humanity is, for us, a step towards that goal. And as you point out, saving your culture would greatly contribute to what we perceive to be the meaning of life and the purpose of the universe. Your efforts and unique culture should not be lost."

"Dina," Langdon added, "I think we need a plan for evacuation, if only as a last resort."

"I agree, Robert," Williams said, acknowledging their current situation. "There's nothing wrong with having a contingency plan. In fact, I think the urgency of our situation dictates that we consider it seriously. Robert, I want you to work with Seth on the logistics of it. Seth, what are the general steps involved?"

"It's just information transfer," Seth replied. "We've finished transferring all external data associated with humanity to one of our data nodes, so this information is already backed up. The remaining data that needs to be transferred is for humans themselves. The DNA for each human will need to be cataloged, as well as the information contained in the neural networks of their brains. This information will also be transferred to our data nodes. The scanning process actually goes quickly. It will only take about one minute per human, but there are over 7.7 billion humans, which means that we'll need to have multiple scanning centers—thousands of them—across the world. We can set this up fairly rapidly, but we can't scan all humans at once. We estimate that it would take two months to complete the scans depending on how many centers there are. Scanning will have to begin before the final decision to evacuate the planet is made, however. The process can't be a last-minute operation for obvious reasons. There would be chaos."

"I will try to get authorization for the process to be started," Williams said. "Nations around the world will have to coordinate their efforts."

"I must caution you that there will also be side-effects to this process," Seth stated. "Those who are scanned near the beginning will lose a portion of their lives."

The faces of those assembled became visibly alarmed.

"What do you mean?" Joshua asked.

"Scanned information is static," Seth explained. "It's a backup at a certain moment of time. When the backup is restored on New Eden, any experiences that a person has had since the time of the backup will be lost."

"I guess that's unavoidable," Langdon said. "Still, having a backup, albeit a dated one, is better than no backup at all. We'll have to have some type of lottery system to determine the order of scanning."

"Another side-effect is age," Seth said. "We'll be growing a clone of each human on New Eden from their DNA. The process is much faster than the actual growth of a normal human. It will take only a couple of months for clones to become mature. Once the clone has reached the desired age, we will infuse its brain with the information we have scanned from the brain of the original person on Earth. A question for you to consider is at what age should we consider the clone to be mature? That's something your population will have to decide."

"What do you mean by mature?" Langdon asked.

"What I'm asking is this: at what age would you want us to do the information transfer to the brain of the clone? Obviously for children, we would grow their clones to the same age they were on Earth. What would you like us to do for adults?"

"What are you getting at?" Liz asked, still confused by Seth's question.

"We could grow each adult clone to any desired age that represents adulthood. From what I understand, adults are defined as any age from eighteen to a hundred years old. We could implement the information transfer to the clone at any point during this range irrespective of what age the original human was when scanned. Should each individual human be given this choice, or should all humans be grown to the age at which they were scanned?"

Seth had said this was a side-effect, and yet this was much more than that. It was tantamount to a fountain of youth.

"I would think that we would have to allow each individual human to choose," Williams answered after some thought. "I can't see it working any other way. I don't think a government could mandate that every individual maintain their current age."

"Wow," Vinod remarked. "How many eighty-year-olds are going to opt out of being in their twenties again? You've all seen the movie *Cocoon*, haven't you?"

"Yeah, somehow I feel that the average age of humanity will definitely be less than it currently is given the possibility of individual choice," Joshua said. "But you're right, Dina. We couldn't mandate that all humans remain their current age. That's really a personal choice. But over long periods of time, this age discrepancy will be diminished. Over generations, humanity will revert back to a more natural distribution."

"Okay," Seth said. "It'll be an individual decision."

"When do you want to start the scanning?" Williams asked.

"As soon as possible, but first I'd like to start backing up humans who currently aren't aging," Seth said.

"What do you mean?" Liz asked. "Everyone's *always* aging."

"I'm referring to humans you have frozen in your cryo facilities," Seth answered. "As you know, we consider them to contain life. They're still human, albeit in a suspended state."

All eyes turned to Rachael, who looked at Seth, shocked. They realized the implications of Seth's statement and knew that Rachael would be directly affected. Her brother Richard had been frozen many years ago. Was there the possibility of his being revived? There was doubt among some of the members present as to whether frozen humans should be backed up at all. They had, in fact, died, although it wasn't the petrin definition of death. Should they be backed up and revived on New Eden? The moral implications of moving humanity to New Eden were many and were multiplying by the minute.

"Would you revive them on New Eden or leave them frozen?" Rachael asked.

"It would be your decision," Seth replied. "We wouldn't leave them frozen as you say. If you didn't want them immediately revived, they would simply be stored as data—as information on one of our nodes. Leaving them on Earth is simply not an option if you want them to be preserved."

"What about their illnesses?" Liz asked. "They all died of various causes."

"You're referring to *your* definition of death," Seth replied. "We consider them to contain life even though they're not currently living. Those who are still able to be cured of whatever afflictions caused them to be frozen can be repaired by us, but there are some conditions we can't repair, such as those with permanent information loss. For example, any human who has been frozen as a result of brain damage cannot be revived. The information loss from their brains is permanent. Remember that our definition of death is the loss of the last copy. Once the last copy of the information from their brains has been lost, it cannot be retrieved."

Rachael tried hard to control her heightening emotions in front of the group. Was there a possibility of seeing Richard again? She was speechless. So many thoughts and emotions coursed through her mind. What would it be like for Richard to wake up on an entirely new world, one he wasn't familiar with? What would he think of a grown-up Rachael? Would he adjust, or would the shock be too great?

Joshua saw Rachael's emotional strife. He reached out to hold her hand and offer comfort.

"I think they should be backed up," Joshua said. "Wasn't that their entire intent when they decided to be frozen in the first place? As far as reviving them, we can make that decision later after further thought. As for Richard's case, he died as a youth. According to what Seth just said, I presume he would be revived as a young boy."

"They should be backed up," Rachael said, still trying to keep her emotions in check.

"That's fine," Seth said. "We will attempt to scan the humans in your cryo facilities. During scanning, we can determine whether or not there has been permanent information loss. Only those we feel can be revived will be stored as information on our data nodes."

Rachael looked at Liz, who in an instant understood her gaze.

Liz remembered the night on the carrier when Rachael was upset because she was afraid that if Richard's information was still on Earth, he wouldn't be in heaven. She wondered what Rachael would want the outcome of Richard's scanning to reveal. Would she want the information to have been preserved so that he had the possibility of being revived, or would she wish that his information had not been retained, which, in Rachael's mind, would mean that he was in heaven? Liz gave Rachael a look of support, the most she could offer in a public setting.

Rachael composed herself and turned to Seth. "When you scan people in the cryo facilities, I think it's very important that you notify their relatives as to the results of the scanning process. They have a right to know if their loved ones are able to be revived or not."

"We will absolutely do that," Seth said.

After a few moments of silence, Vinod took an uncharacteristically serious tone as he thought of a question. It would be one that would be difficult, if not impossible, to answer, but he felt he had to ask it.

"Whose decision will it be to have humanity transported to New Eden?" he asked.

"What do you mean, Vinod?" Williams inquired. "I'd think that if we felt our war with the infiltrators would be lost or that Earth was becoming uninhabitable, humanity would make a collective decision."

"A collective decision?" Vinod said. "You mean one made by some governmental organization like the United Nations?"

"Yes," Williams said. "Something like that."

"Governments notwithstanding, would individuals have a choice about going to New Eden?"

"Of course," Williams answered. "We wouldn't force anyone to go against their will. It would be an individual decision. If we decide to evacuate Earth, however, I feel that any decision to stay would be akin to suicide."

"An individual decision?" Vinod said. "A decision not rendered by society?"

"Yes," Williams said with frustration. "I'm not sure why you're asking these questions. The answers seem obvious."

Vinod looked at Williams' image on the monitor. "What if someone wanted to go to New Eden even though the government decided not to evacuate Earth? Would it still be an individual decision?"

The group was shocked by the question, one that had huge moral implications. Would society dictate that individuals not be allowed to separate from humanity unless the society of which they were a part gave them permission?

Seth gave a knowing smile to Vinod. Vinod was expressing a dilemma that petrins had encountered ages ago when Medusa had first split from the collective. They had allowed her to leave the collective, a decision they later regretted. After the split, petrins had decided that no individual could disconnect from the collective permanently. Seth was curious how humans would respond to this same choice.

"Are you saying you want to split up humanity, Mr. Bhakti?" Porter asked tersely.

"Not split up humanity per se," Vinod replied. "It would simply be a side effect of allowing humans to make their own individual decisions."

"For me, the answer is obvious," Porter stated. "No human should be allowed to go to New Eden unless the government agrees."

"Which country are you sworn to protect, general?" Vinod asked. "Isn't it the land of the free? What freedom are you affording your citizens? Aren't we free to make our own choices?"

"Are you questioning my loyalty to this country?" Porter shouted.

"Let's step back a moment," Williams stated calmly in an effort to de-escalate what was shaping up to be a contentious argument. "It's a valid question, Mr. Bhakti, but not one we need to answer now. It's also not a question that any of us in this meeting can answer. Our first priority is to save this planet and have a backup plan if we can't. I will, however, bring this question to the president and other world leaders for their input. It's not an easy decision by any means. It's one that's going to require much thought and discussion." Williams paused for a moment before continuing. "Seth, I realize that this decision is ultimately up to the petrins. I know that you're willing to transport humanity to New Eden if we so choose, but what would the petrins do if the leadership of humanity—its governments—decided not to evacuate Earth even if some individuals still wanted to go. Would you allow this? Would you transport them to New Eden against their governments' will?"

"It's a universal dilemma," Seth said, "something that many societies have had to deal with. Indeed, it's a moral decision that we ourselves have struggled with. What are the rights of an individual versus the rights of a society? Our view of this has evolved over the millennia. In the beginning, we were more focused on individual rights. This is the reason we allowed Medusa to disconnect from the collective in the first place. But given how that turned out, our thoughts have changed to favor society as a whole. As you know, no one in the collective can disconnect permanently. We feel that life works better in a cooperative fashion. That's why we eventually turned into a collective. Don't get me wrong. We highly value individual rights. Individuality is differentiation that makes life more purposeful and expands its complexity. But life functions best when there's a balance between individualism and communality. When this balance is not achieved, the results are detrimental to the function and purpose of life as a whole. Just think of what happens at the extreme ends of this range. If there's no individuality, you end up with cancer. This is the problem with Medusa—endless clones without differentiation. On the other end of the spectrum is a society that's constantly at war with itself. Any small differences between individuals become a reason for division and conflict. Humanity, especially in its past, has frequently been on this end of the spectrum. Your past is littered with wars that killed large segments of your population over simple differences in beliefs such as religion. This balance between individuality and communality needs to be achieved in all forms of life, even in the cells that make up an organism such as the human body, for an organism or society to function properly."

"What are you saying?" Vinod asked. "We shouldn't divide ourselves along cultural and ideological lines?"

"That's not what I meant. It's beneficial for societies to have different cultural beliefs. This adds to the diversity of a society, but these divisions must not be used as a reason for undermining the ultimate purpose of a society or organism. Even in the human body, cells are divided into large groups for specific purposes. You call these groups your organs. As long as your organs function for their designed purposes and help the organism as a whole, they are beneficial. But if something goes wrong and one organ system starts attacking another, it can become fatal."

Liz thought of Seth's last statement as it related to the human body and her study of medicine.

"He's absolutely right," she stated. "There are disease states in humans that pit one group of cells in the same body against others. These diseases are called autoimmune diseases in which the immune system goes haywire and starts attacking its own tissues. These are some of the most devastating medical conditions in humans. Rheumatoid arthritis is a condition where the body's own immune system starts attacking the cartilage of its joints. As another example, Crohn's disease causes the immune system to attack cells that line the gut."

"Those are apt examples," Seth said. "Vinod, I realize the reason for your question. Believe me, it's something that we still struggle with. However, I think we'd find it extremely difficult to transport individuals to New Eden against the will of society in general. If the government chooses to allow individuals to go even though the entire planet wasn't being evacuated, then we'd allow it. Otherwise, we'd be reluctant to grant individual requests to be transported to New Eden."

"I get it," Vinod said. "It's not that I would want to do that. I was just bringing this up as a point of discussion."

"I understand your reason for this line of questioning," Williams said. "It's very important. As I've said, I'll discuss this with the higher-ups." Williams leaned back in her chair. "We've had a very deep discussion today. There are obviously many questions we don't have definite answers for, but before I end this meeting, is there anything else of importance that anyone wants to bring up?"

"I have one final topic to present," Seth said. "It's a request really."

"What is it?" Langdon asked.

"The primary reason we transported Joshua and Rachael to New Eden was because we wanted to give humanity an idea of what life on New Eden would be like so they could convey this information to everyone else. Much has changed there since their last visit. The entire planet has been terraformed. As I told you before, the dome that Joshua and Rachael encountered has been removed. Additionally, over the past few months, we've introduced more of the flora and fauna that's native to Earth to the planet."

Langdon felt that it was presumptuous of the petrins to assume that humans would decide to occupy New Eden. The decision had not been made, and yet the petrins had already recreated indigenous lifeforms from Earth on New Eden?

"What if we decide not to move there?" he asked. "What will happen to life on New Eden that is native to Earth? Will it be removed?"

Seth stared at Langdon without responding, allowing him time to reflect on his question. He knew that Langdon was a reasonable man, a scientist, one who was good at getting at the truth. Seth knew that sometimes it took humans time to realize the bigger picture. His silence was an effort to give Langdon that time.

As Langdon stared back at Seth and wondered why there was no response to his question, a thought crossed his mind. Did humans have domain over *all* life on Earth? Should *they* be the ones who decided the ultimate fate of all of Earth's biology? Should humans proclaim ownership over life that they, unlike the petrins, had no real hand in? He suddenly understood Seth's non-response.

"You're trying to preserve life, aren't you, Seth?" Langdon asked. "You're just trying to preserve the outcome of the evolution of life on this planet that you yourselves seeded."

"Yes," Seth said quietly. "Just like we tried to preserve humanity during my first visit here."

This was an epiphany for Langdon. He was a man of science and logic, not a person who dwelled much on the morality of science, but this was definitely a moral decision, one that science didn't have an answer for. This one simple instance of the petrins' actions had been a revelation for him, and he understood better the motives of the collective. They were enacting their vision of how they viewed the eventual destiny of the universe—a living entity composed of diverse, interconnected societies. They were the preservers of life in the universe while Medusa, their adversary, was the destroyer.

Hearing no further response from Langdon, Seth continued his request.

"We have preserved Rachael's clone on New Eden. I'm asking that she be transported there to witness the changes we've made and report back to give humanity further information with which to make its decision regarding evacuation if it becomes inevitable."

"Can I go with her?" Joshua asked.

"Yes," Rachael added. "I'd like Josh to join me."

"We didn't preserve Joshua's clone," Seth replied nonchalantly. "Only Rachael's. We can, of course, transport Joshua there later after a new clone of him has been established, but for now, Rachael is the only one who can visit New Eden immediately."

"Why did you only preserve *her* clone?" Joshua asked, somewhat offended. "Why didn't you preserve mine?"

"Redacted," Seth responded.

That was a word that they hadn't heard from Seth in quite some time.

Chapter Forty-One
A Return to Eden

One month later, Seth had set up numerous scanning centers throughout the world, and the scanning of humanity had already started. Frozen humans in cryo facilities were the first humans to be scanned and their scanning was almost complete. For all others, a lottery system had been instituted based on a person's birth date, which would determine the order in which humanity would be scanned.

No one would be forced to undergo the procedure, and while many had said they would refuse, the vast majority consented even though they hoped to remain on Earth.

Four additional bio labs were hastily being constructed in Europe, Asia, Africa, and South America, which were scheduled to grow additional defenders for the surge that had been ordered to eliminate the infiltrators. The production of the additional defenders would hopefully turn the tide of the war.

Rachael saw Seth standing over her with a beaker of biograins in the bat cave as she lay on a padded table. Joshua stood at Seth's side. She was about to return to a place she never thought she would see again, but she was conflicted about returning to New Eden. She fondly remembered the excitement that she and Joshua shared when they had explored the planet, one they had all to themselves. These thoughts were tempered by her memories of their final night there, a night filled with anguish and emotional pain. What would her experience be like after all these years? She looked with trepidation at the beaker over her head.

"Are you ready?" Seth asked.

"Yes," Rachael said as she took Joshua's hand.

"I love you," Joshua stated, kissing her forehead.

"I know."

Rachael closed her eyes as Seth poured the biograins over her skull. Her senses left her body but soon returned. When she opened her eyes, she was in a familiar place, lying on the bed where she and Joshua had shared their last night on New Eden. The turbulent emotions of that evening quickly resurfaced, but soon abated as she sat up and looked around the room. Nothing had changed. It was exactly as she had remembered it.

Rachael lifted up the right sleeve of her outfit and saw no tattoo on her wrist. This validated that she was indeed back on New Eden, and she noticed that there was a watch on her left wrist. It was an old-fashioned mechanical one with a sweeping second hand. She saw that the time read 7:13, but she didn't know if it was morning or evening.

The watch itself looked like an ordinary mechanical wristwatch with a leather-like band, but when Rachael touched its clear cover, she noted that it didn't feel like glass. The cover was somewhat deformable as she pressed on it. Rachael surmised that the watch was biological in origin.

"Rachael," Seth's voice said in her mind. "Can you hear me?"

"Yes."

"Welcome back to New Eden. I realize that you may have mixed emotions about being here, but I hope you will find your time here to be a rewarding experience."

"I hope so too."

"We've made significant changes to New Eden since you were last here. I want you to discover these changes for yourself. One of the most significant changes is that we've introduced more of the flora and fauna of Earth over the last few months. Furthermore, when you and Joshua were here, we wanted to make the planet a completely safe place, one with no dangers. But this is not the case now. Many of the animals from Earth that we've introduced are potentially harmful to humans, but this was the tradeoff in trying to make this planet more Earthlike. What I'm trying to say is that I want you to explore this revised world, but also to be careful. I can't completely protect you while you're here."

"I understand."

"Your original body is back on Earth, so even if anything happens to you here, it won't affect you."

"That's good to know."

"I've made it possible for you to communicate with Earth periodically in order to speak to Joshua. Due to bandwidth constraints of the spookyons, which are mostly being used to control the defenders and to allow you to be on New Eden, I have set specified times at which you can communicate. This connection will be active between nine and nine-thirty p.m. It is currently 7:13 a.m. on New Eden, and your body has already been adjusted to this planet's time. There's approximately a four-hour time difference between New Eden and California, so nine p.m. your time will be five p.m. California time. Also, a day on New Eden is about thirteen minutes shorter than a day on Earth. I've given you a watch so that you'll be able to monitor the time. It's been calibrated to accommodate the slight difference in the length of days between Earth and New Eden. Many of Earth's creatures have already adapted to the shortened days on New Eden, but we've realized that some are having difficulty with this temporal change. Therefore, we are in the process of slowing down the rotation of New Eden in order to match the rotation rate of Earth, but this won't be completed for a few months."

What technology must it take to change the rotation rate of an entire planet? Rachael thought.

"There's a phone in the other room," Seth continued. "When you pick it up, it will dial Joshua's cell phone directly. I'll tell him to wait for your call during the appropriate time. Do you understand all of this?"

Rachael was happy to know that she could periodically speak to Joshua. It would make her feel less lonely while on New Eden.

"Yes, Seth. Thanks for allowing me to communicate with Josh."

"If you have any requests while on New Eden, tell Joshua, and he can relay them to me. For now, New Eden is yours to explore for the next three days. Goodbye."

Rachael sat on the bed and considered her complete isolation from the rest of humanity. It was an overwhelming thought. She was light years away from the nearest human. She wished that Joshua was there with her as before to explore the planet, now completely terraformed for humanity. Seth hadn't revealed why only *her* body had been preserved on New Eden, but she realized that she had a task to perform. She would try her best to explore this world and report back to humanity on its suitableness for habitation if indeed that need arose.

Rachael got up from the bed, walked into the adjacent room, and saw the phone that Seth had referred to on a nightstand. It was a simple hand piece which looked to be made of a plastic-like material. She lifted it and placed it against her ear, but there was no sound. She replaced the phone on the table and touched the cover of the room's only window. The cover quickly and silently opened, affording her a view of the land beyond her home, and she marveled at the splendor of what she saw. She'd forgotten how truly beautiful New Eden was—a true paradise worthy of description by Earth's greatest poets and writers. She took a moment to take in the view. The most incredible aspect of New Eden's creation was that everything had literally been grown using the petrins' genetic engineering skills, even homes, clothing, and furniture. It was all a fully integrated ecosystem designed from the ground up to serve humanity.

And yet the scene was familiar, one that she had experienced years ago. She saw the snow-capped mountain in the distance, surrounded at its base by a dense green forest. Rachael noted several changes, however. The fields of grass she remembered as being close to her abode had been replaced by various types of vegetation, and she saw a swamp close by, with cattails surrounding a small pond.

Another prominent difference was the color of the sky, which was brighter than before. It was a lighter shade of blue than she recalled. She thought this must have been the result of the dome being removed. There was more atmosphere for the sunlight to interact with, and hence the brighter sky.

Rachael exited the dwelling and found herself in bright sunlight. The orchard was still there, with its variety of food, but what struck Rachael first wasn't the sights, but the sounds. She heard birds chirping, something that had been absent on her last visit. In fact, the only animals previously on New Eden were the arachnids. She turned and saw a nest of robins perched in the branches that made up the roof of her home. Their familiar sound made her feel at ease—more comfortable with her surroundings. She noted a monarch butterfly flapping its wings and watched as it bobbed and weaved through the air, finally landing on one of the trees in the orchard.

Rachael walked around the side of the house and saw that the shrubs that had been growing in rows had matured into full-sized houses ready for occupancy. But what immediately caught her attention was an arachnid standing on the grass adjacent to the homes. It was exactly the same as the arachnids she and Joshua had encountered, with long, slender, brown legs and two tentacles on its carapace. Rachael felt that it looked graceful—even beautiful—compared to the utilitarian appearance of the infiltrators and defenders on Earth. The arachnid, slightly smaller than an infiltrator, moved slowly towards her and bent low, offering her a seat.

Rachael climbed on top of the creature and took a seat on the saddle-shaped carapace. She grabbed its handle-shaped horn and lifted it. Rachael rose into the air as the arachnid flapped its clear wings—mere membranes—which were attached to its legs. She looked at the manicured landscape below and realized how much she had missed this experience. She was embarking on a new adventure of discovery—one she was extremely excited to undertake.

Rachael's first destination was the mountaintop. She wanted to get an overview of the landscape to see what to explore next. She flew low over fields, streams, and grasslands, taking in the sights. Shortly into her flight, she spotted a field with animals and flew towards them to get a closer look. She stopped and hovered over the field and saw a herd of deer grazing on the grass. They looked like ordinary deer she would find in the forests of Earth. They didn't seem bothered by the rhythmic hum created by the flapping of the arachnid's wings. She observed the deer for several minutes before continuing on her journey.

Rachael was soon soaring over a vast deciduous forest. The leaves on the tall hardwoods—oaks, maples, beeches, and others—displayed the brilliant red, orange, and yellow hues of autumn. Rachael had been awed by New Eden on her initial visit, but the variety of landscaping that the petrins had introduced exceeded her expectations for the completely terraformed planet.

The deciduous trees gave way to evergreens as Rachael flew higher up the foothills of the mountain. The air was fresh with the scent of pine and spruce trees as the forest rolled by beneath her. As she climbed to higher and cooler elevations, she noted that the material of her outfit became thicker and warmer, just as it had on her first visit. She was now at the snowline and traversed the high-mountain glacier that led to the top. Sunlight glistened on enormous sheets of ice that rivaled the biggest she'd seen back home. She soon reached the summit and landed on the peak.

Rachael dismounted and stood in the ankle-deep snow. She recalled fondly the night she and Joshua had shared at this very spot, warm and cozy in the cocoon that the arachnids had created for them by interlacing their gossamer legs to one another. It had been an intimate and romantic encounter.

At the summit, Rachael gazed in all directions. The ocean that she and Joshua had frolicked in was still to the right, but the red area on the left that they thought was a desert was no longer there. In reality, it had been the boundary of the dome that enclosed them. The desert had been replaced by a vast beige area that Rachael assumed was a grassland, perhaps a savanna. She decided to explore the ocean first, got on the arachnid, and flew swiftly down the right side of the mountain.

The snow fields gave way to pine forests, streams, and waterfalls that plunged off the rock faces. Rachael followed a stream that she knew would lead to the ocean. The crystal-clear stream widened into a river, and she came upon bears wading near the base of a small waterfall, all looking intently at the cascading water. Salmon jumped up the waterfall as the bears leapt at them, occasionally capturing one with their teeth or claws. The bears took the fish to the riverbank, where cubs waited for the meal. *So much like Earth* Rachael thought as she continued towards the ocean.

At the lower elevations, the forests gave way to tropical plants and a rain forest. Monkeys bounded from tree limb to tree limb as she skirted the canopy. A parrot flew from one of the higher branches and glided next to her, curious about the object that had entered its domain. "Hello there," Rachael said to the animal before it descended and perched on a mango tree, its branches heavy with bright red and orange fruit. The petrins had obviously filled the habitats of the planet with the diverse creatures from Earth.

As Rachael approached the ocean, she remembered the orchard where she and Joshua had shared a meal. She was hungry, so she decided to search for the orchard, which she found shortly. She landed the arachnid on the sand next to the ocean and entered the rows of trees. Her arachnid found the base of a nectar tree and drank from one of its vines. In the orchard, there were still many fruits that were unfamiliar to her, but there were many more that she recognized: apples, pears, peaches, mangos, and bananas.

Rachael picked a selection from the orchard, sat on the warm sand, and ate her lunch, looking out over the vast ocean in front of her. *I can't believe I'm light years from Earth. This place seems so utterly familiar.*

After eating, she walked to the water's edge. The ocean was no longer calm as it had been on her last visit. Large waves crashed over rocks in the sand. Rachael surmised that since the dome had been removed, the ocean was buffeted by more wind, and hence the rougher water. Rachael dipped her feet in the surf and noted that the ocean was much cooler than she remembered. A wave crashed on a large boulder, sending water high into the air, splashing her face. Rachael tasted salt on her lips. She dipped her hand in the water and brought a few drops to her mouth. She realized that the petrins had replaced the freshwater ocean with saltwater.

As she looked out over the horizon where the deep blue ocean met the light blue sky, a jet of mist erupted from the ocean surface. *I wonder what that is?* Rachael climbed onto the arachnid and flew over the waves to investigate the phenomenon.

She came upon a humpback whale and her calf swimming gracefully on the surface. The humpback let out another spray of mist before she and her calf dove to deeper waters. She realized that these majestic leviathans would never be hunted on New Eden. Indeed, no animal species need ever become extinct again. No matter what humans did on this world, the petrins had the data stored on their nodes that could recreate the plants and creatures native to Earth if needed. Rachael realized that the petrins were indeed the preservers of life.

Turning her arachnid, Rachael marveled at the panorama of land she saw behind her. The entire planet was teeming with life—land, sky, and ocean. *If it wasn't for my arachnid, I would think I was on Earth.*

Rachael flew towards the land and took a long five-hour flight around the base of the mountain to the other side, noting valleys, crags, and what appeared to be volcanic rock. She was headed towards the savanna she'd seen from the summit. She glided over grasslands, with grazing animals that were identical to their counterparts on Earth. The savanna was parched, and the grass was dry and brown. Acacia trees dotted the horizon with their umbrella-like canopies.

In the distance, Rachael saw a group of animals—giraffes! They were eating leaves from an acacia tree, their long graceful necks arching to reach the desired branches. She circled the majestic creatures and the tree to get a better look before moving off. Farther into the savanna, there were more animals: zebras, gazelles, and wildebeests. Even farther away were herds of animals—mere black specks—that she couldn't identify. Rachael had never visited Africa, but she doubted that the experience would be much different than this. *How did the petrins know so much about Earth to be able to make New Eden so Earthlike?* The data from the Internet, she realized, contained an enormous amount of information about Earth's habitats, and the petrins had obviously used this information to fashion New Eden into a second Earth. But how had they obtained the DNA for all of these creatures? Had Seth created more reconnaissance insects, like the ones that had scanned her body and mind many years ago to allow her to be resurrected on New Eden? She knew it was definitely possible since Seth, once again, had access to a biological lab in the bat cave back on Earth.

It was almost sunset as Rachael looked at her watch, which read 5:58, and she wondered whether she should head back home. She didn't want to miss the opportunity talk to Joshua at nine p.m., but she decided she had more time before she needed to turn back.

At the edge of the savanna, Rachael saw an orchard adjacent to more houses. She landed the arachnid close to the orchard and gathered food before walking to one of the houses and entering through the front door. The inside was identical to her home. *The petrins are good at replication,* she thought, *but design may not be their strong suit.* Rachael sat on a couch in the living room, opened the window covering, and stared at the savanna and the numerous animals grazing there. She felt as if she were on a safari on a dusty African plain.

What impressed her most was the peaceful atmosphere that permeated the planet. The petrins had created a planet-wide biosphere in which perfect harmony was maintained. There was no smog, pollution, traffic, or jackhammers building skyscrapers. New Eden would change, of course, when humanity began arriving, but hopefully people would gain a new appreciation for the environment and learn to cooperate with the land and elements rather than misuse them. The potential to grow as a species was unlimited, and this would be one of the central messages she would convey when Seth returned her to Earth.

Rachael observed that even in this home, there was a phone on the table. *Can I call Joshua from this phone too?* She figured that if the phone were there, it could only have one purpose. Seth was allowing her to explore the planet, and she could do a more thorough job if she didn't have to return to her home base every evening. *Seth has thought of everything.*

Rachael sat on the couch, enjoying her meal as the sky turned a bright orange tapering to gold—a perfect African sunset. She was startled when a pride of lions passed within a few yards of her window. She felt safe, but she would make sure the lions weren't around when she left in the morning. There were definitely more dangers here now, just as Seth had cautioned.

The sky darkened, and she saw the spiral galaxy rise from the horizon. She wondered where she was in the vast universe since the location of Petri or any planet it terraformed was unknown, even to the petrins since they did not engage in space travel. Perhaps astronomers would one day be able to spot familiar galaxies from New Eden and be able to approximate the location of their new home. Mankind, she assumed, would never stop looking to the stars. And spookyon technology did not preclude the possibility that man would still want to build conventional spacecraft and explore whatever galaxy they were in if only to experience its wonders and sheer beauty. Surely there were many space-faring civilizations in the universe.

Promptly at nine p.m., Rachael picked up the phone and placed it to her ear. Joshua had been anticipating her call and picked up after only one ring.

"Hello, Rachael!" he said enthusiastically. "How are you?"

"I'm great, Josh. I wish you were here. Just curious—what did the caller ID on your phone say?"

"New Eden," Joshua replied with a laugh. "Seth's thought of everything. This has to be the longest long-distance call of all time. How's New Eden?"

"It's simply wonderful. The petrins have done a wonderful job of making it more Earthlike. There were many times today when I forgot I wasn't on Earth."

Over the next thirty minutes, Rachael related all of her adventures of the past day. Near the end of their allotted time, she asked, "So how are things back on Earth?"

"No big news since you left. The war drags on as usual, and the scanning of frozen humans is almost completed, and the scanning of living humans is commencing at an accelerated pace. Seth figures that in two months, he will be able to scan all the humans that want to be backed up."

"Has Seth told you anything about Richard?" Rachael asked in a more serious tone.

Joshua knew immediately what Rachael was getting at. She was wondering if Richard had been scanned and if his information was intact.

"No, nothing yet."

"How are you holding up without me?" Rachael asked.

"I'm doing okay. A little lonely, I suppose. I invited Liz, Vinod, and Ted over for dinner tonight."

"Dinner? Really? *You're* going to cook?"

Joshua chuckled at the question. "Rachael, you know me better than that. You're the chef in this relationship. I can barely make mac and cheese. I'm ordering in some Thai food."

"Good idea. Sounds like fun. I wish I was there."

"And I wish *I* was *there*," Joshua countered. "I'd love to experience the revamped New Eden with you. From what you describe, it sounds amazing."

"It *is* a wonderful place, Josh. I completely understand your wanting to experience it with me."

Joshua was still irked that Seth had allowed only Rachael to return to New Eden. He had no idea why his clone hadn't been saved by the petrins.

"Did Seth tell you why only *your* clone was preserved?"

"No, he didn't mention anything about that. Maybe he'll un-redact that before I return to Earth."

Chapter Forty-Two
Solidly Liquid

Ted, Vinod, and Liz arrived at Joshua and Rachael's condo. Vinod had driven, and he and Ted had picked up Liz on the way. Ted had brought a bottle of authentic Louisiana moonshine, a bourbon variety.

"Did you talk to Rach?" Vinod asked after they had taken a seat on couches in the living room. "How's she doing? What's New Eden like?"

"I just spoke to her," Joshua replied. "She's having a wonderful time, although she misses all of us. She also said the petrins have made a lot of changes to New Eden. She says it's much more Earthlike, with many of Earth's animals and plants. She's spending the night in a home near a facsimile of an African savanna."

"It's amazing that the petrins can recreate such a diverse habitat on a planet light years from Earth," Liz said.

"It all about information transfer," Vinod stated. "The petrins have copied the entire data of the Internet. They now know just about everything about this planet and its contents. They've already begun scanning humanity, and I've heard that Seth is even scanning some of our works of art at a molecular level in order to preserve them."

"Interesting," Liz stated, "but would they be the same?"

"Would *what* be the same?" Ted asked.

"The works of art," Liz replied. "If you were to scan the *Mona Lisa* and then recreate an exact copy at the molecular level on New Eden, would it be the same as the original? I mean, da Vinci wouldn't have physically put his brush strokes on the copy."

"I believe it would be the same," Joshua said. "For me, it's not so important which molecules and atoms make up an object. The genius of the *Mona Lisa* is the painting itself. It's what da Vinci created. His unique use of color and brushstrokes would be preserved. Besides, if human clones are the same as their original humans, why not art?"

"Good point," Liz said, "although I think that others may not share your viewpoint. Some may feel that since da Vinci himself hadn't physically interacted with the copy, then it wouldn't be the same. I guess the same might be said for rare books, antiques, and historical artifacts."

"Maybe," Joshua said. "I suppose information transfer has limitations as it pertains to the individual appreciation of certain objects."

"How about we break out some of Ted's homemade bourbon?" Vinod suggested.

"Sure," Ted said. "That's why I brought it."

A few minutes later, Vinod held up a glass of bourbon after taking a sip. "Man, Ted, you really outdid yourself this time. I'm not normally a bourbon drinker, but this stuff is smooth."

"It's a special bottle," Ted said. "It was a batch my daddy made over ten years ago before he died."

"Your father passed away?" Liz asked.

"Yea, about eight years ago now," Ted responded. "Went suddenly—heart attack."

"Sorry to hear that," Joshua remarked.

"Yea, I miss him," Ted said. "I keep this batch of bourbon to remind me of him. It's been aged for quite some time, which is why it's so smooth. I open a bottle from the batch only for special occasions."

"Then I'm honored that you've brought some to my home," Joshua stated. "I wish Rachael was here to enjoy it with us."

"Don't worry," Ted replied. "There's more where this came from. She can try it when she gets back."

After they had finished most of the bourbon, the group ate dinner, which consisted of various Thai curries and noodles, and then sat around a circular patio table located on a wooden deck at the rear of the condo. The home was situated in the hills to the north of Berkeley, affording a magnificent view of the city lights of Berkeley and the Golden Gate in the distance. Moonlight glistened on the waters of the bay in front of the bridge.

"You have an unbelievable view, Josh," Liz remarked.

"Thanks."

Liz turned back towards the group. They were on the last of the bourbon. She raised her glass and said, "I propose a toast. To Ted's dad for this wonderful gift he left us."

The others raised their glasses in tribute and finished their drinks.

"Ted, is your mom alive?" Liz asked.

"Yup, still in Louisiana. Spoke to her today before coming here."

"How's she doing?" Liz asked.

"She's good," Ted replied. "By the way, she told me that she's scheduled to get scanned tomorrow."

"Scanned?" Vinod asked. "Like in one of the petrin scanners?"

"Yup. She had some questions for me about how it works that I couldn't answer. I told her that I'd ask y'all. You know—the scientists."

"Okay," Joshua said. "Go for it."

"She was wondering about the transportation process to New Eden. How does it work exactly?"

Joshua tried to explain the concept for Ted.

"When she gets scanned, the petrins will collect all information about her. This will consist of both the DNA sequence of her cells as well as the information stored in the neural connections of her brain."

"Her brain?" Ted said. "They gonna copy her thoughts?"

"Basically, but not just her thoughts. They'll also copy her memories, her personality—really everything that makes her who she is. This information will be copied as data on one of the petrin data nodes. A clone of her physical body will then be grown on New Eden using her DNA, and the information from her brain on Earth will be transferred into the brain of the clone. She will, in essence, be transported to New Eden. Assuming evacuation becomes necessary, of course."

"I understand the scientific process of how it happens," Ted said, "but her questions were deeper than that. She's wondering if it will really be her?"

"What do you mean?" Joshua asked.

"If you make a copy of someone, is that copy the same as the original? Is it still them? I mean, they're not the same physical body."

"I wish Rachael were here to answer your question," Joshua stated. "She's really the only human who's been through the process, but she told me unequivocally that she's the same person. She feels that she's the same Rachael she's always been even though the actual atoms and molecules that make up her body are completely different."

"There's nothing unique about the atoms and molecules that make up a person," Liz stated matter-of-factly.

"What do you mean?" Vinod asked.

"When I was in medical school and learned how the human body works, I came across a study conducted in the 1950s that simply amazed me. This, of course, all happened prior to our contact with the petrins and being told that life was just purposeful information. Ted, from what I gather, your mom is wondering if a body made of completely different atoms but arranged according to the pattern of the original body is still the same person."

"Yup," Ted replied. "I think that's what she was getting at."

"Well, even the body she has now is not the body she's always had," Liz stated.

"It's not?" Ted asked, perplexed.

"As you all know, our bodies are made of atoms and molecules. About two thirds of the entire mass of a human is water, which is a fluid substance. We consume water every day, but we also lose water daily through urination, respiration, and evaporation from our skin. Water is constantly being cycled through our bodies. Consider your own body. What are the chances that any of the same water molecules that were in your body a year ago are still in your body now?"

"Given the amount of water flowing through our bodies," Vinod answered, "the chances of still having some of the same water molecules that you had a year ago would be very slim."

"Exactly," Liz stated. "So at least two thirds of what constituted your body a year ago has been completely replaced. If we look at the other one third of your body—the part not made of water—it's made of various molecules such as proteins and lipids that are the building blocks of our cells. Cells are constantly dying and being replaced in our bodies. Various cell lines have different rates of replacement. For example, blood cells, skin cells, and the cells that line our intestines are replaced rather frequently. Other cells, such as nerve cells, aren't replaced at all. That's why brain damage is so permanent. The body doesn't have the ability to replace damaged central nervous system cells."

"Interesting," Joshua remarked as he stroked his chin. "Maybe that's why the brain is the place where our thoughts and memories are stored. They're stored on a substrate that doesn't get replaced—that isn't in constant transition. Perhaps that's what allows our thoughts and memories to be more permanent."

"That makes complete sense," Liz said, "but even though neural cells don't replicate after childhood, the molecules in humans that make up our cells are still replaced. These molecules are composed primarily of four kinds of atoms: carbon, oxygen, nitrogen, and hydrogen. These atoms are constantly being exchanged by our bodies. We eat food and drink water, which is a new source of all of these atoms. We also exhale carbon and oxygen in the form of the carbon dioxide, and we release nitrogen and hydrogen in our urine." Liz sat back in her chair and paused before continuing. "As I told you earlier, there was a study conducted in the fifties to look at this exact phenomenon we're discussing."

"I think I know that study," Joshua said. "It was conducted in Oak Ridge, Tennessee, at the nuclear research facility."

"Yes, that's the one," Liz said. "In the study, they tagged certain atoms with a radioactive marker and then measured how long they stayed in the body. The results were astounding. They found that ninety-eight percent of all atoms in humans are replaced every year. I'm sure that over a longer period of time, that number approaches one hundred percent."

"What are you saying?" Ted asked. "Ninety-eight percent of all the atoms in my body right now are new? They weren't there a year ago?"

"That's exactly what the conclusions of the study found."

"I understand where you're coming from, Liz," Vinod stated. "I see this as being possible with a fluid substance such as water, which is continually being taken in and expelled by our bodies, but what about solid substances? I would think that solid structures would retain their molecules."

"There is no such thing as solid structures in humans," Liz answered with a wry smile. "The cells of our organs are continually dying and being replaced."

"No solid structures?" Vinod said. "What about something like bones?"

"Bones may appear solid," Liz said, "but they're not as unchanging as you'd imagine. Bone is a tissue that's in a constant process of remodeling itself even in an adult. There are cells called osteoclasts that continually destroy bone by dissolving it to create tiny channels in the bone. Later, other cells called osteoblasts create new bone in the areas dissolved by the osteoclasts. Bone is actually a fairly dynamic substance."

"What's the purpose of that?" Vinod asked. "Adult humans aren't growing anymore. Why does the body need to keep recycling bone?"

"I believe I know why," Joshua replied. "Is it to prevent fatigue fractures?"

"Exactly!" Liz stated. "Nonliving solid items like a rod of steel will eventually break over time if they're stressed repeatedly. Think of a paper clip. If you bend it back and forth repeatedly, it eventually breaks because every bend of the clip causes small fractures in its metal. This process is called fatigue fracturing. It also happens in bone. Every time you take a step, small micro-fractures occur in the bone as it responds to the weight of your body. If there was no reparative process, all of our bones would break over time even with the simple process of walking. The continuous regeneration of bones using osteoclasts and osteoblasts repairs this microfracturing and prevents them from breaking."

"The human body is an amazing machine," Vinod said. "I guess it's not really a liquid or a solid. It's really something in between the two, something that's dynamic and constantly in flux."

"That's true," Liz agreed, "but back to my original point. As I've said, over the period of a year, the atoms and molecules that make up our bodies are almost completely replaced. But this raised an important question when I learned about this study in medical school. If the material that makes us up now is almost completely different than what it was a year ago, then what *is* it that makes us the same person? I had a notion as to the answer to this question, but it wasn't confirmed until Seth told us about the petrin definition of life."

"It's information that defines us," Vinod said. "The molecules that make us may be completely different from a year ago, but the pattern in which those molecules are arranged is the same. The retention of this information is what makes us . . . *us*."

"That's exactly what I've come to believe," Liz stated. "It answers the question that I pondered during medical school. Even though the molecules that make up our bodies are always being replaced, there is *something* in us that is constantly reorganizing new molecules into the pattern that defines us. Now you understand why I became a member of the 103 Club. Seth's revelations in session 103 clearly answered the conundrum that I've had since medical school. What's truly amazing about the human body is that, even in adulthood, after the pattern of what is represented in our DNA has fully matured, our bodies are still able to maintain their patterns even though ninety-eight percent of their matter is replaced yearly. As we get older, it's not our molecules that age. It's the pattern that defines us that's aging."

Liz turned to Ted. "As far as your mother's question is concerned, you should explain to her that what makes her an individual is this information, the very same information the petrins will be scanning tomorrow. The physical items such as atoms and molecules that make her up are irrelevant. If the petrins recreate *her* information using a *different* set of atoms and molecules on New Eden, then it would still be her."

Ted laughed. "Well, there's one thing I hope the petrins duplicate on New Eden, and I don't care what atoms or molecules they use."

"What's that?" Vinod asked.

"A genuine swamp with gators, snakes, and good fishing. And maybe a cabin deep in the woods with a still for makin' moonshine."

"It's a must," Vinod said. "And they better have uploaded classic rock to their node."

"Don't worry," Joshua said. "I think the petrins can accommodate your need for parties, although that may be low on their priority list."

Chapter Forty-Three
The Crimson Leaf

The next morning, Ted had a little extra spring in his step as he entered the Defender Control Facility at the Bowman Particle Research Center. He had been paired with Seth for his patrol and relished the opportunity to get to know the petrin better. He and Seth would be patrolling an area near the eastern coastline of the Korean peninsula.

Ted lay down on an empty cot in the remote-control ward, and soon a technician came with a beaker of biograins.

"What's the assignment, commander?"

"Big day today, Maurice. I'm patrolling with Seth."

"Wow! That's exciting. Patrolling with the main man," the technician said before pouring biograins over Ted's head. "Good luck."

Ted awoke on the Korean peninsula in defender form. He could see that he was still attached to a nutrition tank but didn't feel thirsty at all, so he knew he had been replenished. He checked his ammo indicator and saw that it was full. He disconnected himself from the feeding tube, which looked as if it were attached to his abdomen. Ted saw a defender standing next to him. Due to the perspective change, the defender seemed much smaller than in real life.

"Seth, is that you?"

"Yes."

The voice entered Ted's mind, but he knew that the defender next to him hadn't actually spoken. The words were injected into his auditory cortex by the biograins via the spookyons they were both connected to.

They were in a barren wasteland. It was daytime, but the sky was dark and overcast. There was no vegetation or anything that had any semblance of life. Large boulders and rubble were strewn about the area. They may as well have been on Mars given the complete lack of life Ted observed. He couldn't believe that this had once been a natural paradise, one filled with trees, grass, and animals. Continuous nuclear bombardment had turned it into a lifeless landscape.

"All set to begin our patrol?" Seth asked.

"Let's do it."

In defender form, Seth and Ted walked northeast towards the coastline. They were still quite a distance away from the ocean, and their patrol wouldn't end until many hours later, when they reached the shore. Their mission was simple: find and destroy any infiltrators or spookyon collector trees in their patrol area. Seth could see in all directions as they walked, but Ted could only see in the direction that he looked. The tentacles that were not being used for direct vision would nevertheless alert him to any movement or heat signatures behind him. The defenders walked for over an hour without spotting anything of significance.

"This place is lifeless," Ted remarked, looking over the barren landscape.

"War destroys indiscriminately," Seth said while continuing his march. "As you know, we believe that life is the purposeful arrangement of molecules and matter, while death is the randomization of that information. All of the purposeful information of this area has been randomized. It's dead."

"We had dinner at Josh's place last night," Ted said as they continued their patrol. "Rachael told him that you've done an amazing job with New Eden in making it more like Earth. What a huge contrast it must be to what we're seeing here. It's interesting that New Eden is more like Earth now than this part of Earth. This area we're patrolling seems like a barren planet."

"An unfortunate consequence of war."

A short time later, Ted and Seth came upon the bodies of two dead infiltrators and one dead defender in close proximity to one another. They paused to inspect the carnage. Smoke still rose from multiple rents in the armor of the carcasses.

"Looks like this battle didn't happen too long ago," Seth remarked, looking at the smoldering corpses. "We have to be alert."

Suddenly, Ted heard a beeping sound coming from behind and to the right as a red indicator lit up in his right visual field.

"Seth!"

"Yes, I see it. Let's go."

The duo ran towards the heat signature, weapons drawn. When they were a hundred yards away, two infiltrators appeared from behind a tall pile of rubble. The infiltrators stood still and unleashed a volley of airfoils. The defenders were immediately struck by the projectiles, which bounced off their armor. Seth charged towards the infiltrators, with Ted following close behind. Seth fired while in a full run, his airfoils not directed at the infiltrators themselves but at the airfoils the infiltrators directed at them. Seth was able to hit the approaching airfoils in mid-flight and disturb their trajectory so that they fell harmlessly to the ground. *How much skill and processing power does it take to be able to target a high-speed projectile while still in flight?* Ted wondered. The airfoils gave off showers of red-hot sparks as they collided with each other. Very few airfoils hit them since most were deflected.

Seth stopped his advance when they had gotten within twenty yards of the infiltrators, but he continued firing. "Aim for the left one first!"

Ted took a position just to the right of Seth and aimed both of his weapons at the base of one of the tentacles of the infiltrator on the left. He opened fire with all eight of his tentacles. The barrage soon severed the tentacle, which fell off, leaving a hole that blasted out blue-green flames. Ted continued firing into the flaming hole, filling the insides of the infiltrator with airfoils and shredding its contents. The infiltrator fell to the ground as a second blast of flames shot from the opening.

Ted saw the underside of its carapace open in multiple spots as juvenile infiltrators scurried out. The second infiltrator stopped its firing and ran away at high speed.

"Go after the juveniles!" Seth shouted as he chased the retreating infiltrator. "I'll take care of the other one."

Ted targeted and blasted the eight juveniles as they tried to escape. He made sure to count each one he killed to make sure none escaped. He looked for Seth and the other infiltrator but saw only a cloud of dust.

"Seth, are you okay?"

"Yes."

Ted surmised from the abbreviated response that Seth was still engaged in battle, but he knew that the infiltrator was no match for Seth and his enhanced capabilities. Ted walked around the large pile of rubble from which the infiltrators had emerged. As he reached the far side, he found a spookyon collector tree, its leaves still a pristine white. He blasted the tree with airfoils, turning it to splinters.

"Second infiltrator and juveniles eliminated," Seth said. "On my way back to you. What's your status?"

"I'm good. All the juveniles are eliminated, and I found a spookyon collector, which I destroyed." After Seth had returned, Ted examined his carapace and noted numerous dents and chips on the surface of his defender's armor. "Looks like you took the brunt of the airfoils. Your armor's sustained damage."

"I'm fine," Seth remarked. "What's your ammo level?"

"Sixty-eight percent."

"I'm at fifty-two. I think we're still good to go. There's a resupply cache about twenty miles away. We should head for that and reload."

"Sounds like a plan."

The duo walked in silence for the next few hours as the desolation of the nuclear wasteland dampened their moods. They both knew that infiltrators were spawning at an alarming rate. Many offspring were escaping, and as Seth had explained at a briefing, each new generation was better adapted to its environment. Each new generation was becoming harder to kill.

We're fighting over an area of land that no human could live in for decades Ted thought as he scanned the desolation that spanned from horizon to horizon.

They came upon a fast-moving stream, its water transporting radioactive contents towards the ocean.

"Are you getting thirsty?" Seth asked in order to gauge Ted's energy level.

"A little."

"We're almost to the cache. We have to follow this stream a little farther. It should be just around the bend."

The duo followed the stream, and as they rounded the bend they saw the cache, still attached to a parachute partially draped on top, that had been dropped some time ago by a high-altitude bomber. There was a tank filled with Ensure, and next to the tank was a large wooden box filled with ammunition. What caught their attention wasn't the cache, but what was to the right of it: four infiltrators.

"Seth!"

"I see them."

One of the infiltrators pointed its tentacles at the cache and opened fire. The white liquid from the tank spilled onto the ground, and the box of ammunition was splintered. Thousands of airfoils lay in a disorganized pile on the dirt.

"Should we call for backup?" Ted asked.

One of the infiltrators suddenly turned all of its tentacles in their direction.

"Too late," Seth replied as the four infiltrators charged in a horizontal line. "I'll take the three on the left. You take the one on the right."

Seth bombarded the left three infiltrators with airfoils as Ted did the same for the one on the right.

The infiltrators stopped their charge and returned fire. Seth and Ted's armor took heavy fire as Seth concentrated his attack solely on the far-left infiltrator. Ted continued his attack on the right one, leaving the two in the middle unchallenged. A tentacle on the left infiltrator was severed and fell to the ground. Seth focused his fire into the burning hole left by the detachment, and in a few moments the infiltrator slumped to the ground, releasing eight juveniles. Seth quickly targeted them as the duo continued taking heavy fire from the remaining infiltrators.

Ted managed to lop off a tentacle on the right infiltrator and quickly destroyed it. He then concentrated his fire on the juveniles that escaped from the carapace while Seth focused on the remaining two infiltrators.

"I'm running low," Seth shouted. "Fifteen percent ammo left!"

Ted checked his ammo meter, which read forty percent. He concentrated his firepower on the infiltrator on the right.

"My armor has been breached!" Seth shouted.

Ted glanced at him and saw a small jet of blue flame erupt from the front of his carapace.

The two remaining infiltrators, seeing the flames coming from Seth's defender, directed all of their fire at the rent in his armor.

"Ammo critical!" Seth shouted before severing a tentacle from the left infiltrator. "I'm out of ammo!"

Ted fired at the hole in the left infiltrator as both infiltrators continued to attack Seth. He watched in horror as Seth's defender slumped to the ground, its body lifeless and burning.

"I'm disconnected," Seth said.

"Goddamn it!" Ted shouted as he continued pouring airfoils into the gaping hole in the left infiltrator. It soon slumped to the ground, and Ted quickly dispatched the juveniles that emerged from it. The one remaining infiltrator stopped its firing and took off down the stream bed.

"Ted, what's your ammo situation?" Seth asked.

"Twenty percent."

"You should wait for backup."

"I got this!" Ted shouted as he sprinted in pursuit of the final infiltrator.

He chased it for over a mile as it ran full speed along the stream bed. The stream flowed into the opening of a cave near the base of a small mountain, into which the infiltrator darted. Ted ran to the entrance of the cave, which was fifteen meters wide.

"Don't go in there without backup," Seth said as he monitored what Ted saw through his spookyon interface.

"It's trapped. I'm going to finish it off."

Ted cautiously entered the cave and walked a short distance, following the stream. He moved forward, weapons drawn, as the cave grew darker, but there was still adequate light for him to see. As he rounded a bend in the stream, he entered a small cavern, which he scanned. The cavern was irregularly shaped, with large stalactites growing from the ceiling, stalagmites rising from the ground. He didn't see the infiltrator, but what caught his attention was a spookyon collector tree a short distance away. Its leaves were all white.

"Why the hell is there a spookyon collector in here?" Ted asked.

"I don't know," Seth replied as he monitored the visual feed from Ted's eyes. "They definitely need airflow in order to work."

Ted kicked up loose dirt from the cave floor and watched as the dust cloud moved farther into the cave. "There must be an exit ahead. There's air flowing through here." Ted blasted the collector with airfoils, and it shattered into thousands of pieces.

Suddenly, the infiltrator emerged from behind a large stalagmite and fired airfoils directly at him. Ted returned fire and saw that his ammo meter read critical—ten percent remaining. The infiltrator ceased firing and ran towards the back of the cavern, Ted following.

The infiltrator stopped again and fired, but it wasn't aiming at Ted. It fired at the ceiling of the cavern above, which crumbled and showered large boulders directly onto Ted, pinning him to the ground.

"Damn smart!" Ted exclaimed.

He lay on the ground, his left arm—and therefore, his left four tentacles—immobile and useless. He could only see out of his right eye as his left visual field went blank. Ted aimed his right weapon at the base of one of the infiltrator's tentacles and fired, but the airfoils didn't hit their target with their usual accuracy. With only one eye working, Ted had lost his depth perception. He continued blasting airfoils at the infiltrator, but he noticed something behind it in a dark recess of the cavern. It was another spookyon collector. Ted's heart sank as he saw that one of the leaves on an upper branch was red.

"Shit, Seth! It's red!"

"You've got to destroy it!"

The infiltrator stopped firing and ran towards the collector. Still pinned by boulders, Ted directed his right gun at the collector and targeted the red leaf. He pulled the trigger and managed to blast the branch to which it was connected before his ammo was depleted.

Ted watched in horror as the red leaf dropped and landed on top of the infiltrator's carapace and slipped into one of its gill slots. The infiltrator slumped, motionless for a moment, and then slowly stood up straight. It pointed all eight tentacles at Ted and unleashed a barrage of airfoils. Ted's vision went black. He had been disconnected.

Medusa had come to Earth . . ..

Chapter Forty-Four
Future Uncertain

Williams, Porter, and Langdon met in a briefing room located in the innermost ring of the Pentagon. Williams had just come from a meeting with the president of the United States. Porter had received an independent briefing from the joint chiefs, and Langdon had been apprised of Earth's status from the satellite imaging departments at NASA and the Jet Propulsion Laboratory in Pasadena. They took seats near the head of a table and opened dossiers without speaking. Recommendations made over the next hour would be relayed to the president and the United Nations.

"So it's come to this," Porter said in an even tone of voice. His military swagger was no longer in evidence. He now spoke more like a diplomat. "Medusa is rapidly gaining more and more control over Earth. Our forces are fighting a valiant battle, but we're losing, and there's no hope of victory. Now that Medusa has arrived, she brings her advanced intelligence to the infiltrators, something they previously lacked."

"We knew this might happen," Langdon said, "but it's still hard to process the intel. Earth . . . our home . . . the place where life evolved on a planet teeming with almost eight billion individuals—conquered by a cosmic megalomaniac, a cancer that has spread to this tiny speck of dust in the Milky Way."

"Yes," Williams stated in a monotone. "We'll save our eulogies for another day, however, since time is of the essence. General, the president has given the order to evacuate, although it comes in the form of a recommendation made in consultation with the Secretary General of the United Nations. There's been a worldwide panic in the form of humans swarming the scanning centers set up by the petrins. They're being overrun. The military has had to step in and control the crowds so that the scanning can be completed in an orderly fashion."

Langdon inhaled deeply, showing obvious frustration.

"Satellite imaging confirms reports from the ground," he said, "which is that large segments of Earth's population are congregating in the areas where the scanners are located. Despite the mad rush, the humans are still being scanned according to the birthday lottery that was set up before. It seems ironic that at the time of the lottery, many wanted a later date in order to lose the least amount of their life experiences as possible, but now those with the earlier dates seem like the lucky ones. There are, however, an estimated billion people that still refuse to be scanned."

"Can you be more specific?" Porter asked.

"They fall into several categories. Many are refusing to evacuate on religious grounds, claiming that what Earth is going through was foretold in their respective scriptures and religious texts. They believe that this is the end of days rather than an alien invasion. Others are not all that different from those who have come to be known as doomsday preppers. They want to stockpile food and ammunition and then hunker down, believing they can escape the destruction that's to come."

"Perhaps we can educate them in the remaining months before the scanning period is over," Porter suggested. "There's no chance of survival for those that stay."

Williams leaned forward, her elbows on the table as she massaged the temples of her head.

"Every effort will be made to do just that, but the president's private advisory council on these matters predicted that many people would refuse for any number of reasons. We're where we are precisely because we're not a homogenized world society. As Seth said—and the president and most world leaders are in full agreement—no one can be forced to leave. Government policies aside, it's an individual choice for everyone. Personally, the thought of losing over a billion people to Medusa is abhorrent to me, but this too was anticipated. We shouldn't have expected a unified response from so many people in so short a time."

"But *why* can't we force them, Dina?" Porter asked. "It would be for their own good."

The chief of staff shook her head. "The president has rejected this idea, and the petrins wouldn't go along with a policy of forced relocation."

"What about the homeless, prisoners, and the elderly residing in nursing homes?" Langdon asked.

"They are being located and given counseling and transportation to a scanning center if requested," Williams answered. "Seth is aware of the diversity of our population and has promised to relocate everyone who desires to do so. We're going to have to do the best we can on our end and rely on petrin guidance to deal with special cases."

Williams paused to take two aspirin and a sip of water.

"There are other reasons why we have to allow people to make an individual decision. Can you imagine the chaos that would ensue if a billion people were forced to move to New Eden against their wills? As it stands, we'll still have to determine how society will be organized—perhaps *re*organized—once the evacuation is complete. Will we have a world government? A police force? Crime? And what about vocations, religious denominations, and universities? What about *all* our institutions and corporations? Humanity is being given a rather severe wake-up call, but Earth's diversity will remain intact. We can't expect all of humanity's problems to disappear overnight if we honor the rights of the individual, which is something we must do at all costs. Forced evacuation would only compound problems that are sure to arise."

"That's true," Langdon agreed, "but poverty and want will be things of the past. Mankind can focus on achieving greater potential."

"We can hope this will be the case," Williams said, "but accurate predictions about the future are not possible, at least as far as the president's advisory council is concerned. The president has agreed with world leaders communicating via the United Nations that a leadership council representing all nations will be set up when the evacuation is complete. That will be an enormous step in maintaining continuity once we arrive on New Eden."

Porter seemed disturbed and shifted in his seat.

"Will mankind continue to evolve technologically?" Porter asked. "All of this talk about paradise is a bit unsettling, especially to a military man like myself."

"A good point, Mitchell," Langdon said. "What's paradise depends on your perspective. It's not in our nature to stagnate. We should continue to study the arts and sciences and explore the galaxy, with or without spookyon technology. The petrin cloning process will leave our innate curiosity about existence intact, not to mention the dynamics of psychology and sociology."

"We don't have firm answers to all of these questions, but they all point in one direction," Williams said.

"Yes?" Langdon said.

"It is going to come down to how much petrin influence we want. This has been the primary focus of the president's dialogue with other heads of state for many months. The overwhelming conclusion is that, at least at the beginning, this entire process cannot be undertaken without petrin supervision and advice. They've relocated other cultures in the universe, and probably only *they* know how to address the possible roadblocks we'll encounter once our new lives have begun on New Eden."

"I hadn't thought of that," Porter said, "but as much as I dislike it, I don't see any way around it. We're going to need their help, if only initially."

"I concur," Langdon said, "but at some point in the future maybe we can disconnect from the collective and chart our own course. For now we're going to need serious guidance. I trust you're aware that there are competing factions about the need for petrin help even among those who are more than willing to be relocated. The 103 Club is advocating that we accept all the help that the petrins are willing to give, and the club is winning followers daily. Others want complete autonomy so that Earth's development can continue on its present trajectory as much as that's possible."

"It's obvious we have a lot that we need to work through," Williams said, "and it's going to take time, but the more issues we can settle before relocation is complete, the better. I'm going to recommend to the president that we accept petrin help in our initial phase of relocation. That may or may not be the view of other governments, of course. Mitchell, how long can we hold off Medusa's forces so that we can complete scanning and make preparation for what the president is calling our final exit, preparations that include addressing many of the questions we're raising today?"

Porter referred to his dossier and scanned several pages before answering.

"The infiltrators are moving quickly out of the Korean peninsula and are spreading through Eastern China and are rapidly gaining strongholds in Eastern Siberia. One of our nuclear submarines in the Sea of Japan spotted a group of infiltrators swimming underwater towards the Japanese mainland. They fired torpedoes at the group but were unable to destroy them. We are moving some defenders to the western Japanese coast as a defense. But realistically, since these bastards can swim, it's only a matter of time before they advance across the Pacific to the Americas. As Seth warned, the infiltrators can adapt after each engagement, enabling them to anticipate our weapons and tactical strategies. They always had that capability, but with Medusa's intelligence directly orchestrating the battle and enhancing the performance of the infiltrators, I'd estimate we have three months left, give or take, but this estimate is predicated on an increased rate of nuclear bombardment of the infected areas. After that, there may still be pockets of civilization, but they'll become more and more isolated."

"There's another variable in this equation," Langdon said, "one that also affects our timeline for ultimate evacuation. Radiation levels are now rising in every area of the globe, even at the research station in Antarctica. Steering currents have continued to carry radioactive fallout around the world. The effects are strongest in Asia, of course, but early symptoms of radiation sickness are presenting in wider and wider areas."

"Can't Seth cure radiation poisoning in the same way that he'll repair diseases in people scanned in cryo facilities?" Porter inquired.

Williams nodded. "Seth has said that the petrins have the ability to do that unless the radiation has caused permanent brain damage, which might be the case in some individuals."

"Time is against us," Langdon warned. "The arrival of Medusa changes everything. Infiltrators, radiation, unrest among certain segments of the population—it's daunting."

"Seth has assured me that he can increase the number of scanning stations exponentially if we give him satellite data to locate the largest pockets of population. To enable this, Joshua is working at the particle center to capture more primordial spookyons to increase the bandwidth for the purposes of scanning. Whether he can capture them quickly enough is another matter."

"We can reallocate spy satellites to provide Seth with the information he needs," Langdon asserted.

"I'll request this from the president," Williams said.

"We're forgetting the most important variable of all," Langdon pointed out, "which is Rachael's report when she returns from New Eden. Seth has placed a great deal of stock in her ability to win over humanity, so the statistics we've discussed today may change for the better."

"Quite true," Williams said. "The president's advisory council has recommended that she be the feature of a worldwide broadcast when she returns assuming global communications are still intact. Certain urban centers have already fallen, and radiation is playing havoc with certain communication channels used by our intelligence agencies right here in D.C."

"We can put her face on every television, phone, tablet, and computer on the planet," Porter said. "We can even use jumbotrons in stadiums and arenas around the world."

"Excellent idea," Williams said. "I'll relay that to the advisory council. She will be the most important diplomatic ambassador Earth has ever had."

No one spoke for several minutes as the challenges to evacuate Earth as quickly as possible sank in. They had previously spoken about the need for evacuation and its ethics. The logistics, however, were proving far more complex than anyone had imagined.

Williams seemed philosophical. "I suppose Mr. Bhakti was getting at many of these issues when he asked who would make the decision to evacuate and how much personal freedom individuals would retain if relocation was imminent. He knew how difficult the entire operation would be and how many moral issues would be raised once the plan was in progress."

Porter laughed. "A thoroughly irritating young man, but his intelligence is not in question. His contribution to our efforts over the past several months has been invaluable."

"I'd like to end our meeting on a positive note," Williams said, "and it's perhaps a variable we haven't taken into account yet. It's Seth revelation about the purpose of the universe."

"How will that mitigate the headaches of relocation?" Porter asked.

"It may not in the short term," Williams replied, "but humanity on New Eden will possibly become a member of a cosmic community of intelligent species, all interconnected to achieve meaningful purpose. I choose to be the eternal optimist in thinking that the population of Earth will be helped in this unprecedented transition by a connection to innumerable intelligent species. Can you imagine the collective wisdom of countless alien cultures feeding into Earth's destiny? Not all at once mind you, but over time, who knows how humans may evolve. Hopefully, we'll turn into a truly enlightened and peaceful species."

"You're right as always, Dina," Langdon said, "but there's one very big hurdle to becoming part of this larger community of connected civilizations."

Dina nodded. She knew what Langdon was about to say.

"What you're theorizing depends on whether we accept long-term guidance from the petrins after the relocation has been completed. If world leaders reject petrin help—if we choose to go it alone and cut ourselves off—we won't have access to that wider community."

"Very astute, Robert," Williams said, "and yet I still think there's hope even if we ultimately reject the petrin offer for long-term supervision and decide to disconnect from the collective."

"I'm not entirely following," Porter said.

"Rachael has always believed that man was meant to claw his way up—to exercise self-determination. It's why she rejected New Eden three years ago. I think it's obvious from our meeting today that utopia won't be handed to us on a platter. We'll still have to do some hard work even if the petrins have a strong advisory voice in our destiny." Williams paused as she looked into a corner of the room, as if thinking of a distant scenario. "Even if we choose to disconnect and go it alone, however, humanity won't stop evolving. I think science and technology will exist on New Eden and will one day surpass what we presently have on Earth. With or without the petrins, I believe mankind will one day take its place in the community that Seth has alluded to. I think we'll find our way."

There was a brief moment of silence as the three figures stood and exited the room.

Chapter Forty-Five
Child of New Eden

Rachael looked at her watch, which read 8:55 p.m. She'd had another wonder-filled day exploring New Eden and couldn't wait to tell Joshua about it. She had explored a desert with tall white sand dunes interspersed with oases bordered by large date palms. She had seen tall grasslands through which elephants had cut various paths with their hulking bodies. She was now in a home on the rim of a canyon that looked out over a lush green valley. There was a river close to her home that fell in large torrents as a waterfall into the valley below causing mist to rise and spray her home with dew. It was a magical place, one that she wanted to share with Joshua.

Promptly at nine that evening, she picked up the phone and connected with Joshua.

"Hi, Josh. How are things? I miss you."

"I miss you too. How was your day?"

"Wonderful. I want to tell you all about it."

Joshua had contemplated telling Rachael about what had happened on Earth over the last twenty-four hours—how Medusa now had direct influence over the planet. He had decided that that news could wait. He wanted her to enjoy her time on New Eden and not be burdened by news from Earth.

"That's nice," he said with as much enthusiasm as he could muster.

It wasn't enough. Rachael immediately noted the subdued tone of Joshua's voice. "What's wrong?"

"What do you mean?" Joshua asked, trying to be more cheerful.

"Josh, don't play coy with me. I know when you're hiding something. Out with it."

There was a pause in the conversation. Joshua wasn't good at keeping a secret. He realized the futility of trying to hide the news, especially from someone so observant.

"I have some bad news," Joshua stated.

"What is it?"

"One of the infiltrators captured a red leaf from a spookyon collector tree."

"What?" Rachael said with a gasp. "Does that mean . . .?"

"Yes. Medusa has made connection with Earth. The president and other world leaders have issued orders for the evacuation process to begin in full swing. Seth feels, as we all do, that this war's eventual outcome, even though it may be many months down the road, is inevitable. We can't win."

We can't win.

The words were a jolt to Rachael. Earth would become uninhabitable for humanity. The die was cast. Humanity had no one to blame but itself for this disaster. Mankind's lack of cohesiveness, its propensity to divide itself along racial and cultural differences, had led to the loss of its home world.

"Oh, Josh," Rachael said with tears flowing down her cheek. "I want to come back right away. I want to be with you on Earth. Ask Seth to bring me home."

"No," Joshua said forcefully. This was the exact scenario he had hoped to avoid. "We know that humanity's new home will be New Eden. You have one more day there. It's important that you explore as much of it as you can in order to explain what it's like for those who are reticent to relocate. I'll see you back here after that. You now have one of the most important duties of any human alive. You're tasked with convincing as many humans as possible to get scanned."

Rachael was silent. She knew better than to argue with Joshua, especially on matters of logic. She knew he was right. Humanity would need to have as much information about New Eden as possible before it could be transported there. The more information it had, the less uncertainty and fear there would be.

"I understand," she said solemnly. "How much time do we have? How is the scanning of humans progressing?"

"Even though there has been some panic, the scanning is progressing quickly. I spoke with Williams and Langdon today, and they believe we have enough time to scan everyone who wants to be evacuated assuming we continue to get cooperation from world governments." Joshua paused before continuing. "So tell me about your day," he stated, trying hard to be optimistic. "I want to learn more about our new home."

*   *   *

Rachael awoke the next morning after a night of fitful sleep. The fate of humanity had weighed heavily on her mind the entire night. Humanity would have a rebirth. Humans would soon occupy a new home world, but there were still many questions and details that needed to be worked out. Would humans still want to divide themselves into countries on New Eden? How much influence would humanity allow the petrins after they had been transported? Joshua hadn't had enough time to go into specifics as to what world leaders had decided or what the president's advisory council was considering. How would humanity cope with such drastic upheaval?

Rachael realized that the petrins had altered New Eden as much as possible to make the relocation easy for humanity. *Will humanity survive this transition?* Her mind awash with thoughts, Rachael lay on her bed, staring at the ceiling.

Yes! Humanity will survive. We must survive!

Humanity had already survived many transitions, even on Earth. It had emerged as the species that had best navigated the survival of the fittest, the principle on which evolution was based. Earth, the now-lost home world, had prepared humanity well for this transition. Humans had always been survivors, and this transition would be no different. It wouldn't be easy—paradise would soon be filled with billions of people—but she had faith that mankind would meet the challenge. Self-preservation was hardwired into human DNA, and that wouldn't be lost in the scanning process.

Rachael knew that she had one more day on New Eden, and she was going to make the best of it. She got out of bed, showered, walked into the living room, and touched the window covering to allow daylight to stream in. The sun was just rising over the valley below. Its brilliant rays were starting to cast rainbows on the rising mist of the waterfall. It was a beautiful and awe-inspiring sight. Seth had named this place New Eden, and it really was an Eden, a magnificent garden of life in all its glory and complexity.

Rachael was startled as she heard a knock at the door and turned with trepidation. Was she not alone on New Eden?

"Who is it?" she asked as she walked to the door.

Rachael was relieved to hear a familiar voice.

"It's me Rachael. It's Seth."

*   *   *

Rachael opened the door and was shocked to see Seth. He was dressed in an outfit identical to hers, but his appearance was somewhat different. Even though it had been difficult to distinguish android Seth from an ordinary man on Earth, the person she was looking at now was entirely human. He looked exactly the same as the android back on Earth, but in human form.

"Seth, is it really you?"

"Yes, it's me."

"How are you here?" she asked, giving him a hug. As she embraced him, she noted that he was warm, made of flesh and blood.

"I've always been here," Seth replied as he walked into the home. "This biological clone of me was created during your last visit to New Eden, although it was never used. The petrins felt that if you and Joshua experienced some unforeseen emergency, there needed to be someone here to help you."

Seth and Rachael sat next to each other on the living room couch.

"So you're . . . human?" Rachael asked, still in shock over Seth's sudden visit.

"No, I'm still a petrin," Seth replied with a smile. "I've taken the form of a human via this clone, which has been designed to resemble the android you created for me. But just like *your* clone, my clone doesn't have a brain. It's being remote-controlled by me from Petri using spookyons."

"So why are you here?"

"I wanted to speak with you in person. What I have to discuss is very important, and I wanted our conversation to be more . . . personal. Joshua told me that he informed you about Medusa connecting to Earth."

"Yes. He also told me about the order for evacuation."

"How do you feel about humanity moving to New Eden?"

Seth knew that it had been Rachael's decision to shun New Eden three years earlier. He wanted to see if her thoughts had changed.

"I have mixed emotions, Seth. I feel sorrow for our home planet and am deeply saddened by what will become of it. But you and the petrins have built an almost identical copy of it here. You've done a wonderful job of creating a place where humans will feel comfortable. I feel very fortunate that you're giving humanity a chance for existence. We will be truly indebted to you."

"I'm happy to hear that. Our intentions have always been to allow you to live in peace and happiness."

"I truly believe that, Seth."

"I have other news for you," Seth said as he grasped Rachael's hand as he had seen Joshua do many times before. "We have finished the process of scanning your brother Richard."

Rachael's heart beat rapidly, her mouth dry. Did Richard have the possibility of being revived on New Eden?

"Is his information intact?" she asked with trepidation.

"Yes," Seth replied. "He can be revived."

Rachael bent forward, sobbing. This was an answer to a question she had agonized over for the past couple of weeks. She was relieved to finally get an answer—one she was overjoyed to hear.

"It was what you were hoping for, right Rachael?"

"Yes," Rachael replied between sobs. "I'm very happy."

Seth paused to allow Rachael to absorb the information. He knew that she had anticipated it for many weeks and that she would be emotionally overcome by it.

When Rachael was more composed, Seth said, "There's something else I need to tell you, but I didn't tell you earlier because I didn't want it to affect your judgment of New Eden. I wanted a truly unbiased opinion about whether you felt humanity will be happy here. But now that it's been decided that humanity's new home will be New Eden, and you feel that humanity will thrive here, I feel comfortable telling you."

"What is it?"

"There's a specific reason why we preserved only *your* body on New Eden and not Joshua's."

"Which is?"

"This clone of you on New Eden is pregnant."

"What?" Rachael said with a gasp as fresh tears filled her eyes.

"You and Joshua are going to have a child."

Rachael leaned on Seth's shoulder, overcome with emotion. Seth wrapped his arms around her to show support. Rachael remembered the night she and Joshua spent on the summit of the mountain during their last visit. They had made love in the cozy confines of their arachnid cocoon.

"Seth . . . I . . . I can't believe it," Rachael managed to say through waves of emotion. "We didn't tell anyone, but Josh and I were unable to conceive a child on Earth."

"Really?" Seth asked. "We didn't note any genetic defect in Joshua or yourself that would cause that."

"It wasn't a genetic defect," Rachael answered. "The doctors think it was the result of an infection Josh had as a child."

Seth gently placed a hand under Rachael's chin and lifted her head so that she was looking directly into his eyes.

"Well, you're going to have a child on New Eden. That was the reason we preserved your body. I know that humans have varying moral ideas about life at its very early stages, and I wasn't sure what your feelings were about the subject. After our connection with you was ended, I had your body preserved in the off chance that you would reconnect with us. As you know, your clone here doesn't have a brain, but one is going to be created for it during the relocation. This will be the permanent body you will have on New Eden in order to preserve your child."

"Thank you so much for thinking of me, Seth. You don't know how much of a gift this is for Josh and me."

"You're welcome, Rachael." Seth stood up from the couch. "I'll leave now and return you to Earth at the end of the day."

Seth walked to the door of the home, turned, and said, "Goodbye, Rachael."

"Goodbye, Seth."

Rachael lay on the couch and placed her hand over her belly. A broad smile came over her face at the thought of her and Joshua raising a child together. She soon collected herself, wiped the tears from her face, and got up from the couch. She had a task to complete. She was charged with exploring New Eden for one more day. She was a reporter at heart, and this was the most important assignment she had ever been given.

Rachael walked out of her home and climbed aboard the arachnid. She soared high into the air and flew directly towards the rising sun as its golden rays warmed her face. Her thoughts turned to the future—her future, humanity's future, Richard's future, and her unborn child's future. As she soared over the living paradise which cascaded underneath her, she knew that the future was uncertain, but she also felt that the future would be glorious in its uncertainty. It would be a future that paid homage to the tapestry of life in the cosmos of which she was a part.

Rachael thought of the child growing inside of her. She would soon be adding something new to that tapestry. She was bearing the first human child ever conceived on another planet—a child conceived on the summit of humanity's immaculate new home.

A child who would know no other home . . . but New Eden.

A REQUEST FROM KISHORE

I hope that you enjoyed reading *The Arachnid*. Please leave a review in the amazon store. You can do so at this link:
https://www.amazon.com/review/create-review?&asin=B08HNCX7Q9.

Medusa's Gauntlet, the final novel in the New Eden trilogy is now available at:
https://getbook.at/MedusasGauntlet

I do plan on authoring more novels in the future. Please join my mailing list at my website to be notified about any new releases:
https://newedenbook.com

Please tell your friends about New Eden or The Arachnid via social media or other methods. Your help in promoting my novels is greatly appreciated. You can use these links to share:

For New Eden use:
https://getbook.at/NewEden

For The Arachnid use:
https://mybook.to/TheArachnid

You can follow me on twitter @SciFiKish.

Many people have asked for a desktop image of the insect from the book cover. You can download it from this link:
https://www.newedenbook.com/wp-content/uploads/2020/09/The_Arachnid_Desktop-scaled.jpg

ABOUT THE AUTHOR

Kishore Tipirneni MD is an orthopedic surgeon who lives in the Phoenix area. He is also a self-taught programmer and serial entrepreneur who in the late 90's developed digital imaging software which became the leading digital imaging solution in the U.S. that was later acquired by Stryker Medical. He owns numerous patents in both the medical and computer science space.

Thanks to my launch partners:

Troy David, Harry Flaxman, Kenneth Green, Cara Marie Guilfoyle, Paul Lockwood, James Lovette-Black, Gregory Moss, Michael Mashel, Robert Mundy, Fred Nelson, Keith A. Roberts, Steve Strickland, Richard Weinberg, and Dean.

.

Made in United States
Orlando, FL
17 January 2022

13579809R00221